ABU BILAAL YAKUB

THE AMULETS OF SIHR

www.ironheartpublishing.com

Text Copyright © 2018 by AbuBilaal Yakub

Illustrations Copyright © 2018 by AbuBilaal Yakub

No part of this publication may be reproduced, transfered, scanned, copied, distributed, leased in printed or electronic form without written permission and consent of the Publisher and Author.

No part of this publication may be reproduced in whole or in part, or stored in a retrieval system, or transmitted in any form or by any means, electronic, mechanical, photocopying, recording or otherwise, without written permission and consent of the Publisher and Author.

The following publication is a work of Art and Fiction. Any Names, Characters, Places, and Events are a product of the author's imagination and any resemblance to any person, living or dead, is purely coincidental.

Paperback ISBN-13: 978-1-9993870-3-7

Hard Cover ISBN-13: 978-1-9993870-1-3

E-Book ISBN 13: 978-1-9993870-2-0

All rights reserved.

Published by Iron Heart Publishing House.

www.ironheartpublishing.com

To
My Grandparents
Ahmed and *Sakina*

Pious are those who strive
to better the lives of others,
and it is our obligation
to honor them by advocating
their legacy.

PART ONE
THE DARK CON OF MAN
15

ONE
THE BLACKSMITH
27

TWO
UNDER THE PALM TREE
41

THREE
RULE OF THE UNJUST
57

FOUR
THE SOUK AND THE BEGGAR
73

FIVE
THE UNSEEN
89

SIX
THE FORTRESS
105

SEVEN
THE RETURN TO KHALIDAH
119

EIGHT
THE DESERT
135

NINE
THE DEAD CITY
149

TEN
THE PARTING OF FRIENDS
165

PART TWO
THE NEW WORLD
181

ELEVEN
THE FOUR ELEMENTS
193

TWELVE
THE CRIMSON WARRIOR
207

THIRTEEN
THE BUTCHER OF AGHARA
221

FOURTEEN
THE STUDY
235

FIFTEEN
MASTERS AND BROTHERS
249

SIXTEEN
THE FLAW
263

SEVENTEEN
THE FEAST
277

EIGHTEEN
FALSE PIETY
293

NINETEEN
SHEIKH RUWAID
307

TWENTY
THE EAVESDROPPER
321

PART THREE
THE QUARTERMASTER
335

TWENTY-ONE
THE SILVER DAGGER
347

TWENTY-TWO
THE PRIESTESS OF AFTARA
361

TWENTY-THREE
SORCERERS AND SLAVES
375

TWENTY-FOUR
THE KEYSTONE
389

TWENTY-FIVE
THE PALACE
403

TWENTY-SIX
OF SIN AND THE SINNER
417

TWENTY-SEVEN
THE TEACHER
433

TWENTY-EIGHT
THE SECRET SISTERS
449

TWENTY-NINE
THE ROYAL REQUEST
465

GLOSSARY
489

ABOUT THE AUTHOR
495

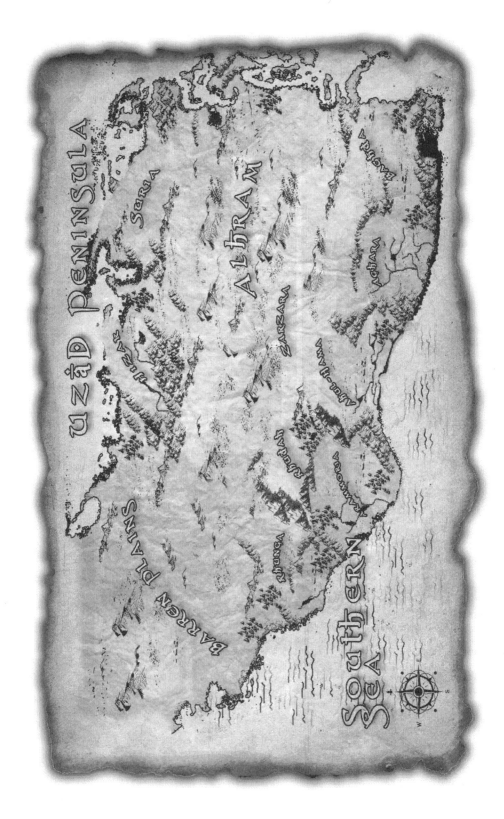

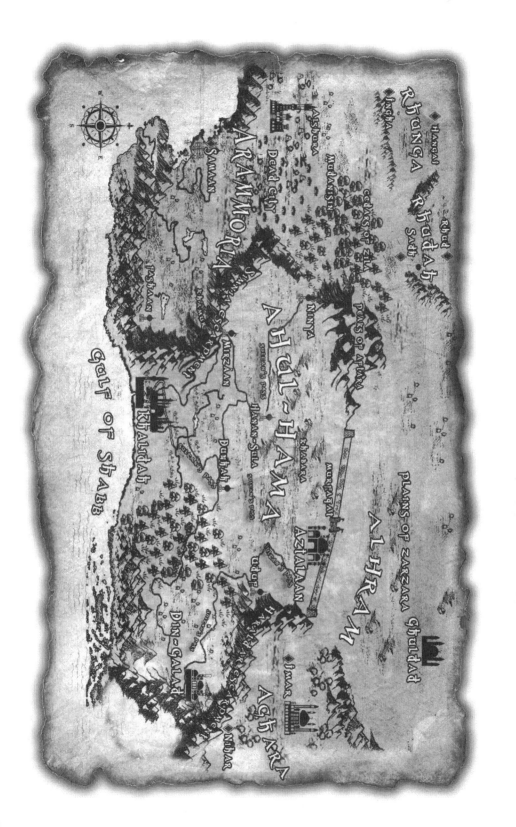

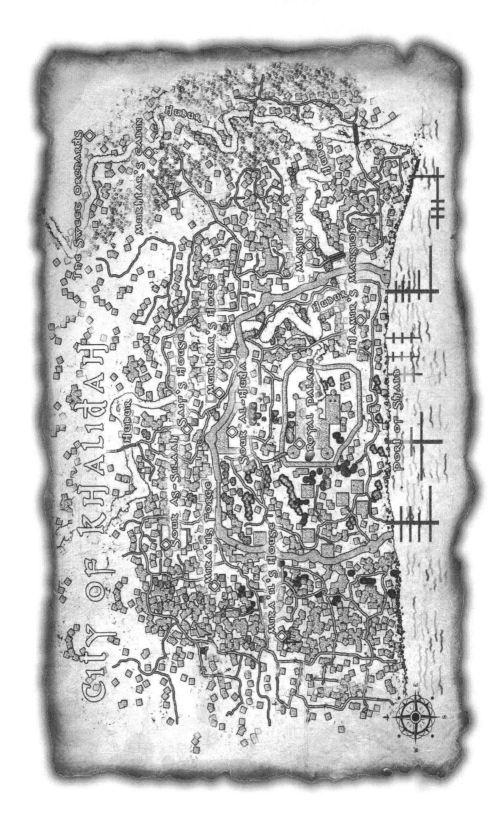

And when We said unto the Angels 'Prostrate yourselves before Adam'; they did obeisance, all save Iblees; he demurred with arrogance and thus became a disbeliever.

Qur'an 2: 34

PART ONE

THE DARK CON OF MAN

20 YEARS AGO

They say, there can be no peace without war. No conquest without bloodshed. One begs the question then, did humanity begin from the loins of war, or peace? Did the first man and woman exist on foundations of turmoil, or harmony?

War begets war. War begets bloodshed. War destroys humanity.

Yet here he was, leading the front with an army on his back. Here he was...

These, and other thoughts, surged through Azhar Babak, General of the First Legion, as he paced back and forth in his tent, with the air of a man desperately awaiting important news.

"Farid!" he stopped and called, his back turned away from the entrance of the tent.

The tent flaps withdrew and in stepped an armed soldier, his heavy armor chinking as he came to an alert halt.

"General." His head inclined slightly.

"Any sight of them?"

Farid shook his head. "It is difficult to see through the dust clouds."

The Legion's camp, a large settlement in and of itself, had been struck by the most terrible storm yet, and even after the sands had somewhat settled, the winds were still high, howling with rage against the canvas tarps and tents of the encampment.

"Have Captain Dimah's scouts returned yet?" Azhar asked.

"No word from them either, General," Farid replied. "However—" he hesitated, jerking his head in an odd way. "It must be nothing," he added as an afterthought.

"Speak with ease, soldier," Azhar urged him. "What is it?"

Farid's tense shoulders relaxed a bit. "One of the party you had sent into the Dead City," he said, "the one who arrived unconscious."

Azhar turned sharply. "What of him?"

"He woke about an hour ago," Farid said. "I hear word that he is speaking to himself, uttering in devilish tongues while the infirmary struggles to attend to him."

Azhar gave a curt nod to acknowledge Farid's concern, but chose not to address it any further. When it came to subordinates, certain things were best left undiscussed. Especially things that tend to vex edgy soldiers who clung to superstitions tighter than their shields and swords.

Over the past several days, in rapid succession, the sandstorms continued to wreak havoc across the dunes of the Khabara Desert. As if that was not enough, a most dismal plague seemed to emanate from the west, engulfing the Legion with a gloomy ordeal, shattering the spirits of his men. If Azhar did not know better, he would have concluded, as his men did, that some devilry was at play here. Most of his cavalry was still recovering from the damage of the storms, and as much as they pleaded and begged, the Legion could not move on— not just yet. Something else was afoot, and he was compelled to see it through.

"Return to your post," Azhar instructed him. "Alert me when the delegates arrive."

Farid inclined his head again and exited the tent. Alone once again, Azhar returned to his pacing, recollecting the events of the previous day.

He sighed with exhaustion. It had been a long and very trying day. After fending off two short skirmishes at the borders of the Dead City, he had to contend with representatives from the Elder Council, who were demanding that he pull back his forces and attack from the south instead, where their spies had reported a weaker defense.

Had it not been for the delay caused by the sandstorms, he would have had the delegates sent on their way. Back to Aztalaan. Back to their Council Halls and courtrooms where they belonged. Despite his outlook on politics, he had to endure several hours of strained diplomacy before they finally understood why he was camped out by the Wells of Ninya. Mere miles from the Dead City, his Legion had conquered, and currently occupied, the only source of water across the Khabara Desert. This was a strategic point on the map, and if he was half the competent man he thought he was, he would not so easily abandon it.

There was another reason why he refused to abandon the Wells of Ninya. A more reticent reason.

A fortnight ago, in the form of a rather vague and imposing message, General Ussam Bashiri of the Third Legion had requested an urgent meeting with his delegates. In his letter, he claimed to have found a way of defeating the enemy and putting an end to the war. It was certainly not the first time that someone had approached Azhar with dubious notions of vanquishing the Dark Prince. A considerable measure of such schemes were more than often voiced around the campfires, and it was a gamble he took when he sent his quartermaster beyond enemy lines, into the Dead City, as per General Ussam Bashiri's letter. In truth, when that expedition yielded strange and unexpected results, he was forced to accept the word of his fellow General. As such, he made all the necessary arrangements. He dismissed the Council delegates earlier in the day and instructed his men to keep an eye out for any approaching emissaries.

Azhar was a tall and muscular man, renowned as a fierce swordsman, a steadfast and disciplined leader. His dedication had more than once nominated him for a seat on the Elder Council of Immorkaan, which governed the nation of Aztalaan, their allies, and all their armies.

The Aztalaan banner commanded three Legions; the second led by General Murad Surukh. Fighting alongside Aztalaan was the Empire of Din-Galad, their forces led by Emperor Adad Babati, and the Kingdom of Aghara whose ranks were led by Queen Sitra. They called this union the Elder Council of Immorkaan, and the truce was forged when it became known that the Nation of Rhudah and the barbaric tribes of Rhunga had pleaded allegiance to Arammoria and sworn their servitude to the Dark Prince.

The wind beat against the tent and Azhar shuddered, glancing at the single candle's wick gradually melting away to the bottom. Dawn was soon approaching, and if Ussam Bashiri's messengers did not arrive before daybreak, he would have to make some very calculated decisions regarding his Legion's progress in the war. General Bashiri had assured him that this would be the night. Alas, it seemed a dim prospect, considering that the storms had caused huge delays for anyone hoping to cross the desert. He had half a mind to call it a night and perhaps catch a few winks before sunrise, but ahead of arriving at that decision, he heard a small cough behind him.

His back stiffened, shoulders tensed, and hand instinctively reached for the hilt of the scimitar by his side. Cautiously, he turned and spotted the silhouettes of two figures hidden in the far shadows of the tent where the candlelight could not reach them.

"Reveal yourself!" Azhar growled menacingly. With a faint chink, his scimitar unsheathed by an inch. He was merely steps away from them, and nothing would hinder him from making a swift attack were he to be provoked. "Sorcerers are unwelcome here!"

Hands raised in quick surrender, the first figure hastily stepped forward into the light so that Azhar could now see his hooded, watery eyes. "I assure you, we intend no malice," the man said. "I am Laban Varda," he gestured to the second figure, who also stepped forward as he was introduced. "This is Ussam Bashiri. We are your allies, not foes."

Disguised as mere travelers, both men wore long, tanned robes and white turbans, hardly besmirched by sand or dust— rather atypical for travelers who had just arrived. Azhar's grip on his scimitar slackened, and he returned it to its sheath with a light snap, but did not unhand the hilt.

"Why would you not announce yourselves like normal people?" he asked. "How did you even enter my tent without my consent?"

"Our presence here must remain a secret," Ussam Bashiri, dark-skinned and taller than either of them, gave a short bow and touched his forehead with his right hand to show his respect. It was an unexpected gesture, and Azhar was prompted to do the same, but exhaustion clouded his mind, and the moment passed.

"Hence our unannounced intrusion," Laban said, somewhat apologetically.

"Your unannounced intrusion warrants an explanation," Azhar demanded, exerting a controlled amount of sternness in his voice.

"Sorcery, General," Ussam replied with equal rigidity. "Laban Varda is well-versed in the Dark Arts. Long has he spied on the enemy for us, and without his assistance, we would have been massacred at the gates of Ghuldad. I owe my victory of the ancient fortress to him."

"An Arammorian spy," Azhar eyed Laban curiously, throwing subtle glances at Ussam, wondering if his fellow General had utterly lost his mind. How *dare* he bring an Arammorian sorcerer into his camp? "A most precarious task," he added, trying not to display any form of antipathy. A strong and competent General would slay them where they stood, but a wise one would ascertain their true intent before doing so, and he aspired to be the latter.

Laban's fingers were interlaced, his thumbs rubbing against each other. "Indeed it is," he said, sounding indifferent.

"You must forgive me," Azhar said. "I did not expect you, but your messengers, and have therefore not made the appropriate preparations for your welcome."

"The blame lies with me, General," Ussam bowed, and Azhar was once again caught in an awkward moment. "But the urgency of the matter could not be left in the hands of an emissary."

"You must be weary from your journey. I can make arrangements, should you wish to rest your eyes and limbs."

Ussam declined with a brisk shake of his head. "As I said, General, our presence here must remain a secret. If the Elder Council were to catch wind of what we are about to propose, our hope of winning this war will be lost."

"We must also make haste," Laban added, betraying a slight sense of unrest. "Alas, I fear we may have arrived at an hour too late."

Something was evidently afoot. Whether he was fomenting ill will, or he was prey to some form of malice, Azhar did not know, but he sensed dire urgency in Laban's voice. He was surely troubled, at the very least. Then again, these were uncertain times. No man could evade the dark shadows of angst and despair.

"Very well," Azhar gave a brisk nod.

"Sit, General Babak, for what I am about to tell you will require your full attention," Laban gestured at the cushions that lay around the tent.

Azhar's eyes narrowed ever so slightly. *Who did this man think he was?* To order *Azhar Babak,* a *General* of the Aztalaan army, in his *own* tent? Azhar was not a proud man, but he did not appreciate his authority abrogated, not by his own men, and much less by someone he had just met. The Arammorian certainly assumed his role with confidence and a good measure of condescension. Azhar knew he would have to establish some clear boundaries before any further ventures were discussed. He sat down across from Laban, keeping a meticulous eye on him.

"Did you procure the items we requested?" Laban asked Azhar, as Ussam joined them.

"If I did not?" Azhar challenged.

Laban raised a dubious eyebrow. "I was under the impression that everything was ready?" He glanced from Ussam to Azhar with uncertainty.

"I was very definitive in my letter, General Babak," Ussam stated. "Did you not heed my instructions and warnings?"

"Heed your *instructions?"* Azhar's temper attained a delicate edge.

"General Bashiri, we are at *war*. You are in *my* camp, so allow me to emphasize that I do not take instructions from persons unknown," he glanced at Laban, "much less from those who fail to recognize my stature."

A stony silence followed and lingered, while the two generals exchanged cold and reserved expressions.

"I beg your forgiveness, General Babak," Laban was first to speak, indeed sounding genuinely apologetic, "I will be honest with you —"

"I would very much appreciate that," Azhar interrupted, not quite prepared to relinquish his displeasure.

"As we have only just met," Laban continued, a touch of impatience in his tone, "much must be discussed before trust can become mutual. I cannot, however, emphasize enough on the severity of this matter. We have to act on what we have discovered, and with haste. Therefore, much of what courtesy would dictate must be overlooked for now. You have to understand and accept that we are just as determined in ending this war. If you believe, for whatever reason, that we cannot work as one, then we will respect your decision. As such we will simply find other means to fulfill our objectives."

Azhar's jaw clenched. "Is that so?" He faced Ussam. "Did you not approach me solely for the position I currently hold at the borders of Arammoria?"

"Does it appear as such?" Ussam countered.

"It certainly does," Azhar tilted his head slightly, giving him a stern look. They needed him. Of that, he was certain. The question was *why?* Were they to just use him to their advantage and discard him thereafter? He hoped not. Not for their own sake. Not if they hoped to survive his wrath. "Who else will you send into the Dead City to raid desolate tombs? And what, if I may ask, do you hope to achieve from this venture you propose?"

The wind howled against the canvas tent, masking the distant murmur of soldiers on guard outside, unaware of the ongoings in their General's tent. Azhar studied Ussam with an unwavering attention, who avoided his eye, appearing impassive and unmoved.

Laban exchanged a brief nod with his partner and said, "This war has been raging for close to a decade, and we are no closer to defeating the Dark Prince than we were when it began. He will become the destroyer of worlds if not stopped, and if you would rather continue to fruitlessly fire arrows and brandish steel at him, you are free to do so. Although we can clearly see that it is hardly making a mark."

Azhar gave him a long hard stare. Did he trust them? Certainly not. Should he? Perhaps. It would be foolish of him to discredit a genuine armament against the wickedness of war, without giving it due consideration. He must first assure himself that their intent was untouched by personal and ulterior motives.

"Is it that you fear his retribution for conquering his second-most prized stronghold?" he challenged Ussam, searching for a reaction.

"He is the Dark Prince," Ussam remained composed, but the glint in his eye became colder with every word his spoke. "His retributions are ever swift and ruthless. If there was a way of forestalling his wrath, would you not take it? General Azhar Babak, would you rather allow countless more souls to endure his endless persecution?"

Ussam was questioning his intent, something Azhar would never tolerate, but he restrained himself from lashing out. Perhaps it was time to lend them an ear at the very least.

"We did indeed procure the items you requested," he said. "They are as you described." He noted the look of relief on their faces and continued, "I am curious, however. Why did you specifically ask me to send a man who is hardly a soldier? He is a simpleton. A blacksmith!"

"Alas, General," Laban replied. "There is more to this blacksmith than meets the eye. We have burned the bones, and the wisps of smoke whispered to us. The man you have in your service is the son of a sorcerer."

Azhar was unable to hide his bewilderment. *The son of a sorcerer serving in his ranks?* He struggled against the impulse to leave the tent and confront Harun Zafar.

Laban, it seemed, was rather surprised at his reaction. "Ah…" he let on softly, "…you did not know?"

Azhar felt the color drain from his face. It was enough to know that his fellow General employed a sorcerer, but to have one in his own ranks without his knowledge… This was utterly unacceptable. "It does not matter," he tried to counter. "Harun is no more sorcerer than I."

"It does matter," Ussam said to him. "Think, General Babak."

Silence endured, during which Azhar gave the matter deep thought. He considered what this information meant, what it could do, and the devastation it may bring upon those he would have to involve. He did not wish to admit, but it did indeed matter that Harun's father was a man embroiled in the dark arts. Azhar had always known Harun to be a devout man, faithful to his wife and son. Soon he would have a second child. Did Harun know of his father's ties to the occult? Was there a life secret to him, a life he did not wish the world to know? And if not, was it fair to drag him into the midst of all this? Would it be fair to intentionally lead him upon a path of destruction?

"You seem unconvinced," Laban peered at him.

"Can I be blamed?" Azhar shrugged. "What is the source of your information?"

Ussam sat up straight, a small grin curling about the corner of his lips. "The conquest of Ghuldad came with a precious bounty," he replied, almost as though he had been waiting for that very moment. "Deep beneath the dungeons, my men uncovered texts and scrolls, remnants of the ancient Kingdom of Zarzara. Indeed, we have scrutinized every page we could set our eyes upon. I urge you to have faith in what we speak of."

"Faith without knowledge is ignorance," Azhar stated. "Enlighten me as to how these items will vanquish the Dark Prince Azazil."

Ussam seemed mildly impressed. "Very few dare speak his name."

"There can be no benefit from the fear of a name," Azhar said, and he waited patiently for his query to be addressed.

"It is with sorcery that he is powerful," Ussam explained, "and it is with sorcery that we will destroy him."

"What you must understand," Laban shifted on his cushion, "is that no man— no human has the power to perform magic. Believing a sorcerer to be powerful is, without doubt, believing in the very illusion he wishes you to see. The power of magic comes from the abilities of entities whose existence is known, but remains unseen."

"What entities?" Azhar asked, unable to disguise the slight quiver in his voice.

"Jinn," Laban replied, and a cold chill wafted into the tent as the candlelight flickered. "Created from a smokeless fire, with the abilities to do that which man cannot. It is with the aid of these beings that *any* magic is performed, but they must be convinced of your allegiance before they can give you theirs. Sorcerers are faced with horrendous tasks when a contract is forged. The Dark Prince is a dominant entity, and his powers are drawn from the sorcerers who worship his being—"

"And by killing his sorcerers, we weaken his forces and his powers," Azhar narrowed his eyes and nodded.

"Alas, if only it were as transparent," Laban said, unperturbed by Azhar's interruption. "To kill those sorcerers, we must first destroy the Jinn who aid them. The Dark Prince's most trusted ally, he who is known as the Hand of Azazil, an ancient demon, commands hosts of the mightiest of these Jinn. In truth, it is near impossible to kill a Jinn, for they are not bound by flesh and bone as we are. They coexist in a world quite unlike ours, disunited by a veil, not only impossible to pierce, but forbidden to attempt."

Azhar was unable to contain his curiosity. "Then *how*—?"

"Thus the items you procured," Laban said simply.

"Is that their significance then?" Azhar asked. "Weapons that can kill Jinn?"

"Where are they?" Ussam looked around the tent, as though hoping to see a display case in one of the corners.

Azhar faced the entrance of the tent. "Farid!" he called, and the armored guard entered the tent. "Bring the chest. And wake Harun. I demand his presence."

ONE

THE BLACKSMITH

PRESENT DAY.

Much could be said of Harun Zafar's youngest son. Not unlike his peers, he grew up whole and healthy, despite the constant hardships and enervating essences of life. Harun and Suha had been praised several times for raising their children well, but were the brothers always well-behaved, obedient, and good-mannered?

Atrocity befell them at a very young age when their father was imprisoned and astonishingly vanished from his prison cell shortly after. With an adamant disregard for rules and authority, Zaki rebelled and attempted pursuit, only to lose himself to the wilderness. He was later discovered to have joined the ranks of the celebrated Red-Guard of Aztalaan.

Like his elder brother, Mukhtar possessed no less a rebellious trait, but coerced by reality, he adapted an early maturity, and his cunningness and tenacity helped him persevere. Fatherless for the better part of his life, he grew up poor but healthy, destitute but happy, and life taught him what he needed to know. Mika'il Abaraina, married to Suha's elder sister, had taken custody of Harun Zafar's forge, and it was under his watchful eye that Mukhtar earned his livelihood as an apprentice blacksmith.

He was later than usual one morning. Weaving in and out of the crowded sweaty streets, he half-walked, half-ran, heading for his uncle's forge located on the eastern side of the district, deeply dreading what surely awaited him. His uncle was a man intolerant of tardiness. He was intolerant of rather everything, in Mukhtar's opinion.

The harbor to the south brought the cawing of seagulls and a salty tinge, making the air heavy with humidity and noisier than ever. Under clear skies and a blazing late-morning sun, carts pulled by stubborn mules and oxen pushed aside people, people pushed other people, and the streets continued to bustle in a strangely harmonized way. Merchant stalls were set up within feet of each other, their owners making every effort to attract customers, while shoppers moved between stalls and stores, hunting for the best bargain.

With the congestion of small market squares and numerous industrious businesses, the air had a faint taste, tinged with stenches of smoke and rot. Piles of rubbish and puddles of sewage, riled by the tropical heat of Khalidah, made it somewhat difficult to breathe. Widely known as the Immortal City, Khalidah was spread out along the rocky shoreline of the Gulf of Shabb, a port of economics and commerce for merchant vessels across the seas, making it a center of all trade routes. Camel-driven caravans traveled from as far away as Aghara and beyond, bringing with them spices and incense, livestock and farmery, silk and cotton to trade for the skills that Khalidans had to offer in craft, artistry, and fishing.

A heavily guarded wall cleft the affluent from the indigent populous that spanned the remainder and greater part of the city well into the outskirts. Pressed for time, Mukhtar did not take his usual, less polluted and less crowded route to work. He ran past the wall, into a maze of twisted, narrow streets and alleys, lined with disorderly houses of mud and clay, and emerged onto Rayis Street, where he was forced to slow his pace. A much larger crowd was gathered around the middle of the street, restricting movement from either side. Cries of prices and offers filled the air, mingled with a frenzy of cheers and roars. His uncle's forge lay further down the street to his right, but curiosity drew him toward the crowd, where he strained his ears to listen in.

'I have twenty gold from this fine man here! Twenty gold! Do I hear twenty-one?'

'Come now... Come now! Look how strong she is! How very young and bright!'

'Do I hear twenty-one?'

At the very back of the crowd, a beady-eyed man was ardently chatting with his companion, spontaneously pointing at the spectacle. Mukhtar approached him and inquired.

Slightly irritated at the interruption, the man turned and frowned. "Slave traders," he grunted. "With merchandise from as far away as Aghara. Or so they claim. Gives them a very good excuse to triple the usual prices." He folded his arms. "I refuse to believe it though. They must have picked this rabble from the sewers of Din-Galad!"

On occasion, Rayis Street was known to attract slave trades when the demand was high, and many corrupt City-Guards greedily partook in the endeavors so long as their share of the profits was guaranteed. Sure enough, as Mukhtar looked about, he spotted a pair of them idling at the corner of the street, deliberately turning a blind eye.

He felt anger boil inside of him. "It is men like you who continue to encourage such poisonous trades!" he snarled at the beady-eyed man.

The man simply pointed to a blank wall further down from Kashif the Carpenter's shop and his brother, Ufuk's Store of Antiquities. Two bodies were sprawled, one on top of the other, their blood spilled and seeping into the sand and dirt.

Mukhtar's throat became dry. *"Dead?"*

"Unless you wish the same fate, keep your piousness to yourself!" The man gave him a shrewd look, then simply turned away. Despite the warning, Mukhtar pushed his way through to the front for a better view.

The opening before the crowd revealed two men, one short and well-built, with long braided hair and a small sack of coin tied to his waist. His accomplice was much taller and broader, with an ugly scar across his face and a large battle-axe mounted on his back.

While buoyantly addressing the crowd, they hungrily circled a young and helpless girl. She looked no older than Mukhtar. Her hands and legs were chained, filthy clothes torn to near shreds, and matted hair hid part of her dirty face with a bleeding lip and bruised cheek. She hung her head in evident shame, staring at her grimy and muddy feet. A large, iron, caged-cart was parked in the alley behind her. Three others sat, trapped behind rusty iron bars, watching the bidding of their companion with hopeless expressions.

The large slave trader nudged his partner and pointed to somewhere in the crowd. He had spotted a customer committing to his price, and he smirked with shameless glee and screamed, *"Sold!* For twenty-one gold coins!"

The last of their merchandise was sold, and as the crowd thinned, Mukhtar was able to get a proper view of the slave-girl, and his heart became heavy with pity. He felt compelled to show her mercy as she was pulled by her hair and dragged like a sack of grain. She let out a small, drained squeal of pain as the slaver removed her chains and threw her ruthlessly into the cage, completing the task with a spit of disgust and a look of pure loathing. The others made room for her, and she curled up into a far corner of the cage, hiding her face behind her knees, tugging on her rags to keep as much of herself concealed as she could.

"Savor these final moments," the slaver growled, his lips curling into a malevolent grin. "Tonight, your new master will devour your chastity—" he lowered his voice to a malicious whisper, "—and I will do the same before you are delivered to him!" He gave a sinister cackle and locked the cage.

Mukhtar, who was leaning against the wall close by, pretending to admire an elderly merchant's display of clay pots, clenched his fists, angered at what he had just heard. The slaver sniffed repulsively at his captives, before entering the antiquities shop with his companion and their customer, Ufuk.

They left the cart unguarded, Mukhtar thought. *Why?*

He glanced at the dead bodies further along the street and the answer was obvious. *Who would dare?*

Cautiously, he approached the cage and stopped to consider

his options— was it worth the risk? It was not his business, not his responsibility, but the manner in which the girl's head was pitifully curled into her knees, silently sobbing, was too much for him to bear. He glanced about nervously. The alley was deserted. There was no one else about.

"You!" he whispered to her. "Slave-girl!"

She ignored him.

"You boy!" One of the other slaves croaked, an old man with long gray hair and beard. He crawled closer to the bars of the cage and Mukhtar's nostrils were filled with a nauseating stench of rot and human waste. "I sense greatness in you. Will you show us mercy? Will you free us from this prison?"

"He is a Khalidan," the third spoke. He was just as gaunt, unkempt, and filthy as his fellows. Mukhtar noted a gap in his beard. His right cheek appeared to have suffered a terrible burn. "Pompous and self-centered, Khalidans care for nothing but themselves! Go away! Your false nobility will not save you when those slavers catch you speaking to us!"

Mukhtar frowned. "I am willing to free you from the wickedness of these men!"

"Will you also gloat before you have even accomplished your deed?"

"I should leave you to rot in that cage!" Mukhtar retorted angrily.

"Do as you please, Khalidan!" The man said recklessly. "Our doom is sealed. Once we were free, now we will die enslaved to man."

Mukhtar ignored him and gave the girl a long and hard stare, trying to resolve the conflict within him. How could he justify his own freedom, when so many others who deserved to be free, lived their lives under their master's whips? No man or woman should have a worth in coin. The large slaver's words continued to ring in his head. He could not stand for such brutality, and may not have the strengths to bring the slavers to justice, but he did possess the tact and the advantage to help the captives escape. What they did with that freedom was their choice.

The ox that pulled the cart gave an uninterested bellow and chewed on its cud innocuously. Mukhtar picked up a fairly large rock, and the slave-girl looked up disbelievingly. Her companions tensed. The scarred man eyed him curiously. The other slave did the same. The old man gave him an encouraging nod and he readied himself to break the lock, but froze before he could strike.

Voices were coming out the front of the shop. The slavers were returning.

"Hide!" The old man hissed, his sunken eyes wide in horror.

Gripped by fear, Mukhtar hastily dropped the rock and scampered away behind a large pile of logs in the otherwise deserted alley, retreating barely a moment before the men appeared.

"I have heard tales of you, Haim Tuma," Ufuk was saying, eyeing the slaver cautiously. "Tales of the Butcher of Aghara."

Haim gave an impish snort, noting the merchant's apprehension. "It was not a title I earned for any misdeeds," he explained. "I was indeed a butcher in Aghara, and carried the title with me when my brother and I were exiled from that cursed land of pompous aristocrats!" He spat on the ground, and Mukhtar raised a dubious eyebrow. Both his mother and aunt were from Aghara, and never had they spoken of it as a cursed land. "Although you cannot deny," Haim continued, "it does strike fear!"

Ufuk coughed nervously. "It does indeed. Forgive my boldness but I must ask, where does most of your merchandise come from?" He gestured at the slaves in the cart.

"From Aghara," Haim's brother replied, "as we had announced to all!"

"Do you take me for a fool, Gussar?" Ufuk eyed the tall slaver. "The girl might pass for an Aghari, but the others..."

"Ah, Ufuk, is it not bad fortune to disclose one's trade secrets?" Haim responded, and then lowered his voice. "I admit, we may have exaggerated to double our profits, but our merchandise has always been unique. Take that old man, for instance," Haim gestured, "a sorcerer. *A sorcerer!* We found him lurking outside the palace walls at a midnight hour, crouched by the stream, murmuring his demented spells and casting seashells into the waters flowing through the gap beneath the wall. He vowed to curse us if we chained him. My superstitious *goat* of a brother—" he chuckled at the large slaver, who gave him a disgruntled look, "—did not want to. Afraid of sorcerers, he is. Alas, the old man has brought nothing but good fortune since. Fetched us a decent forty gold coins himself, and ten for each his accomplices!"

Ufuk almost yelped with excitement, and Mukhtar knew what he was thinking. If this was true, then it certainly seemed as though these slavers were in a lucrative business.

"Come now, Haim, have we not already become friends?" Ufuk appealed, unable to disguise the greedy look on his face. "It is truly unjust to steal your secrets, and I am not an unjust man, but perhaps we can aid each other in future endeavors? She may not seem much now," he gestured at the slave-girl, "although I am certain that after a good scrub and a few square meals, she will be a delight around the house. If she proves her worth, I may yet recommend your name to some of my own clients. Shall we return to my shop and discuss some more? Perhaps we can come to a mutually beneficial arrangement, your merchandise and my clients? I even know a ranking city guard, Ghadan Lahib. He is a close acquaintance and has highly influential friends who can turn the other way and keep the authorities blind to our trades."

Haim seemed to be giving it some thought. "Very well then, why not? I believe we can spare some time. Is that cage locked?" he asked his brother.

Gussar glanced at the lock, seemed satisfied with its integrity, and the three returned to Ufuk's shop to discuss their ventures.

Mukhtar allowed a moment to pass before stepping out. Heart hammering against his chest, he picked up the heavy rock again and swung. The rusty old lock was no match for the blacksmith's powerful arms, and it gave in immediately. The slaves realized their opportunity, and as soon as the cage was open, they jumped out and made their escape. The girl gave a small yelp as her shoulder caught on a jagged edge and tore off a piece of her filthy clothes. Mukhtar glanced around nervously, but no one seemed to have heard her.

The old man was last to step out, and he gazed at his savior for a long moment before saying, "Bless you, child!"

Mukhtar stared into his sunken eyes. "I only freed you from wicked men."

The old man gave him a curious look. "We will never be free," he said. "The devil himself has sworn to haunt us with wickedness!" And he joined the others, disappearing into the crowd, leaving Mukhtar alone in the alley with the cage, staring at the ragged piece of cloth caught on its jagged edge. The ox continued to chew its cud.

A half-hour later, Mukhtar arrived at the forge, still recovering from the rush of adrenaline. He had vanished long before the slavers came out to find an empty cart, but as the adrenaline wore off, anxiety crept in and gripped his innards with piercing claws.

He continuously glanced over his shoulder, half expecting the slavers to be in pursuit. What if they had recognized him? Or followed him? He shook his head, took deep breaths to calm his beating heart, and tried to focus. If the slavers truly suspected *him*, they would already be on his tail. He threw another frightful glance over his shoulder. Not much but a dusty, overcrowded, winding and twisting street of disheveled and mismatched merchant stalls trailed behind. Nothing out of the ordinary. Nothing to cause needless unease. He had to focus on what lay ahead. His uncle was expecting him early. He had already received several prior warnings of poor punctuality and he was arriving nearly four hours later than ever. At this point, the slavers became the least of his concern. He opened the door to the rear entrance and stepped, as quietly as he could, into the stifling hot atmosphere of the forge, breathing in the familiar smell of metal, wood, and leather mingled with dust.

The forge was well sized but windowless. The stifling heat came from the large furnace and kiln, built into the far corner of the forge, which according to Mika'il, had never run cold for nearly three decades. Two wooden benches ran the length of the forge on either side, equipped with stone grinders, anvils, and vices. The walls were covered with a variety of tools, from hammers and chisels to stencils and templates. At the front was a low counter that opened out to the street, behind which his uncle, Mika'il Abaraina, sat on an old and weathered stool, hunched over his ledgers.

Saif was at his usual station by the stone grinder. His duties were primarily to restore old weapons, and was given repairs such as straightening and sharpening. Faraj, a man almost as old as Mika'il, sat on the opposite side, using his wooden dummy to shape an iron chest-brace. He looked up when Mukhtar shut the door, and gave him a *'your-uncle-is-not-pleased'* look, but said nothing more. He was known to be a man of few words and a very skilled blacksmith, having worked with Mika'il and Harun from the very beginning.

Mukhtar knew that his uncle was upset, but whatever the matter, there was nothing he could do about it, and would just need to take it in its stride. He would delay the inevitable if he could, silently slithering to where Saif was working.

Saif and Mukhtar knew each other since they were children, growing up in the same *Madrassa*. He was shorter than Mukhtar, slightly hunched, with a much darker complexion, curly hair and beard. "Where have you *been?*" he asked over the sound of the grinder. "You were meant to be here early and help me finish sharpening these arrowheads!"

"I overslept," Mukhtar said, simply trying to push aside his earlier experience and focus his mind on work. "What have we to do?"

Faraj was still hammering away on the other side, and the noise from the grinder masked their voices so that Mika'il remained hunched over his ledger.

"Much work!" Saif responded urgently. "Abunaki was promised till noon because *you* failed to finish his arrowheads yesterday!"

"We have just about two more hours then," Mukhtar prepared himself for work. "We should manage—"

"Alas! His royal highness has decided to avail himself!"

The grinder halted. Saif's arrowheads fell with a clatter, Faraj stopped hammering his chest-brace, and a stony silence filled the forge. Mukhtar swallowed and turned, slowly and deliberately, to face a fuming Mika'il.

"Explain yourself!"

"Khal..." Mukhtar's ears reddened, "I meant no disrespect—"

"Disrespect?" Mika'il's voice became dangerously quieter, and Mukhtar struggled with the sudden constriction in his throat.

"Forgive me, Khal!"

"You do not deserve forgiveness!" Mika'il remarked. "You deserve a taste of reality! Khalidans roam these streets every day to find decent work, and here you are, taking everything *for granted!*"

Short, broad-chested, heavy-armed and balding, Mika'il was usually kind despite his grumpy attitude and formidable, chiseled features. His beady glittering eyes and thin lips, combined with a wrinkled forehead, made him look very stern. Under the ferocious glare that was usually reserved for him in situations such as these, Mukhtar thought the world may have vanished beneath his feet. Within moments, he was drenched in sweat, and the fiery furnace behind him did nothing to prevent the perspiration.

"Khal, are you not overreacting—?"

"Just because your uncle runs this forge, does not mean you can march in here whenever you feel like!" Mika'il yelled. "And let me tell you something—" pointing at him with a thick, weathered finger, "—were it not for the pleas of your Khala and your mother, I would see you rot in a ditch somewhere, because you deserve nothing more!"

Several Khalidans passing by, drawn by his booming voice, could not resist stopping and watching.

"Khal! How can you say that?" Mukhtar gasped, genuinely abashed.

"This forge only survives on hard work and commitment. *Discipline!*"

Mika'il's voice was steadily becoming louder. "Where is your discipline, if you *cannot— even — wake— up— early— in— the— morning!*"

Mukhtar's fists clenched. To be ridiculed by his own uncle, in the presence of his peers, was convulsing and infuriating. He could think of an array of excuses to explain his lateness, but he would not speak them, nor the one truth. His uncle's reaction would be no different. Perhaps even worse. There were hundreds, if not thousands of retorts that were longing to escape his lips, but he bit them back. There was no sense in taking this any further than it had already gone.

Mika'il, however, was not done. "The world does not circle you, Mukhtar! You are not here to entertain us, and as you can see, we are hardly entertained!"

Except for your audience at the counter! Mukhtar thought, stealing a glance at the front of the forge. He spotted some of their neighbors, craning their necks over others, trying to get a proper view.

"It is time you grew up, Mukhtar! Grow some roots, so that one day you can stand on your own!"

Mukhtar's jaw was set, his gaze focused on a jagged piece of metal under his bench.

"If Abunaki returns —" Mika'il said.

"*Who?*"

"*Do not interrupt me!*" Mika'il yelled again. "If Abunaki returns, and his arrowheads are not done—"

"Oh, *that* Abunaki," Mukhtar mumbled. He wondered if Mika'il would have been any less angered if he hadn't had the urgency of work to push him to the edge.

"—and I have to give them to him free of charge, it will be coming out of *your* wage!"

Mukhtar nodded grumpily.

"And if you *ever* set foot into this forge any later than daybreak, you will be without work!" Mika'il brought his finger frightfully close to Mukhtar's nose. *"Do you understand?"*

Mukhtar had very few memories of confrontations with his uncle, all with unpleasant outcomes. Their most recent conflict was a few months back, involving Zaki, and a physical battle had almost ensued between his uncle and his brother. Over time, Mukhtar had come to learn that in matters involving a family member, it is much simpler to just apologize and walk away, rather than create unpleasant memories that tended to last for years.

"Forgive me, Khal," he repeated his apology, keeping a straight and impassive face.

The effect was immediate. The harshness in Mika'il's voice dropped. "Every morning, I want to see you at the entrance of the forge awaiting my arrival, and I care not how great a calamity you must overcome for that to happen!"

"Yes," Mukhtar mumbled.

Mika'il returned to his seat by the counter. "And I will be having a word with your mother about this!"

Surely not! Mukhtar felt the world vanish beneath his feet once more. "Khal, is not my apology enough? You really needn't—" he began.

Mika'il silenced his feeble pleas with a careless wave of his hand.

TWO

UNDER THE PALM TREE

If only he knew sorcery. He desired nothing but to vanish, perhaps sink into the ground, or even become one with the wall. A glaring glance in Mika'il's direction was all he could muster, and some of his thoughts may have shown on his face.

"Do not even think it," Saif warned him.

"How can you know what I think?" Mukhtar asked him curiously.

"The look on your face says it all," Saif replied. "An evil eye is a treacherous deed, and a most heinous form of sorcery imaginable. You know this!"

Mukhtar glanced at his uncle again. With a cold shoulder, Mika'il sat on his stool, arms crossed, brow furrowed, and a glare that radiated more heat than the forge's furnace, telling off any who passed by, doing whatever it was that they shouldn't. A young boy, playing with wooden blocks just a few feet away from the counter, received the fright of his life when Mika'il unleashed his fury and sent him running for his mother's aid, and she arrived with retaliation.

"The street does not belong to you, Mika'il Abaraina!" she shrieked from across the street. "My child has every right to —"

"Do not preach to me of right and wrong, woman!" Mika'il retorted readily. "I know very well how much *'right'* you have been doing with your husband's business!"

Her husband, Jaul the carpenter, had been gone for several weeks with a trade caravan. Much of his business had suffered during this time, as his wife knew very little about carpentry.

She cast him a look of pure loathing. "Curse you, Mika'il! May misfortune befall you and yours!" she snapped and disappeared into her shop with her son.

"Why they even bring their children to their workplaces, is a wonder!" Mika'il grunted to himself. *"Irresponsible* parents..."

Mukhtar and Saif snickered to themselves, while Faraj indulged him. "Why are you so troubled, brother?"

"Forgive me," Mika'il shook his head slowly. "I have been plagued with an unsettling feeling all morning."

They continued to converse in low voices, and although Mukhtar couldn't hear much, he suspected his name may have come up more than once. He and Saif continued their work, sharpening Abunaki's arrowheads. Abunaki was a renowned swordsman and archer, and all his weaponry and armor had very precise specifications. Aside from Faraj, Mukhtar's eye for detail marked his skill-set, and any work that required such precision was his responsibility. It was with great relief when they completed all the arrowheads, and Abunaki arrived only moments after to collect them.

He was a long-standing client of Mika'il's, well built for his age, with small watery eyes, and a graying beard.

"Are they ready?" he asked with a wide grin on his face. "I hope so for your sake, Mika'il!"

Mika'il laughed confidently. "I know you expected unpaid service if delayed, but not today!"

Mukhtar brought forward the finished arrowheads, and Abunaki's smile faded. He then scrutinized as many as he could, and upon finding no fault, signaled to his son to pick up the goods.

The boy was young and scrawny, his fluffy, curly hair riddled with dirt. Mukhtar half expected him to collapse under the weight of the box, which he lifted with surprising strength. Abunaki cleared his throat and puffed out his chest as he always did before taking out his coin purse, pouring the contents over the counter and separating his money.

"I am curious," Mika'il eyed Abunaki's imperious display of affluence. "Why not just have the arrowheads mounted? I have excellent timber to fashion you sturdy arrows, balanced to your liking."

Abunaki shook his head without looking at him. "No need. Alulim here will do it. I wish him to learn the art of weapon-craft. Very ambitious he is. Claims that he will one day be King!"

He laughed loudly at his own joke, and Alulim's cheeks reddened. Mika'il gave a small chuckle. "Keep alive the dream," he added to the boy, "and you may yet be surprised! I for one would heartily agree that we need a new King."

"Careful what you wish for, Mika'il. Better the devil you know than the angel you don't. Here you are then," Abunaki handed Mika'il his payment, "Fourteen copper coins as agreed. Although I must say, I really did not expect you to complete the order this time. I see you have Mukhtar here. Perhaps he is the reason you managed?"

He laughed again at his own joke, but before Mukhtar could even break into the smile he was yearning to display for his recognition, he was put down by the dark look on his uncle's face.

"Come now, Mika'il," Abunaki seemed to have understood, "let not your anger blemish his youth! He is but a young man with the world at his feet!"

"Take him with you to work your own mediocre of a forge then!" Mika'il snarled. "Rid me of his idiocy. Even with the world at his feet, he himself has turned the other way! What use is he then?"

Fists clenched, jaw set, and with an immense muster over furious emotions, Mukhtar skulked back to his own workbench and focused his gaze on a rusty nail to keep himself restrained.

"They are young, Mika'il Abaraina," Abunaki gave a casual wave. "Have you forgotten your own days?"

"He is old enough to carry the weight and responsibility of a family, yet he behaves like a child sometimes," Mika'il argued. "At his age, I was already married! And what of Alulim here, would you speak the same of him?"

Abunaki's eyes narrowed ever so slightly. "Perhaps you are right. There is much our children should learn from the burdens we have faced in life and the sacrifices we have made for their sake."

Mika'il sighed. "If only."

Abunaki gave a small, thoughtful nod, and decided to change the subject. "Have you not heard the news, Mika'il? Immorkaan has sanctioned greater powers to the Chief of the *Souk As-Silaah*."

"Do not speak to me of that place!" Mika'il spat. "Curse the day Immorkaan appointed Ghulam Mirza as the chief! He is nothing but a warlord in the hide of a false leader who has always oppressed the city's artisans."

"Ease your temper, Mika'il," Abunaki lowered his voice and glanced over his shoulder. "You never know who might be listening." He leaned in closer. "I, for one, have greatly considered approaching him to build an alliance. Rather than contend with them, having such men as allies does tend to have some benefits!"

"Indeed?" Mika'il's eyes narrowed. "Much like your friendship with Thamir, the merchant? You do what you must, Abunaki. I will not partake in their corrupt ways. Will you be needing anything else?"

"Yes, there is one more thing," Abunaki said, quickly noting Mika'il's dismissive tone, "a dear friend has a few things he needs repaired. I highly recommended your name."

"I appreciate the referral," Mika'il acknowledged. "I will take good care of him. And if our transaction bears fruit, I promise to lower the rate for your next order."

Abunaki bade them farewell, and left with his goods, Alulim struggling to keep up with his stride.

Later that hour, Mukhtar was glad to escape the confines of the forge. He and Saif crossed the dusty street to the cooling shade of a palm tree squeezed into a small gap between Jaul the carpenter, and an eatery belonging to one of Mika'il's oldest friends, Tasseem. They had an arrangement that Saif and Mukhtar could eat anything worth two copper coins, paid for by Mika'il. He and Faraj preferred to have their meals in the forge in case a customer required attention.

The sun was at its peak, sweltering without a single cloud to tarnish the blue sky. Mukhtar settled down in his usual spot and watched the citizens of Khalidah pass by in their long, sweeping robes and *thaubs* of brown, white, and the occasional colorful shade of red or blue.

Mukhtar and Saif discussed Abunaki's warning about the Chief of *Souk-As-Silaah* while they waited for Adil Babak to join them. The young guard was about the same age of nineteen as Mukhtar and Saif, tall and muscular, with sharp handsome features that construed royalty despite his simple Khalidan Guard uniform. His blue eyes, straight nose, and lightly tanned skin were an exact replica of his father's, even though Mukhtar rarely had the opportunity of personally meeting General Aarguf Babak, the appointed leader of the Royal Army and older brother to the King.

"Salaam," Adil greeted them as he approached. He was accompanied by members of his squadron, and equally his closest neighbors among the wealthy families of the Rich District. Mukhtar and Saif's least favorite.

"Look here, boys! It is the muck of the city!" Their leader, Yael Varda, sneered at the top of his voice, followed by the laughter of the minions who never left his tail, Nabun, Qurais, and Jubair. Bullies and vandals they were known to be, abusers of the authority of their uniforms.

"Leave them be!" Adil waved them off. It always seemed strange to Mukhtar that he would roam the streets with the likes of Yael, yet he would sit down to eat only with Mukhtar and Saif.

They bade him farewell, threw Mukhtar and Saif dirty and loathsome looks, and disappeared down the street. Adil set his spear against the wall and sat down across from Saif and Mukhtar, who were already halfway through some vegetable stew and rice.

A nearby minaret announced the call for prayer, and Saif stood up as he always did when it was time for prayers. "Coming, Mukhtar?"

"Go," Mukhtar replied without looking at him. "I will follow."

"Never pay heed to Yael," Adil told Mukhtar when they were alone. "He is quick on the tongue, but a good soldier."

Mukhtar was not listening. With Saif gone, his thoughts had drifted to that morning's events.

"Mukhtar?" Adil waved at him when he didn't reply. "What troubles you?"

Mukhtar leaned back comfortably against the wall, as a waiter came out to offer them another pitcher of water.

"He was late this morning, and had to face his uncle's wrath!" The waiter chuckled. "I have been watching his face melt from across the street!"

"Oh, you have, *have you?*" Mukhtar snarled at him. "Mind your own *business,* Halim!"

"I tell you, Adil," Halim continued enthusiastically, ignoring Mukhtar's warning, "I have never seen the mighty Mukhtar so helpless before."

"Adil, might I interest you in a gripping tale?" Mukhtar raised his voice.

"I would be very much pleased!" Adil remarked.

"It is a tale of bravery and valor," Mukhtar claimed. "The tale of a young man and his quest to become most skilled with a short blade and a potato!"

Mukhtar paused for a moment, allowing the words to sink in. Adil was confused, but Halim understood immediately, and his expression became grim.

"Wait— that is not— you vowed never to—!"

"I made no such vow!" Mukhtar pressed mockingly. "Oh, how very tempted I am!"

Halim, red around the ears, glared at Mukhtar, left the pitcher of water, and rushed back to the eatery, cursing under his breath.

"What was *that* all about?" Adil frowned.

For a moment, Mukhtar thought Halim would return with a rolling pin or a wooden spoon as a weapon, but when he didn't, Mukhtar gave a casual wave and shook his head. "Nothing."

"Indeed?"

Mukhtar gave him a sideways glance. "This morning, I stumbled upon an illegal slave trade on Rayis Street."

Adil eyed him cautiously. "And what does that entail?"

"I freed the slaves," Mukhtar told him.

Adil slowly raised both his eyebrows. "You did? *How?*"

Mukhtar gave him the details and watched Adil's face become grimmer by the moment, that when he was done, the young guard only nodded silently.

"Will you say *nothing* to that?" Mukhtar demanded.

"What is there to say?" Adil shrugged. His expression was mildly contemptuous, to which Mukhtar became slightly disturbed, wondering if he had made a mistake by telling him. "You toyed with fire, Mukhtar," he asserted. "Slave traders are not to be trifled with. You need not have involved yourself with them."

Mukhtar's brow furrowed with fury and disbelief. "So turn away from such brutality? Abandon them to be used and abused?"

Adil took a deep breath, chose his words carefully, and gave Mukhtar a stern look. "Did it ever occur to you, that even as slaves, they would still be given food and shelter, provided for by their masters? They now have nothing but the rags on their backs, and by nightfall they will steal, or do worse, just to diminish their hunger. Consider this, Mukhtar— you have endangered not just theirs, but your life too, for if those slavers were to pick up your scent," he paused, "pray, they never find you!"

Mukhtar leaned back against the wall and shut his eyes, as a loaded cart rattled by, its mule braying loudly, shamelessly complaining of its burden. Whatever Adil said, made sense, and Mukhtar had not given it much thought. He knew he was stepping into the wolf's den, but he had escaped undetected. Would the consequences truly follow him so far?

"Say nothing to my mother," he requested, and Adil responded with a reassuring nod. Saif emerged from the *Masjid* along with other devotees who were now returning to their places of work. "And nothing to Saif either?"

"I shall keep it secret for as long as it remains so," Adil assured him.

They both stood up as Saif approached them. "Salaam. You missed prayers, Mukhtar. What kept you?"

"I kept him, Saif," Adil replied instead, and Mukhtar gave him an appreciative look, for he did not want the rest of his day to be all about how big a mistake he had made. "I am still curious, however. Why was Halim displeased with your tale?"

"The tale of a blade and a potato?" Mukhtar grinned and glanced over his shoulder. "Halim Al-Kanaan comes from a long line of miners, but has it never occurred to you why he would work at an eatery?"

"Unskilled with a pickaxe?" Saif shrugged.

Mukhtar shook his head. "A year back, he came across some decent coin, entertained friends at a tavern, and later came to Tasseem's Eatery for a meal. Unknown to him, his coin purse was lost along the way, and they foolishly ate to their fill, but had no money to make payment. He then pleaded and promised to pay later."

"That must have made Tasseem's day," Saif grinned and glanced at the eatery.

"Tasseem simply showed him the kitchen door," Mukhtar gestured at the door of the forge as they approached it. "He had to peel a pail of potatoes to pay his debt, but the man was so frightened and distracted, he peeled an entire sack, twice his size, in one night, and given that he did it in a state of drunkenness, Tasseem was impressed and offered to hire him!"

Saif and Adil burst out laughing in the alley just as Halim, oblivious to them, appeared across the street serving more customers with enthusiasm in his every step. For a moment, Mukhtar felt a distant remorse for backbiting him, and his laughter fizzled away.

With no objection from Mika'il, Adil spent the afternoon at the forge, making jokes to keep them entertained, and only left when a squadron of higher ranking guards patrolled by.

That evening, Mukhtar left the forge hurriedly, wanting nothing but to isolate himself in his room. He had felt as though the day could not possibly be any worse than it had become. Mika'il was in such a bad mood, that Mukhtar wondered if his uncle might even reach home safely without ending up in a fight somewhere along the way.

Everywhere around him, shops were closing, and merchants were packing up their stalls and wares. The city's distinct buzz quietened down to a lower decibel, while the sounds of music drifted into the streets through the now open doors of inns, taverns, and brothels.

Small flickers of light were appearing in various homes, as people lit their lanterns, oil lamps, and candles. He passed the alley where the slave traders had parked their ox-driven, caged cart. All that remained were the darkened residuals of dried blood against the stone, sand, and dirt, further down the street.

He turned his gaze and dragged his feet along, slightly hunched due to exhaustion, as the events of the day reenacted in his mind. Later that afternoon, the most unwelcome of customers had arrived at the forge; representatives from Immorkaan. Captain Ghadan and his Lieutenant, Hassin. Orders from the Elder Council were scarce since much of the Royal Army's requisitions came from the *Souk As-Silaah*, but on such rare occasions, they were Mika'il's least favorite. Never had any dealings with Immorkaan been on fair terms.

Unfortunately, they found Mika'il at a bad time, and he wasted no effort in tolerating them. He blatantly scorned them, demanding that they must first pay off their previous dues, *and* pay him in advance for the new order before he embarked on it. The delegates, just as intolerant, threatened to tax them heavily if Mika'il did not comply. Compelled to defend his livelihood, Mika'il was forced to bow his head in shame and adhere to their demands.

Mukhtar and Saif's morale shattered to bits when Mika'il curtly announced that neither of them would be receiving the day's wages because he now needed the money to requisition supplies. For this, he needed to journey to his hometown of Mirzaan, a single day's ride and a two-day return by caravan, slower with the goods. Hopefully, they would have completed their work by the end of the seventh day, as per the terms.

Mukhtar crossed the street and paused before the doors of his house. Suha would eventually discover Mika'il's four-day absence, and would ultimately learn everything from her sister, including Mukhtar's encounter with Mika'il. He was ardently debating whether or not to disclose anything to her, when someone excitedly called his name.

"Mukhtar!"

Startled, he turned and smiled when he saw...

"Misbah!" He scooped her up into a hug. Nine-year-old Misbah, with her neat headscarf and smiling eyes, had always been fond of Mukhtar. He put her down gently and greeted her mother.

She responded respectfully as she came closer, holding a large dish covered in a plain cloth. Along with a headscarf, and eyes very like her daughter's, Mukhtar noted a darkening bruise on her left cheek. The origin of it was not unknown, but he respectfully refrained from showing discern. Her husband, Gizwani, was known to be a drunk and violent man, and the only reason why Samiya and their daughter would be out at that hour, was if Gizwani himself was away, perhaps drowning in wine at a tavern. She drew her headscarf closer to hide the bruise and again, Mukhtar pretended not to notice.

Misbah chatted merrily, telling him all about her day at the *Madrassa*, and what she and her friends did the previous week. He responded with silent nods and led them into the small courtyard with a non-functioning stone fountain in its center, over which he threw his cloak and followed the aroma of food to the tiny kitchen. Before the small fire pit, Suha stirred a boiling, steaming pot, and sang to herself, unaware of Mukhtar's arrival.

"Salaam, Ummi," he greeted her softly, and she gave a small start. Despite being slightly alarmed, her smile was so warm and welcoming, he could not have asked for anything else in that moment.

"Salaam," she placed a hand on her chest and heaved slightly. "You startled me. Why are you late?"

"It has been a long and trying day."

Her smile fell. "Was there trouble at the forge? Did your Khal punish you?"

"I will tell you later, Ummi," Mukhtar lowered his voice. "Samiya and Misbah are here, and—" he lowered his voice further, "—she has a bruise on her cheek—"

"Mukhtar!" Suha's voice descended to a bare whisper, and she threw a cautious glance out the kitchen door. "Have I not told you before? It is not our concern!"

"Gizwani is becoming relentless, Ummi!" he argued. "How much more must she endure before it becomes our concern?"

Suha reached out and ran her hand through his hair. "There is much that you do not understand." She stepped out into the courtyard, and he trailed behind, looking slightly crestfallen. "Go. Rest. I will call when food is ready. And remove your cloak from the fountain!"

The two women greeted and hugged each other. "I bought pastries from Falami's bakery, and thought of you," Samiya said.

"Oh Samiya, may the Almighty bless your warm heart!" Suha fretted.

"And yours, Suha," Samiya returned the compliment.

Mukhtar left Misbah with a final smile and ascended the short staircase up to the landing above. The two women exchanged more pleasantries down below, and their voices carried away into the kitchen.

Their stay was not long, and Mukhtar knew that Samiya would have to return home before Gizwani found out that she had left.

"Did she tell you then?" Mukhtar prodded Suha for answers when they settled down for their meal. "Did she confirm that Gizwani raised his hand on her?"

Suha's nostrils flared. "How many times must I tell you? *This does not concern you!*"

Mukhtar fell silent and decided not to prod further. Suha would only become angrier.

"What is the matter, Mukhtar?" She sensed his agitation and softened her voice. "Why are you so troubled today?"

Mukhtar narrated to her the events of the day, taking caution not to mention the slave traders. Having witnessed Adil's response, he was not quite ready to share that secret with her just yet. However, he did not hold back his frustrations with Immorkaan. Their unjust way of conducting business had long remained unchallenged, and he had more cause than many to detest them.

"How do they *justify* their actions? They bring nothing but despair with them! We must stand for ourselves! We must challenge their tyranny!"

He had spoken the wrong words without realizing it. Ever since her husband had been taken away by the authorities, Suha absolutely refused to entertain such rebellious talk in her household.

"God forgive me, your tongue be tied and silenced!" She threw a nervous glance over her shoulder, as though expecting the authorities to be listening in. "Have I only raised *rebels?* It pains me, just as much as anyone else, but this is the life we have all chosen, and we must survive it! I too have lost much, your father, your brother—"

"Zaki is still alive, Ummi," Mukhtar said irritably. "You did not *lose* him. He serves the Red-Guard, remember?"

"*Do not argue with me!*" she snapped at him. "Now, you listen to me, Mukhtar, or so help me, I will walk you to Aztalaan and leave you with your rebellious brother. The two of you can bask in all the glory in the world!" She took a strained breath and calmed down. "Your father was a brave man, and so is your brother, but they have always forgotten that their family's needs are greater than their ambitions. Ever have they craved glory and honor, and in the end, it did not matter what they liberated, because the oppression continued, while your father, and others like him, lost more than their lives."

Mukhtar knew why she was upset. Only recently had they received a letter from Zaki, stating that he had been quested to hunt down the fabled Assassins of Ghuldad, a notion that had been greatly opposed by everyone in the family.

A light breeze lazily floated into the room and frisked the flame of the oil lamp. A cricket chirped from somewhere outside. Suha stared at her empty plate and Mukhtar gazed out into the deserted courtyard, wondering if that was indeed what his father and elder brother had done, that they had disregarded their kin for selfish endeavors. The very thought filled him with sorrow. Little did he have, but his father's memory to look up to, and even that seemed to diminish before his very eyes.

Later that night, he lay on his bed, staring at the dark cracks against the whitewashed ceiling of his room, listening to a dog barking in the distance. Too much had happened that day for him to just sleep off and forget. Why would Suha declare her husband's ambitions foolish? *Did I free those slaves for a desire of valor and glory?* He thought.

Was his act of nobility, a weak trait of his father's? He shook his head. *No. Not Glory. Pity.* He had stopped to consider, even doubt his actions, and yet, it was purely out of mercy for a fellow human being.

However, that was not what truly troubled him. It was what Mika'il had said to him about being irresponsible, and Mukhtar's reaction to his uncle's words, regardless of how they were spoken. He felt a pang of guilt in his stomach. Mika'il was like a father to him, and despite his anger, Mukhtar was deeply fond of him. He should not have to bear Mukhtar's irresponsibility. No one should.

He turned over on his side, straightened his pillow, and made a silent vow to improve himself. He knew his uncle. If he showed signs of change, Mika'il would forgo his anger.

The thought gave him some comfort, as he drifted off to sleep and almost immediately fell into a dream.

It was an endless cycle of absurd activities that involved Mika'il crouched inside a cage, yelling at him in a strange language. Then Abunaki appeared behind him, laughing loudly. *'This time he will be for free! Those slavers promised me!'* He pointed at two men who turned out to be Saif and Faraj, cackling away like a pair of jesters.

He was woken by a *Mu'adhin's* call for prayer in the distance, and he reached out for a cup of water by his bedside. Then he turned the other way and fell back to sleep. The dream was different this time.

THREE

RULE OF THE UNJUST

A sense of exhilaration filled him purposefully. There was something here he needed to see, something he needed to do, and its outcome would either benefit or destroy him. The desert storm had engulfed him whole, shifting and unsettling sands, thick and obliterating. Static and lightning flashed high above him, followed by the sounds of thunder, deep and roaring.

Ahead of him was a shimmering bright light, peering through the gaps in the blowing sands. There was a purpose to that light. A firm and resolute purpose. Its existence was divine, yet he sensed its wickedness. Its purpose was bound to an evil beyond anything imaginable, and yet he was drawn to it. Why was he drawn to it? He had to go to it— what if he never reached it?

Something emerged amidst the shifting sands. Eyes subtly glowing behind clouds of dirt and dust, eyes that were blank and milky white. To what did they belong? What devilry was at play here? Fear gripped him. Not the fear of death, but that of loss. The presence will deny him his innermost desire to do good, but will ignite and fulfill his deepest temptations of wickedness. It would not allow him to cross to the other side and reach the light.

The creature had someone. Or something, bound in chains, lying at its feet. It was struggling against its bonds and it spoke...

'Wake up, Mukhtar! Wake up!'

There was a loud knocking. It pounded heavily against the inside of his skull. He pried his eyes open, but remained still, trying to contemplate his surroundings. Sunlight was pouring through his open window with a welcoming, crisp morning breeze and the unmistakable yelling of his neighbor, Gizwani Al-Shura. Perhaps Samiya's venture last night did not go unnoticed. Where was Misbah, he wondered? He hoped that the innocent girl was nowhere about to witness the cruelty inflicted upon her mother.

"Mukhtar? Wake up or you will be late again!" Suha's voice sounded from outside his door.

His window overlooked Misbah's, and there were times,

unknown to her, that he had seen her cry in a corner by herself.

Suha called again. Groggy and a little feverish, he mustered the strength to get up and open the door.

"Mukhtar!" she gasped, her expression solemn. "You are pale and *drenched* in sweat! What is the matter?"

"Nothing," he mumbled and shook off her hand as she tried to feel his forehead.

"Are you unwell?"

"I am fine, Ummi."

The look of a mother, worried for her son, was too much for him to bear, especially when he wanted nothing but to be left alone. Left alone to dwell a while longer on his nightmare. The image of a figure bound in chains at the mercy of some creature, deeply troubled him— had been troubling him since he was a child, an affliction he had struggled to keep secret even from his mother.

He pressed the palms of his hands into his eyes. Shifting sands. Lightning. Gleaming eyes. Flashing images now seeped through the gaps in his fingers. The more of reality that materialized around him, the more of the dream that disappeared. He shuffled to the basin of water and rinsed his mouth with salt and mint leaves. He then dressed while listening to the sounds of conflict drifting in through his window. Perhaps, he thought, Samiya should ask for *Talaaq*. How much longer was she willing to endure her husband's continuing abuse? And where were the damned authorities? Surely, a passing guard patrol should have heard the commotion by now? Why had no one intervened? Why hadn't he?

Should he? He certainly felt the urge. To bring Gizwani to

justice. To free Samiya from her burden. His thoughts went back to the slaves. Was it really his place to intervene?

Suha had prepared a cup of spicy cardamom tea, which scathed his tongue and throat as he gulped it down and hastily left for work.

A groggy and rather disgruntled Saif greeted him when he entered the forge, and Mukhtar had a feeling that he was not the only one who had a restless night.

"Nightmares?" he asked.

"In a manner of speaking," Saif replied. "A talk for another time, though. We have much work. Faraj wants us to clean the forge before embarking on the council's order."

Mukhtar glanced at Faraj, who was scanning through some sort of list by the counter.

"Seven spears and seven wooden shields," Saif responded to his unasked question. "He has called for one of Kaka Jaffar's cart-boys to bring us wood from the lumber yards."

"But that will take all day!" Mukhtar complained. "When has Kaka Jaffar ever delivered anything on time?"

Saif shrugged. "Mika'il has left instructions. He has already informed most of his customers that he will be unavailable for a few days, and Faraj will do the same in his absence. While we await all the material, he wants us to clean the entire forge."

"Indeed?" Mukhtar felt his throat twitch slightly. "With whom did he leave instructions?" And as soon as he said it, he realized how foolish he might have sounded. Was he becoming envious that Mika'il would now entrust instructions to all but him?

"Does it matter?" Saif gave a small chuckle. "The filth of this forge will need several days to scrub clean!" he stated. "It is truly strange how your uncle thinks at times, if I may be so bold."

"Strange indeed," Mukhtar muttered. It seemed his uncle had not forgone their previous day's argument, and would perhaps brood over it his entire journey. He kept any further displeasure to himself and picked up his leather apron from behind the door.

With the forge being a constant hive of activity, it was rare that either of them had the time to grab a sweeper. The floor was littered with pieces of metal and wood shavings. Broken items and random tools were scattered all over. Layers upon layers of dust covered underutilized areas, especially Mukhtar and Saif's bench, unlike Faraj's workbench, which was neat and tidy, tools well-oiled and accounted for.

Mukhtar and Saif practically waged war on the forge, while Faraj focused his efforts on attending to customers who were unwary of Mika'il's absence.

Several months' worth of effects were unearthed along with old and almost forgotten fabrications of various designs, plates of armor, swords and knives, spearheads and arrowheads. An array of broken tools like hammers, mallets, and chisels, were exhumed from mounds of dirt and the darkest, most deserted corners of the forge. Most of all these treasures ended up in a large pile in the alley behind the forge.

Their battle was not without casualties. At some point during the morning, all three of them had suffered at least an injury each. Within the first two hours, Faraj had tripped and fallen over a small crate that Mukhtar had pulled out from under his bench, and had to sit down on Mika'il's stool, massaging his lower back.

Shortly after, Saif had unknowingly thrust his hand into the same crate and caught his forearm on a sharp metal piece. In an attempt to stop the bleeding, Mukhtar had rushed across the street to procure honey and garlic paste from Tasseem, which he applied on the wound, and dressed it up with a piece of cloth.

Mukhtar was no exception. At noon, while they ate, Adil and Saif laughed shamelessly at Mukhtar's face. Below his left eye, a large lump was steadily bruising where a fist had made contact. He had been trying to winch an arrowhead that was stuck to the bottom of the same wooden crate responsible for Saif and Faraj's injuries.

Saif was clutching his ribs with his good arm, strained with laughter. "His hand slipped, and he hit himself right in the face!"

Mukhtar threw him a scathing look. "My hand was sweaty!" he argued, but that only aggravated their laughter.

Later that afternoon, Kaka Jaffar sent a messenger to inform them that the wood would not arrive until the following morning. Hardly in any physical state to get much work done, Faraj awarded them the remainder of the day to rest their injuries.

Saif suggested waiting for Adil's shift to end so they could walk home together. Mukhtar agreed wholeheartedly, wanting to reach home when it was already dark, so that no one else would see his face. They spent the rest of the day discussing politics and playing games of chance to pass the time.

When Mukhtar arrived home in the evening, Suha was knitting in the courtyard, and she shrieked when she saw his face.

The battle that followed was one of many. First, they argued about why, and with whom, he was fighting. Then, they quarreled about his behavior with Mika'il the previous day. His uncle, it seemed, had spared enough time to disclose everything to his aunt before he left and naturally, the sisters conversed. They settled the argument with Mukhtar's numerous apologies and vows to change his ways, after which he had to contend with Suha's insistence to treat his wound.

"Hold still, Mukhtar!" she snarled at him, her voice as dangerous as the warning of a rattlesnake.

"Get it *away* from me!" Mukhtar protested frivolously. "It reeks!"

"Mukhtar Harun Zafar!" She slapped his wrist. "You had better hold still if you know what is good for you!"

It was all he could do not to push away her hand and vomit on the side. It truly did emit a pungent smell, and stung his eye as she applied it.

"Why were you fighting?"

"Have we not discussed this already? I was *not* fighting!"

Despite their previous argument, she still raised a silent and suspicious eyebrow.

"Why would I lie about something this obvious?" he argued.

"You expect me to believe you were hurt at work?" she asked accusingly. "What sort of *blacksmith* are you?"

"Believe what you want then," he mumbled.

"*What was that?*"

"Nothing!" he replied quickly, not wanting another argument. "I am tired. I must rest."

"Not until you have eaten," she said, as she finished applying the ointment. "And I have something to show you," she added in a

kinder tone.

"What is it?" he asked distractedly. The medicine had a strong effect on his eye, and he used the edge of his sleeve to scoop up the tears flowing through. She reached forward and slapped his wrist again. He scowled at her.

"Wash and come down. And don't you *dare* touch that eye!" she warned.

When he went down, his stomach gave a low rumble as an inviting aroma of fresh flatbread and chicken, roasted with spices and yogurt, reached his nostrils.

"Is there a special occasion?" he smiled and sat down on his favorite murky-brown, moth-eaten cushion.

"Does a mother need an occasion to dote upon her son?" she placed a large, glistening piece of chicken on his plate, and pushed forward a bowl of *Humus* and *Tahini*.

"Such food is fit for a wedding!" he commented enthusiastically.

"Perhaps we shall serve it at *your* wedding!" she hinted smartly, and his smile fell. "If and when you finally decide to marry!"

He gave her a look usually reserved for when she brought up such suggestions or complained about how much she longed for grandchildren. Not at all willing to deliberate it any further, he changed the subject.

They ate and discussed their day's activities. Mukhtar told her about how tasking it was to clean the forge, while Suha told him about what had happened while he was at work. Samiya had visited again that afternoon, with another bruise on her cheek. Mukhtar did not meet Suha's eye while she spoke, and his silent protest became evident.

"It is not that we are ignorant or selfish, Mukhtar," she explained. "Samiya herself has forbidden our involvement, and until she does not ask, we cannot intervene. She speaks to me of what happens behind their walls, for she has none other to confide in, and what you hear or see, you must keep to yourself. Understood?"

He nodded sincerely.

"What did you want to show me?" he asked her while they put away the remnants of their meal.

"Wait here," she retreated up the stairs and returned a few moments after, with a small, black, wooden box, bound in dark leather and embossed in gold embroidery, roughly the size of her hands put together.

"What is this?" he received it with a curious frown.

"Open it!" she said excitedly.

Mukhtar opened the box. Padded silk lined the inside, its contents neatly packed beside each other. A scroll, a wrapped object, a bone, feather, claw, what looked like the tail of a scorpion, and a lock of dark hair.

"These items are so peculiar," he held up each one to examine it.

"I questioned your father about them," Suha said, "but he offered no explanation. He only made me vow to keep them safe."

The dirty, tightly bound scroll emitted a putrid scent, far more pungent than the medicine around his eye. To keep from vomiting into the box, he pushed it aside and picked up the object wrapped in dark silk.

At the end of a short, golden chain was a triangular pendant, boasting an embedded, glimmering, icy-blue gemstone, unlike anything he had ever seen. Perfectly circular in shape, it seemed to be emitting a mesmerizing bluish glow from within itself. A strange emotion overcame him; a conflict between love and hate, good and evil, right and wrong, and part of him wanted to fling it across the room, yet another triggered an inner sense of deep possession.

"Your father brought it with him," Suha explained. "A relic he found during his expedition to Ninya," her tone became apologetic, and Mukhtar noted her ears blush ever so slightly. "I felt terrible about what I said last night. Your father was many things, but he truly cared about us. You and Zaki were the jewels of his eyes. I realize that perhaps it is time for me to relinquish what I have been clinging to for all these years. Keep the box and his contents. May they remind you of his strengths, and caution you from his weaknesses."

"Ummi—" Mukhtar began, but was unable to bring the words together.

She acknowledged his emotions with a warm smile, and urged him to indulge in the contents of the box.

Mukhtar returned the Amulet to the box, and turned his attention to the bound scroll. With difficulty, using his one good eye to find a nook, he dug into the knot and eventually loosened the binding.

The scroll was filthy, faded in some areas, and had a familiar scent, acrid like that of a resin he used to bind string on sword handles, only stronger and far more putrid than any resin he had ever used. The writing was in a dark, crimson ink, and a language he could not read. Strange symbols and markings filled-in the edges of the scroll, and emanated a peculiar sense of exhilaration, much like the Amulet kept with it. Absentmindedly, he bade Suha farewell when she retired to bed, and continued to stare at the piece of parchment. He held it up at different angles and tried to decrypt its meanings.

The hour was late when he finally doused the candles and oil lamps, and made his way to bed, tired and exhausted. He moaned as he wrapped himself up in his sheets, remembering that the following day promised to be full of toiling with hammer and anvil.

Under the supervision of Faraj, he and Saif spent the following three days preparing handles for the spears and the backings for the shields, to be completed when Mika'il would arrive with the rest of the materials. This was no simple task, for they would usually give such work to Jaul the Carpenter, who would complete it sooner and better. He was, however, unavailable, and without Mika'il's approval, Faraj was unable to negotiate a trade with other carpenters in the city.

It seemed that misfortune would not cease to follow them. When Mika'il arrived, he did not bring with him readily forged steel. Instead, he had a cartload of ingots, and Mukhtar screamed with frustration when he realized that he and Saif would have to spend the night by the furnace and keep it burning at its hottest in order to melt the metal before forging and fabrication.

"Steel has almost become as rare as gold," Mika'il tried to explain. "Alas, I could not afford it without having to sell an arm and a leg. Jawad Banu-Darr was kind enough to loan me these ingots."

It was only on the sixth day, did they finally begin to beat and shape the metal, but the day ended sooner than expected, and with much disappointment. At the eleventh hour, unable to bear the heat and fumes of the furnace anymore, they put down their tools and gathered in the alley behind the forge. Mika'il commended their efforts, and reluctantly assured them that he would be able to bargain for more time, but Mukhtar knew that it was an impossibility. Immorkaan did not understand leniency.

Barely an hour after reopening the forge the following morning, Hassin and his superior, Ghadan, arrived with a cavalry of five other guards, to collect seven spears and seven shields, and they were not at all pleased. With blatant mockery and scorn, they scrutinized and criticized everything, from the materials used, to the poor craftsmanship.

"You were given a simple task, blacksmith!" Ghadan barked at Mika'il. He was shorter than Mukhtar, bald and hairless, except for his thick, bushy eyebrows that seemed to meet in the middle of his round face. "A spear and shield a day! And I come to find wares that could have been made by *children!*"

Even Mukhtar had to admit to the poor quality and finish of the items. Given more time, they may have done much better. They always did.

"Seven days could never have been enough," Mika'il pleaded. "I made it *very* clear, but you were adamant."

Mukhtar pleaded alongside his uncle. The wood was untreated, and the metal was in no shape to do battle. Improvements could be made if they were given more time.

"Immorkaan does not care for your inadequacy," Ghadan remarked. "I would not pay a dime for such poor instruments!"

"And we do not care for your coin!" Mukhtar retorted. "Take your business elsewhere!"

"Leash your *dog,* blacksmith!" Ghadan warned.

Mika'il raised a hand to silence Mukhtar. "Hassin, you once worked this same forge. Will you not understand? We ask only for a day more to finish. Will you not show leniency for your former companions?"

Light-skinned, curly-haired, and a year older than Mukhtar, Hassin's eyes remained cold and unyielding. Leniency would not cross his mind, not on this day. With fair reason.

Hassin was once a blacksmith, a prodigy of Mika'il's, and he worked hard, with determination and skill, earning the title of Hassin the Iron-Heart, one who understood the metal and how to bend it to his will. All but a short-lived title. Hardly a year back, Mukhtar had destroyed his reputation by accusing him of selling arms to mercenaries, an act frowned upon by any distinguished and respectable weapon-maker across the city.

The battle was lengthy and brutal. Both Hassin and Mukhtar were left with bleeding lips and wounded souls, their friendship disbanded, their unity destroyed, and despite Mika'il's willingness to forgive, Hassin left. Mukhtar did not care then, nor did he care now, and it was because of this bitter memory that they both found themselves on opposite sides of the forge's counter, with little else but hatred for each other.

"You are pleading with a traitor, Khal," Mukhtar scoffed. "He has become an advocate of the corruption of Immorkaan."

Ignoring Mukhtar altogether, Hassin stepped forward. "Do not force their hand, Mika'il. Give them what they want," he spoke very softly, and with an edge to his voice. "You know of whom I speak," he added in an undertone.

It was only meant for Mika'il's ears, but the words carried, and Mukhtar overheard.

"You treacherous—! I *knew* you were up to no good!" Mukhtar growled.

Mika'il's eyes narrowed. "Return to your masters, and take your threats with you!"

Hassin stepped away from the counter, looking very grim. "Do not contend with them, Mika'il. They have much power and authority."

"Then they have more to lose than I!" Mika'il declared.

"What will it be, Mika'il?" Ghadan demanded, and Hassin stepped aside wearing a rather triumphant expression.

"You either pay us in fair for the work we have done," Mika'il folded his arms, "or allow us more time to finish."

"Or take your unworthy trades elsewhere, and never darken our doorstep again!" Mukhtar added angrily.

By now, a small crowd had gathered. Mika'il's neighbors had left their own places of work to come and watch what was happening. Ghadan began to laugh, and his cavalry followed suit. "You speak as if you have a choice, blacksmith!"

"You have no authority!" Mika'il retorted.

"Don't I?" Ghadan smirked. "I bear the Khalidan Seal of Immorkaan," he touched the branded insignia on his uniform, a five-pointed star, bearing the symbols of the Five Cities. "I advocate the rule of the Elder Council. Under my charge were you given this task, and by my measure, you have failed miserably!"

"I do not see what that has to do with seven spears and shields!" Mika'il argued. "They are hardly a speck in the Royal Army's arsenal!"

"No, you do not," Ghadan began pacing back and forth as he spoke, addressing everyone in the vicinity. "If you had such intellect, you would have foreseen this," he whispered to Mika'il, and then raised his voice again, "allow me to enlighten you. Your inadequate weapons could prove fatal in battle, endangering the lives of our citizens. As per the laws of the land, whosoever places the life of another citizen in jeopardy, be it by his own actions, directly or indirectly, is considered a traitor and a threat to society and—"

"And has every right to a fair trial!" Mika'il interrupted. "I know what you are doing, you traitorous *imp!*"

"These are *my* streets!" Ghadan growled. "Here, *I* am judge and executioner! *I* am your *fair trial!* Surrender this mediocre forge and all your shoddy wares, or by the King's name and the laws of this great Empire, all your heads shall be cleaved and hung before the gates of the *Souk As-Silaah!*"

There was an odd ringing in Mukhtar's ears. The injustice had gone too far for too long. Without giving it any thought, he reached under the counter, pulled out a rusty old scimitar and charged forward, clumsily clambering over the forge's counter. Both Mika'il and Saif instinctively grabbed hold, and tried to pull him back. Ghadan took several surprised steps back, and allowed his guards to come forward, all drawing swords with menacing, bloodthirsty snarls, and growls. It took the combined efforts of Mika'il, Faraj, and Saif, to restrain Mukhtar. Hands trembling uncontrollably, he fumbled the scimitar and cut himself. Only then did he allow them to draw him back, clutching his bleeding hand.

Joined by his cavalry, Ghadan cackled loudly. "You wish to fight us when you cannot even wield a blade?" he shrieked. "I warn you, blacksmith. Leash your *dog* before he loses his head!"

"There is no need for this to end in bloodshed," Mika'il's voice trembled slightly. "Perhaps we can come to a peaceful agreement?"

"Your forge," Ghadan replied simply. "And *all* your wares!"

Mukhtar glared at him through watery eyes, his lips curled in a furious attempt to keep from screaming in pain. "We cannot allow them to do this!" he muttered through gritted teeth. "We cannot give in to their injustice! We *must* fight back! We must take a stand!"

"And we will!" Mika'il assured him, his voice heavy with disdain. "At the right time. In the right place."

FOUR

THE SOUK AND THE BEGGAR

The midday sun tore through clear skies, scorching his slumped shoulders as he walked home, sullen that the forge had been taken, angered that it was Hassin and Ghadan who instigated it, and frustrated that he, Mukhtar, failed to prevent it. He still had the urge, the strong compulsion to turn back, confront and force them to undo what they had done.

What would it achieve though? More hatred? More conflict? Will revenge on Hassin and Ghadan bring him comfort, or only more despair? Perhaps Mika'il was right. Perhaps there were other ways of pursuing the matter without hostility.

"Salaam, Mukhtar," came his mother's voice.

He jumped and looked around. So occupied were his thoughts,

that he had already reached home and was standing in the center of the courtyard, with nearly no recollection of the journey.

"Salaam, Ummi," he responded with an exhausting yawn, took off his cloak, and threw it over the fountain in the middle of the courtyard.

"How many times have I told you *not* to do that?" she asked rhetorically.

"When has it ever sprung water?" Mukhtar responded irritably. "It is a *useless* pile of stone!"

"It is also the foundation of the house of your father and forefathers. *Remove* your cloak!"

"Fine!"

The cloak swept the ground behind him, as he fumed up the stairs and slammed the door. He did not wish to leave his room. Suha called for him twice more, but he did not reply. He knew that he would eventually have to break the news to her, and at dawn the following day, he would have to trek the city streets to find work. A weary prospect in and of itself.

He hung his cloak on a nail behind the door, sat down against the edge of his bed, and buried his face in his hands. What was the reason? What was the purpose behind it all? Perhaps it was a sign, for him to make a change, to pursue a newer course, and find an ambition larger than toiling a forge until old age, like his uncle.

"Mukhtar!" Suha called.

Why must there be so much loss and destruction for change to occur? Such absurdity. Such oppression. The strong continue to impose, and the weak give in because they *believe* themselves to be weak. Were *they* weak? Mika'il was never weak, so why did he surrender? Mukhtar raised his head slowly and blinked in the light.

"Mukhtar?"

Did Mika'il know something that Mukhtar did not?

"I have prepared food for you!"

A mere argument. Only a marginal effort and not even a fight? Mika'il was a man who did not tolerate any form of misbehavior or mischief. A man known to stand up to authority, and defend his own. Mika'il, the *real* Mika'il, would never have allowed *anyone* to step over him. And yet…

"Mukhtar? Hurry, or it will become cold."

Something was afoot. Something was amiss, and Mukhtar had to find out. For now, he would behave as if nothing had happened. He would say nothing to Suha, until he himself had a clear understanding of things, and right after dawn the following day, he would go to Mika'il and demand some answers. His livelihood depended on it.

"Mukhtar!"

"Coming!"

At the crack of dawn, Mukhtar rose sharply out of bed, and with a strong sense of purpose, he left home.

A hazy, purple sky loomed overhead, while a crisp morning chill ensured that everyone was cloaked. The streets were just about showing signs of early activity as he walked to Mika'il's, a dwelling much smaller than his own, south of the *Souk As-Silaah,* the weapons market. Some of the neighbors were already awake and about with their chores and duties, and those who recognized the blacksmith's nephew, sent him greetings. An eight-guard patrol marched boldly down the street, and Mukhtar waited until they had turned the corner before knocking on Mika'il's door. Since his encounter with Ghadan and Hassin, he did not trust any man in uniform.

A small latch opened and closed, the lock was undone, the weathered door swung open, and Mukhtar gazed upon the ever smiling face of his mother's elder sister, Fariebah.

"Mukhtar!" She beamed.

"Salaam, Khala," he greeted her.

Although five years older than Suha, she simply looked like a taller and slimmer version of her sister. Her hair was streaked with silver and plaited like Suha's, and she even wore her headscarf in the same manner. "Salaam," she led him into their tiny living room. "Have you come to wake your Khal?"

"Is he still abed at this hour?" Mukhtar asked.

"Odd, I know," her smile faded and she lowered her voice. "Last night, he spoke of giving up his trade. He did not even wake for prayer this morning. I must admit, I am concerned."

"What does he intend?"

"Little do I know," she shrugged. "He has been rather *strange* of late."

"Stranger than usual?" Mukhtar raised an eyebrow.

She seemed uneasy to him. "He eats little, sleeps little, and spends more time alone, billowing clouds of smoke from his *hukah*."

Mukhtar would not have seen cause for alarm if circumstances were otherwise, and coming from his aunt in a manner that seemed to trouble her deeply, he felt the need to assure her. "I will speak with him, Khala. Perhaps he will reveal what plagues him."

She gave him a warm smile. "Oh, you need not concern yourself with the worries of an old man. Whatever it is, I am certain it will come to pass. He will be up momentarily. Will you have some breakfast?"

Mukhtar did not have to wait long. Mika'il's shadow soon appeared in the doorway, a silhouette that was slouched and carried itself in a weary manner.

"Salaam, Khal," Mukhtar aired a greeting, trying his utmost to sound as respectful as he could.

"Salaam," Mika'il replied indifferently and settled down on a cushion. His voice was croaky, and as the light fell on his face, his eyes were dark, sunken and exhausted.

Mukhtar assured himself not to be the first to speak. It was the only way to force his uncle into disclosure. Silence trailed while Fariebah brought in a tray of *Kaymak* and bread with black tea, and left to carry on her daily chores. More silence followed while they ate. Then Mika'il took a sip of his tea and spoke.

"I know why you have come," he said without looking up.

"Do you?" Mukhtar responded without thinking.

Mika'il threw him a warning look. "I am beginning to dislike your tone."

He had always been stern and demanding, but Mukhtar was no different. This was no longer a moment for niceties. "And I dislike your deception," he kept his gaze on Mika'il.

It was a bold statement, but one he felt was necessary. He waited patiently for a response.

"Who are you to question my decisions?" Mika'il's voice became harsh.

"Your nephew!" Mukhtar countered. "And I do not question. I *demand* you speak to me openly!"

Another bold statement. A daring move. Either he will get the answers he sought, or he will be shown the door, and it would be a long while before they would speak to each other again.

Mika'il said nothing, and so Mukhtar was driven to press him further. "I heard Hassin's threat. You cannot deny it. Their objective was set beforehand. They were sent!"

"Yes, you heard Hassin," Mika'il replied. "Ghulam Mirza has need for skills such as mine and—"

"Enough!" Mukhtar slapped the moth-eaten rug they were seated upon. His wound from the previous day had hardly healed, and it was forced open again, bleeding through the dirty bandage wrapped around it. "If you cannot be honest with me, then where is the sense in calling ourselves kin?" The cut seared terribly, and he wished he hadn't done that, but there were more pressing matters to be concerned with, and Mika'il's reaction distracted him from the pain. There was anger on his face, and a distinct fear in his eyes.

He took a sip of tea, lowered his cup, and gazed out the door. He sighed deeply.

"True. They were sent. Their motives were ulterior but unclear, perhaps even to themselves. They have been misguided like ignorant puppets, and their puppeteers are true masters of deception."

Mukhtar blinked.

"Unknown to them, Hassin, Ghadan, and so many others, share a secret bond," Mika'il continued. "One that I have remained oblivious to for a long time."

"How do you know this?" Mukhtar asked, unable to hide his surprise.

"Your father knew," Mika'il replied. "And he tried to warn me. But he has been away for the last decade, and his warnings have faded. Alas, would I have paid heed, I would not have had to see this day!"

Confusion was etched on Mukhtar's face. "You speak in riddles, Khal. I do not understand."

Mika'il stared at the open door, into the light pouring from the small courtyard outside. He toyed with the obsidian-stoned ring on his finger. His brow was furrowed and his eyes narrowed. He was thinking deeply.

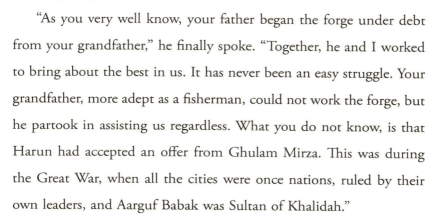

"As you very well know, your father began the forge under debt from your grandfather," he finally spoke. "Together, he and I worked to bring about the best in us. It has never been an easy struggle. Your grandfather, more adept as a fisherman, could not work the forge, but he partook in assisting us regardless. What you do not know, is that Harun had accepted an offer from Ghulam Mirza. This was during the Great War, when all the cities were once nations, ruled by their own leaders, and Aarguf Babak was Sultan of Khalidah."

"Adil's father was *Sultan?*" Mukhtar gaped. "He never spoke of this!"

"Indeed," Mika'il nodded. "And perhaps he does not speak of it with good reason. The politics between brothers at the time, as it is today, was kept secret, but it is widely known that Azhar Babak brought together all the Kings and Sultans and Emperors, and united them under a single banner called Ahul-Hama. It was with this unity that the war was won."

Mukhtar nodded, "I know of this tale, but I fail to see its relevance." Everyone, from the very old to the very young, knew of Azhar Babak's triumphs. Songs and ballads were a capstone of every festivity. Pledges were recited by children in every *Madrassa*. Monuments erected around the city were all engraved with praises and poems. The endless praises and accolades to Immorkaan and Azhar Babak meant little to Mukhtar. "Tell me more about Ghulam Mirza."

Mika'il gave him a sideways glance. "As Azhar's lieutenant at the time, Ghulam Mirza tasked Harun and I as quartermasters of their Legion…"

Mukhtar's thoughts were drawn away while Mika'il narrated his tale. Upon defeating the Dark Prince's forces, Azhar Babak had declared his throne to be in Khalidah, and reduced his elder brother, Aarguf, to a General. Harun was raised to a seat on his council, and Ghulam became overshadowed by a simple blacksmith.

Mika'il took another sip of his tea. "Aarguf never retaliated, but those he recruited did. Ghulam was appointed quartermaster of the Royal Army, and was given all the influence and power he needed to build his *Souk,* but that was never enough for him. His enmity toward your father never diminished."

Mukhtar was stunned. He could only imagine how deep the murky waters ran. So intricate were his father's relationships with the likes of Aarguf, Ghulam, and the King, yet none of them had ever stopped to consider the family he had left behind. None of them had ever stopped to care for Suha and her sons. Mukhtar was filled with an even grimmer thought; all of them, to a remarkable extent, would have had a hand in his imprisonment.

Mika'il cleared his throat, and Mukhtar gave a small start.

"What I have said is not meant to stir you," Mika'il said in a calmer and softer tone, "but to help you understand, so that your choices will be wiser. So that you are not misguided by bitterness and anger."

Mukhtar nodded calmly, acknowledging his uncle's advice. "What will we do now, Khal? How will we survive?"

Mika'il gave him a reassuring smile. "I will find us work. Do not despair, for we will find a way to reopen the forge. Mika'il Abaraina is not without friends in this city."

Mukhtar had sensed Suha's dubiety when he returned home and informed her (as Mika'il instructed) that he had been allowed a few days to recuperate from the strenuous work they recently did for Immorkaan. At the time, she did not prod much, but Mukhtar knew that she would dig deeper, and he only hoped that Mika'il would find a resolution before the truth unearthed. He wondered whether Fariebah had also been kept in the dark. How much longer would his uncle be able to keep his secrets?

The days, however, turned to weeks, with little or no success in their efforts. Eventually, those acquainted with the trade, came to learn that Mika'il Abaraina had been bullied into surrendering his prized forge to the *Souk As-Silaah*. Driven by shame and desperation, Mika'il and Mukhtar attempted to seek audience with Ghulam Mirza, but without a written consent from the Chief himself, they were barred entry into his fortified *Souk*. Mukhtar even pleaded with Adil to arrange a hearing with his father, assuming that the General of the Royal Army may have enough influence to turn the tide in their favor. Rather than meet with them, Aarguf Babak sent Adil with a curt message, stating that the affairs of the *Souk* were not his, and without Immorkaan's sanction, he could do nothing.

Mukhtar made every attempt to keep the matter secret from his mother, leaving early in the morning and pretending to return home in the evening after a long day at the forge. Instead, he and Saif trekked the city streets in search of work, earning meager wages, only enough to sustain their livelihoods. As his resource of coin depleted, Mukhtar desperately struggled with withholding from Suha, yet he could not bring himself to depriving her the necessities of their lifestyle. One hot and humid afternoon, with nothing else to do, Mukhtar reluctantly accompanied her to the *Souk Al-Huda,* the largest sheltered market in Khalidah, named after King Azhar Babak's late wife.

The *Souk* was a hive of activity, even more so as the rainy season drew closer. As soon as they crossed the large open gates into its bustling threshold, they were engulfed by a turbulent medley of sights and sounds quite unlike the city streets. There were noises, both strange and familiar, accents and dialects both local and foreign, belonging to people from lands far and wide. All kinds of scents greeted their nostrils, oils, perfumes, incense, vegetables, meats, and fruits.

Aside from the chaos and the stifling heat of the *Souk*, what irritated Mukhtar the most were the stragglers and brokers who attacked the moment anyone stepped into the market. They were swindlers who blended with crowds to avoid suspicion, picking out vulnerable shoppers. Typically, they earned through commissions or frauds, and the guards would leave them be, as long as they received their share of the profits.

Mukhtar and Suha had to push and pull their way through a group of near seven or eight of them.

"Look at this!" said one, with an accent that may have been from somewhere far north, possibly Rhudah. The filthy-robed man was brandishing a tiny glass bottle with very suspicious looking contents. "It is a medicine for the cure of rash. Simply apply on rash, and rash go away. Only two silver!"

"I am not interested!"

"This is pure white gold. Look, it is pure!" said another, almost shoving a ring up Mukhtar's nose.

"No, we don't want—"

Another one grabbed his shoulder from behind and wheeled him around. "What of your sandals, young man? Do they embarrass you? Are they the reason why the women do not come closer? Take these instead! Look at the craftsmanship. Look at the stitching!"

"Get off me!" Mukhtar shoved him angrily. The man staggered back, stepped on the hem of his own *thaub* and fell to the hard, dusty ground.

"Mukhtar!" Suha pulled him away before the man had any time to react.

"What?" Mukhtar protested, checking his waistline to make sure his money-bag was still there.

"Perhaps he is right," she glanced over her shoulder nervously. The man was craning his neck over the crowds, searching for Mukhtar, but they had already taken a different path now. "Perhaps if your sandals were in better shape, it would be easier to find you a wife!"

She had been mentioning his marriage one too many times of late. Rather than give a grumpy scowl, he smirked. "Were *you* attracted to Abha's sandals before you married him?" he asked, gently nudging her arm with his elbow. He distinctly noted her cheeks flushing, before she was drawn away by a merchant selling cloth.

They trailed along narrow and twisted pathways, looking into different stalls and shops, as their owners shouted out their wares and special prices.

"Three for the price of only two, sister!" said one.

"There is not a better quality in all of the Souk! Shall I make it ready for you?" said another.

And another, *"If you can bring me a better price, I will throw my uncle into the Hubur!"*

Suha was beside herself with excitement, admiring different wares, and bargaining to her utmost to get whatever she wanted, while Mukhtar dragged along behind her, carrying everything they bought. He did enjoy her company for a while, but was now becoming bored and frustrated, wanting nothing but to get out of the market as soon as he could. He hated the overcrowded alleys between stalls; hot, sweaty, and noisy. All afternoon, he continued to spot rather conspicuous drug-dealers, squatting around corners, vigilantly offering potential clients merchandises such as *Hashish,* Blue-Lotus, and Opium. He kept a wary eye out, for such felons were prone to having mercenaries lurking about, safeguarding their trades, and the consequences could be grave if he mistakenly wrong-footed them.

After what felt like hours, they arrived at a much cleaner area of the *Souk,* one that was not riddled with the mingled stenches of fruit and vegetables among other noxious bouquets, but filled with the sweet scents of *Oudh* and incense. It was known only as the Incense Lane.

The shops primarily traded in perfumes, scented oils, frankincense, *Bakhoor,* Ambergris, Sandalwood, and *Oudh,* all imported from distant lands. There were also shops that traded *hukah* equipment, refills, vials, and components.

"The hour is late," Suha said as they strolled along the aisles.

"I am glad you noticed," Mukhtar grunted sarcastically, hauling several small sacks of goods, wondering at this point how they would survive, for Suha still did not know that her son was without work. "My limbs are screaming of exhaustion."

"There is a *Musalla* up ahead. We should pray before we leave," she led the way forward.

"Can we not just head home?" Mukhtar pleaded. "I am riddled with the filth of the *Souk,* and do not wish to offer prayers in such an impure state."

"One should learn the art of making excuses from *you,* Mukhtar!" Suha replied over her shoulder. "I wish you would offer your prayers with a devout heart. Perhaps then you would find peace."

Mukhtar wrinkled his nose and followed her down the narrow aisle to a relatively small, stone enclosure, where men offered their prayers. A walled room next to it was set for women, and there was running water behind the enclosure for devotees to wash and make ablution.

"What of all our belongings?" Mukhtar asked in what only sounded like another feeble excuse. "It is not safe to leave them out here."

"Everything in your hands has been provided by your Creator," Suha responded. "No one will steal it if *He* protects it. Take everything inside with you."

She removed her slippers and entered the small room while Mukhtar pretended to do the same, but as soon as she disappeared, he remained behind instead and sat down against the low wall.

For reasons he could not quite justify, even to himself, he did not really see the need to enter the *Musalla*. He did not even realize how ill-advised his own thoughts were.

How his fate would have changed had he followed his mother's advice.

The overwhelming scents and fumes from the perfume shops, riled by the stifling heat, were beginning to have an influence over him. He felt drowsy, and had to shake himself awake several times. The *Souk* was not the right place to fall asleep unless he wished to be robbed blindly. He drew the sacks of goods closer and looked around, trying to find something that would keep drowsiness at bay.

He watched the people walk by, chattering away excitedly, laden with all manner of wares, many displaying gleeful expressions to advocate their recent requisitions. Khalidans truly were exceptional folk, always pretending to be concerned only with minding their own business, but ever prepared to scrutinize the misdemeanors of others. In Mukhtar's case— sitting in the dirt against the wall of a holy place was not something that was socially acceptable. Even a toothless old beggar, across the aisle, cast him repulsive looks.

Uncomfortable under the man's gaze, Mukhtar stood, leaned against the low wall instead, and ignored him. A few moments later, another beggar approached and rattled an old wooden bowl under his nose. The stench was unbearable; a mixture of bad eggs and rotting fish, and Mukhtar recoiled, wrinkling his nose as he waved her away.

That is when something utterly disturbing caught his eye, and he glanced at the beggar's legs in fright. Bloody and bruised skin was horribly stretched and mangled over protruding bones that made it look like they were twisted from the knee, so far back, that her feet pointed backward. Beneath the layers and mounds of dirt and mud, behind curtains of long and filthy, matted hair, she looked horribly familiar. Someone dreadful. Someone terrifying.

Was it a trick of the eye? Was it the heat inside the *Souk*?

The world spun around him. A sudden sharp and burning sensation hit the pit of his stomach, as if he had been stabbed with a hot iron rod. He doubled over in immense pain, searing through his entire body, stifling his very nerves, such that the resultant scream that left his open mouth, was no more than a strangled and muted cry of agony. His eyes were forcibly shut and his face contorted in agony.

For a brief moment, he had all but forgotten where he was, whether he was sitting, standing, lying down, or for that matter, even flying in the air. There were people shouting. There were people screaming. Were they screaming for him, or at something else? Robbed of all energy, unable to keep his eyes open, he fell to the ground in a cloud of dust.

And lay there.

Unknown to Mukhtar, roughly about an hour before, Haim Tuma and his brother, Gussar, entered the derelict hut of an infamous witch, somewhere on the eastern outskirts of the city. She had served his needs before with rather uncanny results.

The witch sat on a worn sisal mat, heavy shawls drawn over her gaunt and hunched body, her skin riddled with leprosy, her eyes yellowing with gray, watery pupils. "Coin the pot, before we begin," she spoke in a shrilly, crackling, high-pitched voice that made the fine hairs on the back of Haim's neck to rise in fright.

He nudged his brother to comply. Gussar gave him a flinty look. He nervously tugged at the collar of his armor, struggling to breathe in the filthy, decaying, revolting and stifling stench of the tiny, windowless room riddled with pots of acrid incense and eerily glowing orbs. He removed a few copper coins and threw them into the pot.

"I am in need of your services," Haim said. "My slaves have escaped." He threw a blood-stained, filthy piece of cloth onto the mat before her. "*That* must belong to one of them."

The witch grinned under her cowl, exposing gaps in her decaying teeth. After a long while of muttering feverish incantations and falling into several trances, she said, "cannot find the slaves... A sorcerer conceals them..."

"I *told* you!" Gussar snarled at his brother. "We should *never* have captured him!"

"It was not sorcery!" Haim retorted. "The lock was broken!" He turned back to the witch. "Someone must have helped them escape!"

The witch glanced at the coin-pot, making her intentions clear. With a grumpy snort, Haim tossed a few more copper coins into the pot.

The witch's grin widened. More devilish mutterings. Chantings. Supplications to evil beings.

"Follow the girl…"

"What *girl?*"

Heavy beads, amulets, bracelets of bone, and other grotesque artifacts, jingled as the witch raised a gnarled finger and pointed to the entrance of the room. The brothers turned slowly and deliberately. Haim suppressed a shudder. Gussar nearly shrieked with fright. She bore a horrific resemblance to one of the slaves. But she could not be. She was not even human.

The Jinn's feet were horribly twisted around its ankles and to add to its eccentricity, it turned its head almost entirely without so much as a twitch of its shoulders. Eyeing its mistress and the human slavers, it twisted its lips and curled them into a most devilish grin, nudging the slavers to follow.

FIVE

THE UNSEEN

Mukhtar raised his head an inch off the dirt. It throbbed with unimaginable pain. The beggar had vanished, and Incense Lane had erupted in chaos and disarray, as four, perhaps five men, pushed through the crowd with murderous intent.

"There he is!" One of them screeched, pointing directly at him. *"Seize him!"*

There was no mistaking the large battle-axe, heavy build and the scar on his face— it was Gussar, the large slave trader. On his heel was his brother, Haim.

Instinct, pure instinct took over Mukhtar. His mind became blank for a brief moment and then sprung back, alive and awake.

Without any further thought, he scrambled to his feet and tore into the crowd, ignoring all the cries, shouts, and insults that followed.

Forcefully, he shoved through to make way for himself, fear gripping him like an iron clamp, twisting his insides.

"*Seize that whelp!*" A yell followed him from behind.

A man in a faded gray *thaub*, perhaps thought him a petty thief, attempted to bar his path, but Mukhtar was prepared and feinted left, then right, then left again, twisted and slipped through his narrow grasp.

"Hold him! *Hold him!*" Someone else screamed.

A city guard appeared before him, spear at the ready. Mukhtar attempted to jump over a stack of barrels on the side, but his foot slipped and caught the edge of a barrel. He fumbled his arms clumsily in midair and crashed into a fruit stall. Covered in crushed oranges and banana paste, he slipped and slid as he tried to get up, hastily glancing about to find his bearings. In wake of the wreckage, stall owners and shoppers broke into a brawl, and the city guard was overcome with the chaos. Further behind him, the agitated crowd slowed his pursuers. Seeing that his window of escape was still open, Mukhtar took the opportunity and continued to pursue the exit.

"I will *kill* you!" Another scream came from behind.

A crossbow-bolt whirled past his right ear, briefly disorienting him. It struck a wooden pole, and Mukhtar's eyes widened with horror as he passed the rod lodged into the thick cedar. Drenched in sweat and breathing heavily, his heart beat in a frenzy inside his chest, lungs burned, and legs screamed for mercy. He exerted all his efforts into squeezing through the crowds and maneuvering past obstacles. Adrenaline and fear were flooding through him, but that was all he needed to keep moving forward.

Frightened by the advancing pursuers, the screaming crowds thinned to give them way, and the gap between them and Mukhtar shrunk with every passing moment. His only escape was to lose them in the streets. Another bolt was fired, made its mark and pierced his right shoulder. The force of it threw him several feet forward, and with an agonizing scream, he crumbled to the ground before a fish-stall, as a scarlet stain spread over his *thaub* and the wound bled out.

Is this it? Is this my end? He thought wildly. *No! I will not die this way. Not in this manner! Not in the filth and dirt of the Souk. No! On your feet, Mukhtar! Freedom is not a luxury. You must fight for it!*

Swearing in pain, he pushed himself up and glanced back, ducking almost immediately to evade a third crossbow-bolt that brushed his hair as it whizzed over his head, and struck a blue-robed man in his thigh. The man let out a startling howl and collapsed to the ground, while the crowd dispersed in utter disarray, shrieking and yelling. The chaotic *Souk* became far more aggravated than it ever was, as everyone now charged for the exits, not at all wanting to be the next crossbow victim. This made Mukhtar's task even more difficult, trying to push his way through with an injured shoulder, the crowd failing to realize that *he* was the target, not them.

A large man with a thick mustache, unknowingly barred his path, carrying an immensely large basket of vegetables, and Mukhtar blindly ran into him. They both tumbled to the ground in a messy heap of produce. Infuriated, the man groped for him, clutching his injured shoulder. Mukhtar screamed in agony, squirming to escape his grasp. Slippery with blood, Mukhtar's shoulder wriggled free and he scrambled to his feet once more, slightly disoriented but determined to pursue the exit.

Almost at the gates of the *Souk*, he caught a brief glimpse of daylight and nearly tasted fresh air, when he felt a dull heavy blow to the back of his head, and as the world spun out from under his feet, a mangy sack descended over his head and absorbed him into a dark void.

A starry night. A bright morning. A cloudy afternoon followed by a stormy night. Iron bars. Neighing horses and bleating camels. It took two days for him to fully regain consciousness. With him were six others, cramped into a caged cart, perhaps the very same cart that once stood in an alley not so long ago. The journey was bumpy, rugged, and rough, along the stony and treacherous Sultan's Pass. Neither had a clue to their destination, only that they were headed north as they deduced from the slithering shadows of the horses, camels, and carts upon the craggy ground. From tropical lands, over rocky terrains, through scorching deserts and dry climates, seven days into their journey, no one dared speak a single word. They were whipped mercilessly if they uttered even a bare whisper.

Their escorts were ruthless mercenaries on horseback, armed to the teeth with powerful steel and thick armor. When they arrived at the Red-City of Aztalaan, it was nightfall, and their caravan passed through unchecked and unhindered. Sacks of coin exchanged hands under the shadows, as corrupt Red-Guards were bribed to allow them passage through the Walls of Murfaqat, and after six more days under the scorching sun, they arrived at a formidable, ancient fortress. The Assassin Fortress of Ghuldad.

They were dragged out and forced to wear black sacks over their heads. Like he, those who struggled and resisted, were met with heavy blows to the back of their heads. There was no further struggle. Only an endless and dreamless sleep.

When next he woke, it was in complete darkness. The skin on one-half of his body touched cold stone, and blinking did little to acknowledge his environs, leaving him utterly incapable of instrumenting neither form nor the extent of his surroundings. In a frightful flash, he was gripped by the most incongruous thought of being buried alive. He shrieked, swung out his good arm, and touched nothing but the air around him, while his shrill eerily ricocheted off a wall not so far off. Not entombed then; isn't *that* a relief? Or was that merely an illusion? Suddenly he remembered, he did not know what it was like to be buried, and fear and panic flooded into him with a pungent broil.

He ran a shivery hand over his sore, throbbing head to discover a swollen and tangled bit at the back, where the skin had been split by a heavy impact upon an already existing wound. The cut had not been treated and was swollen so badly, it felt to him like a second head was growing right where his hair had revoltingly matted with dried blood.

A soft and airy sensation around certain secretive parts of his body told him, with a nasty pang, that he was unclothed, and he frantically ran his hands down his body, relieved to find every bit of him unimpaired. His hand remained at his midsection, hiding his shame from no one in particular. Or were there eyes in the darkness that he could not see? He remained still and held his breath, listening for any concealed company.

It was long before he tried to get off the floor, but his shoulder capitulated excruciatingly, and he fell back down as the image of a crossbow-bolt flashed his mind. He ran a sensitive finger over the wound, which stung at his touch. The bolt had been removed three days into their journey as captives, but the wound was left untreated. A trace of dried blood clung to his skin down his arm, shoulder and back, as well as his chest.

With a sickening howl, he made another attempt at rising, this time succeeding and stumbling forward. He dragged his feet and reached out with his left hand (while his right safeguarded his manhood). His fingers touched cold stone and followed it through two corners, coming to a halt where the stone vanished into a gap of wood and metal that felt like a door. He covered the distance in a few short steps, and the sudden visualization of the room being far smaller than he had anticipated, made him feel claustrophobic and petrified that he was now compactly congested along with all his thoughts and fears. Knowing that crying out for help would avail for nothing, he succumbed to his inner fears and collapsed by the door, pathetically breaking down into a session of tears.

Curled up like a fetus, he faced the door where a fluttering breeze is all that escaped from the gap below it, a scent of freedom behind the mass of wood and metal. How long he cried, he did not know. The sound of his own voice startled him, croaky and parched.

The urge to urinate overcame him, and was enough to venture the darkness to find the closest corner to relieve himself. Here, he shuddered with inconceivable shame and humiliation. A tremulous thought in his subconscious continued to tell him that all this was a dream, nothing but an apocryphal conception; but there was nothing imaginary about this room if the walls felt apparent enough to his touch. There was only the overpowering, gloomy blackness, and the indefinite silence reverberating his introspections in a manner that instilled terror in the deepest trenches of his consciousness.

Back at the spot by the door, he shut his eyes in an attempt to sleep off his misery, eventually dissolving into a disturbing slumber of horrible nightmares. When he woke, his sense of smell directed him back to the grotesque corner where he relieved himself again, wondering at this point, how he would replenish his body, if at all his captives would feed him.

Just then, the door unbolted with a thunderous clap, and burst open, making him shrivel in fear and panic. An orange glow covered his shoulders, but before he had time to turn, two pairs of strong rough hands picked him right off the ground. He wriggled his legs like a fish, while a filthy sack descended over his head, filling his nostrils with the stench of rot and decay. He was slammed into a chair, limbs bound firmly against the wood, and without any admonition, several lashes of a whip crackled in the air and seared through the skin on his torso, branding him for a sin he once believed to be an act of nobility.

He screamed, praying beyond his own belief, to be relieved, that they would stop and it would end; but it did not, and when he could no longer think, no longer feel anything, he dissolved into darkness.

Is this it? Is this my death?

Cold water splashed on him, and his body screamed in agony as he woke. Not dead. Not yet? His breath shortened with anxiety, eyes darted in every direction, trying to make out the moving figures beyond the intricate mesh of the filthy sack, while pleas for mercy escaped his lips impetuously until a deep, calm voice silenced him with dread. "We are honored to have you among us."

Several derisive laughs and cackles followed the statement. There were others in the room, how many others, he did not know. The voice that spoke sounded horribly familiar, but dare he trace it to its origin? Dare he question and face its owner?

Cold water clung to his skin, making him tremble silently, but little did he believe it to be the cause of his shivers. It was fear. A dark, unnerving contemplation of what was yet to come.

Then he felt it.

A piercing pain, newly inflicted upon his chest. He screamed in agony as a sharp blade cut slowly through the skin on his right breast, and warm blood trickled down his torso.

"*No! I beg you! God, I beg you!*" He writhed against his holds.

Another cut. Another scream of pain.

"There is a culture, somewhere far beyond the Barren Plains of the Uzad Peninsula—" the man spoke slowly and deliberately, his voice filled with awe and excitement.

"—that has a rather... *unique* form of torture—"

Another cut on his torso.

"—They cut their victim, *slowly and painfully.* Deliberate—"

Another cut, another scream.

"—small cuts, just on the surface of the skin— an enduring process until eventually, the victim..."

Cut. Scream.

"...surrenders..."

Cut. Scream.

"...*all!*"

He paused. Mukhtar whimpered, dreadfully anticipating more.

The man spoke softly now. "It ends when you want it to end. So, tell me... where have you hidden the Keystone?"

Mukhtar shuddered and trembled under the pain, struggling, recoiling, and writhing like a trapped animal. "I do not know what you speak of," he whined helplessly. "Please, let me go!"

"Do you take me for a *fool?*"

Another cut. This time on his leg, forcing him to thrash uncontrollably and instinctively under the pain. The struggle only engendered immense torment, as the man's hand slipped and drove the blade deeper than his intent.

Mukhtar wriggled and wrestled against his holds, as the suffering attained unfathomable heights. His eyes shut, and the last remaining sounds of agony escaped his trembling lips in a grappling groan.

Darkness beyond darkness. A void he could not dream of escaping. What did it feel like, to lose hope, to give up and accept your end? Is this how he would depart from this world, lying naked on the floor, cold, bleeding and hurting? His own dignity abandoned him, and he relieved himself where he lay, unable to move a single muscle in his body, weak, hungry, broken, and bent. How long had it been since he smelt fresh air, ate food, or drank water?

Soon after, they fed him. Moldy bread and stale water, food fit for rodents and maggots, given to him once a day through the dark gap beneath the door. Aside from this small act of mercy, he was deprived of any human contact. The ramification of it, was that he began to have random conversations with himself in an attempt to keep insanity at bay. Little did he realize, by doing so, insanity was slowly becoming an inevitability. The days passed on in this manner, and he slowly lost all sense of himself. He could not tell when the day ended and night begun. He slept when sleep came. When he woke, the darkness was no different than when his eyes were shut. How long he was there, he did not know.

"How long your stay, matters not if it ends with your death," a voice whispered in his ear. A female voice he had never heard before. It was cool, melodious, yet eerie and had an unidentifiable accent.

"Wh— who's there?" he whimpered.

There was no response. Only a deafening moment of silence,

punctured by a vicious sound. Hissing and spitting, constricted and irregular, halting at spontaneous intervals, until he realized with horror, what he was hearing.

It was laughter.

He lifted his head an inch off the ground, searching the gloom for its source, but could determine nothing. Terrified, he began to pant heavily, and scrambled up against the cold wall, drawing his knees closer to his chest. The laughter grew louder and louder until it had completely engulfed him, and he pressed his palms over his ears to shut it out, but it did not subside.

The laughter suddenly ceased and he whimpered. Something slithered across the room with the dry noise of cloth scraping against the ground.

"Do you not recognize me, Mukhtar?" The voice grew closer and closer. "It was you who freed me... from my cage... from the prison I was bound to..."

The sounds of tiny bells, like those of anklets, jingled and echoed across the walls, and the edge of something silky soft brushed his foot, touching the raw flesh of his inflicted wounds, and he remembered the horror he had seen in the *Souk*.

He had seen the slave-girl. How could this be? Had she betrayed him after he had risked all to liberate her? That was impossible. No. It had to be a trick, an apparition of some sort. This was sorcery.

"You c—cannot b—b—be *her*—" he slithered back against the wall, "not p—possible. This is all in m—m—my head—"

"*I am in your head! In your heart, your flesh, and your bones. I have never left you, never will. I can cure your suffering, or worsen it!*"

Mukhtar pressed his hands firmly on his ears and muttered feverishly under his breath. "The cripple— the beggar— the slave—"

"*Abandon this turmoil, and join me, Mukhtar,*" the voice was as clear as though it came from inside his head. "*Together we will pierce the very veil of heaven itself— or hell; whichever you desire.*"

"Get away from me!" he shrieked.

The laughter rang in his ears, burying him in fear. Sweat dripped down his forehead and chest, leaving his skin colder than it already was. Amidst the overwhelming emotions and agitations, it was a while before he realized what the unseen presence was.

"*Bones, bones, cold bones,*" it sang. "*Soon you will meet your maker. Soon you will die!*"

"You are a *Jinn*!"

"*That I am, my love, my sweet...that I am...*"

"Kill me then! Be done with it!"

"*To kill... now that would be tempting, it would. But senseless,*" it hissed. "*There is yet a purpose to your being. Your father's debt must be paid, son of Zafar!*"

"I owe you *nothing!*"

"*That is but an illusion you have projected to sway me away from you, but sway I will never. Choose it or not, we are bound and burdened by divine purpose!*"

"Go away!" he screamed.

"*Stubborn, stubborn creature!*" she clucked her tongue. "*There is none here to impress! Your life here will pass unseen. Have a little pride and end it on your own terms, or accept mine and live to see tomorrow.*"

"Your terms are lies!"

"*You would not know the truth, if it seduced you!*" her tone was becoming melodramatic as she continued to toy with him.

Mukhtar began to pray, but it seemed to have no effect. He raised his voice louder and louder, and yet she remained.

"You are forsaken, son of Zafar!" she cackled. *"Abandoned by your fathers, and forced to bear their sins. The hunt will never cease until you relinquish what your captors desire. They are men without moral or virtue, for they are servants of Azazil, practitioners of evil. Theirs is sin, and in it shall they abide. Do you truly believe that he who is reading the stars and worshiping the devil, cares if you live a traitor or die a martyr?"*

"I am no traitor," Mukhtar mumbled between a continuous ramble of supplications.

"Denial!" she shrieked. *"You think we have just met? I have been with you all your life, the little whispers in your veins, numbing and keeping you within the confines of your own little prison. I have been the nightmares that wake you in the night, reminding you of your own wretchedness!"*

"I refuse to believe you!"

An angry hiss.

"If you knew what to believe, you would not be here. Faith has always been the greatest weakness of your kind. Blind faith and the illusion of hope. Part of you still has hope, and that hope makes you believe that the door will open and you will walk out of here with your sanity intact. It is that part you must kill if you want to survive. Prostrate before me, Son of Adam, and live. Or die in here, and rot."

The laughter came again, the air grew colder and thinner, and he shivered uncontrollably.

Faith. Hope. He thought desperately. *Was there hope? Our greatest weakness and also our greatest strength. Remember, remember, He who created you from a clot of blood, and the Jinn from a smokeless fire. Faith. Pray with your heart, Mukhtar. Pray to Him.*

It became evident to him. He sobbed and prayed. With all his heart, he recited, "I seek refuge in The Almighty from the *Shaytaan*, the accursed one. Say, I seek refuge in The Lord of the dawn. From the evil of what He has created. And from the evil of the darkening night when it settles. And from the evil of mortal witchcraft. And from the evil of the envier when he envieth."

The laughter turned into a shriek that rose to an unnatural decibel, rattling the room in fading reverberations, until it became indistinguishable from the ringing inside his own head. He ran out of breath just as the door burst open, and light poured through. His eyes shut slowly, unwillingly embracing the dark abyss.

He struggled to open them, but felt that his eyelids were made of lead, as were his arms when he tried to lift them. His senses were slowly coming around, and he realized he was lying on a soft surface. His head hurt terribly, and all he wanted to do was to lay there until it all stopped.

A prickling sense of reality descended upon him, flashes of his memory playing piece by piece in his mind— *the beggar, the armed men, the chase*— he became restless— *the voices, the terror, the pain*— he moaned— screams; his own screams of agony. The turmoil continued while his consciousness slowly resurfaced.

It was dark, and he gasped in horror. Had nothing changed? Was all that an illusion? He was unable to move his limbs, and for a moment, thought that he was still bound to the chair. Then his eyes slowly adjusted. A window to his left brought in the dull moonlight, and he was lying flat on what appeared to be a woolly mattress on the floor. He cried in pain as he attempted to move his head and look around.

"Calm yourself," a soft whisper came from somewhere in the dark.

"Who is th —that? Where a— where am I?" His voice was croaky and dry, and his throat hurt with every sound he made. Pulses of pain were firing through his head.

"We must bring down the fever..." the voice said again, sounding muffled and distant, "...bring the pail..."

Mukhtar groaned. He felt very weak and feverish. More words were spoken, but he paid them no heed. The pain became unbearable. A few moments passed, and an orange glow flickered to his right where someone was lighting the wick of an oil lamp. Seasoned rough hands reached under his head and back, lifting him up into an upright position. The motion alone drained him of all energy, and he felt the world darken again.

"Drink this. It will ease the pain," the voice was soft and soothing, and carried with it a scent of lavender, which instantly diminished when a small clay pot, emitting a very foul smell, touched his lips. He tried to push it away, but was met with resistance. Reluctantly, he took a bitter tasting sip, causing him to vomit all over his front. He was forced to take yet another sip, and felt the medicine tear at his throat and chest. His soiled shirt was forced over his head, and his chest wiped clean with a warm damp cloth. His scars burned and seared, but he did not even have the strength to scream in pain. When he overcame his grogginess, he sat up against the wall, head hung to one side, sweating and breathing heavily.

The room was a tiny square with a single wooden door and barred window. The walls were made of bare stone, as was the floor and ceiling. A man sat, cross-legged, on a thin cushion across from him. He wore a white *thaub* under leather armor, his face concealed beneath a white cowl.

Mukhtar turned to his right, where an elderly, slightly stooped man, tore leaves and crushed them into a paste in a small bowl. He had a long gray beard, and wore a white cap over his equally long gray hair, his sunken eyes concealed by the deep shadows on his gaunt face. The light from the oil lamp brought into effect the wrinkles on his face, etched with the shadow of an aged wolf.

Looking down at his own body, he noticed the various bandages around his leg and torso. With sensitive fingers, he traced the one around his head until he felt the swelling. It stung at his touch and he flinched at the pain.

"Do not aggravate the wound," the old man warned in a hoarse whisper. "If you do not heal in good time, you will be rendered useless. And those rendered useless, face the gallows."

Mukhtar blinked. "Who are you? Where am I?"

"I am tasked with keeping you alive, and you are. Only just. At dawn, they will come for you. Unless you give them what they seek." The old man turned and spoke to the other by the door. Beside him was a fully robed and veiled woman, so that all Mukhtar could see of her was a set of gleaming eyes adorned with *Kohl*. They both gave curt nods to show that they had understood the old man's instructions, and left.

"Who are you?" he asked again, confused and frightened. Was this a trick? Were his captors preparing to enact some new form of torture? He remembered the blood-curdling voice that preyed upon him in the darkness. "I refuse to be haunted by your devilry!" he shrieked, and as he did, his throat burned and he coughed and spat out blood.

The old man stroked his beard, but otherwise remained silent, as though he had not heard him. Just then, the door opened and the woman reappeared, bringing with her a strange whiff of lavender mingled with boiled potatoes, fresh bread, and spicy lentils. She placed the tray on the ground beside him, and left again. Mukhtar looked at the tray suspiciously. *It is most certainly poisoned.* He would *not* touch that. However, the savory aroma and uncomfortable pang in his stomach assured him that if he did not eat, he would eventually die of hunger.

"The devil has sworn to haunt mankind," the old man stated, eyeing the manner in which Mukhtar ravaged the dish of food. "Why should you be any different?" And he left, shutting the door behind him, leaving Mukhtar with hundreds of unanswered questions.

As soon as he put down his empty vessels, he felt a surge of drowsiness. With his head and body still aching and throbbing, he lay back down, listening to a cricket chirp outside his window, and slowly descended into a deep and dreamless sleep.

It was morning when the door burst open, startling him awake. Clad in white robes and armor, three men stepped in, barely giving him a moment to contemplate his surroundings.

"Haul that *swine* to his feet!"

six

THE FORTRESS

His hands were shackled, feet chained and an iron disk clamped around his neck. Mirthlessly, he was dragged through the dark, stone corridors and out into the brightly lit world where a blazing morning sun burned through his eyelids. His head throbbed, his leg hurt and every wound on his body screamed. He was greeted with a frenzy of shouts and screams, jeers and scorns, name-calling and insults.

They lead him past enclosures where men were furiously engaged in training battles. Past archery ranges where arrows blurred through the air before tearing into targets of hay. Dark, loathsome eyes and loud flagrant derisions followed him with every step.

They flung him through the air and he landed hard in the dirt. Sand filled his eyes, nostrils, and ears, bringing him even more discomfort, but his captors showed no mercy. Their intent was vile and apparent, and the realization tore through him viciously— if he did not adhere, he would cease to exist.

Was there need to exist anymore, to live without his will? Is this what the remainder of his life promised to be? Would he ever escape it? Would he ever return home?

The whip cracked through the air and lashed on his back. He screamed. Images tore through his mind, bringing back memories, bringing more pain. So it began.

Every day, from that moment, Mukhtar became what he had never before dreamt of being. He was one of three others who pushed a massive wooden wheel that turned a complexity of gears which powered a gale of cool air into an even larger forge, while a whip occasionally lashed their backs, coercing them onward. Twice a day, they were relieved with bread and water to replenish themselves, only sufficient enough to sustain their task.

The days persisted. His mind and body were tested upon sand, rock, cedar, and iron. Two of his companions, Baqil and Khurn, were anglers from northern Hizak. The fourth, Dymek, was a basket-weaver from Suria. Far from learning their names and origins, conversations were forbidden. Even a hushed whisper was enough to earn ten lashes. As time went on, Baqil and Khurn were replaced after the burden of the wheel surpassed their will to live, and Mukhtar soon realized the bitterness of loss.

Eventually, he became just another face, another able-bodied slave, and was only alive for as long as his limbs continued to push forward. The guard who stood watch over them was a large man, ruthless to the bone. Shahzad the Impaler, as he was known by his peers. No one knew his lineage, not even himself, and many others called him the Son of No Man.

Theirs was not the only forge in the vast, immensely large courtyard, its boundaries vanishing into a distant blur, at least from where he sat and slept, outside in the open, chained to the wheel with nothing but a woven sisal shroud to keep away the cold. Under starry skies, he thought of home. He thought of his mother, uncle, and aunt. His friends, Adil and Saif. He wept to grief's end, as day by day, the fleeting hope of ever seeing them again, slipped through his fingers. He prayed, in whatever state of purity he thought his prayer may be heard. He prayed for forgiveness, repenting, crying, pleading and begging to his Creator, to save him from this nightmare and return him home to his kin. Whether his prayers were heard or not, he did not know, but it was all that he had left of his consciousness that kept him human. Kept him from losing himself to insanity.

Soon he became accustomed to his environs. On the far side of the courtyard was the large enclosure where men fought against other men, with the simple air of sport and an unwavering affinity of brotherhood.

The walls around them were almost as high as the sky, and the citadel overlooking the training enclosure, even higher. Every day it loomed its formidable shadow over them, that when the sun crossed its apex, it was no longer visible, creating the illusion of night coming sooner than anticipated.

He could not see the gates of the fortress, but deduced its location to the east by following the neighing of horses and bleating of camels. Stables were always built closer to the exits and away from the citadel. It kept the stench and noise away from its occupants. He placed the kitchens to the north of the courtyard by sniffing the air. The aroma of food touched his nostrils thrice a day even if the taste did not.

When his mind did not fixate on the dread of the whips and canes, or the daunting thoughts of facing the gallows, his thoughts wandered. Ghuldad, the atrocious alcazar of high walls and fearsome warriors. He remembered the slavers who chased him in the *Souk*, Haim, and his brother Gussar. Were *they* the masters of this great stone structure? Or were they merely cogs that turned a greater wheel? The thought that there were people far more gruesome and powerful than the slavers who captured him, only made him feel forsaken and doomed.

He saw much. Shackled men and women toiled like slaves and servants, most of them covered in filthy rags that barely concealed their shame. Overseers whipped and pushed them to the cusp of their endurance. He saw men who marched like soldiers and others who slunk like assassins, all dressed in short white robes, clad in armor and weapons of the finest steel.

There were those who walked by and snarled at him, spat on him, called him names that were not his own. There were those who whipped him, caned him, and threw rocks at him just for the sport of it. And then, there were those who pitied him.

Her name was Nuzhah, and he associated her with a fragrance of lavender and *Oudh*, and a pair of almond-shaped eyes that gleamed a light shade of brown whenever the moon waned. Aside from these alluring, intoxicating eyes, her face remained concealed behind a dark veil, always baiting his curiosity. She spoke very little, but tended to his wounds and brought him food whenever she could spare some. He was thankful of her presence. It kept him sane. It kept him alive. Deep within him, her kindness kindled hope and kept his spirit from shattering.

Time passed and the days became almost innumerable. His beard grew into an untethered bush, his hair even longer. His body reshaped itself, grew leaner and muscular. Scorched by the sun, his skin became darker, and every lash of his masters' whips made it thicker and tougher. He became a man who was stronger than he realized, and his freedom would come soon. He could sense it. However, the wheel needed turning and so he turned. He pressed hard on the wooden handle, dug his feet into the blistering dry sands, every scorch, every splinter reminiscing a life, long lost.

He heard conversations, arguments and discussions, some hushed, others open and loud.

"...the fresh batch will cultivate the fields..."

"...the fields need less cultivation..."

"...and what will he feed his soldiers?"

"What does it matter? So long as they are armed!"

"It will matter not if they haven't the strength to bear arms."

"There will be no arms to bear if there remains none to work the forges!"

They needed more men to work the forges. More men like him? More slaves to push the wheels and feed the fires? More men to beat metal into shape?

There were even stranger conversations that took place within close proximity.

"They arrived fewer than anticipated."

"It must have been a hard battle."

"No battle is ever simple, Shahzad. That is why they call it a *battle!*"

"Were I to be schooled by the likes of you, Ghasif!"

The one called Ghasif chuckled. It was a sarcastic laugh. Mukhtar was not too far beyond insanity to perceive it, and could not help but grin. Anything that brought Shahzad displeasure was comforting for him, no matter how small.

Shahzad did not seem insulted.

"Have you ever known anything harsher than a whip, Shahzad?" Ghasif pressed on. He was taller than Shahzad by a few inches, thick bushy eyebrows and a beard that touched his chest brace. "Have you ever known a foe greater than a slave in chains who couldn't even fight back?"

Shahzad's nostrils flared. "Were you to meet me on the battlefield, you would know no greater foe, *Ghasif!*"

They glared at each other for a moment and burst into laughter. "Did you hear the news?" Shahzad asked when the laughter died.

"There is little I have heard while on my mission. What has transpired since?" Ghasif asked.

"The Master has summoned his sorcerers to the citadel," Shahzad sounded excited, as though he longed to speak of it. "They will be here in two days. Their emissaries have already arrived. There hasn't been a gathering of such in decades."

Ghasif's eyes narrowed and his voice became stony. "No... there hasn't."

"You should prepare yourself," Shahzad continued. "The Captains will be given new orders. Soon, the trumpets of war will sound."

"That is news indeed," Ghasif threw Mukhtar a most indiscreet glance as he made his pass. "Does the Master seek a truce with Arammoria then?" he asked Shahzad in an undertone.

Shahzad tensed and hissed, urging Ghasif to lower his tone. He nervously searched their vicinity for any unknown eavesdroppers.

Ghasif did not seem troubled. He knew they were alone. Aside from the slaves, that is. "Well?" he pressed.

"Such are the rumors," Shahzad whispered. "I heard it from Kassim in the citadel. A truce with Arammoria will give us the strength to advance."

"But you think otherwise?"

Shahzad nodded. "It bodes ill."

"Certainly does," Ghasif agreed.

Shahzad tilted his head slightly, eyes still darting in every direction. "I have never marched to war," his voice was grim. "Our missions dwindle to the cries of battle and bloodshed. I must admit, I dread the prospect. It will only be a matter of time, though," he shrugged. "At least I will be able to leave these forges. My duties are lax, I will admit to that, but the smell," he finished with a lighter tone. "Oh, the smell is a torture!"

They laughed, but it was distorted and unsynchronized. Shahzad nearly wept with laughter, clutching his gut at the wit of what he said, whereas Ghasif only seemed to accommodate his companion's joke. As he made another pass with the wheel, Mukhtar sensed a discomfort in Ghasif. His slightly raised, bushy eyebrows seemed to indicate a distinct dread, as though the unanticipated had happened.

"What is the meaning of this?" A more authoritative voice called.

Ghasif and Shahzad both stood still. Mukhtar tensed. He would not so easily forget it. It was the same voice that had tortured him, demanding the whereabouts of a keystone.

Two guards escorted him. The manner in which he held the hilt of his sheathed scimitar marked him as not only skilled, but also vigilant and wary with every step. That is not what intrigued Mukhtar though. It was the blank patch of skin on his right cheek where his beard refused to grow, and when Mukhtar made another round, he struggled to suppress a gasp of horror.

"General Masri." Ghasif and Shahzad both gave synchronized military-like bows.

General? Mukhtar tried not to make eye contact. *The slave became a General? A slaver himself?*

"You have returned from your mission," Masri addressed Ghasif. His tone carried an arrogance far more elevated than when he was a caged slave. How he ever came to be a General of Ghuldad was certainly beyond comprehension.

"Indeed, I have," Ghasif replied calmly.

"Tell me, Captain Majtaba, have you all but forgotten the Creed of Ghuldad?"

Ghasif's beard twitched. "I was born into it. Raised with it. I will never forget my *true* creed."

Upon emphasis of the word 'true', Mukhtar made a mental note to ask him, if he ever got the opportunity; what was the *true* creed of Ghuldad, if not slavery, coercion, and war?

Masri's lips curled into a sneering grin. "A poor impression it will cast upon you and your late father, were you to dishonor our ways."

"Indeed, it will," Ghasif's voice remained calm and controlled, although Mukhtar could sense the restraint.

"Why then would you keep the Master waiting after your mission?" Masri asked. "And is it not forbidden to engage in meaningless conversations within the fortress walls?"

Ghasif's beard twitched again. As Mukhtar made another pass, he noted a glint in the Captain's eye, a fiery glare. He wished nothing but to spring forth and tear the General to pieces.

"Indeed, it is forbidden," Ghasif gave another short bow. "Forgive us, General. It will not happen again."

"No. It will not," Masri gave a satisfied smirk. "If it does, you will be stripped of your rank. Understood?"

Ghasif's jaw was set. Wordlessly, he hastened away, and Mukhtar continued to push the wheel.

The *Sorcerers* had been *summoned?* The Captains were ordered and the Legions armed? Mukhtar had heard talk of war before. Mere rumors and conversations exchanged between idle men who discussed politics over stale *hashish* and acrid coffee. However, this was information that instilled fear in him. He cared less that these people were on a path of destruction. He cared less that his own freedom was forfeit. He cared more for those who would fall victim. Whom did Ghuldad intend to wage war against? The brutish hordes of Rhudah? The barbaric tribes of Rhunga? Or the peaceful lands of Aghara? Or, and he thought this with an even deeper fear, the Empire of Ahul-Hama. The cities of Aztalaan and Din-Galad. The very doorsteps of Khalidah. Did Immorkaan know of this advancing army? Were they prepared to face what was coming?

A truce with Arammoria? Mukhtar had heard the tales of the Great War. The dread and anxiety they were told with. It seemed that such dread was imminent in the two-decade, hard-earned peace after the war. For the moment, he could think of little else but to come free of his irons and escape this incarceration. The safety of his kin depended on it.

He curled up in his usual spot by the massive neck of the wheel, shuddered under his sisal shroud, and stared into the inky black sky. The air was heavy with the scent of rain, and a distant rumbling foretold of an approaching storm. He hadn't yet spent a single day or night under a deluge and wondered how he would survive it. Would he and the other slaves be given shelter, or would they have to cower under their sisal shrouds and desperately try to keep warm and dry? Dymek grunted and mumbled in his sleep while his limbs twitched. He was exhausted and weary beyond either of them. Death was close for him, Mukhtar could sense it, and the thought filled him with grief. It was only a matter of time. He would fall at the wheel or be dragged away to the gallows, for a man no longer able to work the forges was a man rendered useless. And those rendered useless, faced the gallows.

Far across the fields were pockets of light. Fires lit to keep the night guard warm. He glanced at the parapets above. Archers patrolled the top of the walls in every direction. Would he even be able to muster the strength to climb the walls? Or risk death and find a way through the main gates? Mere ten feet away from the wheel and the archers will reign down their arrows on him. He gave a small snort, a tiny chuckle to his own silly thoughts and distant ambitions. He tugged at the shackles on his wrists and ankles, and laughed a little louder. He could not even undo the iron binding him to the wheel. How could he ever fathom crossing the courtyard, the guards, and the gates to freedom? He laughed even louder, but only as loud as he alone could hear. He had not laughed for a long time. Even though his own voice frightened him, he continued to laugh. Then he heard footsteps and fell silent.

Fear gripped him. He was discovered. He should not have disturbed the silent night. Now the whip would be unleashed. He would be punished. Worse, he would be unchained and taken to a more treacherous task. One he would not have the strength to complete, which would only see him to the gallows and hanged until he found death, because those who were rendered useless, were taken to the gallows. His teeth trembled as the footsteps grew closer. He brought his fists to his mouth to keep from crying out. Tears filled his eyes and he began to weep.

'Why does it cry?' A voice hissed in the dark. The footsteps grew louder. The sounds of anklets jingled. *'Is it fear? Why is it afraid?'*

It was the same voice. The same sound of fabric rustling the ground, scraping the inner walls of his deepest thoughts.

'Cold be your heart, cold be your bones, and foolish be your thoughts. Did I not offer you asylum? Did I not offer you freedom?'

"This is the evil of the *Shaytaan*," he murmured feverishly under his breath. "This is his vile manipulation, his deliverance of wickedness. I believe in the power of the One true God. Save me from this endless torture, O' mighty Creator of the worlds, with whom lies the benefaction of life and the sovereignty of death."

'Pray, oh pray,' she mocked. *'You are nothing but an inferior spawn of a creation of mud and clay! You have no divinity! You have no power!'*

"All power belongs to Him," Mukhtar continued to mutter relentlessly. "He is the Lord of all creation. He who parted the

Heavens and the earth. He who created the light, the fire, and the clay."

"*Your thoughts are puny, your efforts futile,*" the Jinn cackled mirthlessly. "*There is no other power here, save that which trickles from the essences of the ultimate evildoer.*"

"Go away!" he whimpered.

The Jinn laughed even louder. *'Go away?'* it shrieked hysterically. *'And leave you here to rot in your own filth? There must be a greater purpose to your existence than that. Pray... Pray... Pray. Who will save you now? The Hand of Azazil awakens with vengeance on mankind. Arisen will he, arisen with scars. He will wage his war and become the destroyer of worlds. Who will save you then, Mukhtar?'*

'...Mukhtar...'

'...Mukhtar?'

"Mukhtar?"

"Mukhtar!"

Someone shook him. He struggled, swinging his arms in fury to fend off an unknown attacker, or so he thought.

"Mukhtar! Cease your struggle—!" A scruffy voice and strong arms tried to restrain him.

"I will not yield!" he yelled. "Unhand me! I will *not* face the gallows—" the rest of his statement was muffled. A heavy hand had clamped his mouth shut. His shackles clanged, his chains jingled. Eventually, he was subdued and forced to gaze into a pair of brown, almond-shaped eyes belonging to a face hidden behind a dark veil and a lingering scent of lavender and *Oudh*.

"Calm yourself," Nuzhah ushered him quietly.

"You said this would be simple!" The scruffy voice spoke to his left. "He will have alerted all the guards by now! Why are we even wasting our efforts on this slave? He knows nothing!"

"Do *you* know enough to judge?" Nuzhah remarked angrily. "Do as you have been instructed!"

"I do not take orders from *servants!*" Came a rude response.

"Restrain yourself, Rauf!" Another voice said. A rather familiar voice.

By now, Mukhtar had gained better focus. He recognized Ghasif, who held him firmly by his right shoulder, and another man who could only be Rauf. Rauf had one hand clasped over Mukhtar's mouth and another that pinned his left shoulder to the ground.

"Unhand me!" Mukhtar tried to yell over Rauf's hand.

"Calm yourself, Mukhtar," Nuzhah told him again. "We will remove your shackles!"

Remove his shackles? Was this the rescue he longed for? Was this the freedom he yearned? It was instantaneous. He let go his skirmish and they released him. Ghasif helped him up while Rauf struggled with the shackles. Mukhtar searched the gloom nervously.

"Where is the other?" he asked, unable to keep the quiver from his voice. He realized he was trembling uncontrollably, the sisal rags covering his body were drenched in sweat and the perspiration clung to his skin with an unforgivable chill.

Through the darkness, Ghasif gave him a quizzical look, "There is no one else. The guards have been sedated."

"Sedated?" Mukhtar gasped. "No! Not sedated! Not them! Where is... *She?*"

"Whom do you speak of, Mukhtar?" Nuzhah gazed at him. "There is no one else here."

Rauf undid the chain that bound him to the wheel, but was unable to break his braces. Even without the chains, Mukhtar was grateful. He rubbed the skin beneath the iron on his wrists, ankles, and neck, and winced. They hurt with soreness, but a soreness he adored more than anything in that moment. He was rid of the chains.

"This is Captain Ghasif Majtaba and his Lieutenant, Rauf Ibn Anbar. They are..." Nuzhah made an unnecessary introduction, but Mukhtar allowed her to speak. Her voice provided a distraction. A moment for him to consider other matters. The Jinn had come to him, once before and again tonight. His eyes continued to search the shadows, but aside from the four of them, there was no one else about.

"...are you listening?" Nuzhah demanded. He nodded inattentively. "They will take you to Aztalaan...," she continued speaking. Her voice became muffled by his thoughts, wandering and searching for the unknown, the unseen.

Its existence was inexplicable. Undeniable. He believed it to be a fragment of his imagination, but now it was absolute. It filled him with fear. It would come to haunt him again.

SEVEN

THE RETURN TO KHALIDAH

They had brought clothes. A ragged shirt, worn trousers, tattered sandals and a faded cloak. While he wore them, Ghasif conversed with Nuzhah in aggressive whispers, and Rauf clucked impatiently nearby, which Mukhtar found to be very irritable.

Rauf's long hair touched his shoulders and partially concealed his pockmarked, unshaven face. He was clad, just as Ghasif, in short white robes and leather armor. A bow and quiver of arrows were strapped to his back, along with a pair of daggers around his waist. The Lieutenant was an archer. An archer with keen eyes, penetrating the dark in every direction. "We *must* hurry!" he hissed at Ghasif.

Ghasif shortened his heated conversation with Nuzhah and returned to them as Mukhtar tied the straps of his sandals.

"What of Dymek?" Mukhtar asked him, nudging his head at the Surian also chained to the same wheel. He was snoring lightly, his limbs continuously twitching from exhaustion.

Ghasif shook his head. "We cannot take anyone else with us. The journey is perilous. Leave him be."

Mukhtar wanted to protest, but his desire to be free prevented him from arguing with his rescuers. He threw a final pitiful glance at Dymek, silently praying for his burdens to be eased.

"How will we escape?" he asked.

"Did you not hear what the servant said?" Rauf remarked.

Mukhtar shook his head.

"Are we to *hold* his hand every step of the way, Captain?" Rauf complained to his superior.

"Enough, Rauf!" Ghasif ordered the Lieutenant. "We have no time to bicker amongst ourselves. Come!" He ushered them to follow.

"Try to keep up, slave!" Rauf snarled.

The more Rauf used words like *servant* and *slave,* the more Mukhtar disliked him. His jaw was clenched, but he decided against retaliation. His eyes were fixed on Nuzhah. She had not taken a step forward. Her almond eyes shimmered in the moonlight, her expression unreadable behind her veil. "Will you not come with us?" he asked

She shook her head jerkily.

His eyes widened. He remained rooted to the spot. "They will *know* you helped me!"

"Our road is treacherous and perilous," Ghasif answered instead, a slight quiver in his voice almost betraying his true intent. "She is safer here. Ma'alim will protect her. Come now, we haven't much time!"

Mukhtar refused to move. He did not know who this *Ma'alim* was, nor did he care. He suspected some treachery afoot but could not bring himself to saying anything at that moment. Much was obscure, much more may be at stake, and his freedom was at hand. He did not wish to compromise that for anything. Instead, he gazed at her earnestly, struggling to find the right words. "I cannot thank you enough for what you have done—"

"Enough with the pleasantries!" Rauf interrupted harshly.

Mukhtar ignored him. "Farewell," he said to Nuzhah. "Peace be upon you."

"And upon you, Mukhtar," she responded kindly. "Until our paths cross again."

He regarded her with a final, amiable gaze, and followed Ghasif and Rauf across the unmanned, unguarded courtyard to the other side of the field. When he glanced over his shoulder, she had already been swallowed by the darkness. Despite his heightened sense of freedom at hand, Mukhtar could not help but feel heavy at heart. He would dearly miss her.

He was surprised to see guards and slaves alike, asleep and oblivious to the three of them. When Ghasif said they had sedated the guards, Mukhtar did not take it to mean *all* of them.

Rauf slipped him one of his daggers as they approached the gates. "Be vigilant," he muttered under his breath. Mukhtar tensed and held up the dagger firmly.

"I said vigilant, not *'prepare to strike!'* Keep up!"

Mukhtar lowered the dagger and cursed Rauf under his breath.

Contrary to what he had assumed, not all the guards had been sedated. Four, strong and heavily armed men barred their path under the large stone archway. Behind them, at twenty-feet tall and as wide four horse-carriages, was a heavy iron gate. A dancing flame threw their shadows against the stone walls in a frenzy of darkness over light.

"Who goes there?" The call came from a fifth guard hidden in the shadows.

"One who will not look back," Ghasif responded. "Will you see us passage, or will you spill the blood of kin?"

"Kin does not betray kin," the guard declared, still hidden in the shadows.

"Long have we been betrayed, brother. I have seen it, you have not," Ghasif said as they came closer to the gate. "What will it be, Iyad? Will you see us passage?"

"To abandon your creed, bears great consequence," Iyad warned and stepped forward into the firelight. "To free a slave without the Master's permission, and to escape with him... even greater. You tread on loose sands, brother."

"Do not assume that I have taken lightly your counsel, brother," Ghasif responded with equal acerbity. "But I am burdened with greater purpose. I must see it through."

"Then you have made a decision that is sound by you," Iyad folded his arms and leaned back slightly. "You bear, not only the consequences of your own, but also the actions of those who accompany you. Their loss will be your responsibility, mark my words."

"Consider them marked," Ghasif's tone remained as cold as ever.

Upon Iyad's silent command, his companions unbolted the gates. In a low squeal of metal on metal, the ancient gates swung a fraction to allow them through. As he came closer to Iyad, Mukhtar was able to fully look upon him, wondering why the Gatekeeper had not been sedated like the other guards, as Ghasif had claimed.

He stood taller than his peers, his knitted eyebrows and cold dark eyes against a scarred and beardless face made him look very perverse. It was enough to deduce from his features alone that Iyad was a ruthless, stern and sharp leader, one who obeyed orders without question and held a high regard for rules. Perhaps his willingness to help Ghasif may only have come from a love of coin or a favor owed. Either way, it seemed to be wearing out, and Mukhtar hastened behind Ghasif, with Rauf bringing up the rear. As soon as they stepped beyond the gate, he breathed an air that felt lighter and cleaner. The air of freedom.

They trekked along a wide, rocky path down the hill, and Mukhtar threw a final glance over his shoulders to the gates closing behind them. Somehow, Iyad's cold eyes continued to gleam at them from beyond the iron bars. Never would he return to those gates. Never would he allow himself to be enslaved by them. And what of Ghasif and Rauf, the disparate two who were so willing to risk all to help him? What truly lay in their hearts?

Be wary, he cautioned himself. *Vigilant. You only need them as far as Aztalaan.*

However, restraint had never been Mukhtar's strength, not when curiosity stung him like an angry bee. They had barely walked a few paces and he asked, "Why are you helping me?"

"Keep your questions to yourself, slave!" Rauf warned in an undertone. "At least until we are clear of the village!"

"I am no slave!" Mukhtar retorted angrily.

"You will *always* be a slave!" Rauf remarked. "Be it by chains, or your own thoughts!"

"What is your—?" Mukhtar rounded on him.

"Keep silent!" Ghasif hissed at them. "We have a long road ahead of us, and if we cannot journey as one, then all our efforts will be for nothing! Wait until we have passed the village and *then* we can converse!"

There was nothing but the sounds of fluttering shrubbery along the path and the crunch of dirt beneath their feet, and in a few short moments, tiny flickers of lights appeared before them. Against the darkened horizon, Mukhtar saw the silhouette of short mismatched huts and cottages.

The village was silent and asleep, and their path to the other side remained undisturbed. Here, three horses had been made ready for their journey. The stable-boy, young and scrawny, was handed a small sack of coin which he hurried away with, hardly giving them a second glance. It was an action that raised suspicion and warranted scrutiny, but Mukhtar remained as silent as he had been instructed. He was slowly beginning to contemplate how much effort the two assassins had put into his escape.

Their journey, as Ghasif explained, was a two-day ride west, and three days further south to the Walls of Murfaqat, an ancient structure built to protect Ahul-Hama from the northern realms. The Wall was famously guarded by the formidable Army of the Red-Guard, soldiers of Aztalaan, feared and renowned in every battle ever fought. Ghuldad was their greatest foe, which made Mukhtar wonder what Ghasif and Rauf really intended. What mysterious strategy did they have in mind when they arrived at Murfaqat?

"Am I allowed to speak now?" he asked when they were barely an hour into their journey. "Or must we still be cautious lest the *scorpions* overhear us?"

Ghasif gave a nervous chuckle while Rauf muttered, what Mukhtar assumed were only more insults under his breath.

Angered, Mukhtar pulled the reins of his horse and rounded on Rauf. "Why do you resent me?"

They all halted. Rauf opened his mouth to argue, but Ghasif replied instead, "He does not think you worth the effort."

"Rescue a *slave*, when we could be doing far more important things!" Rauf announced.

"Turn your horse around then!" Mukhtar retorted.

Rauf opened his mouth but Ghasif intervened again. "He hasn't a choice. We follow the orders of *The Teacher*. It is *he* who finds you important."

"A *ridiculous* notion!" Rauf commented blatantly.

"Rauf!" Ghasif warned him again. "Refrain from such talk!"

"Greater perils are afoot, and the Teacher places more importance on this slave!" Rauf retorted back.

"No man is unimportant! Not slave nor master!" Mukhtar glared at him.

"It is that very thought that has brought you thus far!" Rauf did not care to disguise his sneer. "Ask yourself— *was it worth it?*"

Mukhtar fell silent. Rauf's words struck him. He had been asking himself the same question since he woke in the dark cell.

They rode on in silence until dawn approached, and before mid-morning, they stopped for breakfast. Ghasif pointed due west and explained their journey further. They would ride to sundown, through two more villages before the road took them south across the *Plains of Zarzara*. Mukhtar had heard tales of the Plains, rumors that an ancient Kingdom once thrived there, overrun by an army of Jinn who still haunt the plains and prey on unwary travelers. He made no mention of such tales to Ghasif or Rauf. The last thing he wanted was to be ridiculed by them.

"Who is this *Teacher* you speak of?" He nudged his horse forward to ride beside Ghasif.

"He is our true leader," Ghasif answered. "A man of spirituality and wisdom. We call him Ma'alim, *The Teacher*. You have met him. He tended your wounds before you were cast to the wheel. He has secretly risen against the unjust authority of Ussam Bashiri, the Master of Ghuldad."

Mukhtar recalled the old man who had promised to visit him but never did. So *he* was Ma'alim. Indeed, he felt a rush of gratitude for him. He had both healed Mukhtar of his injuries and aided his rescue from slavery.

"Your conversation with General Masri..." Mukhtar began.

Ghasif cursed loudly, and behind them, Rauf did the same. "Masri is a vile and ruthless man!" Ghasif said bitterly. "He arrived with Ma'alim, as humble as a lamb, seeking asylum. God only knows the devilry that man has embraced, that has seen him rise to the rank of a General, while Ma'alim struggles to free us from the tyranny of his kind!"

Mukhtar kept secret his engagement with Masri in the cell, as well as their much earlier encounter in Khalidah. He was not prepared to trust the Assassins just yet. "And the slavers who captured me?" he asked instead.

"They sold you to mercenaries from Din-Galad," Ghasif explained. "They did not know your true identity, and only meant to recover what you cost them."

"And what is my true identity?" Mukhtar asked curiously.

"The name of Zafar is known to Ussam Bashiri," Ghasif gave him a sideways glance. "Your father aided him, Azhar Babak and the High Chancellor Laban Varda, in ending the war two decades ago."

And they betrayed him after, Mukhtar thought to himself. "What does he intend with me?"

"Little do we know," Ghasif replied, and Mukhtar sensed a lie, "only that Ma'alim saw a deeper motive behind your capture and instructed us to take you away from there. We are to leave you at the gates of Murfaqat, under the care of your brother. You must make your own way from there on."

Mukhtar gazed at the open, rocky landscape under clear blue skies. An endless barren stretch lay before them, hot sands gathering into a fiery storm far behind, the horizon ahead smeared by a thin dark line of distant mountains.

"We must be vigilant," Ghasif warned. "Ussam's sorcerers will already have caught our scent."

"*Sorcerers?*" Mukhtar raised an eyebrow.

"Four sorcerers of a demonic race," Rauf replied from behind them. Despite his earlier outbursts, he seemed to be coming to terms with his designated mission. "Fallen agents of a fallen Dark Prince. *Sahir Idumea, Sahir Eth, Sahir Ahumai* and *Sahir Elzafaan*. For reasons and circumstances that do not make sense to *anyone*, they now serve Ussam Bashiri. *That* should speak for how powerful and wicked he has become."

Ghasif nudged his horse forward. "Come, Mukhtar, we must hasten to Aztalaan. Pray the enemy has not yet infiltrated the Red-City."

"And what of the sorcerers?" Mukhtar threw a nervous glance over his shoulder, trying to disguise his trepidation. "How will we escape *them?*"

Ghasif held up his left hand and touched the ring on his forefinger. The gold band reflected a glint of sunlight into Mukhtar's eye. On its crown sat a polished red stone. "It was given to me by Ma'alim. It is a Ring of Power that will keep us masked from the eyes of Ghuldad for as long as I wear and command it."

Mukhtar fell silent and nudged his horse forward. Protected by a magic ring provided by an unknown savior, and hunted by assassins and sorcerers with demonic powers. If life had been difficult enough in chains, why did freedom suddenly seem worse?

'They will never cease the hunt!' A whisper echoed around him and he shuddered, suddenly overcome with immense fright and anxiety. They had made camp for the night, and as per their arrangements, he had taken the third watch. He shivered, pulled his cloak tighter, and continued to stare into the crackling flames of the campfire, uttering strings of divine supplications to keep his fears at bay. The sooner he returned to Khalidah, the better he will be, safe once again behind the four walls of his home.

The journey through the Plains of Zarzara was uneventful and, contrary to all popular beliefs, did not avail an army of Jinn. Perhaps, and Mukhtar was very skeptical about it, Ghasif's ring may have truly masked their presence from preying entities.

Two more days under the scorching desert sun, with very little food and water remaining, the renowned walls loomed closer into view. They entered the village bordering the Wall after dusk, worn beyond imagining, longing for nothing but a hot meal, cooling water to drink and a place to rest their heads.

Torches in brackets illuminated the red stone as far as the eye could see. Its thickness measured a ten-camel caravan, and its length ran from escarpment to escarpment, east to west. The only way in was through the King's Passage, an elegant archway of intricate architecture, and large iron gates manned by the Red-Guard. Several watchtowers stood tall at regular intervals every mile or so, each with a beacon at its peak for signaling at times of siege.

It was built during the reign of King Hamasi, some four centuries prior, as a defense against northern foes. Now it was only used as a poor excuse to extort taxes from anyone entering or leaving the Empire.

Like so many others, they made camp by the wall, awaiting dawn when the gates would open and they would be allowed in. Mukhtar could hardly remember the last time he crossed over. When he was barely conscious, and the Red-Guard was bribed to allow them passage under cover of darkness.

"Why did he yield so easily, I wonder?" He heard Rauf whisper to Ghasif while they ate.

Ghasif did not reply and Rauf, it seemed, did not wish to press him. However, Mukhtar was curious, and he knew exactly what the subject matter was. Rauf was referring to Iyad's leniency at the gates.

"I have wondered the same," he joined the conversation. "Why did he give us passage so easily? I did not hear the jingle of coin."

Ghasif's beard twitched and his eyebrows curled. Anger flashed in his eyes. "Captain Iyad is *not* a petty thief. Do not impugn his honor, especially when you know *nothing* of the sacrifice he has just made only for *your* freedom!"

Mukhtar was slightly taken aback, but did not show intimidation and instead humbled himself. "I did not mean to insult. I only meant to understand how we escaped. Why did we not take a more secluded pass? Why the front gate?"

"Ghuldad is an ancient fortress, once the stronghold of the Dark Prince's most trusted ally, Sahir Idumea," Ghasif replied after a brief hesitation, while Rauf turned away and became busy with sharpening his daggers. "Idumea was defeated by General Ussam Bashiri, and he and his brethren were forced into servitude. Over the years, Ussam has learned from them the Dark Arts and amassed his powers. In order to keep Immorkaan at bay, he forged Ghuldad into a sanctuary for those who lost their ways and sought asylum, secretly building his army. As such, its greatest weakness became its doorstep, but its greatest strengths are men like Captain Iyad. If he has seen us passage, then he has also understood the truth in our purpose."

"I fail to understand—" Mukhtar began and hesitated, unable to phrase his query.

"You fail to understand why a man such as Ussam," Rauf interrupted, "a General of the Aztalaan army, would defeat a Dark Sorcerer and force him into servitude for his own benefit, while proclaiming himself a saint to the world?" He exchanged a grim expression with his Captain.

"A man's true faith is tested when he allows the devil to manipulate his thoughts," Ghasif stated, which seemed to put Mukhtar's query at rest. Ussam desired power, has desired so from the very beginning. He would stop at nothing until he has conquered all, no matter the cost, no matter the detriment.

Dawn came with haste, leaving behind a sleepless and restless night, that when Mukhtar woke, he was still instilled with the fear of being chained to the wheel. He stood in the long queue leading up to the gate, awaiting his turn to be interrogated by the guards, while Ghasif and Rauf lingered patiently nearby.

"State your name and business!" The guard barked at him when his turn came.

"Mukhtar."

"Your full name, peasant!" The guard barked at him again. He was beardless, clad in a crimson tunic under heavy armor, and held an intimidating spear in one hand. Mukhtar drew his cloak closer to conceal his shackles. If the Red-Guard suspected him to be an escaped slave, they would chain and imprison him no less, forcing him into servitude at the wall, like his brother.

"Mukhtar Harun Zafar," he said, stealing a glance over the guard's shoulder with the hope of spotting his brother.

"Zafar?" The guard narrowed his eyes. "You are kin to Zaki Harun Zafar?"

"My brother," Mukhtar nodded. "He is a Captain of the Red-Guard."

"Ah, Captain Zafar is an honorable man," the guard stated with a raised chin. "We will inform him of your arrival. You may wait by the wall there."

Mukhtar shuffled back to where Ghasif and Rauf sat with their horses by the wall, covered in large blankets to disguise their Assassin uniforms.

"Well?" Ghasif enquired.

"They have sent for my brother," Mukhtar said.

"Then we wait."

"How long are you willing to wait?" Mukhtar asked.

"Long enough to meet your brother and explain to him the gravity of the matter," Ghasif replied.

"I hardly believe he will be pleased to see you!" Mukhtar raised an eyebrow. "He was only recently tasked with hunting your kind. Are you willing to risk meeting him?"

Rauf scowled at him irritably. "You ask too many questions for a slave!"

Mukhtar threw him a scathing look. "I truly *despise* that word."

Ghasif kept a wary eye in the direction of the gates while Rauf threw a rock at the wall and watched it interestingly, as though wondering how many he would need to bring down the massive stone structure. This irritated Mukhtar even more.

"You need not remain here," he declared. "My brother will come soon."

"We will leave when our task is done," Rauf stated.

"I can fend for myself!"

"*Fend* for yourself?" Rauf mocked. "You would not survive a day in the desert on your own. Still be shackled were it not for us!"

Mukhtar's nostrils flared. "I need not saviors who are arrogant and keep secrets from me!"

"You are truly an ungrateful—" Rauf started forward.

"Keep your voices down!" Ghasif warned in an undertone, his eyes narrowed, scanning something over Mukhtar's shoulder.

A young Red-Guard approached them and they tensed. Mukhtar distinctly noted Rauf's arm reach for a dagger inside his cloak. The assassins would not yield without a fight. They would die before facing the horrors they would be subjected to in the dungeons of the Aztalaan citadel. How would they contend with Zaki, and why they would even risk coming this close to the wall, was beyond him.

This guard, however, was not a soldier of rank. He wore the colors and the armor, but aside from a simple short sickle-sword by his side, he carried no intent of a fight. He was a messenger.

"You there!" he declared when he was only feet away from them. "Who among you is Mukhtar Harun Zafar, brother of Captain Zaki Zafar?"

"It is I," Mukhtar responded.

"I have been tasked to inform you that Captain Zafar will be unable to avail himself," the guard stated, reciting what he had obviously memorized on the way there. "You must come to the gates with me to be questioned by his Lieutenant for your reasons of crossing into the Empire. Lieutenant Sameer has expressly declared that your needs will be catered for by the Red-Guard under the Captain's honors, and you will remain in Aztalaan until he arrives. Please, accompany me to the gate."

Mukhtar nodded and almost instinctively started forward, but was held back by Ghasif's hand on his shoulder.

"Wait!" he warned in an undertone, then spoke to the guard, "Allow us a moment to make farewell. Inform Lieutenant Sameer that we will bring him to the gate within the hour."

The guard looked confused. His jaw was clenched. He was unprepared for such a response. "I was instructed to bring the Captain's brother with me."

Ghasif returned what Mukhtar assumed was a friendly smile. "Long will it be before we see our cousin again. Good soldier of the Red-Guard, will you not give us the hour to make farewell and exchange parting gifts? Perhaps sit down for a final meal?"

The guard shuffled on the spot. "But I have been instructed…"

"Only an hour, O' Soldier of the Wall," Ghasif's voice had become humbler than Mukhtar had ever noted. "I am certain the good Lieutenant will understand. After all, you are a man of honor, are you not? You are a man who understands virtue, are you not? Know that Captain Zafar will most certainly hear of your hospitality for his brother and he will, without doubt, show his gratitude."

The confusion on the guard's face could not have been more evident. He was young, perhaps even a mere apprentice. He yearned to be ambitious, to prove his worth to his superiors so that one day, he too might be given Captaincy. Ghasif had pleaded the right note.

He nodded curtly. "Within the hour then, citizen." And he left.

As soon as he was clear of them, Mukhtar wheeled around to face Ghasif. "Explain what you have just done! Why did you turn him away? Why did you lie to him?"

Ghasif did not take his eyes off the guard, and only replied when he was a fair distance away. "They are lying to *you,* Mukhtar. Your brother is not here!"

Mukhtar shook his head disbelievingly. "I *know* that. The guard said so. He also said that they will give me sanctuary until Zaki returns."

"Into a trap!" Rauf stated. He was already packing their belongings. "It is as we suspected. Ghuldad has infiltrated Aztalaan as well."

"What do you mean?" Mukhtar became angered again. Why were they speaking to him in riddles? Why the secrecy?

"We must come away from here, immediately!" Ghasif warned.

"No!" Mukhtar stepped away from Ghasif. "Enough of this! I demand—!"

"And you have every right to demand so," Ghasif pleaded, "but not here. Not now. They are watching us. They are waiting for you. As we stand, we are still in Alhram, No Man's Land. They cannot do anything to you while you remain on this side of the Wall, but once you cross the gate, you *will* become their prisoner. We must leave. Now!"

EIGHT

THE DESERT

The sun's fiery hot glare tore through his *thaub*, searing his shoulders and neck. His head was throbbing, his heart filled with emotions he could not understand. Fear for his brother. Disappointed that he was not there to receive him. The dread of what lay ahead or what might follow, and disdain that he was yet again at the mercy of Ghasif and Rauf. Helpless and desperate, he followed them through the winding village lanes. Agitated, he waited while they procured supplies for the journey.

What journey? Mukhtar wondered. Where will they lead him now? How far will they take him, and will he survive it? He leaned back, slid down against the mud wall of a bread-maker's stall and buried his face in his arms while a mule, laden with heavy sacks, passed them by, braying loudly.

"Further west, past the *Peaks of Aftara*," Rauf told him without him asking. "South through the *Cedars of Zila*, the tallest, most ancient forest in those lands. Seven days to the edge of the cedars and Arammoria will avail itself. It is the road we must now take to the Immortal City."

Mukhtar raised his head sharply, squinting at Rauf's silhouette against the midday sun.

"You will lead us through the wastelands of Arammoria?" he growled. "Have you *lost* all sense? Those lands are *riddled* with wickedness!"

Rauf chuckled, as did Ghasif. "Only the strongest will survive, Mukhtar!"

Mukhtar stared at them disbelievingly. "You would *jeer?* I have heard the tales! And what of *Aftara* and *Zila*, the Gods of old? They are known to plague the mountains *and* the forests! We cross their lands and they will slaughter us!"

"*Pagan gods,* or ancient Jinn *worshipped* as gods," Ghasif stated. "Both the mountain and forest tribes were forced to submit to the Dark Prince, and their demon-gods became mere servants of his. Their worship is idolatry and their faith is profane, unworthy fear. The can do us no harm."

Mukhtar avoided his gaze. He did not wish for them to know, nor did he wish to further the conversation, but he had more reason than many to fear the Unseen. They had not heard, not *felt*, what he had in the darkness.

"Whom did they worship after the Dark Prince fell?" he asked.

Ghasif gave him a dark look and said, "The Priestesses of Aftara, and the *Sufis* of Zila, still hold their beliefs of old. Their sacrilegious rites and rituals only pave a path to the Abysmal Flame. Pity them for theirs is a fate of sin."

Their seven-day journey began as soon as the sun sank beyond the horizon and the stars availed themselves to light their path. After the first night, they continued to travel only by day. It would have been more sensible to travel by night and escape the scorching sun, but Ghasif simply refused. Deserts were known to play host to *Ghuls* among other mischievous entities. They could not risk wandering into something *unnatural* in the darkness.

The barren landscape of Alhram was rocky and uneven, unlike the massive, smooth dunes and soft sands of the Khabara Desert south of Aztalaan, or the empty vastness beyond the horizons of Rhunga. When the sun scorched the earth, the sky was reflected against the sands in shimmering illusions and mirages, sometimes giving them false hopes of an oasis in the distance. When the inky blackness covered the skies, when the stars above twinkled in divine harmony and the sands beneath their sandals became cool and soothing, the desert upheld a beauty that was ethereal. Silent and calming, where one would find themselves in solitude only with their Creator.

Odd formations of towering rocks, molded by thousands of years of treacherous winds, safeguarded the illusive distances from the road, playing host to foxes and hyenas. Eagles and falcons soared high above them, scanning the hot and dry sands for their next prey. Ravenous vultures sometimes hovered close by preying upon their will to surrender to the desert.

They wore headdresses and turbans to shade them from the scorching sun, drawn tight over their ears to keep at bay the hollow, howling wind, and over their noses to filter out the dust blown up by the constantly passing gales. Although weary and exhausted, Ghasif, on his white mare, silently but vigilantly led the way past desolate and fallow rocks, Mukhtar followed in equally scorned silence on his chestnut, and Rauf, on his black steed, brought up the rear.

The silence was not mutual, had endured since they departed from Murfaqat, and was one of the reasons why Mukhtar was upset and contemptuous. All attempts to seek out answers fell on deaf ears, while Ghasif and Rauf continued to discuss their plans in hushed tones. Frustration continued to fill him as he pondered over how much longer he would need to remain at the mercy of the two assassins, and several times he had to fight the urge to escape on his steed and find his own way back to Khalidah. If only he knew the way.

They took the road west as Rauf had indicated, maintaining their disguises as mere travelers. The closer they approached the borders of Rhudah, the harsher the desert became, but to their utter surprise, not as abandoned as they had assumed.

Bedouin tribes were scattered all over the rocky vastness, their tents fluttering in the winds, veils drawn close to keep away the drifting dust and lingering smell of waste from their camels. Some of the tribes welcomed and gave them sanctuary, while others made it very clear that they were not taking any visitors. One particular tribesman was banished by his own people when he allowed Mukhtar, Ghasif, and Rauf to follow him back to his camp. The chief of the tribe, a gaunt man with a pet falcon on his shoulder, released the bird with instructions to peck at them until they were clear of his sight while his warriors brandished their spears and shields, arming their bows with crude arrows. It was only when Rauf fired a warning shot from his bow, as they rode away from the camp in haste, that the bird was called back. Mukhtar wondered what would have happened if Rauf's intent was to kill it.

If the desert was harsh, the Cedars were no less. Towering high above them, the ancient trees created a canopy of shade from the sun, but the cold mist hovering above the ground concealed more than just wild predators. Eerie and gloomy, they felt watchful eyes on them, as though whatever resided there, be it Jinn or the forest tribes of Zila, only waited with bated breath to attack them were they to be provoked. Once again, Mukhtar only suspected that their passage remained unseen because of the ring Ghasif wore, and the more he thought of it, the more distant he felt from divinity and true faith. Having spent his childhood with Saif in *Madrassa,* he had acquired enough knowledge to distinguish evil from good— and there was no doubt in his mind with regards to Ghasif's ring.

Eight days later, they made camp at the edge of the forest. Mukhtar completed his task of tending to the horses, and climbed over a large rock to scan the ghastly landscape. The wind howled eerily across the barren lands, bringing about a dry and destitute stench of decay. Even though they were still miles away, he could sense the uncanny, mysterious aura of the ruined and desecrated wastelands, something he had only heard of in tales. "Strange," he squinted. "Not a soul in sight."

Below him, Ghasif pitched their tattered tent, while Rauf

prepared some meat to roast for their meal.

"No one dares venture here," Ghasif stood and pointed to the east. "Those watchtowers outside Ninya are manned by the Red-Guard. It is difficult to see much from that distance, but as long as people know that the wastelands are being watched, they keep away."

Ninya was a once small military camp that bordered the Dead City, and the only safe haven between Arammoria and the Dunes of Khabara. It became a settlement when the Aztalaan army remained there for too long during the Great War. Mukhtar had heard several rumors claiming that Azhar Babak had built himself a private home in Ninya, a secret retreat for when he sought solitude.

"Tall tales and rumors," Ghasif responded when Mukhtar mentioned it. "There is no such retreat for the King. No secret coterie of exotic concubines or hidden treasures. Ninya is just as daunting and bleak as the wastelands it neighbors, and the garrison only remains there as it is commanded. No one would dare venture close to these lands, no matter how insane they are."

"How insane are we then?" Mukhtar asked.

Rauf chuckled. "Come down. Let us eat!"

The night sky was cold and dark, devoid of the moon or the stars, but they had the crackling fire to give them light and warmth. After setting up their tent, they settled down around the fire and helped themselves to roasted meat and bread.

"I understand your urge to seek answers—" Ghasif began.

"You need not explain it if you do not want to, Ghasif," Mukhtar stopped him there. "I care not anymore, only that

I return to Khalidah in one piece. We can go our separate ways then."

This was the first time they had spoken openly since their departure from Murfaqat, and he did not wish to destroy it by engaging in heated arguments.

"No, Mukhtar," Ghasif held up his hand, and Mukhtar sensed the urgency in his voice. "That is untrue. We do not wish to part ways with you, at least not in bitter faith. Rauf and I have discussed at length, and realize that our mission does not truly end when we enter Khalidah. We are all faced with a calamity, and only with unity can we overcome it."

Mukhtar, who had now finished his meal, hid his astonishment at this abrupt divulgence by casually leaning back against the large rock. He folded his arms and gazed at Ghasif for a long while.

"The tales of Ghuldad are as ancient and obscure as the mists of the Dead City," Ghasif began explaining. "No one truly knows how Ussam defeated Idumea, only that he led a small group of his most skilled warriors and conquered the fortress from within. Some say High Chancellor Laban Varda, who at the time was an Arammorian spy, fed Ussam with crucial information that aided him in his mission. Upon succeeding, Ussam and Laban discovered the means by which Idumea and his brethren, Ahumai, Eth, and Elzafaan, became powerful. Ussam wasted no time in forging his alliances, Azhar Babak who was camped at Ninya, being the first."

"Who recruited my father," Mukhtar gazed into the fire.

"They found the magical objects and weapons they needed to win the war," Rauf continued.

"Magical objects," Mukhtar murmured, his thoughts wandering

to the box Suha had given him. The peculiar items Harun had found during the Great War. He refrained from saying anything. Could this perhaps be the reason why the two assassins were adamant on escorting him to Khalidah? *Tread carefully, Mukhtar.*

"When Azhar became King," Ghasif continued unwarily, "he named his Council of Elders. Himself, his brother Abidan, Adad Babati, Laban Varda and—"

"My father," Mukhtar finished.

Ussam was cast aside. Discarded and left to roam the desolate hallways of the conquered Ghuldad. Just as Mika'il had described Ghulam Mirza's motives, Mukhtar was slowly beginning to understand Ussam's thirst for revenge. He sought to overthrow Azhar Babak and claim the throne for himself. All it takes to conceive a war is the whim of a madman riddled with wicked thoughts. However, Mukhtar sensed a greater power at play. The Jinn in the cell and by the wheel, only a few days ago, could not have been a solitary ploy of Ussam Bashiri.

Mukhtar leaned forward, stroked the fire, then scanned the darkened landscape in the direction of the Dead City, and could not suppress the shudder that ran up his spine at the mere thought of venturing there. These were lands accursed to be lifeless, home to evil Jinn and wicked men.

"Is there no other way?" he asked grimly.

For all his talk of strength and bravery, Rauf kept hidden a similar expression of concern behind his curtain of long hair.

"Khabara is a desert impossible to cross without proper provisions, of which we now have very little," Ghasif explained, "and we cannot risk coming too close to Ninya or Aztalaan. All is lost if we are discovered."

Rauf remained unconvinced, as did Mukhtar. He suspected that the Lieutenant might attempt to talk his Captain into pursuing an alternative route, and Mukhtar was dearly praying for his success.

The following morning, they set out again, heading further south. The climate became cooler by the hour, and by the end of the day, all three of them shuddered under their cloaks and blankets.

Rather than cut through the barren wastelands, Ghasif guided them around its borders. The journey would take longer this way, but they would avoid the eyes of the Ninyan watchtowers and the desecrated gloom of the Dead City, an area Mukhtar came to realize was larger than the cities of Khalidah, Din-Galad and Aztalaan all put together.

The uneven plains were a canvas of blackened stone, as if razed by flames for days at end, stretching out as far as the eye could see. Much of what they came across was rubble and rock, ruins of the outskirts of the city, and further in, beyond thick strands of unnatural mists, were obscure contours of much larger stone structures. Low dark clouds hovered across the lands, thick and ominous, barely keeping the sun alive.

The night was swift, and morning approached without any sign of warmth. The horses grew restless, and all attempts to mount them became futile. Rauf was able to keep them calm by feeding them some herbs. They pulled them by their reins, and although this lengthened the journey, they were at least able to leave their belongings on the horses' backs, and walk unburdened.

"I have never seen a beast so agitated," Rauf said with deep concern. "I fear they will not survive the journey."

His prediction was right. In the following two days, the effects of Rauf's herbs began to wane the further they ventured, and the horses were now showing signs of brutality. They had no choice but to release them and continue the journey afoot.

"They will trample us if not run away with our belongings!" Ghasif remarked as they wrestled to control the reins. "We can procure fresher horses in Mirzaan if, God willing, we make it there."

Using the dimmed sun to maintain his bearings, he continued to lead the way in a single file, followed by Mukhtar and Rauf bringing up the rear. With all their belongings strapped to their backs, they trekked along what appeared to be a long, winding, brick-road, something Mukhtar had never seen before. Most of the roads and streets in Khalidah were of plain dirt and sand, mud or rock, but never made of brick and stone. Ghasif explained that they were entering an area known as *Mudanisin,* Land of the Defilers, a once vibrant town of Arammoria, and home to thousands of witches and sorcerers who supported the Dark Prince's ambitions. The ground was barren, the soil contaminated with soot and coal, littered with skulls and bones of man and beast.

A foul stench, the crunching of dirt under their feet, and the distant rustle of dried leaves, filled the air around them. Two days passed on this lonely trail and destitute landscape. Dark clouds blotted out the sun, and soon they lost track of time, for it was no longer possible to tell whether it was day or night. Desperate to meet their destination, they only stopped for short intervals to replenish themselves, and were on their feet after mere moments of rest.

Rauf was pleading with Ghasif to make a stop, but the Captain insisted they must move on. They had been walking silently for several long hours until Ghasif finally declared they make camp for the night.

Rauf dropped his supplies and sunk to the ground, heaving. Ghasif and Mukhtar set about gathering firewood and pitching the tent. He had never felt so exhausted before, and struggled to keep his eyes open, peering through the mist and fog. "I can barely see the tip of my nose!"

"How much further, Ghasif?" Rauf moaned.

"We crossed the borders of *Mudanisin* only two hours ago," Ghasif stated, "and are now in *Alshura,* Land of the Royal and Loyal. Three more days to the mountain pass of Khamur."

"How can you be certain?" Mukhtar squinted at the sky. With such dark and ominous clouds, it was difficult to place the sun during the day and the stars at night, without which, it was almost impossible to plot a heading.

In response, Ghasif pointed at the only tree within their reach, under which Rauf was now snoring. Its branches hung like shriveled arms stretching out into the night sky, their tips like claws, barren of any leaves. On its withered trunk was tied, a long fluttering piece of white cloth, torn, tattered and stained. "To become an assassin, I had to endure the gloom of Arammoria for seven days, a journey from the Cedars of Zila to the town of Fashaan. This was years ago."

"It must have been a tasking journey," Mukhtar said, silently commending Ghasif's ability to navigate the labyrinthine landscape of ruins and mists.

"It was indeed," Ghasif nodded, "and if I were to be honest, it did not feel as daunting an ordeal as it does now. *Get up*, Rauf!" He kicked his lieutenant's foot to wake him.

They settled down for a silent meal of dried meat and bread. While they ate, Mukhtar could not help but continuously glance over his shoulder. It was a strange feeling, having to search for something that could not be seen.

All his life, uncanny and otherworldly matters always seemed to lurk nearby. He could not deny his fascination about the Unseen, and never forfeited an opportunity to pour through the numerous subjective books and tomes that lay in his grandfather's cabin, a simple shack hugging the banks of the Hubur. Perhaps, he assumed, it was the reason why he had more than often been a victim of strange and vivid nightmares.

As far as his most recent encounters in the darkness were concerned, he was still unsure, and could only explain them as illusive thoughts. His greatest fear, however, his most despised state of existence, was one without knowledge of what guided his hand. What was and why it was.

As such, he began that night's conversation with a query he hoped would lessen his burden. "Tell me more about your leader—Ma'alim. When did he come to Ghuldad?"

Rauf shrugged. "Several weeks before your arrival. He came seeking sanctuary, as do many. By proving his skill in medicine, weaponry, and witchcraft, he secured himself a seat on Ussam's council."

"You would follow a man who practices sorcery and witchcraft?" Mukhtar narrowed his eyes.

Ghasif held up his left hand to show his ring. "His sorcery has kept us safe from the eyes of the enemy. He has bound a Jinn to this ring, tasked with keeping us disguised for as long as I wear it. Do not be so hasty to judge, Mukhtar. You may disagree with his methods, but they have protected us thus far, kept us from harm."

Mukhtar decided not to argue back.

"Within a few short weeks, Ma'alim began to rally a select few to his cause," Rauf continued. "Nuzhah and the other maidservants. Ghasif was the first from among the assassins. I followed his footsteps as Ussam's reign of power grew."

"Rauf had much to learn," Ghasif eyed his lieutenant. "Still has much to learn. And Ma'alim always had much to teach."

"He spoke of freedom," Rauf said. "He spoke of destroying Ussam's tyrannical reaches, vanquishing his corrupt doctrines, and rebuilding Ghuldad as it once was. He preached a free and united guild of assassins who no longer needed to live in secrecy. He sees no reason why the inhabitants of Ghuldad cannot give up arms to live normal lives and be one with the free peoples of Ahul-Hama and Aghara, in trade and knowledge."

Mukhtar gazed into the fire before him. The more he heard about Ma'alim, the more he longed to meet him again. It was as though the Teacher echoed every thought in Mukhtar's mind. "A leader who values freedom is a shield for his people."

Ghasif gave a light chuckle. "Ma'alim believes otherwise. Freedom is an illusion, he always said to me. A sympathy for emotion. A mask of delusion."

They cleared away the remnants of their meal, after which Mukhtar and Rauf slept while Ghasif, fully armed, remained awake against the tree to keep watch over the first shift. It was not long before the fog had picked up around them, and he fed the fire to keep it alive, but aside from their brief vicinity, everything else was a dark and misty blur.

Mukhtar's sleep was uneasy and horrid. His nights had been that way since he woke in the darkened cell. Before shutting his eyes, his thoughts were abuzz with all what Ghasif and Rauf had told him. Much of it seeped into his dreams, twisting and coiling into torturous visions. When Rauf shook him, he woke with fright and alarm. "What is the matter, Rauf?"

"We are not alone!"

NINE

THE DEAD CITY

Dawn was still far off. The crisp chill dug deep into his bones as he tried to contemplate his dark surroundings. The silence was almost deafening, and the only source of light they had was an ember in the ashes of their smoldering campfire.

"*Hurry!*" Ghasif hissed, and it took a moment for Mukhtar to find him in the dark.

Their journey continued without a sound or second thought. Ghasif led, Mukhtar followed, and Rauf trailed behind, his bow armed with an arrow, his eyes peering the darkness for a reason to set it loose.

The air was brisk, every breath escaping their lungs in a misty cloud. Mukhtar was still unclear as to who or *what* was watching them, but refrained from sounding his query, making every effort to deter his feet from rustling the ground while his senses vigilantly hunted the gloom for anything that moved. He cursed the mist. He cursed the dark. Without the ability to see, he felt vulnerable and disadvantaged; he tightened his grip on the dagger Rauf had given him at the gates of Ghuldad, and tried to keep Ghasif within his reach. An undesirable sensation stole through him, forcing him to anticipate an imminent and inescapable notion of bloodshed. His innermost urge was to give in to his fears and run. He remembered reading something in his grandfather's books.

> When the night is darkest, when the silence is deepest, beware the Hour of the Witch. Beware the free will of the Unseen.

He shuddered.

Something rustled. An unnatural screech erupted the silence. Its echo of response followed imminently. Ghasif halted, stilled his breath, and peered through the mist and the darkness. The air rang with a deep, horrid, bloodcurdling roar that raised the hairs on the back of their necks. They squatted low and followed Ghasif silently through the maze of derelict tombstones.

Something rustled again and they froze. It sounded much closer and heavier. Was Ghasif leading them into the path of the enemy, or perhaps into the den of some ferocious beast? An image of several ravenous, bloodthirsty creatures came to mind as Mukhtar braced himself for a fight he was unprepared and untrained for.

The rasping growl, low, deep, and somewhat strained, drew closer and much faster. Its footsteps were becoming heavier, irregular, and uncontrolled.

The curtain of mist parted. A large, furry figure caught itself in the path of an unseen rock and fell forward, grazing the ground with its built momentum. It came to a halt merely feet before them, palpitating deeply.

They all shriveled back and cowered against the ancient stones, eyeing the four-legged, massive beast of thick, black-and-white, striped-fur, and yellowing fangs. Rauf quietly drew an arrow while Ghasif carefully released his scimitar. Mukhtar gripped his dagger with a sweaty palm, watchful of the beast's claws protruding through thick paws that could crush him to death within seconds. Never had he seen a tiger of such enormity. Would it have stood, it would have looked him in the eye, and with very little effort, torn his neck with a single strike.

It was injured. Its savagery was painfully suppressed, its muscular body twitched as darkened blood soaked the fur beneath its ribs. It must have been stalking the wastelands, hunting for its meal, treading through the mists like a silent wraith. What atrocity had weakened it as such?

Despite Ghasif's silent warning, Rauf set aside his bow and crawled forward. Mukhtar watched with mingled interest and bewilderment, as the Assassin reached out, lay a calming hand over the beast's head, and whispered unknown words with melodic benevolence. He then removed from his bag, the same herb they had given their horses, chewed on the leaves, and placed them on the tiger's drooling lips. With his fingers still intact, he cautiously retreated to where Mukhtar and Ghasif squatted and stared in awe.

Mukhtar realized he was still holding his breath. They watched as the herb began to take effect, dulling its pain and the rush of fear. It rose and stood before them, taller and broader, its striped fur fluttering calmly. It regarded them with its piercing, icy-blue eyes for a long moment before turning and trotting away awkwardly to compensate the pain in its side.

Mukhtar glanced at the other two. Ghasif's expression was stony, his eyes locked on Rauf. He sheathed his scimitar and continued to lead the way forward.

They were only gone a few yards when Ghasif froze again and signaled them to remain silent and hidden. Angered voices, painful whimpers, and muffled cries were coming from a few feet ahead of them where a flickering glow ignited the mists.

A clearing in the fog revealed three, tall, dark figures, cloaked and hooded. One of them held a burning torch. Ghasif, Rauf, and Mukhtar made every effort to keep their presence unknown.

"We *must* move on!" One of the figures snarled and brandished his spear threateningly, a trickle of blood distinctly noticeable on its abnormally long, harsh and crude, steely tip. Mukhtar had never before seen a weapon of such savagery before.

"Patience, Barish," his companion responded. On his waist hung an even harsher scimitar.

"Patience?" Barish rounded on him. "Patience will see you lose a limb like your brother if that beast were to return!" He pointed to a fourth man who was crouched low, clutching a bloody arm.

"Impatience will not see Khuru's arm returned!"

"Stop your bickering!" another gave an angry growl, and they fell silent. He spoke to them in a strange dialect, full of rasping and spitting sounds. *Was this their leader?* Mukhtar wondered.

"He is right," Khuru gasped in pain, acknowledging whatever the Leader said to them. "If they reach the mountains, they will be beyond us."

"Then the mountains will take them!" Barish argued. "I say we return to the fortress and leave these *rebels* to the mercy of the mists and the mountains!"

"You will do no such thing!" Khuru barked at him. "I would rather *die* than return to the citadel in shame because *you* lack the nerve! Use your heads, you fools! Sahir Elzafaan will see us fed to his *demons* if we return to him with nothing!"

"I am more than willing to fulfill your desires, my dear Khuru," Barish sneered blatantly. "It won't be long before your arm bleeds out. Let us linger a while longer and return to the Sahir with your corpse then!"

Nechem dropped his torch, brandished his own spear, and started forward.

The leader stepped between them. "Enough!" his voice echoed off the mausoleum behind them. "Calm yourself, Nechem, and see to your brother! And both of you," he turned to Barish, "hold your tongues, or the Sahir *will* hear of your insubordination!"

They tensed and became silent. None of them desired to face the wrath of Sahir Elzafaan.

"Send out your *Ghul*, Barish," the leader instructed.

"And allow it to be devoured by the monstrosities of this plagued land?" Barish declined. "Have you not always claimed that your *Sila* is far more powerful? Send *her* instead!"

The leader growled angrily. Within two short strides, he stood so close to Barish, their noses seemed to touch. "Your insolence knows no bounds!"

"I did not ask to be here, Hitu!" Barish put on a brave face, but still took a cautious step back.

"Since you are, you *will* listen and obey, or so help me, when our task here is done, I will see your head on a spike for treason!"

Without taking his eyes off Barish, Hitu, the leader, rolled up his left sleeve, revealing the golden band of a bracelet embedded with several small, obsidian stones. On his forearm, a scar gleamed in Nechem's torchlight. It looked like a burn mark in the shape of a triangle enclosing a circle. The symbol intrigued Mukhtar while he watched Hitu rub the bracelet with his forefinger, reciting feverishly under his breath. So tasking was this deed that beads of sweat appeared on his forehead, and he was heaving and wheezing when he finished.

A stench of rotting eggs reached Mukhtar's nostrils, adding to the already lingering foulness of death and decay. The mist parted in a rush. There was a strange sound, a distant scream twisted into a howling wind, and in the blink of an eye, from the very air before them, materialized a dark smoke, eerily coiling and forming itself as if it were alive. The smoke grew and mutated into shape, and there appeared a hooded figure.

Its cloak was a shredded and tattering dark fabric, and Mukhtar could hear the unmistakably steady raucous sound of breath coming from under its drawn hood. The hem of its cloak dissipated in a blurry edge of smoke and mist, and against the dark background, its much darker figure was a strangely shaped silhouette. A badly stooped back revealed a hump that was taller than its head, and unnaturally long arms almost scraped against the ground. The figure turned, and twice, concealed eyes swept but did not see the hidden three. Mukhtar caught sight of a gaping hole in the dark shadow of its hood, and felt his stomach churn. It had a mouth and it spoke.

"You summoned?" Its voice was discordant, crackling, and abnormally high-pitched. It sent shivers up Mukhtar's spine, and beside him, both Ghasif and Rauf stiffened.

"Can you see him?" Hitu asked in a bare whisper and a slight whimper, as if he was speaking to something divine.

"I can *smell him*," the *Sila* hissed. "A Jinn conceals his presence."

"Send it to the dark abyss!" Came the order. "Find the boy, and let us be rid of this place!"

"What of I?" the *Sila* demanded.

"A sacrifice in your name, Great Mirah," Hitu gave a bow.

"A human child will suffice," the *Sila* hissed.

Mukhtar felt a chill creep up his spine, and he suppressed a frightful gasp as felt Ghasif's hand grip his shoulder.

"Your demands are becoming steep!" Hitu remarked. "Very well..." he sighed, "...upon my return to the citadel!"

Mirah, the *Sila*, stooped ever so slightly, as though to bow was against the very essence of its existence. Then, it slithered away and vanished behind the forlorn walls of the mausoleum.

The four men exchanged grim and silent nods, and then followed stealthily in its wake, Khuru supported by one arm around his brother's shoulder.

Mukhtar turned to look upon the equally awestruck faces of Ghasif and Rauf. They were silent for several moments, each one contemplating the reality of what they had just witnessed.

Rauf was the first to speak. "Witchcraft!"

"The demon will become the least of our worries if it arouses other entities to our presence," Ghasif said grimly. "We will be safer once we reach the mountain pass of Khamur."

"And what monstrosity does the mountain conceal?" Mukhtar tried to keep the shiver from his voice, remembering what Nechem had said.

Rauf gave a hysterical laugh. "Monstrosities, wild mountain folk, a tribe of Jinn, or a herd of sheep! Does it matter? Whatever resides there is an evil that can frighten men capable of witchcraft, and we are foolish enough to walk into its den!"

Ghasif was unimpressed with his lieutenant's wit. "Steel yourself, Rauf! I too dread what we might find in the mountains, but we have no other way now. Come, we must make haste. And pray the remainder of our journey goes unnoticed."

Pray, oh pray they did, but the hunt was not abandoned. Several more hooded-figures had joined their earlier counterparts, slithering silhouettes against the fogs in the distance. The pursuants, however, soon became the least of their worries.

A greater peril arose ahead of them. Beyond the fog and mist, towering into the blotted skies, was a monolith of darkened stone, hewn as if from the very rocks it was built upon, spawning the fabled might of Arammoria. Even at a distance of what seemed to be half a day's ride, the clarity of its facade alarmed their impression of its enormity and awe. The sheer heights of its walls were marred with battlements and parapets, manned with archers and strange devices of war. The precipitous towers, with long pointy tips, vanished into thick dark clouds above, and were, without a doubt, fortified with watchful eyes tearing across the horizon in every direction. Tiny flickers of orange and yellow adorned the perimeter, indicating guard patrols, and a low rumble suggested perpetual activity. Not as abandoned and ruined, nor as desolate as the stories told.

"Keep out of sight," Ghasif warned in a low whisper.

"What now, Captain?" Rauf had a hint of panic in his voice. "We have ventured right onto the devil's doorstep!"

Mukhtar glanced at Ghasif, and became frightened with what he saw. There was doubt on his face, uncertainty too. Ghasif, their assumed leader, was without guidance, without a heading. What now?

"What now?" Mukhtar echoed Rauf.

"We must take a different path," Rauf stated. "We should never have come this way."

"There is no other road!" Ghasif argued impatiently.

"What of the desert road?" Rauf held up an arm and pointed west.

"What of it?" Ghasif demanded.

"We can take the road east to the Desert City of Hanan-Sula. From there we can take the Sultan's Pass to Dunhah and south to Khalidah."

Ghasif shook his head without a moment's thought. "The desert road takes us too close to Ninya, and the oasis town of Dunhah will be crawling with Ussam's spies." He gestured for them to sit before him, and drew a rough map in the desecrated dirt. "This is Arammoria. This is where we are. If we keep our current course, we should reach the foot of the Simnian Escarpments in two days or less."

"Lest we be discovered," Rauf hinted. "Are you willing to take that risk?"

Ghasif eyed him for a moment, then sounded his argument. "Every road we take bears risk. Trust me as you always have, Rauf. We can use the cover of the mists to carve a safe path to the mountains. Every step, a cautious one. Fate has brought us thus far, and I refuse to believe that we cannot make it further. *Come!*"

Unconvinced, Mukhtar and Rauf both followed Ghasif as he

led them further away from the fortress and closer to Simnia, the escarpments that marked the borders of Arammoria and Ahul-Hama. They did not dare make camp, nor stay any longer than was necessary. After only brief moments of rest, they continued afoot, worn and exhausted, sore in limb, body, and mind. The need to distance themselves from the dark lands, gave them the strength they required, and by dawn, the colossal citadel and its prodigious towers became shadows in the distance.

As they ascended the rocky slopes of the escarpments, the sun's rays peered through the clouds, brighter and warmer than Mukhtar had ever felt before. Mirzaan would avail itself on the other side after a two-day journey through the pass of Khamur. Tired and laden with sleep, they finally stopped to rest. They had eaten nothing since the day before, and Rauf took off to hunt while Mukhtar and Ghasif remained behind to make camp.

"You are troubled," Ghasif said to him while they enjoyed the soft meat of the birds that Rauf had hunted.

"'*Troubled*' is an understatement," Mukhtar replied.

"Do not allow the gloom of this barren land to inhibit your thoughts," Ghasif spoke softly, and Mukhtar understood that he was only trying to comfort him.

He was far from comfort, however. "I too have become burdened with a greater purpose," he echoed Ghasif's own words.

"What do you mean?" Rauf enquired. "Have we not witnessed wicked man, beast, and demon, all in one night? Have we not seen and survived what very few ever have?"

Mukhtar gave him a sideways glance. "Have you then seen a symbol so strange, it burned through your conscience and capsized your very existence?"

"A symbol?" Ghasif raised an eyebrow.

"An eye, enclosed in a shell, like this..." he held up both his hands and touched the tips of his forefingers and thumbs to form a triangle, "...branded on the arm of the man who summoned a demon before our very eyes."

"A symbol of his faith to his masters," Ghasif shrugged. "Or to the demons he worships. A pagan symbol. What of it? Why does it trouble you?"

Mukhtar hesitated. He stood, walked a few paces away from the campfire, and then back. "It had nearly faded from memory until I saw it again. Tucked away in a tiny box beneath my bed, at the end of a golden chain hangs an amulet that resembles that very same symbol!" He squatted on the ground and drew a tiny circle inside an enclosed triangle. "Coincidence? Or fate?"

"Or perhaps the very reason we are on this road?" Rauf stared at Mukhtar's sketch in the dirt. "It could very well be what the enemy seeks."

"All the more reason to hasten our journey!" Ghasif pressed.

The Pass of Khamur may have been the most trying part of their journey yet. Whether it was indeed a tribe of Jinn, or the witchcraft of evil and wild mountain people, Mukhtar did not know, but barely an hour into the pass, they were overcome with unfathomable grief and depression.

Without admonition, Rauf would drop to the ground and succumb to tears, whimpering about all the wrong he had done to his parents, blaming himself for their deaths. Barely able to lead the way forward, Ghasif would speak with himself in angered whispers, aggravating into temperamental outbursts. When Mukhtar was not comforting the Lieutenant or calming the Captain, he was battling his own inner demons. Childhood memories haunted his every step. Several times, he could have sworn to an apparition of his father or grandfather, urging him to kill Ghasif and Rauf in their sleep.

Ghasif's ring may have concealed them from watchful eyes, but the gloomy and depressing effect that the mountain pass foisted, deterred them from normalcy.

After two long days of enduring unnatural despondency, with most of their sanity still intact, they stood at the edge of a low cliff, overlooking the prosperous mining town of Mirzaan.

"Such is the monstrosity of Khamur," Rauf mumbled. His eyes were puffy with lack of sleep, his nose runny with the cold.

Ghasif fidgeted with the ring on his finger, rubbing the obsidian stone with his thumb. "It could have been worse."

"Shall we vow never to make mention of it?" Mukhtar suggested.

Rauf nodded. "It would be best."

"We can seek assistance in Mirzaan," Mukhtar attempted a reassuring tone. "I know a man, Jawad Banu-Darr, a miner, merchant, and close friend of my uncle's."

Eager to escape the mountain and recover from its adversities, they made their way into town, taking caution not to draw any attention.

Mirzaan was a small, densely populated mining town at the foot of the long escarpments of Simnia. Its wealth came from iron ore and coal, amidst other minerals, but the skill of Mirzaan distinguished them above all others, for they were well versed in the art of forging steel.

Merchants were just about closing their businesses for the day and heading home, as night approached with a cold and fiery wind that thrashed against the escarpment wall. Cloaks held close against the chill, hoods drawn to keep away prying eyes, they made their way along the narrow, winding lanes, between double-storied buildings of rough-cut stone, quite unlike the mud and clay structures of Khalidah.

After asking around, they were shown the way to Jawad Banu-Darr's warehouse, a large stone building with heavy oak doors and a smoking chimney. Mukhtar swung the brass knockers on the door and they waited patiently, throwing cautious glances over their shoulders. A series of locks were undone, and shortly after, a portly, thick-bearded man appeared through the door.

"We are closed for the day," he grunted. "Trades will resume after dawn tomorrow."

"We do not need to purchase anything," Mukhtar said.

"Why are you wasting my time then?" came a blunt reply.

"Forgive me, Jawad," Mukhtar said. "I did not properly introduce myself. I am the nephew of Mika'il Abaraina."

"Mika'il Abaraina of Khalidah?" Jawad grunted.

"The very same," Mukhtar replied.

"That man owes me money!" Jawad claimed, and Mukhtar's face fell. "Have you come to pay his debt?"

Mukhtar shook his head. "We are in need of assistance, Jawad. For the sake of your friendship with Mika'il, will you help us?"

Jawad folded his arms and leaned back against the doorframe. "So finely do you boast your uncle's name, if you but knew how tainted it has become."

Mukhtar was unable to disguise his bewilderment.

"You do not know?" Jawad raised a dubious eyebrow.

"It matters not what my uncle's misdeeds are," Mukhtar said boldly. "Whenever he speaks of Mirzaan, he speaks of the kindness of Jawad Banu-Darr. Will you not, out of the decency of your heart, give us aid— be it but a little?"

The portly miner gazed at him for a long while, then eyed Ghasif and Rauf, as though sizing them up. "You have traveled long, and your journey still remains. I cannot provide you with beasts to carry your burdens, but I can give you a place to rest for the night and provisions for the long road."

Mukhtar let out a sigh of relief. "We cannot thank you enough—!"

Jawad held up a seasoned hand that looked more like a thick glove than anything. "You need not thank me."

Mukhtar looked confused, but Ghasif seemed to have understood. "What can we do to repay your kindness?" he asked.

"One of my men has been severely injured," Jawad stated. "The other is out of town, and I have three wagons that need to be loaded with iron ingots before dawn, or else I will have lost a fortuitous trade."

Mukhtar glanced at Ghasif and Rauf. They both gave two short nods, and Mukhtar shook hands with Jawad.

Loading the wagons, however, was no simple task. It was at the stroke of midnight when they finally laid their heads to rest, well fed and warm. It may not have been comfortable on the straw hewn floor of Jawad's storerooms, but the closed walls gave Mukhtar a sense of protection from the outside world. This was a relief he would not take for granted, for it was the first time in many months that he had found sanctuary from the howling winds.

It was close to midday when they woke. Jawad's daughters had prepared a decent meal of rice and chicken with an array of flavors and spices.

"How far have you traveled?" Jawad asked as they ate from a large dish before them.

"From the open stretches of Alhram," Ghasif replied. "Ask us not our true origin, for it may cause you to be displeased with our company."

"I do not need to," Jawad replied. "Your attire says it all. Your kind has a widespread infamy of inciting dread. However, a man's business is a man's business, so long as it does not affect mine. I would not have trusted you had Mukhtar not mentioned his uncle, regardless of my relationship with him. So tell me, by which road did you come? One would think you crossed the gates and followed the wall to Ninya and south to Hanan-Sula, but I suspect otherwise, for you are far wearier than any traveler I have seen."

Ghasif eyed him cautiously. "We journeyed west to the borders of Rhudah and took the road south, past the Peaks of Aftara and through the Cedars of Zila—"

"And through the Dead City!" Jawad gasped, his hand halfway up his mouth with food. "Only *fools* take that road! Fools who never return, and those who do, bring nothing but despair and talk of war. If at all they return with sanity."

Ghasif smiled. "Had we a choice, we would not take that path."

"I would think not," Jawad said, "for you do not seem like fools to me. Indeed the Pass of Khamur has been riddled by an unknown evil, causing the Simnian Mines to be abandoned. This has disrupted the wealth of Mirzaan. Tradesmen such as I, suffer greatly due to a scarcity of iron ore. So, tell me," he turned to Mukhtar, "how long has Mika'il Abaraina's nephew been a slave?"

Mukhtar turned his gaze.

"You have trekked through dangerous lands of cut-throat thieves, devious sorcerers, and blood-thirsty assassins," Jawad stated. "Which of those are you?"

"Neither!" Mukhtar replied, a little harsher than he intended to.

"Then you are a slave to one of their kind. The irons on your wrists and ankles are not for adornment, of that I am certain. How long were you a slave?"

"Too long," Mukhtar struggled to avoid eye contact with Ghasif and Rauf.

Jawad nodded slowly. "Then I am glad it is no longer."

An hour before their departure, Jawad did them a final act of kindness and cut the iron shackles from Mukhtar's neck, wrists, and ankles. Despite his earlier statement, he also assisted them in bargaining for three strong horses.

Mukhtar's spirits began to soar as they crossed over familiar landscapes. They were passing through villages, fishing camps closer to the river Hubur, farms, lumber mills and tropical terrains. They approached the outskirts of Khalidah at noon on the second day, its vast infrastructure and tall buildings looming closer into view.

TEN

THE PARTING OF FRIENDS

A mile or so, north of the city, concealed by overhanging palm trees, tamarisks and mild shrubbery hugging the banks of the Hubur, was an array of mismatched shacks and cabins of wood and straw. One of those shacks was in dire need of repair, neglected for years since the death of Salim Zafar, Mukhtar's grandfather.

Mukhtar guided the Assassins to the cabin. It seemed a safer refuge than his home in the city, isolated in the woods, further away from the prying eyes of any authorities and enemies alike.

The floorboards creaked under their feet when they entered the desolate shack. A large chest sat at the foot of a simple, wood-frame bed against the wall. Beside it was an antique bedstand, marred with dripping candle wax and an assortment of scrolls and books. Such assortments were hewn across the entire floor, piled up by the chest of drawers, and all around the worn floor desk that sat upon a tattered sisal mat. The air was damp and heavy with a distinct decaying stench of some dead animal. Ghasif threw open the window above the bed, while Rauf unlatched the one on the opposite wall, and cool, fresh air rushed in with the pleasant sounds of streaming water, the rustle of the forest and chirping of birds.

"No one has been here in a very long time," Rauf commented, eyeing the buildup of cobwebs and layers of dust.

"A favorable fact," Ghasif responded. "It will do us well to clean it."

"There is a woman, further down the pathway, who sells good food," Mukhtar pointed toward the door. "A taste of her famous *Falafel,* and you will never eat anything else in Khalidah!"

"Not while our enemies are afoot!" Ghasif stated. "Lead us to the Amulet, Mukhtar. With haste!"

Mukhtar shook his head calmly. He had expected this, and did not wish for them to accompany him home. "The City-Watch will recognize your armor. Remain here. Rest. I will return with the Amulet before dusk."

"We cannot risk losing you to Ussam's agents!" Rauf stated.

"This is *my* city!" Mukhtar argued. "I know the streets well enough to avoid conflict!"

He could see the uncertainty on both their faces. They would not abandon their mission. They would not abandon him, but he detested being in their debt, and the longer they remained to protect him, the more he owed. In truth, he still did not trust them, and there was only one way he could think of to ascertain for himself that they were not aligned with the enemy.

"You are weary," he tried to convince them. "Rest now, and trust that I will return safely with the Amulet."

Ghasif eyed him dubiously before finally understanding his plea, and he made a quick motion to keep Rauf from bursting into arguments. "Very well," he agreed. "Return with haste and steer clear of any trouble. We do not wish to raise attention to ourselves."

Taking care to avoid the watchful eyes of the city's archers, and the brutish glares of patrolling guards, he headed into the city, steeling the excitement in his heart. He was home at last. How he had longed for this, fantasized about it over and over again. The excitement, however, was short-lived.

As he walked the streets, he realized how much of the city had changed. Fewer people were about, engaging in trades of both the legal and illegal kind, the latter being far more dominating and perceptible than ever. Women wept and wailed at the mercy of barbaric men, while corrupt city guards stood aside and did very little, if at all. Mercenaries and slave-traders roamed the streets, unchecked, unquestioned, and those who did not comply with their demands, were met with due savagery.

He entered a deserted alley to cut through to the other side and avoid any open conflicts on the main street. Had Ussam's wickedness spread so far south into Khalidah? Mukhtar was sickened and disheartened. Cruelty had substituted humanity, as his fellow citizens were crushed beneath the feet of corruption, and he could do nothing but watch. However strong the urge, he did not dare intervene. The harsh memories of whips and iron shackles were still too fresh.

So engrossed were his thoughts, he did not see where he was headed. He collided with another man, and they both fell to the ground.

"Fool!" The person retorted angrily. "Can you not see?"

"My apologies, I did not mean—" he hastily stood to help the other person, "— *Adil?*"

"How do you know— *Mukhtar!*"

"Am I glad to see you!" Mukhtar held out his hand.

When Adil declined to take it, Mukhtar took an uneasy step back, and watched his friend pick himself up.

"You have returned," Adil said calmly.

"I have," Mukhtar approached him warmly. "It has been too long."

"Indeed, it has," Adil's voice could not have been colder.

Mukhtar froze. Something was wrong. "Are you not pleased to see me?" he asked.

"Pleased?" Adil responded harshly. "Should I be?"

Mukhtar was abashed. "What is the matter, Adil?"

"Where have you been?" Adil yelled. "How do you *justify* deserting your kin, like your traitorous brother?"

"Watch your tone, Adil!"

"Do you *know* how much damage you have caused?"

"I am warning you!"

"Do you know how much pain and grief your selfishness has brought upon others?"

"I was taken captive!" Mukhtar yelled. "Chained by malicious men, tortured and abused! I long for nothing but to return to my home!"

"That is a most absurd lie!" Adil snarled and Mukhtar became bewildered. *"Taken captive? Tortured?* You seem fine to me, considering you are walking so freely the streets of Khalidah!"

"How *dare* you—?"

"Let me *show* you!" Adil took a menacing step forward, causing Mukhtar to instinctively draw his dagger.

The buildings on either side did little to shelter them from the scorching sun. Pungent piles of garbage filled up half the alley against the mud walls, putrid streams seeping into the dirt while flies buzzed around in festivity. Two cats fought ferociously at the end of the alley, battling over a dead rodent until it was torn to bloody shreds. Mukhtar could not help but think to himself, *would that perhaps be the result of this encounter?* How had their friendship become so distant? There was a time when Mukhtar would reveal all his secrets to Adil, and the latter would do the same. Not that there had never been any disputes. They had had their equal shares of quarrels, but none that had ever resulted in a draw of steel and an air of hatred.

"Put that away before you cut yourself!" Adil sneered, bringing Mukhtar's thoughts back to the matter at hand.

Rather than comply, Mukhtar held up the dagger, ready to strike.

With a menacing step forward, Adil brandished his spear. "Do you really want to fight me, Mukhtar?"

"Do not force my hand, Adil!" Mukhtar braced himself. "What is the meaning of this crudeness? Explain yourself!"

Adil gave a small chuckle. "We have spent months in your search. *You* owe *me* an explanation."

"I owe you nothing!" Mukhtar declared. "I will *give* you *nothing* until I have seen mother!"

"So speaks the Mighty Mukhtar," Adil mocked. "You return on your high horse, making demands and issuing commands, as if nothing wrong has happened!"

Mukhtar stared at him disbelievingly. "Why are you speaking that way?"

"Why did you do really do it?" Adil pressed.

Mukhtar gave him a puzzled look. "Why did I do what? What has happened, Adil? Why are you speaking this way?"

"Did you find what you sought?" Adil almost sounded hysterical. "Did you find the glory and valor? Will you now proclaim yourself a savior?"

Mukhtar gaped at him. "Whatever is troubling you, I will explain. I will tell you all what has happened," his temper was steadily rising. His hands were beginning to tremble and blood was rushing to his head, forcibly so by the scorching sun and the repulsive stench of garbage in the alley. "But I must see my Ummi first. I must see my Khal and Khala. Now, step aside and let me return to my home, or brace yourself for a fight you will regret!"

More to Mukhtar's bewilderment, Adil's lips curled into a small grin. "Very well," he casually drew back his spear and his voice became suspiciously calmer. "Follow me."

Angered and confused, Mukhtar concealed his dagger inside his sleeve and followed Adil into the streets. A half hour later, they approached the wooden doors of the House of Zafar.

"Step aside!" Mukhtar furiously elbowed Adil before he could swing the iron knocker on the door.

Whatever the repercussions of his actions at that moment, he did not care. This was *his* home. Long had he envisioned himself returning to it, and he would not allow his desires to be ruined by Adil's arrogance, not in that moment. He could feel Adil's eyes puncturing the back of his skull. When the door opened, Adil forcefully brushed him aside, and stepped through the doors.

"Look who showed up!" he declared to Mika'il, who stood at the door and gaped at Mukhtar as though he had seen a ghost.

"Salaam, Khal," Mukhtar said.

Mika'il's eyes became teary as he moved forward with trembling hands and pulled his nephew into a fatherly embrace. "Mukhtar!" he croaked. "God Almighty be praised!" He began to sob, and Mukhtar was unable to control himself. Mika'il's voice was more than enough to shatter his heart with emotion.

"Ummi?"

"In there," Mika'il nudged his head, gesturing past the fountain.

Mukhtar crossed the brief courtyard in four short strides, and stepped through the door. He caught a glimpse of the semi-dark room with its moth-eaten rug and worn cushions, then there was a yelp, followed by an even louder shriek, and his vision was completely obscured by cloth and hair — Suha had thrown herself onto him in a hug so tight, it knocked the breath out him.

"Mukhtar! He has returned to us, Fariebah! Oh, *Praise be the Almighty, The Lord of the Worlds. The most Gracious, The most Merciful!* Truly, he has returned you to us! Oh, my poor boy! I searched for you in the *Souk*— then I went home! I prayed for your return! And I waited— we searched *everywhere*—"

"You— are— squeezing— the— life— out— of— me!"

"Let him breathe, Suha," Mika'il entered the room with a hearty chuckle, followed by Adil. Mukhtar could almost have sworn he saw his friend give his uncle a discreet nudge.

Fariebah came forward and hugged Mukhtar as well. She gave him a small kiss on his cheek and smiled happily. "Praise be to God Almighty who has returned you to us safely!"

Mika'il sat down on a cushion against the wall, pulled his *hukah* closer, and inhaled deeply from it, blowing out a large white cloud that engulfed him whole. He may have seemed pleased to see his nephew moments before, but a coldness had settled into his tone when he demanded an explanation for Mukhtar's absence.

"Perhaps he should rest—" Suha protested, reaching out to feel Mukhtar's forehead, but Mika'il held up a hand and insisted.

Mukhtar gave his mother a reassuring look, and settled down across his uncle, choosing his words carefully. He began with hesitation, only to find that he could no longer resist from speaking. The only bits he left out of his grim and dismal tale were his experiences with the unknown voice, his journey through Arammoria, and all the specifics he had discussed with Ghasif and Rauf regarding the Amulet. He did his best to paint them as mere travelers who had taken pity and helped him journey home.

"I escaped," he said when they pressed him for details, "they were careless, and I saw an opportunity."

"Both my sons in grave danger!" Suha gasped when Mukhtar told them what had happened at the Walls of Murfaqat. "What have they done to deserve this?"

"Mukhtar has done nothing to deserve this," Mika'il commented. "It is Zaki who is to blame."

"Why would you say that?" Fariebah asked her husband angrily. "He is your nephew!"

"He deserted his kin to become a Red-Guard!" Mika'il argued. "Every decision he ever made has been thoughtless to the repercussions."

"That is untrue!" Suha remarked.

"*Untrue?* His willingness to accept the mission of pursuing the Assassins of Ghuldad is what has brought such a fate upon your sons, Suha. There can be no other explanation."

Mukhtar kept silent. Suha was right. Zaki's captaincy in the Red-Guard, and his mission to pursue the Assassins, had nothing to do with Mukhtar's tragedy. He did not wish to hear his brother slandered, but as long as their thoughts were drawn away from the grim truth of the matter, he pursed his lips and allowed the conversation to steer in that direction.

"Do not speak of my son that way, Mika'il!" Suha's voice trembled with anger and Mukhtar nearly gasped. He had never heard his mother address his uncle by name. It was usually a respectable title of *'Brother Mika'il'* or just *'Brother'*. "It is true that he left on his own accord, but his fate was never his own to choose!"

"They are bound by oath," Fariebah supported her sister's outlook in defending Zaki. "It was never his choice to make. Long has he tried to return home—"

Mika'il brushed aside everything the sisters said. "You give that man too much credit, Fariebah, but you understand very little about him—"

"And *you* know *my* son better than I?" Suha snapped.

"Get a hold of yourself, Suha!" Mika'il said sternly. "The Red-Guard sends their most celebrated Captain into the wolf's den, and if what Mukhtar says is true, then Zaki is now a branded traitor and deserter. You must ask yourself; what has he done to become their prey?"

They all fell silent. Fariebah gave her husband a disgruntled look before opening a window to ventilate the room of Mika'il's *hashish* smoke, while Mukhtar's thoughts strayed to the Amulet that remained hidden under his bed upstairs, and he was overcome with a sense of urgency. *What if it was no longer there?*

"I must leave!" he declared. "I have left Ghasif and Rauf in *Babu's* old cabin by the river."

"Why must they remain there?" Fariebah suggested. "We have room to accommodate them. Perhaps you should invite them for a meal?" She suggested to her husband. "We owe them so much for bringing Mukhtar home. It would be most discourteous if we do not show them hospitality."

Mukhtar shook his head and became irritated. "Their business is their own, and they will depart when their work is done. You need not burden yourselves."

"Do you not hear yourself?" Adil asked in a contemptuous tone. Mukhtar turned sharply and cricked his neck. He had almost forgotten that Adil was there.

"Stay out of this, Adil," Mukhtar warned.

"And allow you to break your mother's heart again?" Adil stated. "How are you so different from your brother then?" His head tilted to his side.

Mukhtar tensed. Their earlier encounter was still afresh in his mind. "This is a matter between kin," he said through gritted teeth, *"and not one that should concern you!"*

"How very courteous of you to appreciate the efforts of others," Adil mocked. "I am sure you thought about us on your travels!"

"Did you listen to *nothing* I said?" Mukhtar struggled to keep his temper under control. "I was *enslaved! Tortured!*"

"Call it what you will!" Adil gave a casual wave.

"Are you *insane?*" Mukhtar remarked.

"Just like your brother, you are!" Adil affronted. "Pretend that you were without choice!"

Mukhtar stared at him disbelievingly, and it suddenly dawned on him that they had discussed his disappearance to some extent, and had drawn their own obvious conclusions.

"You can allow your him to take all the blame for you," Adil continued to assert, "but it was *your* involvement with those slaves that has brought all this trouble."

As the words were spoken, they struck Mukhtar like a bolt of lightning.

In that moment alone, he regretted ever saying anything to Adil.

"Adil!" Mika'il flashed him look of warning.

"No!" Adil held up his hand. "Why have you fallen silent, Mukhtar? Do not try to mask the truth! *Tell* them what really happened!"

"Adil!" Mika'il warned him again.

Fariebah had covered her mouth, her expression terrified. Suha's eyes darted from Adil to Mukhtar disbelievingly, her mouth slightly ajar. "What is he saying, Mukhtar? What slaves?"

Mukhtar shook with anger. The hatred in his eyes was meant only for Adil. They saw only betrayal. Fury tingling through his body, he curled his fists and stood. "You *treacherous*—"

"Enough!" Mika'il yelled, suddenly appearing between them and spreading his arms out to keep them from hurling at each other.

"Your defiance is disrespectful to *everyone* in this room and all their efforts to bring you home safely!" Adil remarked, not taking his eyes off Mukhtar.

"Your efforts have only shown me your true colors!" Mukhtar did not bother disguising the contempt in his voice. "You are no friend of mine, *traitor!"*

A stony silence engulfed them. Adil was the first to leave. With a look of pure loathing for Mukhtar, he turned and walked out of the room. They heard him cursing loudly in the courtyard, followed by a slam of the front door.

Mika'il gave a deep, strained sigh, and spoke to Suha and Fariebah as calmly as he could, "Prepare some food for Mukhtar to take for his guests."

Suha began to protest, but was pulled aside by her sister, and she reluctantly left the room.

"Typically," Mika'il began, once he and Mukhtar were alone, "I would have prodded you further to understand how deep you have sunk. The evidence, however, is conspicuous based on what you have been through and what you have told us. Regardless, you must never forget, that even though anger sometimes takes hold of the best of us, it has never been, nor will it ever be of any substantial benefit."

Mukhtar gave him an odd look. "What do you mean?"

"There was no need to speak that way!" Mika'il asserted, pointing at the door, and Mukhtar knew he was referring to Adil's departure.

"And what of how he spoke?" Mukhtar argued, with a rather harsh tone. "Was there any need for *that?* I have endured endless battles for months, and all he could think of was his comfort!"

"He does not think that way at all—" Mika'il said.

"I care not what he thinks!" Mukhtar interrupted, even though he knew he did not mean it.

"Mukhtar!" Mika'il's tone became stony and stern. "I plead you to understand. Such actions have grave consequences, and you will have to bear them for a lifetime!"

Unspoken words were exchanged between them, and as he gazed intently into Mika'il's beady eyes, he suddenly realized something he should have years ago.

"You *knew* my father was to be arrested?" Mukhtar gasped. "You knew, and did nothing of it!"

"Before you continue to throw accusations, *understand* what I am trying to tell you," Mika'il responded with immense effort. "No one knew anything about your father. He became a changed man after the war. Although related through family, your father and I were also the very best of friends. But our friendship waned as his ambitions thrived to a point where we could no longer see eye to eye. His choices and actions had consequences. Grave consequences. When Immorkaan came through those very doors—" he pointed toward the courtyard, "— and took him away, he had none to blame but himself."

Suha's voice sounded from the courtyard.

"I urge you Mukhtar," Mika'il continued in a lower tone, "do not follow the same path as your father; do not echo his sins." He toyed with the ring on his finger for a brief moment, lost in thought. Pure silver, with a dark obsidian stone embedded into its crown gleaming as though it had recently been polished. He pulled it out and handed it to Mukhtar. "Keep it."

"Khal?"

"I once rescued an elderly man from a pair of corrupt city guards," Mika'il explained. "I was young then, energetic. Much like you, I would not stand for oppression. Like me, the old man had no successor to bear his name forward, no sons or daughters to bear his heirloom. You are the closest I have to a son, and I praise The Almighty for gifting me with you."

Mukhtar felt his throat twitch as tears threatened to engulf him. Suha called for him again, and he glanced at the door.

"He rewarded me with this ring," Mika'il continued. "He called me son. I am calling you son. May it enlighten you as it has enlightened me."

Suha called a third time.

"Do not carry the burdens of your kin on such a path," he continued. "The only way you can bring peace to her is by undoing what wrong was done by your forebearers. She will be saddened, but time will heal all wounds."

Mukhtar nodded again, and with one last look upon his uncle, he left the room to meet his mother awaiting him in the courtyard with a package wrapped in cloth.

However, the look on her face said it all. She had heard every word, and her eyes were filled with tears. She said nothing more, turned and headed up the stairs to her room. The emotional turmoils were overwhelming him such that the strain caused his old wounds to bear new pain. Not only had his best friend walked out on him in anger, now his mother was doing the same.

He reached the cabin without realizing it, and entered to find Ghasif asleep on the bed, and Rauf sitting at his grandfather's old floor-desk, reading.

"I brought food," Mukhtar held up the package his mother had wrapped.

"And the Amulet?" Ghasif woke sharply when he heard Mukhtar's voice.

Mukhtar nodded and pulled the golden chain over his head to show them the gleaming icy-blue stone. Before returning to the cabin, he had retreated to his own room to retrieve the Amulet. Upsetting clouds of dust under his bed, he breathed a sigh of relief to find it untouched and undisturbed. He had thought of waiting for the cover of darkness to smuggle it out, but was overpowered by the uncomfortable silence that lingered around the house.

"By God, it is a beauty to behold!" Ghasif whispered, eyeing it with interest.

"Its resemblance to the symbol is irrefutable!" Rauf snatched it from his hand.

"Indeed it is," Mukhtar responded.

Ghasif snatched it back, giving the Lieutenant an angry scowl. "We have discovered more about the symbol."

"What do you mean?" Mukhtar asked.

"Have you not noticed?" Rauf gestured around the cabin, at the neat piles of books and scrolls beside the floor-desk. "We cleaned while you were gone, and began to read whatever was legible. They contain an abundance of the Occult, Black Magic, and the Dark Arts. But there is more to it than mere symbolism. Sorcery, witchcraft, idolatry. What *was* your grandfather involved in?"

"I too have questioned the same," Mukhtar eyed the books and scrolls. "I have read most of them, yet I have never truly understood their meaning, or why they ever belonged to my grandfather." Or did he understand, but was never prepared to accept that sorcery had always tainted the bloodlines of his forefathers? Texts depicting the Dark Arts lay abundant in his grandfather's cabin, and an amulet presumed to be a weapon of sorcery passed down to him by his father. What more was there to the name of Zafar that he did not know of?

"There is a passage here —" Ghasif held up a tattered book, titled *The Disguise of The Unseen*, and read aloud;

> ...of an entity as ancient as the world itself, so gruesome, so evil, so corrupt! It is said, that since the beginning of time, this entity, favored by The Heavens, corrupted by its own arrogance, vowed to lead mankind astray and claim dominion over them as a superior being. He is named Shaytaan. He is named Iblees. He is named Azazil. He is named The Deceiver. He who has claimed the Throne of Ithm, is named The Hand of Azazil.

PART TWO

THE NEW WORLD

TWENTY YEARS AGO.

The quartermaster's tent was surrounded by stockpiles of weaponry, spears, shields, and swords, amidst supplies essential to the advancement of the Legion. Large fluttering tarps shielded them against the pernicious adversities of the recent sandstorm. Farid arrived at the quartermaster's tent to relay the General's orders. A lone soldier guarded the entrance, leaning against his spear to ease his exhaustion.

"Galel," he inclined his head in greeting.

"Farid," slightly groggy, Galel responded in kind, "how fares the night watch? I haven't left my post since dusk."

"Cold, gloomy and somewhat troubling," Farid replied.

"Indeed," Galel said. "That last storm has been the most devastating, and the eeriness of Arammoria..." he gave a shudder. "I long for an end to this war, that I may return home."

"The end will come soon, my brother," Farid assured him.

It was the tone with which he said it that made Galel raise his eyebrows. "What news from the General's tent?" he lowered his voice, putting on a grave tone.

"Nothing in stone yet," Farid replied with equal solemnity, "but there seems to be something at play. We will speak later. Wake the blacksmith," he nudged at the tent's entrance. "He has been summoned by the General."

He left, and Galel, mildly confused and curious, poked his head through the tent flaps and searched the darkness.

"Brother Harun," he whispered, and the man closest to him grunted in his sleep. "Brother Harun!"

The man stirred slowly and opened his eyes. "Galel?" he whispered groggily, not intending to wake his companion. "What is it? Has something happened?"

"General Babak requests your presence," Galel said.

Harun sat up, rubbed his eyes, and stared at Galel's outline in the dark. "Why?"

Galel shrugged

Harun sighed wearily. "Very well."

Galel left the tent, and Harun remained seated for a few moments, gathering his thoughts. The wind lashed against the tent with dreadful intent, but it held resistantly. He prided himself on pitching it well, and was not at all eager to leave it for the chill outside. It was dreadfully dark, but much of the night had passed. Dawn would be approaching soon. What did Babak want to see him for at this hour? Even as he asked himself that question, he already knew the answer to it. This certainly had something to do with the unsanctioned, secret expedition into the Dead City. Azhar better not be considering it again. That haunted wasteland was the last place Harun wished to set foot upon. Not something he had bargained for when he accepted the army's proposal to serve as quartermaster.

Mika'il was snoring gingerly on his mat across the ground, his dark silhouette moving up and down with deep breathing. Should he wake him? Perhaps not. There was no need to trouble the man. Azhar relentlessly searched for every opportunity to discuss the expedition's findings, and keeping it all a secret from Mika'il was no simple task.

He pulled on a *thaub* and cloak to shield himself against the ghastly gale, stifled a yawn, rubbed his drowsy eyes, and reluctantly left the warm and cozy tent. Cloak tightly drawn, he made his way to the center of the camp where the General's Pavilion stood tall, easily distinguishable with Aztalaan banners caught in the high winds.

Guards on duty were patrolling the maze of canvas tarps and fluttering banners, while others stood alert at stationed posts. Tasked as quartermasters, Harun and Mika'il not only supplied weapons and armor, but also food and bedding. Ghulam Mirza had secured them a healthy compensation for their services. Regardless, Harun had to admit he was growing weary of his tasks, and dearly missed his home and family in Khalidah. Almost as if to exacerbate his dilemmas, the location of their camp was hardly an exotic haven of tranquility.

He arrived at the General's tent, and Farid stood aside to allow him through.

"Salaam, General," Harun aired a greeting, stifling another yawn as he stepped in.

Azhar sat in the company of two other men, on cushions surrounding a tray laden with dates, cups, and a steaming pot of spicy cardamom tea.

"My apologies," Harun glanced at the two men. "I did not mean to intrude upon your company."

"Ah— Harun," the General stood to receive him, which Harun found to be unusual. Azhar was not widely known for subtlety or courtesy, unless he wished to draw some benefit. "Come, join us. There is something we must discuss."

He caught a brief glimpse of the wooden box on the far side of the tent. It was all too familiar, for he had packed its contents himself and surrendered it to Azhar, who had further placed it under heavy guard. Indeed, only a mere handful of the entire legion knew of its existence. Why then was it unguarded and out in the open? Harun tried not to betray his curiosity. He did not wish to reveal his thoughts until Azhar had ascertained his true intent behind its purpose.

"Laban Varda, and General Ussam Bashiri of the Third Legion," Azhar gestured at the two men.

Harun felt drained and sleepy, and swallowed the yawn that was yearning to escape. He nodded courteously as they were introduced, and took a seat beside Azhar, who poured him a cup of the sweet and spicy tea.

Laban excused himself to find a lavatory, and Azhar called for Farid to escort him. While they waited for him to return, Harun could not help but notice Ussam's eyes on him.

"I must commend you on your victory over Ghuldad," he said in an attempt to break the awkward silence.

Ussam gave a courteous nod.

After another long and silent moment, Harun asked, "What will become of the ancient fortress?"

Ussam gazed at him thoughtfully. "Ghuldad stands upon Alhram. In No Man's Land, Aztalaan alone cannot claim it."

"Will it be left abandoned then?" Harun enquired.

"The Queen Sitra and Emperor Babati will soon convene with the rest of the Council," Ussam replied. "They will decide the fate of Ghuldad."

Harun shrugged indifferently. "It would be a shame to leave it to the ruin of the desert. The fortress may prove to be a powerful front beyond the Wall."

Ussam tilted his head slightly and gave him a strange look. "Indeed, it would."

Laban joined them shortly, and Azhar refilled their cups with tea before offering Harun a plate of dried dates. Another unusual gesture from the General. Harun gave the plate a mildly apprehensive look before helping himself.

"Laban and Ussam have come to me with an astounding proposition," Azhar told Harun, who tried to listen attentively. "Would you care to elaborate?" he added to Laban.

Laban took a short sip of his tea and cleared his throat. "The artifacts you procured," he gestured at the box behind them, "are ancient relics of a very powerful nature. No other magical instrument can even remotely come close to their abilities. Legend has it that these items were crafted beyond the Veil."

"The Veil of the Unseen?" Harun nearly choked on a date seed. "The World of the Jinn?"

"Do not be startled," Ussam said.

Do not be startled? Harun gave him a long hard stare. How could someone discuss the occult and the evil so casually and calmly, without so much as a shadow of qualm?

"The crafts and skills of Jinn-kind are unknown to humans," Laban continued with the same composure as his companion. "The Amulets and weapons you acquired are ancient crafts that can be used to rival the Dark Prince's forces."

Harun stared at him. Drowsiness clouded his mind. They found weapons to defeat the Dark Prince, and it sounded like good news. *But what does it all have to do with me?*

"When a Jinn—" Laban went on.

"This information is sensitive," Ussam interrupted his companion. "What we discuss, must remain within this tent."

The air was steadily becoming chilly and crisp with the approach of dawn, but the winds were still high and they beat against the tent, threatening to uproot it.

Laban returned Ussam's caution with a curt nod. "To be a sorcerer, is to submit one's soul to the will of the Jinn, the demons, and the devil himself. Very rarely can a Jinn be enslaved, but when it is, it owes allegiance only to its master, and to those true in blood. There are rituals and sacraments involved, both irrevocably arduous and taxing to body and soul."

Harun frowned and shook his head. "I do not understand."

"Neither do I," Azhar added. "Come clear, Laban."

Laban gave a slow nod as if requesting their patience. "Each of the four Amulets binds an Elemental Jinn, first brought into existence to further the Dark Prince's wicked ambitions. However, with the right rituals and sacraments employed, the same Elemental Jinn can also be used to debilitate him."

Harun's attention was now fully drawn. Sleep had long abandoned him.

"The Dark Prince's most trusted," Laban continued to explain, "the Hand of Azazil, commands hosts of evil Jinn, and draws power from witchcraft. Need I elaborate more?"

Harun did not care to hide his uncertainty. Did these men truly believe that *witchcraft* could win the war for them? The lands of Arammoria had been home to sorcerers since ancient times, and every battle was tainted with witchcraft. Hundreds of sorcerers from Imar and Uduff have been tasked to find a way, yielding murky and mediocre results. And from the mists emerge two men with an averred elucidation? He scoffed loudly.

Laban became offended. "Incredulous as it may seem to you, *blacksmith*; our claim is true! If you have the luxury to scorn so blatantly, then you have not fully realized the gravity of the matter. The Dark Prince's forces and allies grow ever stronger and powerful. Our provisions run thinner by the day, and our foothold in this war weakens irreversibly."

"Our? When did it become *our?"* Harun protested. "Arammorians were the first to give him sanction because he promised you power above all others. Now this war has become *your* concern as well? We are surrounded by betrayers and usurpers!" He looked at Ussam, "You. Galadian. Are not the rumors true that Aghara and Din-Galad seek secret allegiances with Arammoria on similar promises? What will your Emperor say when you come to him with this proposal?"

"I may be born of the Mountain, but I command an Aztalaan banner," Ussam declared. "Therefore, I cannot speak for Emperor Babati. Din-Galad has its own standing in this war and little can we gain by brooding over politics. If the rumors are indeed true, then we must look to our own."

Harun glared at him. "Why have you come to me? You three are capable soldiers. Why do you need a blacksmith?"

Laban and Ussam glanced at each other. Azhar folded his arms and leaned back slightly. "They carry with them a bold claim."

"Do they?" Harun raised his eyebrows.

"Your father is a sorcerer," Azhar said.

"And what of it?" Harun asked harshly. "His foolishness of indulging in despicable acts is driving him to his own destruction."

"There is more to it than mere stargazing or palm-reading," Laban said. "Your father had discovered the existence of the Amulets long before your birth. It was he, and three others, who buried them in the Dead City."

Harun blinked. An odd ringing filled his ears. "Careful, Arammorian," his voice became dangerously soft. "I may be a simple blacksmith, but I *know* how to wield a blade. You are making a very serious allegation!"

Laban gave a soft chuckle. "I do not threaten, Harun Zafar. And I do not twist lies. Your father discovered those Amulets and hid them, for their powers are too great to be wielded by man. We have come here tonight for a very specific reason."

Azhar reached out and touched Harun's trembling hand. "Steel yourself, Harun. There is sense in what they say."

Harun took a deep breath and tried to calm himself.

"We must face fact," Ussam urged. "The only way to end this war is by use of the Amulets. And the only way we can control them is by true blood. Your blood, Harun Zafar. Your father commanded one of the Amulets, and you have inherited the same legacy. Whether you choose it or not, the same blood flows through your veins. The same fragility. You can allow that weakness to consume you, or you can claim your birthright and use it for good."

Harun said nothing. He shot a glance at Azhar, who had focused his gaze on the teapot.

"Look around you, Harun," Laban pressed on. "War and corruption are consuming our very existence. What more evidence do you require?"

"What do you seek to gain from all this?" Azhar asked him simply. "We have spoken for a long while now. Dawn has come and gone, yet I fail to perceive your true intent."

Laban looked abashed. "An end to war," he blinked. "Is that not all there is to gain?"

"An Arammorian does nothing without first securing his own interests," Harun stated. "Even the spoils of war are a profit to your kind! It is a shame to see one of our own, side with the enemy!" he added to Ussam.

"*Side with the enemy?*" Ussam made a sudden sharp move, reaching under his cloak, only to be stopped by his companion. "Is this how you would treat your guests? You insult us when we bring glad tidings?"

"That is not our intent," Azhar's expression was impassive. "We are not dishonorable men, but if you want us to plunge into the depths of witchcraft, you must first earn our trust. And you will not earn it by the edge of a blade, General."

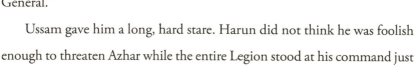

Ussam gave him a long, hard stare. Harun did not think he was foolish enough to threaten Azhar while the entire Legion stood at his command just outside the tent, but his mistrust in the man grew with every passing moment.

"What you say is true," Ussam spoke in a restrained tone. "Babati and Sitra seek to lay down their arms and join forces with Arammoria. They are desperate and they see surrender as a means to survival, but they only face betrayal, and they know it not. Their lands will crumble into scattered tribes and leaderless clans, and the Dark Prince's forces will tear at them even more until they no longer exist."

"They must stand united," Laban said. "Under a single banner. Behind strong leadership. *We* will unite them!"

Harun nearly scoffed again. "They will *never* follow a single leader," he stated. "And what makes you think that the other nations and kingdoms will accept a unified Empire? It is an absurd notion!"

"He is right," Azhar nodded slowly. "Our focus is this war. Our focus is to bring peace to the land."

"Peace is beyond your reach," Ussam gave him a grim look.

Azhar's eyes narrowed and his beard twitched slightly.

"General Babak," Ussam leaned in an inch closer, "a host, larger than any you have ever faced before, approaches from the west. We have seen the banners of forty-thousand strong, thundering the earth on their way to annihilate this legion. Another force, twice as large, marches from Rhudah to General Murad's camp outside the Walls of Murfaqat. My Legion marches to the Wall to join forces with his, but if our defenses fail, then so ends this war with Arammoria as the victors, and the streets of our cities turned to rivers of blood."

Silence deafened the tent. Although nearly diminished, the single candle's wick continued to boast a strong flame, but that was not the only source of light. As the winds fluttered the entrance flaps of the tent, a thin slither of gold appeared and disappeared, growing larger upon the rugs and loose sand as the desert sun began impending itself upon the lands. Dawn had broken into first light, and if Ussam's claim was true, before nightfall, the camp will be deserted, as the First Legion will either be marching out to meet this force, or retreating in shameful surrender. Retreating, because the enemy was not known to take prisoners of war. The enemy was not known to leave any survivors. Azhar and Harun exchanged nervous glances.

"We have no other choice," Laban also leaned forward and whispered with urgency in his voice. "Embrace this humble proposal, and together, we can drive back these evil forces to the dark abyss from whence they come. The four of us, here, today, *must* walk into the fiery pit for the sake of a free nation. I believe in that future. I believe in that New World, and I want to be there to guide and sculpt it into my own image, so that my children, and those after them, can live a life of peace, tranquility, and order."

Harun had heard enough. He stood briskly, urging Azhar to accompany him. They exited the tent and breathed in the crisp morning chill, squinting against the glare of the rising sun. Azhar dismissed Farid and turned to Harun once they were alone.

"This is folly!" Harun declared. "How do we even know if their claims are true? Why have our own scouts not reported of such an army?"

"I cannot ignore such a warning from another General, Harun!"

"Then we can take heed his warning and prepare ourselves for battle!" Harun pressed on. "We can send out for aid from the Council. We can stand and fight this force," he pointed at the entrance of the tent, *"without* their so-called sorcery!"

"We can do no such thing," Azhar stated calmly.

"We *cannot* resort to such measures, Azhar," Harun argued. "You cannot subject your men to sorcery. You have no right!"

"And you have no authority over me!" Azhar remarked with a stern and commanding voice, forcing Harun to withdraw his assertiveness. "You heard Ussam, the enemy is already on their doorstep, just as it is on ours. And even if, by the miracle of God, can the Council spare reinforcements, no army can arrive here on time. The sandstorm moves further east. It will take several days for anyone to cross the desert and come to our aid. Laban is right, we have no other choice."

"Do not agree to this, Azhar," Harun pleaded with him earnestly. "I have witnessed my father rot his life away to the wickedness of sorcery."

"I will not allow us to reach that dark horizon," Azhar said sincerely. "I must look to the safety of my men. I must look to the dire need of ending this war. Trust in your General as you always have, Harun. We will survive this. With unity. With you by my side."

He turned and entered the tent. Harun followed and they returned to their seats. "You seem to have given this quite some thought," Azhar said to Laban and Ussam.

"We have," Ussam answered, "and so should you. Without a clear understanding, we cannot hope to achieve the impossible, and there is no point in taking this any further. We have before us an opportunity to redefine the fate of mankind. Will you allow it to pass because of petty differences, or will you seize it for the greater good?"

Harun struggled to demur, but their statements were irrefutable. He felt Azhar's gaze on him and when he met his eye, they exchanged unspoken, consenting words. Defeating the Dark Prince's ruthless and merciless forces, took precedence above all, and if it meant sacrificing their own lives for the sake of a greater good, then so be it. After a long and silent moment, they both gave assentive nods, to which Ussam and Laban breathed sighs of relief and triumph.

Laban stood briskly, cleared his throat, and went to the wooden box, returning with a small leather pouch. From the pouch, he removed the four amulets. They gleamed in the candlelight. Fiery red. Icy blue. Emerald green. Citrine yellow. Each one glowing from within, mesmerizing and mystically alluring.

"These are the Four Elements of Power," he held each one up to show them. "The Elements of Creation. Fire. Water. Earth. Air. Each element with its unique strengths and weaknesses. With the blood of Zafar, the Rituals will be complete. The *Four* will awaken, and their elements will guide us, protect us, enlighten us, and one day, destroy us. This is our sacrifice for the betterment of mankind. For the greater good. From this hour henceforth, we are sworn to this Order and its Creed. Together we will build a better tomorrow. We will bring peace and prosperity, order and unity. We will build a New World."

ELEVEN

THE FOUR ELEMENTS

PRESENT DAY.

The two Assassins remained as Mukhtar's guests at the cabin for the following days, plotting every possible course of action, each seemingly more foolish and aimless than the last. Ghasif had sent a cryptic letter with a caravan to Aztalaan, where one of Ma'alim's spies would receive the message that the three were safe and sound in Khalidah. They had not heard back from the Teacher for several days, and while they waited, the only subject of their discussion remained the Amulet.

Rauf suggested its destruction. If one of the Amulets was destroyed, the enemy would be crippled. Upon closer scrutiny, however, this only seemed rash and unachievable. They did not know what powers were contained within the bluish gemstone, and therefore, did not know what it might unleash if it were destroyed. In addition, Ghasif argued that to destroy it would not necessarily hold the enemy off the hunt, and Mukhtar sided with him purely because he secretly did not wish to part with it.

Whether it was sorcery or something of a more ethereal nature, he was deeply drawn to it, and the notion of destroying it disharmonized his thoughts in ways he could not quite understand.

They had seen much in the Dead City, and time was against them. Although they wished to maintain secrecy for as long as possible, neither of them could deny the urgency to prepare for an inevitable war. Ghasif hoped to rally as many as he could under Ma'alim's banner, but did not want to take any preemptive steps without the Teacher's approval, and he remained adamant about it no matter how much Mukhtar itched to take some action.

While they awaited word from the Ma'alim, Ghasif offered to train him in combat, something he had been looking forward to since his days as a slave of Ghuldad. It kept his agitation at bay, and gave him the opportunity to better his skills in preparation for what seemed to be an imminent war.

Rather than dawdle, Rauf took on the responsibility to learn all he could about the Amulets and the Four Sorcerers of Ghuldad. This saw him disappear amidst books and scrolls for long hours, and Mukhtar participated wherever he could by researching through all the material in his grandfather's cabin. When he was not reading appalling texts of witchcraft and the dark arts, or training with Ghasif, he spent his time within the confines of home.

"Where should I keep these clothes, Ummi?" he asked Suha. The afternoon was the hottest yet, and rather than laze about, he decided to aid his mother with household chores. He hoped, perhaps, even to stir a conversation that may lead to some resolution.

She gestured at the door of the storeroom and continued to pull the covers off cushions. Her silence had ceaselessly endured since his return, and required no interpretation. His conversation with Mika'il had clearly been overheard, and (according to Mukhtar) misunderstood. She was saddened by it, regardless. How heavy her heart must be, Mukhtar could only imagine. For a mother to have lost her son for many months, to have assumed his death, to bear the burden, the guilt and the grief of such a thought, only for his return to be marked with yet another departure. She would not find peace for a long while, and every time Mukhtar left the house to go to the cabin, there would be a shadow of anxiety in her eyes.

"Forgive me, Ummi," he laid the bundle of dirty clothes by the door, and helped her with the worn cushions. "I have no intention of bringing you sorrow. I will stand by you, as you have always stood by me."

She was neither sad nor angry. In a soft but firm voice, she said, "The time will come when you will build a home of your own, and bear the burdens of your kin. The time will come when you will leave me to age and wither by myself, for that time is inevitable. When you will feel the joy and grief of a parent, and what you do in the present will determine the future of your children. You were always destined for great things, Mukhtar, as do all who crave ambition, but there is no shame in leading a simple life. Whatever greatness you are pursuing, however, I can only give you my blessing, and pray to my Creator that he grants you success, and guides you to the right path."

Abashed, Mukhtar dropped the murky-brown cushion. His hands were clammy, his throat constricted. He had expected an objection, a disapproval, even anger. Not a consent. It felt more like an acceptance; the acknowledgment of an inevitability. Mukhtar hated it because it felt inaccurate. It did injustice to his inner motives. He never sought glory nor valor. He never sought a greatness of any kind, but in the end, he could not allow evil and wickedness to endure. Not while he still breathed. Did she not see how much suffering there was in the world? Did she not see the suffering of her neighbor and dear friend, Samiya, who was at the mercy of a drunken husband?

It happened more frequently than ever before. Mukhtar was woken by her woeful wails, sometimes during the darkest hours of the night, as Gizwani continued to exert his cruelty upon her. It was all Mukhtar could do to remain within the confines of his own home and not storm through the doors with his dagger in hand. Suha knew, and expressly forbade him from intervening. This was a matter between husband and wife, she had said.

It had saddened him even more, to learn that Mika'il had long forsaken his forge to the hands of Ghulam Mirza. It was a battle he claimed to have lost, long before he even thought of fighting.

"Would you give up your life's work so easily?" Mukhtar questioned.

"I am old, Mukhtar," Mika'il replied wearily. "I can no longer battle the tedious and unjust tribunals of Immorkaan. Let them have the forge. There is no more wealth nor bounty left to it. I have decided. Fariebah and I will go to Mirzaan. We will use what little we have left, and recede to a simple life of toiling soil and herding cattle."

Mukhtar chuckled, unable to picture his uncle before the udder of a cow. *"Farming?"*

"What is wrong with farming?" Mika'il raised an eyebrow.

"Nothing," Mukhtar said quickly. "Nothing at all. I wish it for you, if it will help you be at peace with yourself."

Mika'il raised another eyebrow. "And have *you* made peace with *yourself?"* he asked after a brief pause.

Mukhtar became grim. He knew what his uncle was referring to. It had taken him several days to muster the courage and confront Adil. His intention was to seek absolution, but their conversation failed to bear any fruit.

Two days before, he had found Adil in the company of none other than Yael Varda, now Captain of their squadron, and his usual accomplices Nabun, Qurais, and Jubair.

Since his Captaincy, Yael and his accomplices found no reason to remain dutiful to their uniforms. They were commonly found playing games of chance to pass the time, or bullying merchants and extorting bribes to fill their pockets. They were doing just that, under the canopy of a teashop close to the *Souk Al-Huda*. Noon was ablaze with a scorching sun and the streets were a hive of activity, throngs pouring in and out of the *Souk*.

"What do *you* want?" Adil spat. He was leaning against the mud wall, chewing *Khat* while watching the others play.

"I wish to speak with you," Mukhtar glanced at the others. He was not afraid of them, but he was outnumbered. To pick a fight would be foolish and reckless, regardless of all the skills he was learning from Ghasif.

"He does not *wish* to speak with you, *imbecile!*" Nabun retorted. "Now go away!"

Mukhtar ignored him. He had not come to contend with the likes of Yael and Nabun. "Adil..." he called, in as respectful a voice as he could muster.

Adil folded his arms and looked away, as if the pebble to which his gaze was drawn was far more interesting than Mukhtar. His jaw moved up and down, slowly churning a mound of the green, intoxicating substance in his mouth. This only infuriated Mukhtar more than he already was.

Adil was never one to indulge in intoxications, nor was he ever so arrogant and disdainful towards Mukhtar. Would this be an end to what they had held dear for so many years?

Yael confirmed it. He and the others stood, drawing their swords and spears as they advanced toward him.

"Leave, *cur!* Or we will send you to your mother in a bucket!"

Mukhtar glanced at Adil disbelievingly. Never before had he stood aside and allowed Yael to bully Mukhtar. How things had changed.

That was the last Mukhtar had seen or heard of him. He visited Saif that very afternoon, and narrated what had happened.

"He is angered," Saif told him. "And this anger has caused him to be misguided. Give him time. He will find his way."

"They drew swords on me, Saif!" Mukhtar asserted. "In broad daylight! And Adil did nothing but look away with hateful eyes. I suspect his heart is filled with jealousy."

"Jealousy?" Saif frowned slightly. "Perhaps," he gave a meek shrug. "I have never known him to be jealous, but he is human. It is only natural that he should feel that way. Ever has he wanted to shine with glory, to be the man his father has become. Yet it is Yael that takes Captaincy of his squad. It is from him that he must take orders."

"And is that justifiable cause to disband our friendship?"

"Do you not see?" Saif urged. "He blames you for freeing the slaves. It should have been *him,* not you. He blames you for taking away his ambitions and chances of valor. You should have gone to *him*, called for *his* aid to free those slaves. To him, that was his opportunity to show his worth."

"That is absurd of him!" Mukhtar growled. "His father is wealthy. He is *born* of royal blood. How much more *glory* does he seek? And what glory is to be found in freeing slaves? *Absurdity!*" he muttered an afterthought. "*Small-minded thinking!*"

Saif gave a lighthearted chuckle. "Having the General as your father may not be as astounding as you assume, Mukhtar. Ever have you failed to understand his intricate relations with the royal family. He has defied them all to have a bond with the likes of you and I. We are leagues apart Mukhtar. The very air we breathe is different, you must always remember that. Only then will you understand him."

"That is untrue, Saif," Mukhtar argued. "Have I not always stood by him when he was faced with such predicaments? Have I not always comforted him when he spoke of troubles with his relations? There can be no justification for his behavior. It is envy, I tell you!"

"Envy is the religion of the wicked," Saif affirmed. "Adil is not wicked. Give him time, Mukhtar. Time will mend what is broken between you and him."

Saif regularly attended lectures and sermons at the local *Masjid,* and was known to speak words of wisdom when the occasion arose. However, despite his sound counsel, the days endured, and Mukhtar heard nothing from Adil. Whether more time was needed, or their friendship had indeed run its course, Mukhtar did not know. Instead, he focused his efforts on helping Ghasif and Rauf. Much to his disappointment and frustration, they were making just as much progress as his attempts at reconciling with Adil.

One hot and humid afternoon, Ghasif sat quietly on the bed, reading, while Mukhtar and Rauf dawdled lazily on the porch of the cabin.

"Do you think Ussam will march upon the Empire?" Mukhtar asked Rauf.

Rauf shrugged lightly. He was lying beside Mukhtar, staring at the branches above. The melodic chirping of birds, and cooling shade of the leaves below a scorching sun, seemed to invite nothing short of a nap.

"Warfare courses through his veins relentlessly," he replied lazily. "He has refined his tactics over the years. His methods and ideologies have shaped us into the Assassins we are. But he is no fool. He will not risk open war if he can avoid it. He will seek a more insidious approach."

"All the more dangerous," Mukhtar commented.

"Indeed," Rauf said. "He no longer honors the rules of engagement, and a man without honor is limitless in deceit."

"Come in here, you two!" Ghasif called.

"You come here!" Rauf responded, and Mukhtar did not object.

They heard him mutter something that sounded like 'lazy fools' before he stepped out, reading aloud from a book titled *'The Disguise of The Unseen'*.

> "Pagan belief has always looked to the stars for divinity and power. From predicting the future to determining birth rites and destinies, the depiction of a star has become a symbol for the occult. In sorcery, the five tips of the pentagram star each represent a key instrument. Upon discovery of the Amulets, the elements fundamental to creation were embraced as symbols of power. Their existence is ambiguous, hypothetical, and forever questionable, or perhaps it is knowledge divine."

Up-side-down, Mukhtar stared at him with a dazed look. "I understood very little of what you just said." Then he coughed. "Truthfully— I understood nothing."

"I have read that book, Ghasif," Rauf pointed out. "It contains nothing but the ramblings of a storyteller."

"You have seen the Khalidan insignia?" Ghasif rolled his eyes. "The tips of the star? The symbol of the Five Cities?"

"And what of it?" Rauf mumbled.

Ghasif sighed. "It is a symbol of sorcery, a mark used to summon that which resides beyond the veil. Picture *five* Amulets rearranged to form that very shape. You spent so many hours through all the books in there," he pointed into the cabin, "how could you not have seen this symbol?"

Nothing more was needed to waken Mukhtar and Rauf from their afternoon muse.

"I did see the symbol, but thought nothing of it," Rauf said indifferently, but his eyes were wide with interest.

The Khalidan insignia was first forged by the Council of Elders when the Great War was won. When Azhar emerged victorious and called for a unified Empire. Under the governance of a newly formed Immorkaan, the Elder Council he appointed declared the forging of the insignia of a five-pointed star to signify the unity of the five nations that were now the largest cities in all of the Uzad Peninsula. Each point of the star, symbolized by a unique portrayal of a majestic being, advocated each city. Khalidah, the Lion, the bottom tip of the star. Din-Galad, the Eagle, to its left. Arammoria, the Snake, to its right. Aztalaan, the Wolf, at its upper-most left, and Ninya, the Jackal, to its right.

It was widely disputed by most local authorities, tribes, clans and religious societies, condemning it to be a mark of wickedness and sorcery, and the fact that Arammoria, a nation known as the enemy, could even be considered to be part of this unified Empire.

"Is that why they seek the Amulets?" Mukhtar asked. "To summon Jinn? Is that their weapon?"

"That makes little sense," Rauf argued. "Ussam has his sorcerers for that. Even so how many Jinn can they possibly summon?"

"An entire army?" Ghasif gave them a grim look. "A powerful but unseen force? No man would dare oppose him. The question is— how does one control such a force? Listen to this:

> Very little is known of the Fundamentals of Creation, for very little has ever been understood. Fire, Water, Earth, and Air are the physical elements that embody our world, yet seldom does mankind appreciate such abundance. Grievous it is, that those who seek out the knowledge of these elements, seek them for personal ambition, and not for knowledge's sake—

"Those are four," Mukhtar interrupted. "What of the fifth?"

"Patience, Mukhtar!" Ghasif gave him an irritated look, and continued to read;

> Knowledge, however, is only a piece of what construes the complex being that is the creation of the Almighty— mankind. There is good in man as there is evil; and evil is always conquering. Jealousy. Lust. Greed. Overpowering temptations. Witchcraft will forever remain the most common way to draw a vile satisfaction from the turmoil of others. Throughout history, mankind has delved deeper and deeper in its quest to seek out the extraordinary. The aspiration to be better than others, purely out of a desire to become more prominent. Before mankind, there roamed on this earth, beings created from smokeless fire, living beyond an Unseen Veil, in civilizations, nations, tribes, religions—

"I know about the Jinn," Mukhtar interrupted again, and Ghasif shut the book with a snap.

"Would *you* prefer to recount then?" he asked as if he were offering a cup of tea, and Rauf gave a silent snicker.

Mukhtar scowled at him. "Elements and Jinn. I fail to see any relevance to Ussam, the Assassins, or my father!"

Rauf answered instead. "Witchcraft evolved as sorcerers began to find ways to manipulate the elements. If man could do so much, then it was assumed that Jinn could do a hundredfold. The four sorcerers found a way to bridge our worlds, and entrap demons, whose sole purpose was to manipulate the four elements. Four elements. Four Amulets."

"You spoke of a fifth?" Mukhtar pressed his question.

"It is mentioned, but is unclear," Ghasif replied. "Listen;

> The human soul is a power beyond reckoning. It can cross to the heavens and return, a breath of life divine. The element of Creation itself. The Element of Life.

"The fifth element is a *human soul?*" Rauf frowned. "Speak sense, Ghasif!"

Ghasif shrugged lightly. "What happens to our soul after death? What happens when we sleep? Of our very existence, our souls are the most perplexing of all. It is, indeed, *Knowledge Divine!*"

Mukhtar was very distracted while returning home that evening. The blazing sun had baked the walls of Khalidah's mud, clay, and brick buildings all day, such that they continued to radiate heat despite the approach of a cooling dusk. The dirt and sand on the streets were still hot and they burned through his sandals. Much of the populous walked with exhaustion, feet trailing in the dirt, backs hunched, worn by a long day of toiling.

In an attempt to escape the heat, Mukhtar took secluded and narrow alleyways, where the sun had not had much of a chance to fully exert its wrath during the day. His mind was a hive of activity, for the more that made sense, the more that did not. The more answers they uncovered, the more questions they raised.

How could this even be possible? How could such common aspects of everyday life, fire, water, earth, and air, become associated with elements of sorcery? How could such a thing as sorcery even exist? It seemed utterly impossible. Something unseen and unfelt, yet clearly and undoubtedly, known to tarnish everyday life. In the hands of vile men, such treacherous powers existed to serve their own evil thoughts. How could such men even exist? He felt anger. He felt hatred. These were wicked men who brought nothing but misfortune, ruining the lives of others for nothing but greed. These were men who needed to have their heads parted from their bodies, to be hunted and destroyed, so that their evil would have no chance of spreading.

These thoughts were coursing through his mind with the zeal of an agitated beast, and he lost track of time and place, allowing his lower limbs to guide him along instinctive paths, barely flinching against the hot sands burning the soles of his feet.

"You must keep your focus, Mukhtar," someone said to him, "lest you step into a pile of dung."

It was a moment's notice. He leaped as soon as he realized, and bumped into a passerby. After receiving his share of scorns and insults, he searched his surroundings for the Good Samaritan who gave him fair warning.

Leaning against a wooden pole holding up a canopy, was a man concealed beneath its shade. Clad in the armor of the Khalidan City Guard, his curly hair fluttering with the wind, his scimitar hanging loosely by his side. His grin was remarkably comfortable and ordinary, as though his friendship with Mukhtar had lasted long years. But it hadn't. Mukhtar felt a rush of poisonous hatred as he stared at the one person whose existence he had almost forgotten many months ago.

It was Hassin.

"You!" Mukhtar forwent all prior gratitude.

"I just saved you from soiling your feet," Hassin remarked lightly. "Is this how you thank me?"

Mukhtar gave a hysterical chuckle. "Save your false piety!"

"Harsh," Hassin replied coolly. "Why do you insult me?"

"Why?" Mukhtar threw him a dirty look. "If you have to ask, then you are just as foolish as you are traitorous!"

Hassin showed humility by holding up his hands and taking a step back.

"You have only ever sought personal benefit," Mukhtar scoffed, "even if it means stepping over the dead bodies of those you falsely claim to be your friends. Tell me then, why have you come to me?"

"I wish to look upon you, Mukhtar," he replied calmly. "I have heard tales of your misfortune."

"Is not my misfortune, your muse?" Mukhtar challenged. "Show your pretense to another, Hassin. I have no need for it!" He turned and continued to walk down the street.

Hassin jogged behind him and caught up. "I come with glad tidings, Mukhtar," he said. "I have heard of your woes, and wish to empathize."

"You robbed us!" Mukhtar yelled angrily. "Our entire livelihood! I cannot trust *anything* you say!"

"Mukhtar!" Hassin pulled him by the elbow. "I wish to relinquish this enmity, and reunite the brotherhood we once had."

"Unhand me!" Mukhtar shook him off furiously and glared at him. "I have held myself for long, but push me, and you *will* learn the meaning of pain!"

"You *must* listen!" Hassin pleaded. "I have seen the error of my ways! I seek absolution."

"You seek absolution?" Mukhtar's eyes narrowed. "Was it not you who traded weapons with mercenaries? Did you not betray us when you took away our livelihood? Not absolution! You deserve to have had your hands cleaved!"

Hassin turned red with anger. "You know *nothing* of my struggles!"

Mukhtar, however, was beyond sympathies. Over time, he may have forgiven Hassin, but when their sustenance was taken from them, Mukhtar had vowed never to let go. Too much had happened to turn back time. Too much had changed. Shaking with anger, he took a menacing step forward. "You want absolution?" he snarled a whisper and pressed a threatening finger onto Hassin's chest-brace. "Prove that you deserve it!"

With that, he turned on his heel and left Hassin by himself with his head hung.

TWELVE

THE CRIMSON WARRIOR

His anger had not subsided, and it took immense effort to escape Suha's continued attempts to have him eat before retiring to his room, for he wanted nothing but to be left alone with his thoughts. He sat on the stone ledge of his window, allowing the cool night breeze to toy with his face.

In his hand, he held his father's Amulet, its icy-blue gemstone reflecting the moonlight like an orb within an orb. Below him, a black cat scratched the wall with its pink paws, sharpening its claws for the night hunt. Mukhtar knew the cat, somewhat. It had lived in the alley for as long as he could remember, and when he called to her, she gave him a long, curious stare, her yellow eyes gleaming in the dark.

Misbah had often suspected the cat to be a Jinn in animal form, a notion she had come to learn through tales of old tinged with a trickle of knowledge she gained in Madrassa. Although, Mukhtar knew that the *Ustaadhi* in the *Madrassa's* often refrained from divulging too much unless they wished to give the children nightmares. He too had heard the same tales, the same cautions, to speak the name of the Almighty in true faith when a Jinn crossed your path. To seek refuge from the devil when a donkey brayed in vain or when a dog howled endlessly into the night.

Indeed such beliefs were true, and were awed upon when read in books or discussed in sessions. But when faced with its reality, be it but a glimpse, fear became a hungry beast, feasting upon one's very essence. It is how he felt when he stared into the glowing allure of the Amulet, a tangible testimony to that which was beyond the comprehension of man. Palpable evidence that the Unseen, may be unseen, but existed nonetheless, perhaps even in equal magnitudes to the ambiguous actuality of mankind.

The moon was slowly waning behind light clouds, as Mukhtar intently studied the mysterious object in his hand, pondering, his thoughts drawn deep into its enigmatic charms. Why did he feel so enticed by it?

The cat stopped scratching, licked its paws, barred its teeth at him, and slunk away, disappearing along the dark alley. *The hour is late,* he decided, and he stepped down from the window, returning the Amulet to its place around his neck. Tired and weary, he lay on his bed and within moments, fell into deep sleep. His dreams were irrational and illogical, reflecting bizarre occurrences in his daily life, and as a bright day wanes to an end, a night sky slowly imposing darkness unto all, the lucidity of his dreams slipped through his grasp and he was forced to endure a trying ordeal.

Along the streets of Khalidah, he walked with a sense of purpose, heading for his place of work. His heart was filled with joy, for he had heard the good news— that Mika'il had found success in reopening the forge.

He arrived, pulled on his tattered and stained leather apron, and began to search for his tools.

"They are outside," Mika'il told him.

Mukhtar turned and beamed at his uncle, who sat upon the back of a cow, holding a rooster in his hands. They both laughed heartily, sharing a long, deserving and delightful moment, after which he opened the door to go outside, and found that the alley was no more. Instead, he stood before a large, empty field. The ground was freshly cultivated, and there he found Saif and Faraj, digging and pulling a plow. He knew very little about toiling the earth, and chose a large hammer to join Saif in digging, hoping it would suffice.

Instead of working, however, they leaned casually against their tools and talked about Adil, about Jinn, about Ussam and Ghulam Mirza, until Mika'il approached them and said, "Mukhtar, Hassin has come to visit," he pointed at the door of the forge. "He brings you glad tidings, and hopes to bargain for your Amulet. You must not deny him, for I fear his malice. He may harm you!"

Mukhtar tensed. He had no desire to surrender his amulet. He will never surrender it. It was his, and his alone. He tugged on the golden chain, pulled it over his head and held it affectionately. After securely storing it in the pocket of his thaub, he stepped inside. He would speak to Hassin and reason with him first. He would fight him if he had to, but would not yield his precious Amulet.

It was in that moment that he realized he was not in the forge.

Fear gripped him. Darkness engulfed him. His screams were muffled. A deep rumbling sound shook the ground as the walls began to close in. Slowly but surely, he felt the approach of death.

The very air around him seemed to have been sucked out. He gagged. Instinctively, he struggled against the confining space, wriggling for room only in an attempt to bargain a few more moments of life. But the walls drew closer and tighter, closer and tighter...

Then it stopped.

Silence endured. It was a while before he realized that he could reach out into empty space. The walls were no more.

He sunk to the depths, further and further below, fathoms and fathoms deep under water. He struggled for breath. He felt something chained to his feet, dragging him down.

There was laughter, eerie, irregular, and agnate to the hissing of a snake.

Fear and panic flooded into him in a rush of reminiscent horrors. 'Not this again!'

The screeching laughter of the dreadfully demented entity rang through his eardrums. 'It is this!'

The cackling continued the deeper he sunk. He looked down and screamed soundlessly. A hand. A veined, bony, cold hand had wrapped itself around his ankle, its pale fingers stretching into long, translucent, gruesome talons, digging into his flesh. The rest of the hand, a horrid pale arm, dissipated into the darkening depths, beyond which a startling, icy-blue gleam hinted from a pair of snakelike eyes.

'There is a morbid sense of satisfaction in watching you succumb to your own deliriums,' it hissed.

'I have done nothing to deserve this!' Mukhtar thought desperately.

'You reap what you sow, sinner!' it shrieked with hatred, and the hand dug deeper into his flesh, inflicting a new kind of pain.

The searing agony of thousands of needles prickling every inch of his body. He writhed and squirmed in anguish, wriggling his limbs, struggling to escape. The hissing and spitting, screaming and cackling, dug deeper and deeper into his skull.

Then it ceased. Despite the crushing depths, there was a hollow silence, followed by a horrid whisper, 'It cannot be!'

There was a struggle, and the gruesome hand clutching his ankle, relinquished its hold, but even though he sensed his freedom, he could not move. Fear was paramount in him.

There was another whimper. 'You were destroyed with the ring,' the voice screeched in denial. 'I was there! I was one of them! Unless... but... impossible!'

'Inevitable!' the response was roaring and shattering, as heavy as thunder, as piercing as lightning, commanding, assertive, and dominating.

Then there was a rasping, spitting sound, as if something struggled to speak but could not. There followed an ear-splitting scream and a powerful rush of water. Mukhtar was taken against his will, forcefully carried by a *powerful source. After several failed attempts to struggle, he conceded to its might. Water is a powerful entity. To fight would be futile. He allowed it to exert its will, until its will was done. Until its tempers were allayed. And silence descended once more.*

Mukhtar peered through the waters and saw a figure swim toward him. Was this an illusion? Were his eyes deceived, or was the creature before him, truly of beast and man?

Scorched and scaly wings spanned far wide into nothingness. Long, muscular arms with foot-long claws for fingers, hung on either side of the torso of what appeared to be a man supported by the legs of a mule, furry and matted with blood, its hooves upsetting the cold wastes of the ground it trod upon.

The waters had long vanished. There was only sand and dust. He was engulfed by a sandstorm, unlike anything he had ever seen, for the grains appeared not to shift with the wind nor the pull of the ground, rising instead in defined paths toward treacherous skies.

Glaring eyes of a goat's head described what could only be a nameless impiety, as the creature shifted and Mukhtar saw what lay at its feet, bound in chains. The wind screamed and he screamed with it. The sound burst forth from his lungs and mouth, with a decibel high enough to wake him from his nightmare.

Terror and panic gripped his heart. His immediate thought was to reach for the candle by his bed, and ignite it to bring light into the room, but was afraid to even try. He remained there, his mind still trying to comprehend what he had just seen and heard. It was long before he could convince himself that it was only a dream.

When he became aware of his tongue and his lips, he prayed, uttering strings of Divine Verses.

A series of loud knocks echoed through the room, and he froze. Something unnatural was about to happen, and he was unprepared.

Another set of knocks on his door made him jump and pray feverishly, and it took him several moments to muster the courage and investigate.

God Almighty, give me strength! He grabbed the dagger on his bedstand and took a cautious step forward.

The door swung open before he reached it, and his heart almost stopped beating. Saif stood before him, drenched in sweat, his clothes stained with what could only be blood. He was heaving, his fingers trembled, and upon his face was etched a horror quite unlike Mukhtar's.

"You must come with me! Now!"

"Saif? What is the matter?"

"A most disturbing thing has happened," Saif's voice shook. "Hasten, Mukhtar! You *must* come with me!"

It did not take Mukhtar longer than a few seconds to tie his trousers and sandals. Panicky and breathing heavily, he followed Saif with only his dagger in hand.

They peered through the front doors before exiting the house, and aside from the lone horseman further down the street, there was not a soul in sight. With a cautious peek around every corner, they silently crept along the dark, empty streets, and arrived at Saif's tiny house, unhindered. Saif fumbled about in the dark and lit an oil lamp, enlivening a most horrific sight.

Mukhtar gasped and stumbled back frightfully.

On Saif's shabby mattress lay a limp body. The left leg was broken, its shard of a bone protruding through flesh, skin, and cloth. Several deep cuts and lashes bleeding into the sheets. The face was disfigured with gruesome bruises, a dislocated jaw, and oozing cuts. It took several moments for Mukhtar to recognize who it was.

"Hassin," Saif nudged him awake and began to tend to his wounds. "He is here."

Hassin choked, coughed, spluttered, and groaned. "I must— speak— with him!"

"By God Almighty!" Mukhtar's voice trembled. "What has happened to you?"

"You— wanted— proof," Hassin's croak was barely audible, his face twisted into what may have been an attempted grin, displaying a bloody mouth and several missing teeth. He stretched out a bloodied hand and extended a tattered, crumpled piece of parchment. "I have— proof!"

Mukhtar had some difficulty reading the blood-stained scribblings.

"You fool!" he remarked. "I only spoke out of anger! You needn't have climbed into the wolf's den for *this!*"

Hassin's jaw slackened, bloody spit drooling into the sheets. He was utterly pitiful. Mukhtar did not know whether to feel horrified at his state, or startled at what he had procured. More so, he felt guilt, remorse, and a deepening dread that Hassin might not last the night. He read the note again. His fists clenched with rage.

"Where can I find them?" he snarled.

"Spice Street!" Hassin whispered hoarsely. "Forgive— me— brother—"

"Mukhtar! You must not!" Saif warned. "Whatever your thoughts, they are nothing but the devil's whispers!"

Mukhtar ignored his admonitions. "Bring him medicine. Tend to his wounds. Tonight, blood will be spilled on Spice Street!"

"Be it your *own* blood?" Saif remarked. "Think before you act, Mukhtar!"

Mukhtar left with an animosity he had not felt since the day they had been coerced into surrendering the forge.

Spice Street was close to Saif's house. He sniffed the air, and his nostrils were filled with the acrid scents of clove, cardamom, and nutmeg among various other spices and seasonings. The flame of a torchlight flickered at the far end of the narrow street, and the closer he approached, the better he could see its bearer.

"Look who comes to us in the dead of the night!" Ghadan sneered blatantly, his smug voice echoing off the walls and shutters of the shops and stalls on either side of the street. "The Bullheaded Blacksmith! Ghuldad hunts your very existence! How have you remained hidden from their demonic eyes, I wonder?"

"The traitor must have told him everything!" One of the guards grunted.

"It matters not," Ghadan sneered. "He will not live to see the light of dawn! We will tear him limb from limb, and then, we will return his corpse to Ghuldad and claim a sack-full of gold!" His grin widened maliciously, and Mukhtar realized the wickedness of the man. He had worsened since the day the forge was surrendered. He had a spring in his step, pride in his voice, and an arrogance that could only have been acquired through wicked and malicious intent.

What now?

There was no turning back. No escape. Mukhtar shook his head. He would not run away, not this time. He would not turn his back on his pursuers. He will not cower— not from the likes of Ghadan! He took a step forward and drew his dagger.

"Have you come to *die*, boy?" Ghadan screeched.

To kill! Mukhtar took another step forward, and froze.

High above, and unknown to them, a figure leaped from rooftop to rooftop. A shadow among shadows. Spice Street was a long, winding lane of merchant stalls and shops of the finest herbs and seasonings in all the empire. A fine place for a fight? *Very rash, Mukhtar,* the figure thought to itself. Then again, the boy had always been stubborn and thoughtless when it came to picking a fight, and this one was not thought out at all.

From its perch, it watched, hawk-like, as the two parties approached each other. Threats were traded. Three swords and a dagger were drawn.

This was it.

The figure took a few calculated steps back and let out a controlled breath. A quick sprint, an agile leap over the edge, and it sprung forth.

There was a rush of air and a jingle of metal above Mukhtar, and they all raised their heads to search the night sky.

It was as if time had slowed. Against the cloudy, moonless sky, there appeared to be a winged creature flying through the air. They took several hasty steps away from its projectile path.

What devilry is this? Mukhtar thought, and only when it landed, did he become stunned rather than terrified. With a heavy thud and a cloud of unsettling dust, it touched the ground only a few paces before him and remained there, as if a barrier between him and Ghadan. What Mukhtar had assumed to be the wings of an unknown creature, were the deep crimson robes of a hooded figure, sheathed in studded, leather armor. By its side hung a single long scimitar. A crossbow and a quiver of bolts on its shoulder. When it moved, it was a blur.

It drew the crossbow and set it loose, striking its mark in the chest.

One of Ghadan's men fell to the ground, howling and rasping for breath before succumbing to his death. The second guard fumbled with his sword and started forward. The crimson figure did not have time to load a second bolt, and instead charged forward with a drawn scimitar.

Surprisingly enough, this left Mukhtar alone with Ghadan, who seemed to have frozen in horror. Taking advantage of this, Mukhtar charged forward, filled with a rush of adrenaline and rage, and plunged his dagger into the crevice between Ghadan's armor.

The sensitivity in Mukhtar's fingers was paramount. He felt the cold steel drive through layers of skin, vessel, and organ, penetrating deep into Ghadan's belly. A greater terror was etched on the man's perspiring, trembling face. He wanted to scream in pain, but all he could do was gag and choke, darkened blood drooling from his mouth.

"How— can this— *be?*" he croaked, his eyes bloodshot and bulging. "You are— just a boy! *A rat! Vermin!* You are— *nothing!*"

Mukhtar's lips curled with mirthless hatred. He released his hold on the dagger and allowed Ghadan to stagger aimlessly until his feet gave out and he crumbled to the ground. Behind him, the hooded stranger was still engaged in a fierce clash of steel. His adversary was larger and stronger than him, with heavy armor and no less skilled in combat. His attacks were brutal, but not nearly enough to overpower the Crimson Warrior, who was evidently agiler and quick-footed enough to evade his strikes. While they battled, Mukhtar knelt in the dirt beside Ghadan and held him up by the scruff of his armor.

"Who are your masters?" he growled. "To whom do you answer?"

Despite the magnitude of his pain, Ghadan managed to breathe a curse. "You will— *never* know— *cur!* Turn back— return to the loins— of your penniless uncle! This— is war. And war— is the province of men!"

"In this war, you met your defeat by my hand," Mukhtar said crudely, yanking the dagger out and stabbing him twice more with a surge of loathing. "So it shall be to the disgrace of your name!"

Ghadan could not even bear the strength to struggle. His body curled up into a fetal position, his arms pressing into the fatal wounds. He trembled and writhed in acute agony, until he breathed his last.

Mukhtar was not done. His hatred had not dissipated. Rage was still charging through him, and he unleashed it upon the corpse of the vile man who had destroyed their lives, who had spilled the blood of his friend, his brother. He kicked Ghadan's body several times, grunting with every blow, breathing every appalling insult in every language he knew.

"— *Infidel! Cur!* Long have you persecuted the innocent! May you burn in hell for all eternity—!"

The Crimson stranger rushed forward after defeating his foe, and drew Mukhtar back. "Stay yourself! Death must be respected, not abused!"

"*Respect?*" Mukhtar retorted and struggled against the stranger's hold. "Did *he* show respect when he mauled Hassin like a wild animal?"

"Hold yourself!" The stranger cautioned again.

Mukhtar took a step back and frowned at the hooded man. Why would this stranger come to his aid? A stranger both skilled and competent in combat. There was something familiar about him. The way he held himself. His attire. His voice.

"I must thank you for your aid," Mukhtar said. "But this was not your battle."

The figure drew its hood.

"My brother's battles will always be my own," the man said. "And I will forever come to your aid."

Mukhtar gasped, staring at the man disbelievingly. There was no denying the sharp features. He was broad and muscular, with shoulder-length, dark hair, and a beard in dire need of grooming. A scar across his left cheek glinted in the fallen torchlight, and despite a shadow of utter exhaustion, Zaki's smile was broader than ever.

"I left Bisrah, my horse, at home and followed you," he said.

"The horseman at the end of the street," Mukhtar stepped forward and embraced his brother. "That was you!"

"Indeed," Zaki nodded as they parted. "We must come away from here." He glanced at Ghadan's body. "Another guard patrol will have heard all the commotion."

Without wasting a moment more, they turned away from the three corpses bleeding into the street, Mukhtar still slightly trembling from the rush of adrenaline he had amassed since he left Saif's house.

"How have you been?" Zaki asked him. "I heard you were faced with grave ordeal. Ummi sent me a letter."

"Indeed," Mukhtar said darkly, and he began narrating his tale, just as he done to Mika'il. However, he made sure to give his brother every detail. There was no sense in hiding anything from the one person he knew he could trust his life to.

"When I arrived at Aztalaan, the guard said you were not there," he stated. "A lieutenant named Sameer, sought to keep me imprisoned. We hastily slipped away before they could enchain us."

Zaki's expression became stony. "I had already deserted the Red-Guard then. They may have hoped to learn of my whereabouts from you. Alas, it has taken me so long to return to Khalidah. My journey had to be lengthened to evade any bounty-hunters on my tail. It is no simple matter to desert the Red-Guard. I must shed these colors before they betray me," he gestured at his crimson robes.

Mukhtar gave an appreciative smile. "Needless to say, I am grateful you are here, by my side."

Zaki gave him a pat on his shoulder as they came closer to Saif's house. "You must now tell me why you pursued those guards."

Mukhtar handed him the bloodied piece of parchment he had received from Hassin.

> *Master,*
>
> *The wisdom of the Dark Prince could never have misled us. We have discovered that the Keystone is not ornamental, but a mark to hidden treasures which will bring us victory and enlightenment. However, we have searched the blacksmith's forge, but found nothing meaningful. We need a more aggressive approach if we are to see any success. I present this information to you in the hands of Haim, and await your further instructions.*
>
> *Ghadan.*

THIRTEEN

THE BUTCHER OF AGHARA

Nearly ten years back, while journeying from Aghara, Hassin's father fell terribly ill and died before his arrival to Khalidah. He was buried along the Sultan's Pass, close to The Desert City of Hanan-Sula.

Fatherless like Mukhtar and Zaki, Hassin took to the streets, desperate to earn a living and support his mother. When he was shunned away after continuous honest approaches, thieving became an easy escape. As children, Mukhtar and Saif used to watch with awe and amusement, while Hassin invented creative ways to defraud their *Ustaadh* or their peers, and make away with his effects. Much to Saif's displeasure, Mukhtar more than often partook in some of these petty misdeeds, but as time went on, Hassin was slowly drawn to more dangerous crowds. He had faced arrest and imprisonment twice, rescued by the combined efforts of a distraught mother and bitter relatives. In a desperate attempt to save her son from destruction, she pleaded with Mika'il, and in honor of his friendship with Hassin's father, Mika'il accepted him as an apprentice and gave him the tools to survive.

A son of Khalidah's oldest families, Hassin Al-Haddad, the Iron-Heart, died of his injuries close to daybreak when Mukhtar and Zaki returned to his broken, bloody, and lifeless body on Saif's mattress.

Saif was beside himself, and it took great effort on Mukhtar's part to calm him, while not succumbing to tears himself. Together, they carted his body to his mother and three younger sisters, disguised under a heap of random objects, cushions, sheets, and sacks, found in Saif's house.

To bring ill news of her son's death, refrain from telling her the truth, and lie to her only for her own protection, while she is distressed and distraught with a grief beyond imagination. It took Mukhtar, Zaki, and Saif an even greater effort to support the widow and her daughters, until the news had been spread to those of closest kin. He was, as they very well knew, their only source of sustenance. Her daughters were married, were unable to find decent work, and were constantly shunned by even their closest relatives for reasons bound to an age-old family feud.

Under the supervision of the local *Masjid*, Hassin's body was washed, shrouded, and buried, that very afternoon, in the graveyard outside the city. Prayers were later held at their house, and many among friends and families had come to pay their respects.

Isolated from mourners and well-wishers, Mukhtar's heart hung heavy, his mind abuzz with what he had faced the previous day and night. He could not bear to remain any longer than the burial. His revenge on Hassin's killers brought him no comfort, no satisfaction. There was more to his death than just the involvement of Ghadan. What they had discovered, was enough to cause bloodshed, and Mukhtar was now compelled to find and end it before it spread. Ghadan did not act alone. There were others. He would find them. He would bring them to justice. Only then would he find peace.

Mukhtar acquainted Zaki with Ghasif and Rauf. There was an awkward moment when the Red-Guard and the two Assassins met and greeted each other while struggling to keep their swords sheathed and enmity contained. When the moment passed, Ghasif wasted no time in expressing his displeasure towards Mukhtar's act of vengeance the night before.

"That was very foolish of you!"

Mukhtar glanced at Rauf, who was silently wearing a disappointed look.

"Irrational and unwise!" Ghasif continued. "There *will* be repercussions! Their hunt for us will now multiply tenfold!"

"They cannot possibly know!" Mukhtar argued. He was seated cross-legged on the floor, leaning back against the wall, arms folded.

"You fool!" Ghasif countered. "Have you forgotten how powerful our enemies are? We have remained hidden for so long. You have killed *three* of their vital acquaintances. *Think!* Your one act of vengeance will draw all their attention to us!"

Mukhtar brandished the piece of parchment he had been clutching in his hand since the previous night. "Hassin sacrificed himself to bring us *this!* We now know what they are after. We know whom to follow next, and battle them *before* they have a chance to advance their dark agendas, and if you would rather cower, and wait for the world to fall, then you are an even bigger fool!"

"Are you truly seeking an end to their agendas?" Rauf questioned.

"How can you ask that?" Mukhtar's eyes narrowed. "Is that not what we sought since we left Ghuldad?"

"Is it?" Rauf approached him menacingly.

Mukhtar gaped at him.

"Revenge will not bring you peace," Rauf went on.

"This has nothing to do with—"

Rauf shook his head disbelievingly.

"There were other ways of pursuing Ghadan," Ghasif added. "Subtle, discreet and far more effective. But you let vengeance cloud your judgment. You let your emotions take a hold of you, as they still are, and your rashness has jeopardized everything we could possibly do to end their vile ambitions!"

Mukhtar bit his lip. There was no denying Ghasif's point, but what else was he to have done? Hassin was lying on his deathbed, and had Mukhtar wasted time to seek the Assassin's aid first, Ghadan would have slipped through his fingers. As he recalled, Hassin had not mentioned Ghadan by name. If Mukhtar would not have arrived at Spice Street when he did, he would never have made the discovery he did. "Read the note again, Ghasif!" He held up the piece of parchment. "They seek a *'keystone'*, and claim to have found it. This information was due to change hands. Had Hassin not intervened, had we not silenced Ghadan, the enemy would be a step further than us. We now know what they do not!"

"Whatever it is they seek," Rauf remarked, paying no heed to

Mukhtar's statement, "had you involved us before you struck, we could have subdued Ghadan into divulging more. We now have nothing but a bloody piece of parchment and a vague description of something that may not even exist!"

"So Hassin died for *nothing?*" Mukhtar's throat became dry. "This Keystone is what General Masri tried to torture out of me, and you want me to ignore it all?"

Silence fell in the cabin. Dusk was approaching and the day was ending, yet it felt to Mukhtar as though ages had gone by since he last spoke to Hassin. He felt as though there could be no more room for happiness in his heart, and the only way to fill the void was to trace what Hassin had discovered. He glanced at his brother. Zaki, who was sitting cross-legged on the bed, watching their conflict with mild interest, chose to say nothing, but discreetly gave his brother an encouraging nod.

"We share your grief, Mukhtar," Rauf placed a hand on his shoulder. "But perhaps we should rethink our strategies."

Ghasif spoke in a calmer voice. "The killing of three city guards will not go unpunished. Their retribution will be swift, and the people will pay the price!"

"The people are already paying the price!" Mukhtar argued. "Look around you! We cannot just take matters so lightly anymore. We must do *something!*"

Ghasif shook his head defiantly. "We must let the dust settle, and reevaluate our position."

Mukhtar became irritated again. "By which time the enemy will be stronger!" he growled. "Do you not see? The longer we wait, the more time they have to fortify. We cannot allow them to find

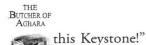

this Keystone!"

"We know nothing of this Keystone!" Ghasif argued.

"How else will we know?" Mukhtar snarled at him.

Ghasif threw his hands in the air, and Rauf intervened. "What then do you suggest?"

"We have a name. Haim," Mukhtar recalled the note he had taken from Ghadan. "Haim Tuma is the slave trader who captured me in the *Souk*. I know where to find him. We can make him speak, and learn everything we need before the dust settles."

Ghasif shook his head. "I will not sanction this!"

"Then remain here with your head between your knees!" Mukhtar stood up angrily. "I will do this by myself!"

Ghasif also stood. "You have no right!"

"I have *every* right!"

"This is *not* your decision to make!"

"I do not need your sanction, nor your blessing! Nor do I ask for your assistance!"

"We must await word from Ma'alim before we do *anything* further!"

"He is *your* leader. Not mine!" Mukhtar lifted his cloak from the wall. "It is strange indeed for *Assassins* to preach freedom, yet they tie their own hands to await authority before doing what is right!"

Angered, Ghasif took a threatening step forward, and Zaki intervened before a physical battle was fought.

"Calm yourselves!" He stepped between them. "Our quarrels only strengthen our enemies. As much as our methods may differ, our objectives remain the same. Let Mukhtar and I pursue the slaver, while you await word from Ma'alim, and perhaps we will come to common ground. It is true; we cannot wait and allow them to fortify themselves. We have an upper hand now. We have a lead. Let us make haste."

It was not a favorable notion. Ghasif turned a cold shoulder, as did Rauf, and the two brothers left the cabin without another word. There was no sense in awaiting orders from an unknown master when the objective ahead was clear. Besides, Mukhtar had an ulterior motive, and he was not ashamed to show it.

They arrived at Rayis Street just as the sun sank beyond the horizon. By the familiar alley was Ufuk's shop of antiquities. Mukhtar and Zaki watched as the man came out, emptied the contents of his pail by the roadside, and returned, shutting the door behind him.

At this hour, aside from the taverns and brothels, most of the populous was confined to their homes, leaving behind thieves, stragglers, beggars, and the homeless, searching for the warmest, softest corner to retreat to for the night.

"We haven't much time," Mukhtar glanced around as they crossed the street. "Guards will be patrolling these streets soon."

Zaki acknowledged with a nod, and they entered the shop.

"We are closed for the day," Ufuk announced without looking at them. He was hunched over his floor-desk, scribbling in his ledger. "Return tomorrow. And unless you have coin, do not waste my time."

"Coin we do not have," Mukhtar declared, "but we are interested in a trade of a much valuable nature. You come highly recommended by a mutual friend, Ghadan Lahib."

Ufuk looked up, his expression stony. The oil lamp beside him illuminated his wrinkly, furrowed face.

"Our master is a wealthy son of a prominent family of Khalidah," Mukhtar went on. "You may have heard the name of Halim Al-Kanaan?" He felt guilty using it, but it was the first name that came to mind.

Ufuk glanced from one to the other. The suspicion in his eyes was apparent. It did not matter to Mukhtar, however. If subtlety failed, they could always resort to steel.

"You are a friend of Ghadan's, you say?" the merchant asked, and both Mukhtar and Zaki nodded. "Then it will grieve you to know that he passed away this morning. Murdered by one of his own men, they say. I hear the traitor was ruthlessly punished, and his corpse was buried earlier today," he scoffed lightly, "serves him right!"

"Indeed, we have heard the news," Mukhtar's fists clenched. Clearly, it had not taken long for false rumors to spread, and since they did not know who truly killed Ghadan, it was easier for the City Watch to blame Hassin. It angered Mukhtar to hear Hassin's name soiled as a murderer. He struggled with the turmoil that arose within him, and felt Zaki's subtle nudge to remain calm.

They all nodded in silence, Ufuk in solemn sorrow, the brothers in pretense.

"What is this trade your master seeks?" Ufuk offered them tea and welcomed them to sit.

"What could be more valuable than human labor?" Mukhtar hinted.

Ufuk raised his eyebrows. "I see. Well..." he gestured at

his display of traditional pottery and a variety of artifacts and instruments, "...as you can see, I am a merchant of antiquities. Not slaves."

"Noble merchant, we mean you no insult," Zaki put up a most apologetic tone. "Like you, we do not wish to draw attention. But our beloved Ghadan could not have been lying when he said that you knew a certain slave trader who could assist us."

"I know no such slave trader!" Ufuk shook his head, his tone becoming heavier.

"Come now, Ufuk," Mukhtar pleaded in a softer voice. "To call Ghadan a liar would be to insult his memory—" and he immediately noted the guilt on his face, "—but let us not trouble the spirit of Ghadan anymore—"

"—perhaps we can come to a mutual understanding?" Zaki picked up and suggested. "Were you to merely *point* us in the right direction, I can assure you, our master will be most gracious."

The greed on Ufuk's face became apparent. Zaki had struck the right nerve, and Mukhtar continued to build on it.

"Halim Al-Kanaan is a most notable and influential nobleman, and we do not wish to return to him with petty excuses," he said. "Were we to be successful and benefit from your directive, we would vow to see that you also benefit from our venture. Would it be a portion of the trade, or perhaps valuable clients from one of the most prominent families in Khalidah? We can assure you that these are a people who can make generous acquisitions on our word alone."

Upon hearing wondrous tales of the wealth of Halim Al-Kanaan, Ufuk became more and more receptive. He divulged more than what was expected. Mukhtar and Zaki had left him with vows upon vows and false promises of endless fortuitous ventures.

Ufuk told them of his meeting with Haim the slave trader earlier during the day, and the most likely place to find him would be in a tavern further down the street, drowning in wine, buried in *Khat* and all other manner of intoxication.

"Perfect," Mukhtar stated. "The man does not even have the ability to control his limbs. This will be easy."

"Look," Zaki pointed. Under the canvas tarps of the open tavern were other mercenaries and city guards. "He is not alone. Do not underestimate your opponent. Caution, little brother."

"Then we must draw him away," Mukhtar asserted.

"Patience," Zaki assured him. "Sooner or later, he will come out. Let us hope our *friends* have followed."

"They could not possibly have resisted," Mukhtar glanced over his shoulder for a moment, and turned again to watch the tavern.

Haim was sprawled on filthy cushions, drenched in wine. Two partially clothed women indulged him in vile and wicked manners, and the brothers waited patiently with disgruntled looks. After what felt like hours, he parted himself from the women and wine, and crossed the street to relieve himself.

Mukhtar and Zaki silently followed him into a deserted alley. The drunk slaver seemed oblivious to his pursuers, and the brothers waited until he was done before confronting him.

In a blur of shadows, Zaki drew a dagger and pinned Haim against the mud wall of the alley. Driven by a sudden rush of adrenaline, Mukhtar drew his own dagger and joined his brother.

"Who are your masters and what do they seek?" Zaki growled.

"Speak! Or I will have your head!"

With two daggers pinned to his throat, Haim seemed to have forgone all intoxication, and for a brief moment, Mukhtar thought that he was truly intimidated. But his expression changed. His gleaming eyes narrowed, his lips curled and parted, revealing yellowed teeth. He was grinning.

Mukhtar unhanded him and turned, dagger at the ready. Dark figures appeared at both ends of the alley, barring their path. Mukhtar counted two and three on either side.

Zaki did not move a muscle. His dagger was still pinned against Haim's throat, their eyes locked with hatred.

"You should never have come here!" Haim sneered menacingly. "The Red-Guard will reward me handsomely for the head of a traitor, as will Ghuldad when I return your brother's corpse to them!"

Haim's guards advanced menacingly, slowly closing in on them. The air rang with the sounds of drawn swords. Mukhtar held his dagger as firmly as he could, mustering all his strength to keep from showing fright.

Zaki's dagger had not moved an inch, neither had his gaze. "Are you *that* certain, or merely just as foolish, to think that I will withdraw my blade without parting with your head! Speak, slaver! What did Ghadan hope to find in Mika'il Abaraina's forge?"

Haim gave a rasping chuckle and yelled, *"Kill them!"*

Acting on his order, they advanced, and Mukhtar tensed. He shifted on his feet, trying to pick out his targets.

There was a *swishing* sound in the air above them, followed by an *umph* and a *thud*. The mercenary closest to Mukhtar, fell to the ground, and his companions froze. Three more arrows were fired consecutively, and three more bodies fell to the ground. Dead.

If Mukhtar's expression was bewildered, it was nothing compared to that of Haim. No longer grinning, his eyes darted in every direction, looking from his dead mercenaries to the night sky, and resting upon the last remaining hope he had. The lone mercenary was stupidly gaping at the top of the walls on either side, searching for the unknown archer.

A gleam of silver flashed before his eyes. There was blood, a horrific gurgling, and the dying man was carefully laid on the ground by none other than Ghasif Majtaba himself. He then walked between the bodies, stopping at each one to shut their eyes and say a silent prayer.

"Has he squealed?" he growled in a low voice.

"He will now," Zaki responded without taking his eyes off Haim.

Haim's lips trembled. His eyes, filled with panic and disbelief, continued to dart over his dead companions. Zaki gave the dagger a slight nudge, and the slave trader began to speak feverishly.

"They seek a Keystone!"

"What is this Keystone?" Zaki asked harshly.

"An insignia forged by Harun Zafar. It marks a lost treasure from Arammoria. A weapon of some sort."

"Describe it!" Zaki demanded.

"Two Blades, crossing each other," Haim began to weep. "This is all I know. I swear it!"

"And the name of your master?" The softness with which Ghasif spoke was far more dangerous than Zaki's dagger.

"Ghulam Mirza!" Haim wept even more. It was strange for Mukhtar to see the very man who had enslaved him and so many others, now at their mercy. "Many mercenaries are in his employ. He has been using them to search for the Keystone, relentlessly. Will you spare me now?" he whimpered. "I have given you everything!"

"There is much you have yet to account for!" Zaki threatened. He had not taken his eyes off Haim, and Mukhtar knew what he was thinking. In that moment alone, Mukhtar felt more fear than he had all night. He was afraid of his brother's intent. Zaki would avenge his kin, no matter the consequence. "It is time to meet your maker, and answer for your sins!"

Haim's eyes widened in horror.

It was quick and effortless. Zaki's dagger ran swift and sharp over skin, through flesh and vein, and Haim Tuma, the Butcher of Aghara was dead before he hit the ground.

Daybreak was mere hours away. When the sun came up, Khalidans poured into the streets, looking forward to another long day of seeking a means to earn a livelihood. The alley off Rayis Street openly displayed a most horrifying scene.

Six corpses of mercenaries and slave traders were perfectly lined up with each other, slumped against the wall of the alley, blood and innards sprawled and seeping into the dirt and sand.

Rayis Street became far more chaotic and aggravated than it had ever been, and by mid-morning, the entire street was flooded with more guards than civilians. Many shops were closed. Trades had been ceased for the day, and by noon word had spread to every corner of the city, mostly in the form of exaggerated rumors.

With the citizens on edge and a second night of brutal deaths,

Immorkaan could not remain silent. By dusk, a citywide curfew had been declared. Any civilian found in the streets after sundown, would be subject to interrogation and open persecution, and the guards had been given limitless powers to enforce this law.

People rebelled in desperation, as more and more aspects of their lives quickly fell under Immorkaan's control. In the following days, riots erupted the streets of Khalidah, growing in magnitude. When the rioting showed signs of spiraling out of control, politicians and viziers took to the streets in an attempt to divert the thoughts of the populous. Soon, the finger-pointing turned inwards. Blame was shifted between tribes and clans. Marks against religions were made. Fundamentalists and extremists incited the youth into crimes of hate. Places of worship were raided and desecrated, Clerics and *Imams* were shackled, and before long, the city of Khalidah had fallen into a state of civil unrest.

FOURTEEN

THE STUDY

Despite their timely intervention, the Assassins would not so easily advocate the brothers. Indeed, they made it quite clear— had it not been for Ma'alim's strict orders, they would have abandoned him in Aztalaan and left him to his fate with the Red-Guard. Mukhtar did not know whether to feel grateful for that act of generosity, or frustrated that he should have disallowed it when he had the opportunity. To contend with the Red-Guard would have been a trying endeavor, but he would have at least relinquished the Assassin's hold over him. He was strongly compelled to evict them from the cabin, but could not shake off the guilt of doing so.

"Get rid of them!" Zaki seemed to be reading his thoughts. "Send them on their way. It is enough that we are housing assassins in Babu's cabin, but do we have to tolerate them as well?"

The Study

Mukhtar was strongly tempted to follow his brother's advice, but could not quite come to reconcile with turning away Ghasif and Rauf, not after all they had endured through the wastelands of Arammoria and the mountain pass of Khamur.

"They saved me from slavery," he told Zaki. "They saw me safely back home. I owe them this much. We should keep them within reach. If they follow Ma'alim's orders, then perhaps their mission will soon turn in our favor. I would rather not side with them, but they may yet prove to be useful."

As such, the brothers distanced themselves. Communication became limited to sharing news and recent developments when they met. Conversations were short, straightforward, and nearly always belligerent.

While Mukhtar roamed the city to find work and bring food to the table, Zaki confined himself to home, using the storage room as his own. As a Red-Guard deserter, he was restricted from openly seeking work, and with skills limited to swords he could do little else but spend the entire day napping and lazing.

Saif had all but cut ties with Mukhtar, or so it seemed. Mukhtar could not blame him. Saif held him responsible for Hassin's death, and regardless of what had transpired, Mukhtar was unable to deny the fact that had he not provoked him the evening before, Hassin would never have ventured into Ghadan's den.

More than once, the brothers attempted to break into the forge and search for the so-called Keystone, but they were heavily outnumbered. After the death of Haim and his mercenaries, the City Watch had been doubled, and suspiciously enough, more guards had been stationed about the forge, which made it difficult for the brothers to approach from any direction.

Eventually, they decided to prod Mika'il for answers, something Mukhtar had secretly been avoiding lest he be coerced by his uncle into speaking about Hassin.

Mika'il openly denied any knowledge about the Keystone. "Were it a blemish on the walls of my own forge, I would have seen it. Strange, that you would ask me about such a thing in wake of Hassin's death. What do you know that I do not?"

Mukhtar struggled to keep the emotional jolt in his throat under control. Zaki handed Mika'il the piece of parchment, stained with Hassin's dried blood. "This is the reason he died."

"And where did he find this information?" Mika'il's eyes narrowed. "*'We have searched the forge but found nothing'* ?" he read from the note. "What is the meaning of this treachery? Did Hassin truly know? Did he battle with Ghadan? Is that why he died?"

"We know only as much as you do, Khal," Zaki replied. "We wish to follow the parchment and learn the truth."

"Their treachery runs deeper than we assumed," Mukhtar urged. "They claim that *Abha* had concealed some sort of weapon and marked its location with an insignia which they call a 'keystone'."

"I forbid you to pursue this madness!" Mika'il asserted angrily. "There is grave danger in indulging with these people."

Mukhtar raised a silent hand, urging his uncle to calm down and try to understand. "We do not pursue this with recklessness. We are cautious and responsible enough to know where to draw the line. I beg you, Khal, *understand* why we are on this path. Much of Abha's life remains concealed, even to his own sons!"

Mika'il poured them coffee, taking his time as he pondered. "Your father was a curious man," he said. "He always thirsted for a quest.

For knowledge. As noble and virtuous as these goals may sound, such temptations always come at a price. Always. His family suffered, his livelihood suffered, and so did any who called themselves his kin. Distant became his relations, and all that he had acquired was never enough to hold his life together."

"It does not matter," Zaki said. "We need to know what he knew. We need that knowledge!"

Mika'il gave a small chuckle and shook his head. "You are just as headstrong as your father! Knowledge is *learned*. It is not given. It is earned, deduced, absorbed, ascertained, and then it is preserved—" he put a finger to his temple, "—in here. We can only keep traces of that knowledge, on stone and parchment, to remind us of what was, is, and what may be."

"Stop spinning our words, Khal!" Zaki's tone became stern. "Where are these traces of stone and parchment?"

Mika'il gave a deep sigh, gazing at them for a long while before he spoke. "Why are you pursuing Ghulam Mirza?"

The question, simple and straightforward, was not unexpected.

"We are not," Mukhtar tried to keep a straight face. It was a lie, and as soon as he said it, he felt a strong impulse to stand up and run into the wall.

"Have you taken your uncle for a *fool?*" Mika'il raised his eyebrows, as well as his voice, and his anger was now directed at Mukhtar's lie. "Hassin dies on Saif's bed. Ghadan dies on the same night. The city has been gripped by fear, worsened by Immorkaan and those they command, and all this began with the deaths of their own pawns. Ghadan was a perpetrator and a pest, but never was he canny enough to think for himself. And this note?" He brandished the piece of bloody parchment. "What am I to make of this? Do *not lie* to me, Mukhtar!"

Mukhtar's ears reddened. He opened his mouth to speak, but Zaki interrupted, "Ghulam Mirza is responsible for Hassin's death. He is responsible for taking away your livelihood."

"And *you* are responsible for bringing him to justice?" Mika'il snapped at him. "What do you really want from me, Zaki? Do you seek sanction? My permission? Have you not already done enough without my counsel?"

Zaki's eyes narrowed. "If you cannot help us, we will find another way!"

Mika'il shook his head disbelievingly, and Mukhtar gave Zaki a nervous glance. This was not the first time he had seen his uncle shake his head that way. It was a year back when, on yet another occasion, Zaki had argued and defended his actions of leaving home to search for their father. As much as Mika'il continued to express how wrong he was, Zaki continued to argue his right to do so. This time was no different, as Zaki was once again on the same path.

"Your father was—" Mika'il's voice trembled with much restraint, "— your father was many things. Very much gifted in secrecy, his greatest attribute, and also his greatest failure. He kept many secrets within the four walls of his study, the windowless room where he spent hours upon hours, pouring over script and scroll." He reached forward and returned the note to Mukhtar. "Your mother has kept the key safe."

Zaki nodded curtly, and Mukhtar stood up with haste.

"Do not look for comfort in that room," Mika'il warned, just as they were about to leave. "Do not look for hope. Much of what you may see, has been preserved since the day he was arrested." He looked at them earnestly. "Your father was lost on this path. Whatever you find, I urge you both, do not pursue the same madness."

The Study

Suha had always struggled to keep Harun's past a secret from her children, succeeding for the most part. Harun's study was, for the past ten years, the most close-guarded secret. She never went in, not even to clean, and kept the key on her person at all times. The last time Mukhtar had entered his father's study was when he was only a child. After his father's imprisonment, every attempt to gain entry was foiled and barred.

Over time, Mukhtar had mostly given up much of his father's memory, holding on to a mere handful of pieces that distinguished him from Zaki and his adamant belief that Harun might still be alive, lost to the wilderness or else locked away in a dingy dark cell for the last ten years. How else— was Zaki's reasoning— could Harun's disappearance be explained? How could a man just vanish from a locked cell in the dungeons of the Royal Palace? How can a man just disappear off the face of the earth, with not a shimmer of evidence? Zaki believed that Harun was still alive, and that had been his drive in life since he ran away in pursuit.

If Mukhtar thought it a difficult task to acquire information from Mika'il, he had yet to face a greater challenge. It took no short amount of pleading and bargaining to convince their mother to relinquish the key while keeping secret their reasons and motives. She was even more tenacious than Mika'il, angered at them merely asking for the key. It was a long, lengthy and rather emotional battle. She eventually surrendered when Mukhtar's relentlessly reminded her of her vow to relinquish her hold over the past.

The study shared a wall with Mukhtar's room, half the size, windowless, and nearly full to the brim with piles of books, heaps of parchment, and an assortment of strange and intricate instruments of brass, copper, iron, and glass. A worn floor-desk sat over a moth-eaten rug, littered with quills, stained with dried ink, and dripping with candle wax. Layers of dust were upset with every step they took as they shuffled into the room.

Zaki, using an oil lamp, browsed through one section while Mukhtar did the other side with a goat-wax candle.

"Careful with that," Zaki warned, and Mukhtar held his dripping candle upright.

"This is gruesome!" Mukhtar could not keep the recoil from his voice. He was flipping through a book titled *The Eye of the Sun,* filled with horrifying images and diagrams. He held the light closer to other books, and read their titles aloud, *"Scriptures of the Mountain Sufis. A Brief Study of Mythical Creatures. What to Do When a Ma'arid Attacks.* What is a Ma'arid, do you know?"

Zaki was not listening. "Never have I seen stranger scripts…" he muttered, searching through a pile of tattered parchments on the floor. "Look," he fished out a book from the pile, "Abha's journal," and began flipping through the pages. "This name…" he said after a short while. *"Siyaad…* have you heard it before? It is mentioned in nearly every one of his recollections."

"Yes," Mukhtar replied, much to Zaki's surprise. "I have heard Ummi and Khala speak of him more than once. He was Abha's half-brother, died as a child."

"This seems to speak otherwise," Zaki indicated the journal. "See for yourself!"

Mukhtar shrugged, but did not care to even glance at it. Zaki gave him a puzzled look and demanded an explanation with raised eyebrows.

"It matters not what the journal says," Mukhtar responded. "For all we know, these could be entirely different entities. The name I have heard belonged to an infant, born in Uduff, taken by the fever and buried beside its mother on the slopes of Mount *Hifa.*"

The Study

"You have a strange way of constituting the aberrant," Zaki stated.

"I am not fabricating tales!" Mukhtar scowled.

"Then why would Abha write of him as if he were still alive?" Zaki pressed.

"It may not be the same person, Zaki," Mukhtar argued. "And why should it even matter? Abha chose to keep it secret. He kept *everything* secret from us! That journal, and everything it contains, is just as dead as he!"

"Just as dead?" Zaki's nostrils flared.

"Abha is dead, Zaki!" Mukhtar did not bother disguising it, as much as it pained to say. "It is time you learned to accept it!"

"I *refuse* to accept it!" Zaki threw down the journal, upsetting a puff of dust.

"Had you remained instead of running off with the Red-Guard, perhaps you would have!" Mukhtar retorted.

Rage became apparent and etched on his scarred face. His jaw was set, and a vein twitched in his temple. Mukhtar was not intimidated. Cautious, yes, but otherwise prepared for a fight. He knew Zaki's temper would not hold for long. He was consumed by guilt. The realization of an impulsive act that had brought him this far, made him what he was, and the trail of anguish and sorrow he had left behind.

It had happened soon after Harun was said to have vanished from his prison cell, and everything around them erupted in chaos. Amidst the confusion, Zaki departed in pursuit of Harun. Lost in the wilderness, he was taken captive by a Red-Guard patrol on the Sultan's Pass somewhere close to Aztalaan, and brought before Abidan Babak, the King's younger brother, who charged him to serve at the Wall.

"The Red-Guard conceals many secrets," Zaki spoke in a grim voice.

"One of these secrets is a breed of soldiers, taken from the catacombs of Din-Galad, from the City beneath the Mountain. Discarded inbreds, hunchbacks, and lepers. They are trained, their deformities strengthened. Their arms are embedded with claws, and given new purpose. They are known as the Cleavers."

Mukhtar raised an eyebrow.

"When a deserter is caught," Zaki continued, "his neck is placed on a pedestal, and a cleaver's arm beheads him. It serves as a grave warning to any who think they can betray the Red-Guard. The last deserter was discovered fleeing north to Suria. They tied his feet to a camel and dragged him across Alhram for forty days, where he was finally put to rest at the Wall."

"They dragged him across No Man's Land only to behead him at the wall?" Mukhtar stared at him disbelievingly.

"He died in the desert," Zaki said darkly and Mukhtar's eyes widened in horror.

"After mere three days of no food or water," Zaki went on, "his backside torn to shreds by the rocky desert, his will to live surpassed him. They dragged his corpse to the Wall and cleaved his head only to prove their might. To send a clear message. He who betrays the Red-Guard faces more than death."

Mukhtar gulped and felt something icy cold hit the bottom of his stomach. He finally understood what Zaki was trying to tell him. It was not that he did not intend to return. It was that he could not. He suddenly realized the magnitude of the sacrifice his brother had made for him.

Silently, they continued their search. For at least an hour, Zaki was engrossed in Harun's journal, something Mukhtar felt a strong compulsion to avoid. He did not want to, could not bring himself to look upon it. He

THE
STUDY

 felt that the secrets their father kept from them were no less a betrayal. Instead, he became absorbed in a book titled, *Kingdoms of the Underworld*.

> – The Jinn are ancient beings, dwelling upon the earth long before the creation of mankind. Religions, nations, tribes, clans, races, and ranks, each one governed by the abilities and powers they wield –

> – The Ifreet are of the most powerful, monstrous and dangerous beings. They are fiery and prodigious, many among the rulers and leaders of their world. They are the Jinn of Fire –

> – The Ma'arid, as mighty and powerful as the Ifreet they may be, have only the desire to exist in solitude, and have no interest in the meddles and politics of man or Jinn, unless driven to. They are the Jinn of Water –

> – The Qa'reen is a Jinn of Spirit, decreed by The Almighty to accompany every human, from the cradle to the grave. They are the beings that whisper and manipulate the human conscience, with the sole purpose of leading it astray –

> – The Ghul are the Jinn of the Earth. Commonly found in places uninhabitable by humans, such as in the vast emptiness of deserts, they are known to be hunters of exceptional skill, luring unwary travelers into their traps –

> – The Sila are the Jinn of Air. They have the ability to soar the gusts, the gales and the winds. Be wary, Sons of Adam, when the wind blows with fiery intent, bethink the power of your Creator and seek His protection –

— Shayateen. Long have they been known to be the followers of the Dark Prince Azazil, the disobeyer, the betrayer, the scapegoat of evil. They are a spawn of his wickedness. They outnumber their fellow Jinn, thousands to one, and ever have they sought to bring malice upon man —

— Little else is known of the many other sects of the Jinn. The tribes of Khubuth, Khizab, and Khabaith, are known to lurk in places abhorred by humans. The tribes of Udhrut, Nasnas, and Shiqq, are also among sister tribes, and have long been the most favored to human sorcerers —

Mukhtar jumped when Zaki gave a sudden gasp.

"Have you seen this?" he remarked excitedly.

"I do not care for Abha's journal, Zaki," Mukhtar said dismissively.

"Not that!" Zaki's remarked. *"This!"*

Mukhtar followed his brother's trembling finger, to a thick, worn, leather-bound book atop their father's old floor-desk. "What of it?"

"I cannot say," Zaki's voice sounded shaky, and Mukhtar frowned at him. "It just— I cannot really say— it feels—"

Mukhtar rolled his eyes. "Open it then!"

Zaki began rocking back and forth in a very eerie manner, his vision slipping in and out of focus. His finger hovered in midair, pointing at the book with a slight quiver.

"Well?" Mukhtar pressed.

"It will not allow me," he replied in a distant voice.

"What do you mean?" Mukhtar frowned. "Have you lost all sense? It is just a *book!*"

Zaki seemed to be battling some intangible, perhaps imaginary force.

"I cannot!" he gasped, and for a moment, Mukhtar became terrified, for there was a strange and frightful look on his brother's face. He moved forward to see the book for himself.

There was nothing extraordinary about it, at least not to *his* eyes. The intricate gold imprint was fading off the worn leather, exposing the inner skeleton of its structure. The title, embedded into the leather, was barely legible, and he had trouble making sense of it. In the end, he was able to discern out a single word— *Kufr*.

Mukhtar shuddered. He felt a strange sensation as he reached for it. He ran a finger along its spine and around the edge, undid the worn, leather straps and turned over the front cover, but shut it almost immediately, and recoiled away, masking his nose.

The stench was so putrid, so fetid, permeating through the heat and dust, and into their nostrils. Mukhtar gagged several times, barely able to hold himself.

"What devilry is this?" Zaki's remarked, his nostrils pinched between his thumb and forefinger.

"Lower your voice!" Mukhtar hissed through a handful of his *thaub*. "Do you wish to bring Ummi upon us?"

"It allures you with strange sensations, and attacks you with such foul odors!"

"It is only resin, Zaki!" Mukhtar waved his hand in the air to drive away the smell. "Binding resin always carries an acrid stench."

"That is not resin!" Zaki opened the door and allowed the smell to air out.

There was some truth in Mukhtar's assumption. Binding resin typically carried such an odor, but considering the age of the book, the smell should have died away a very long time ago. Even then, there was a lingering aftereffect, the stench of rotting eggs, sulfur, and a distinct whiff of —

A piece of parchment protruding beneath the book, caught his eye. On it was a seal of wax, defined and intact, unimpaired by time or environ. This suggested one thing— the seal formed would have been the last thing done in that room before it was shut to outside world. He pulled it out and stared at it.

The seal bore twin swords, propped across each other, blades pointing up, hilts below. Fingers slightly trembling, Mukhtar broke the seal, opened and read what it concealed. He then handed the parchment to Zaki whose expression darkened as he read.

"This can no longer remain secret," he declared, his voice a bare whisper. "We must take it with us. The book too. Can you make another key?"

"I am a *blacksmith,* not *locksmith!*" Mukhtar pointed out.

"You are *useless,* is what you are!" Zaki muttered irritably.

Mukhtar scowled at him. "Ummi will be most displeased if she comes to find out."

"She will not know," Zaki shook his head. "Go see where she is. Keep her distracted, and I will hide them. Tonight, after she is asleep, we will take them with us."

"What of the curfew?" Mukhtar argued. Since the night they hunted Haim Tuma, neither of them had ventured out after dark. It had seemed strange to Mukhtar when he had climbed the roof of the house to scan the city. Never had he seen Khalidah so lifeless.

"Not tonight then," Zaki agreed. "At dawn. Perhaps Ghasif and Rauf will be able to make sense of the book."

Mukhtar's shoulders stiffened and he folded his arms. They had not indulged the other two since that night either, and he was hesitant to share anything with them.

"I do not wish for them to see into Abha's life," he objected. "This matter should be kept a secret between us."

Zaki gave an exasperated sigh. "I despise their involvement just as you but we need answers, and they *might* have them! Put aside your pride, Mukhtar. We need not show them the journal or the letter, nor do we need to tell them where we found the book."

Mukhtar was still hesitant, but he agreed. While he kept Suha distracted, Zaki wrapped the items in a piece of cloth and hid them on the roof.

After dark, when she had succumbed to exhaustion and retreated to bed, Zaki retrieved the package and kept it safe with him, and at dawn, the brothers set out for the cabin.

Even after daybreak, much of the city was still confined, as many of its citizens, dreadful of the repercussions of breaking curfew, kept to their homes until it was safe to leave them. The brothers were cautious of the streets, avoiding areas known to be patrolled.

The package was tucked under Zaki's arm, its odor disguised with several grains of frankincense. "Pray that the guards have weaker noses, lest they are drawn to us by this infernal stench!"

FIFTEEN

MASTERS AND BROTHERS

"Open it!" Ghasif's eyes gleamed with deepening curiosity.

"It wreaks!" Zaki complained.

"You have brought the Immortal City of Khalidah into a state of unrest," Ghasif scoffed irritably, "and you are unable to face the stench of binding resin? Open it!"

"I can assure you, that is not resin!" Zaki cast a dark look upon the book before passing it to Mukhtar, who opened it with unnecessary farce and a rather childish hesitation. Despite the horrid and unbearable stink, there was a heightened sense of anticipation, but one that only lasted for a prickling moment.

The first page was empty, and so was the second. Every yellowing, tattering, and stained page remained hopelessly blank, as Mukhtar flipped through each one, wrinkling his nose with every turn.

"An empty book, with nothing but an ominous title and the stench of a thousand rotting corpses!" Rauf filled the silence.

"It must *mean* something!" Mukhtar desperately flipped through the pages. "Why else would Abha keep it?"

"What about invisible ink?" Rauf suggested.

Mukhtar snorted loudly. "There is no such thing! Is there?" He glanced at his brother uncertainly.

"Yes, there is!" Ghasif gave him an annoyed look. "Little do you know of the skills of the Assassins. We use the waters of lime as ink to write hidden messages. Exposing the page to heat will reveal the text. Use the candle."

"And *burn* it?" Mukhtar frowned. "Look at it, the parchment could barely survive sunlight!"

"This parchment is strange," Rauf ran a finger over it. "It cannot be animal skin."

"Does it matter?" Mukhtar gave him an obvious stare. "It can still burn!"

"Give it here!" Ghasif reached for the book, and Mukhtar surrendered willingly.

Zaki, who was pacing the short space in the cabin, paused to watch as the Assassin lit a candle and brought its flame as close as he could to the page, taking delicate care to keep it from scorching. If this had any effect, it was that the heat only made the smell stronger.

"*Invisible ink* indeed!" Mukhtar scoffed, and Zaki threw him a subtle wink, while Ghasif turned slightly red around his ears.

"There must be another kind," he muttered almost to himself, flicking the page as if urging it to reveal its contents.

"Hmm..." Zaki gave a meek shrug meant to irritate Ghasif, and continued his pacing. "Should we allow you a moment to find it?"

Ghasif's nostrils flared, and he followed Zaki's pacing with a loathsome glare. "I *will* find it!"

"We have faith in your abilities," Zaki patted him on the back as he passed.

"I am beginning to lose faith in yours, *Red-Guard!*" Ghasif responded irritably.

"You have yet to witness my abilities, *Assassin!*"

"If and when you begin to show them. They seem to be lacking in more *intellectual* matters," Ghasif said pointedly.

"Is that so?" Zaki asked coolly.

"If otherwise, your thoughts and actions would not have disrupted the norm," Ghasif responded. His hint was obvious. He and Rauf still disapproved of Mukhtar and Zaki's pursuit of Ghadan and Haim.

"Disrupted the norm, but unearthed more than *you* have in months!" Zaki's lip trembled slightly, and his voice gained a decibel with every word. "Do not patronize me, Assassin! Unless you have a directive, keep your remarks to yourself!"

Ghasif's jaw was set. After a long and stony moment, during which murderous glares were exchanged, he cleared his throat and said, "We do have a directive." He gestured to Rauf who handed Zaki a note. "It has taken long to evade Ussam's spies and the eyes of the Empire, but Ma'alim finally responded to my letter. This is his wise counsel."

> *Brothers,*
>
> *It has been long since we last spoke. We have much to discuss and achieve, but little time and resources to do so. For now, we must maintain secrecy. We are yet too weak to expose ourselves.*
>
> *I must admit, I am most displeased with your insubordination. You were to leave the boy in the hands of his brother, but I would be foolish not to commend your efforts. I trusted you and you have shown your loyalty. You kept the boy safe.*
>
> *With what little you have told me, we are now faced with a much greater calamity, and we must seize every opportunity. The enemy must not discover the Keystone nor the weapon. Reach it before they do, and destroy it.*
>
> *I give you sanction, and my blessing to further your mission. Our spies have informed us of certain key individuals in Khalidah, allied with the enemy's ambitions.*
>
> *Ghulam Mirza, Rasha bint Sumrah, Yusri Abdi, and Nizaam Ibn Jalal.*
>
> *Rid us of these conspirators, so that society can prosper.*
>
> *May the beacon of knowledge and enlightenment forever be our guide.*

"He gives us sanction," Mukhtar could not stop himself from sneering. *"Your* leader approves of what we did."

"So it would seem," Rauf nodded, and took back the note from Zaki.

"Your orders were also to leave me at the wall," Mukhtar pressed on. "You disobeyed them. Why?"

Ghasif's beard twitched. "Our orders were to protect you, not dispose you at the mercy of the Red-Guard. We are your allies, Mukhtar. Have not already proven so?"

Mukhtar avoided his gaze. He could not question their loyalty, regardless of whatever conflicts they had.

Ghasif turned to Zaki. "We are in this together!" He clenched his fist before them to symbolize their unity. "What say you?"

Mukhtar glanced at Zaki. "Red-Guard and Assassin, working as one?"

Rauf gave a light chuckle. Ghasif shrugged. "In another age, Assassins wore crimson colors too."

"Indeed," Zaki held out his right arm, and Ghasif met it with his. "Let us hope we can keep the peace. Where do you suggest we begin?"

"We begin with Ghulam Mirza," Mukhtar declared. "Too long has he oppressed the weak! He will die by my own hand, and none other. He who disapproves, speak now with reason."

No one disagreed. Zaki nodded, "Very well. Go to the *Souk As-Silaah,*" he instructed. "See what you can learn. I will take to the harbor. If Ghulam is trading weapons across the seas, he will have affiliations with merchant vessels."

"I will search the caravan stables outside the city," Rauf added. "If what you say is true, he will have affiliations there as well."

"Ghulam's foul play must have some protection from the law," Ghasif said.

"Yusri Abdi is the man you seek then," Zaki said. "He is Khalidah's lawmaker and *Qadhi.*"

Ghasif gave a curt nod. "I will track him."

"We will need weapons," Mukhtar was eyeing Ghasif's scimitar hanging behind the door, in dire need of proper care, "and tools to repair them."

"I will see what I can do," Ghasif nodded. "Let us meet back here at dusk."

Without any particular strategy in mind, Mukhtar went to the *Souk As-Silaah*. Here, he would begin his search by keeping an eye and an ear out for anything that might give him information about the Chief of the *Souk*.

Aside from the Royal Palace, no other establishment in the city was so heavily guarded. It was a fort by itself, a stronghold that manufactured, housed, and safeguarded the Royal Army's arsenal. Archers paced the parapets and battlements above, while guards patrolled the gates and perimeters. Mukhtar would need a miracle to slip in and out unnoticed.

He needed to improvise. Something he had learned from Zaki, is that soldiers liked to gossip, and that the more there were, the more injudicious and indiscreet they were likely to be. Perhaps he might learn everything he needed without having to enter the *Souk*.

He sat down by the side of the road, pretending to rest his feet while admiring the large facade of the *Souk* with its fluttering pennants boasting the Khalidan insignia. Not too far off, an entertainer was calling to the crowds to watch him perform, and although none bothered, he carried on anyway, drumming a set of *Tefs* and singing ballads to glorify the city. Mukhtar watched him interestingly, but his ears were straining to hear a conversation across the street. A cluster of guards was chattering away like fishwives. From what he could gather, they were discussing Ghulam's sword fighting skills. It sounded like the Chief spent his afternoons in the *Souk's* training courtyard, practicing with a new opponent every day, ranking those he found favorable as his personal guard.

As Mukhtar watched, a short man in a bloodstained butcher's apron was discreetly signaling to one of the guards. When the guard caught his eye, he nodded almost imperceptibly, slipped away from the group, and crossed the street to follow the butcher. Mukhtar maintained a fair distance, enough to keep them within earshot. The two men moved away from the hustle and bustle to the secluded and shaded alley across the street from the gates of the *Souk*. Mukhtar scrambled up the wall of a single-story building in the front, and climbed onto the roof. He squatted by the edge and listened to the conversation taking place in the alley below, positioning himself as close as he could as the guard spoke.

"Why have you brought me here, Bayzar?" he hissed. "We cannot be seen together! And where is Nasar? I have been waiting to see him for two days!"

"There has been a development," Bayzar the butcher replied calmly. "I have been tasked in Nasar's stead. The Master is rethinking his options with the deaths of Haim and Ghadan. He believes we made a grave mistake in trusting Ghulam."

The guard seemed to be thinking along the same lines. "I *told* you he was a two-faced traitor. He could never be trusted. Arrogant and rash. Lacks the basic understanding of subtlety. He will expose us prematurely if not stopped."

The butcher looked grim. "We need him, Yabis. His resources are plenty, as are his influences. What more can you report?"

"Everything is in this," Yabis slipped him a folded piece of parchment. Bayzar read it once and folded it away into a pouch tied to his waist. "I await the Master's command. All else has been made ready. The carts leave by caravan at dawn. Ghulam will be overseeing the transaction himself."

"And how is the General?" Bayzar asked. "Does he suspect anything?"

"Oblivious," Yabis replied. "My sources tell me that he will be attending the feast."

"Did Ghulam merit an invitation?" Bayzar sneered.

Yabis gave a small nod. "He will need to keep that temper of his under control. He *must not* compromise the Brotherhood!"

"He will not," the butcher assured him. "The Master has already warned me to keep an eye on him. He is to be *removed* if things get out of hand. It is General Aarguf we must concern ourselves with."

"In due time," Yabis said. "Let us hope they will keep a civil tongue at the feast!"

"They have their differences, but both Aarguf and Ghulam know to keep up their appearances," the butcher reassured him. "That being said, very few can hold their tongues after wine has been drunk."

"Ah, the redundant stipulations of politics in a state of inebriety."

"Fear not. The Master has a plan, and we must trust in him. Even now he presses his advantage."

Master? Brothers? Mukhtar wondered. *Were they referring to Ussam, or is there some other master we have yet to discover?*

"What does he intend?" Bayzar asked. "Do you know?"

Just the question Mukhtar was waiting for.

"The less you know, the better," Yabis replied curtly, and the butcher raised a suspicious eyebrow to which Yabis responded by saying, "Sincerely speaking, like you, I too am a messenger, and know just as much. Do as you have been instructed. Ensure this letter reaches the Merchant."

They bade each other farewell, and Yabis returned to his post.

Mukhtar silently dropped down behind Bayzar, who exited the alley to join the crowds. He discreetly followed the butcher, gradually closing the gap between them. It was no simple task, as Bayzar constantly kept glancing over his shoulder, but when he was close enough, Mukhtar stealthily reached for the butcher's pouch. A quick lift and the scroll was his, and he slipped into an alley to read it.

> Master,
>
> Our work in the Souk continues, but we are concerned about The Chief's abilities to see things through. He has begun overworking the artisans and taxing them heavily. I fear that the people may come to reject him when the time comes. We cannot afford to have a rebellion which may come to the attention of the King, and that may destroy our plans. I would suggest you find another to take his place, simply as a precaution to secure our interests.
>
> We also worry that our man at Nazdak may have become increasingly unstable. Some of the merchant caravans complain of his inability to resolve matters, increasing the tax charges along the trade routes, spending more of his time locked in the citadel, drowning himself in wine. We have heard rumors that the Mountain City and its Citadel have already been infiltrated by Aghari spies, unmarked and unchecked.
>
> We must consider replacing him with one of our own, before they do so with one of their own. We await your command and remain ever so faithful to the cause.
>
> We are your brothers in light and darkness.

Mukhtar folded the letter, tucked it into his *thaub,* and returned to the *Souk As-Silaah* to try and see what else he could unearth. He sat down across the gates once again and looked about, his thoughts lost amid what he had just read. The drummer continued his act ever so enthusiastically, for he now had a larger audience. Then, something else caught his eye.

Not far away, a speaker had taken a stand at the corner of the street under the shade of a large palm tree, and was calling people forward. His dark oily hair gleamed in the sunlight and his beady eyes occasionally stole a glance at a pair of guards stationed a short distance away. "Aarguf Babak cares *nothing* for the people of Khalidah, else he would not entertain the likes of Ghulam Mirza and Sheikh Ruwaid," he was saying.

Mukhtar loitered to listen, keeping a keen eye on him. His voice carried a distinct tone, smooth and calming, but at the same time, assertive and confident. He was a gifted speaker, and every word ended with a unique period and desired impact. If only they had fallen on the right ears. The crowd, upon realizing the speaker's true affairs, slowly began to disperse.

However, the speaker carried on determinedly. "While we starve, the men in his keep want for nothing, growing fat upon the fruits of *your* hard work and labor. Now they seek to control every bit of our lives! Who will answer for the killings at the Monasteries and *Masjids*? Who will care for the families of the wrongfully arrested Clerics and *Imams?*"

A woman paused to readjust the heavy basket she was carrying. "Be quiet!" she hissed and gestured at the two guards who were peering along the street, suspecting some rabble-rousing afoot.

"Ignorance!" the speaker pointed at her. "Ignorance! Fools you have become, imprisoned by your own ignorance! Our leaders are selfish men who only seek to conquer all! To control us like mere sheep and cattle! Open your eyes! Rise up people of Khalidah. Join us in our protest and liberate this city!"

"They will behead you for this!" said another man, turning away with a dismissive wave of his hand.

"Your words will see you hanged!" another slunk away.

If a higher authority was brainwashing the masses, they seem to be succeeding, Mukhtar thought. He felt an urge to approach the speaker and invite him to join forces, but decided against it. He watched closely as the speaker cast a wary eye at the crowd, and joined another man who was waiting for him.

"How many have you gathered to our cause?" he asked the speaker.

"None," the speaker replied. "They are too afraid."

"We must not give up," said his companion. "Come. We will find another market, another square. Aarguf Babak must be dethroned for our cause to bear fruit."

Mukhtar hurried back to the cabin, desperate to tell the others what he had discovered.

"Ghulam's influence is deep, and his resources are widespread. Many men call him master, but his strength is failing. Now is the time to strike him. There is a wealthy merchant by the harbor. He and Ghulam do not see eye to eye, and this works to our advantage."

"How so?" Ghasif raised a dubious eyebrow.

"From what I gather, the merchant has invited Ghulam to a

feast," Mukhtar explained. "They will need to keep their differences suppressed. Ghulam will be too distracted to expect an attack."

"I believe I may have discovered the same," Zaki said. "Thamir Ar-Rushdi is the wealthiest merchant in the city. His influence regulates the entire harbor, and many use his ships to smuggle goods across the sea, Ghulam being one of them. It is how he has amassed his wealth. In ten days, Thamir will be hosting a feast to celebrate the good news of his eldest daughter's betrothal."

"Then it seems I may have discovered who will be supplying the food and wine," Rauf added excitedly. "Before leaving the city, Ghulam's caravans stop by the Sweet Orchards further north from here. The Sweet Orchards belong to Rasha bint Sumrah, who provides them with food and supplies. She will also be attending the feast."

They all looked at Ghasif, who suddenly became very grim.

"Did you procure weapons?" Rauf asked him.

Ghasif pointed to a small leather-wrapped bundle in the corner. "Daggers. That is all I could find. No weapon maker in the city was willing to sell me anything bigger or even sharper than a rusty blade. They may as well have given me wooden sticks. These will need to be restored before they can do any killing."

"Mukhtar can do that," Zaki said simply. "What has you vexed though, I wonder. Much as I detest empathizing, I cannot help but notice, you have been annoyingly quiet."

Ghasif gave him an irritated look. He removed a few artifacts and pieces of parchment from a small pouch strapped to the sash around his waist. Among them were a bunch of feathers, the fang of some animal, and a ring with a black obsidian stone very similar to the one Mukhtar wore on his finger, as well as a medallion shaped like the Amulet. "This is what I found in Yusri Abdi's mansion."

"Is it —?" he began.

"Another Amulet?" Ghasif asked. "No. An imitation, perhaps. He had a secret room in his mansion. The walls were stained with what looked like dried blood and carved with strange symbols. An eerie presence lingered and I could not bear to stay any longer than a few moments. With haste, I grabbed what I could and fled."

The parchments were filled with scribblings of hieroglyphs, occult symbols, and strange languages. They looked no different than most of the texts they had unearthed in the cabin and Mukhtar felt his insides recoil, knowing full well that it was all associated with sorcery.

"I have studied them as much as I could," Ghasif continued. "The symbol of the Amulet continues to make an appearance. This circle with a dot in its center, represents the Sun God, a symbol of worship to some of the Arammorian Sect. I believe the same symbol is associated with the image of the eye, which relates to an *'all-seeing God';* a pagan belief. This here, however, is the most intriguing image I have ever seen. It was placed under an idol of the very same image, adorned with all manner of pagan ornamentation, bones and skulls of small animals."

Mukhtar stared at a drawing of what appeared to be part goat, part man, with tall horns. The creature's hands were long, horribly extended into lethal-looking claws. The outline of a hand with an eye on its palm was drawn on its scaly chest. Around the entire figure, each limb touched a tip of a large pentagram star, and a smaller pentagram was etched on its forehead.

It seemed strange to Mukhtar, seeing that image. Not strange in the sense that he was frightened by it, but that he had seen it before, almost in its entirety. The creature had peered at him through shifting sands. He was not sure how he knew, or how deeply it concerned him, but its name lingered on the very tip of his tongue.

"The Hand of Azazil," he whispered to himself.

SIXTEEN

THE FLAW

With just under nine days to prepare for their mission, Mukhtar was overcome with a strange sense of determination. He slept late but rose early, worked hard, and barely spoke more than a few words at a time.

He resumed his training with Ghasif. Zaki, determined to outshine his assassin counterpart, offered to teach him his own skills. There was no denying the air of competition between the two, and Mukhtar continued to humor himself for hours each day, as both Assassin and Red-Guard struggled to outwit each other. Regardless, Mukhtar benefited from the best of both sects. He followed their every instruction, honing his skills and learning new ones. His body, strong and sculpted by pushing the wheel in Ghuldad, required nothing more than to be taught the right moves. Within a short span of time, he had become accustomed to the use of twin short-swords and throwing-knives, and was more than capable of clearing an obstacle course without difficulty. He wished he had the same agility and speed on the day he was captured in the *Souk*.

Without Mika'il's knowledge, Fariebah scrambled a handful of his personal tools for them. She was very suspicious at first, but Mukhtar and Zaki managed to convince her that they needed the tools to do some repairs at home.

Rauf surprised Mukhtar when he showed proficiency with hammer and anvil. "I worked the forges of Ghuldad during my early years as Ghasif's apprentice," he replied when Mukhtar enquired.

Together, he and Mukhtar managed to restore most of their weapons to usable conditions for the mission. They diverted from conventional methods of weapon-making, redesigning their daggers to cleverly fit and remain hidden in their sleeves. A dagger would be strapped to a leather band around the forearm and held in place under spring tension. When triggered, the mechanism would release the dagger and the wielder would have to catch it before it escaped. It was not the perfect build nor the most elegant design, considering the limitation of their resources, but it would serve their need, and facilitate an easier way to smuggle their daggers into the feast.

Stealth and precision became everything. They needed to infiltrate, remain invisible, do what needed to be done, and vanish. With what Mukhtar had discovered, Ghulam had many personal and well-trained guards protecting him. The Feast provided the perfect opportunity to face him alone. They only needed to draw him away from the rest of the guests, and execute him in isolation. They would have vanished long before anyone would realize he was dead. They took all the time they needed to tail and learn their target, investigating all his strengths and weaknesses.

In addition to Ghulam, Rauf also kept watch over Rasha bint Sumrah, while Mukhtar and Ghasif focused on Yusri Abdi and Nizaam ibn Jalal. They had agreed only to target Ghulam, but if the opportunity presented itself, they wanted to be prepared to face the others. Zaki had infiltrated Thamir's mansion, disguised as a servant, and returned every night with fresh details about its layout and occupants. It was also his task to establish a way into the feast, as none of them could qualify the guest list.

On the night before, Mukhtar could hardly shut his eyes. He lay on his mat, staring at the dark ceiling, visualizing every step of their mission, and the more he thought about it, the more agitated he became. He eventually fell asleep to the steady and rhythmic croaking of frogs outside the cabin. After a mere three hours of restless sleep, he was up again, only to find that he was not the only one.

An unoccupied mat to his left meant that Rauf was also awake, and judging by the scraping sounds of stone on metal, he was outside, sharpening his daggers. Mukhtar wrapped himself in a cloak to shield against the crisp chill of dawn, and joined him by the steps on the porch. "Is it that you lack faith in my skills?" he asked.

"I have yet to meet a blacksmith to match your skills," Rauf replied, and Mukhtar gave an appreciative grin.

"And I have always shown to be a skilled and experienced assassin," he said.

"What are you implying?"

"That you are restless," Mukhtar replied simply. "I did not think this mission would agitate an assassin like you."

Rauf gave a small sigh and gazed into the trees. "Our *mission* was to leave you at the gates of Murfaqat. Had I any choice, I would never have partaken it in the first place."

"You made that abundantly clear," Mukhtar commented, recalling Rauf's numerous complains during their journey.

"I did," Rauf chuckled, "and I beg your forgiveness."

Mukhtar placed a hand on his shoulder.

"In all honesty," Rauf continued, "I was displeased with Ma'alim's agendas. But now I realize, I was wrong. He did what was necessary to stall the enemy's vile ambitions."

"But that is not what vexes you?"

"As resolute, honorable, and determined as Ma'alim may be," Rauf explained, "I still cannot unravel his thoughts and intentions. He strongly cautioned us to avoid any conflict, any form of exposure. Now he furthers a mission to assassinate prominent Khalidans whose deaths are bound to draw attention, and we have no defenses, no reinforcements. Everything can go wrong and we have only enough to take care of a tiny handful."

"You make it sound like a strange game of chance," Mukhtar stated.

"Strange indeed," Rauf looked at the shimmering sky above. "Stare at the stars, and allow your thoughts to disperse among them. Across *any* realm. Beyond *any* horizon. In a complex paradox, limitless iterations of infinite populations strive to achieve the illusion that has been created for them, and very few ever realize that they are nothing but pawns in a much larger and stranger game of chance. Those were his final words to Ghasif and I, before we escaped Ghuldad."

Their day passed quickly but productively. Zaki left for the mansion at sunrise, while Rauf and Ghasif assisted Mukhtar in cleaning the cabin and preparing for the night. As the afternoon wore off, they began their short journey out of the tiny fishing village, through the forest, and up the Sultan's Pass to the harbor. Thamir's mansion loomed into view in a magnificence of architecture against the setting sun, one of the few structures in the city to adorn an elegance to match the Royal Palace.

The streets were thinning, but for a few stragglers and last-minute shoppers, as merchants closed their shops and stalls earlier than usual. Most of the populous was making their way to the mansion, even though none were formally invited. It may have seemed odd to an outsider, but Khalidans knew what to expect when the wealthiest man in the city threw a feast. No doubt, food would be sent out from the kitchens to the people, even though they were not welcome to join the dignitaries inside. Thamir was one of those aristocrats who always looked to maintain popularity among the citizens by boasting benefaction.

The streets displayed obvious signs of anticipated festivity. Several more guards and archers were posted along specific routes to Thamir's mansion, safeguarding the processions of dignitaries attending.

The three managed to slip past the guards by detouring through alleyways and over rooftops. Just before sunset, they climbed over the mansion's perimeter walls, crossed the gardens, and arrived at the large, open doors of the kitchens.

Thamir's mansion overlooked the Gulf of Shabb with a magnificent and breathtaking view. They could hear the waves crashing upon the shoreline, as the seagulls made every effort to make their presence known, squawking and screeching endlessly.

Unlike the magnificent marble front, the rear was built of bare, graying stone, adorned with and structural indentations and strategic wooden parapets above. Just like their frequent reconnaissance trips, there were no guards about, nor archers on the parapets. It may not have seemed odd before, but it certainly called for concern, considering that some of the most prominent figures of the Empire would be attending the feast.

The bolstering aromas of sweet and spice wafted through the air, as large pots brewed on huge fires in the open kitchen, which was so vast, four of Mika'il's forges would have comfortably squeezed inside. Mukhtar counted about fifteen different cooks and servants, moving about with chaotic coordination, which told him they were well-trained and experienced in this sort of thing. The heat coming from the kitchen was so steamy and overwhelming, they had to stand several feet away from the door in order to breathe comfortably.

Mukhtar tugged at the collar of his yellowing *thaub*, and complained loudly about how hot it was. Rauf was wearing a brown tattered one, while Ghasif wore tattered trousers and a stained shirt held in place by his white sash.

"The deserts of Alhram are far more treacherous," he responded. "This heat is bearable. It is the smell of food I cannot endure on an empty stomach."

"I hear you," Rauf agreed. "Just look at all that rice! How many people does Thamir intend on feeding tonight?"

"The entire city, it seems," Ghasif suggested, "judging by the throngs of peasants at the front gates."

"What a waste though," Mukhtar shook his head in disapproval.

"Is it a waste?" Rauf glanced at him.

"Is it not?" Mukhtar countered. "All this, just for the sake of keeping his image? All the coin he has spent on this one night, if he was just a shade more humble, generous and sincere, by distributing even a small portion of his wealth, he could have easily improved the lives of many poor families."

"If he has spared no expense for the celebration feast," Rauf stated, "I have yet to see how much he will spend on the actual wedding. I can hardly even begin to envision it."

"Why would you be thinking about the wedding?" Mukhtar sneered. "Did you merit an invitation?"

Rauf scowled at him. "*You* certainly would not merit an invitation!"

"And *you* would?" Mukhtar scoffed. "You make a beggar look like royalty!"

"You are not so charming yourself, in those rags!" Rauf countered. "Never have I seen a more ridiculous attire!"

"Stop bickering, you two," Ghasif sighed. "Look, Zaki is coming."

Zaki was almost a ghostly silhouette amidst the smoke and steam pouring from the kitchen. He was accompanied by a large, bald-headed man with a bushy mustache. Mukhtar frowned at his brother's outfit, a navy-blue tunic adorned with threaded embroidery, and a tall white cap with a large peacock feather fluttering in the breeze. "What is he *wearing*, and who is that man with him?"

"I stand corrected," Rauf muttered, eyeing Zaki's apparel.

"Salaam," Zaki greeted when he came closer.

"Salaam," they replied in unison.

"Are these your kin?" the large man asked with a deep growl.

A large apron was drawn tight over his round belly, and his bushy mustache made him look like an overgrown walrus.

"Yes," Zaki replied. "Sons of my uncles. Strong and loyal. I will be very grateful if you would give them work for tonight. It would feed their poor households."

The large man scratched his cleanly shaven chin ambiguously. "Palace work will need to be approved by her Ladyship."

"Please, be merciful," Zaki pleaded.

The man's gaze rested on Mukhtar, and remained there for a long while, as if he was recalling something from his past. "This must be your brother," he said. "He bears your likeness."

Zaki exchanged a brief glance with Mukhtar. "Yes," he nodded.

Feeling rather uncomfortable, Mukhtar was urged to break away from his somewhat dazed look. He focused his gaze on a stray seagull by the kitchen doors, attempting to sneak in.

"Wait here," the man said, turning and returning to the kitchen.

As soon as he was gone, Rauf took a menacing step forward and demanded an explanation, "Who is that man, and who is this *'Ladyship'*?"

"Kazimi is in charge of the kitchens," Zaki replied, "and her Ladyship is Nabiha Altaf, Thamir's personal aide."

"Are you *mad?*" Rauf glared at him. "Why would you involve them personally?"

"How else are you to gain entry into the feast?" Zaki asked simply. "I slipped in unnoticed, but three more faces will certainly draw suspicion, considering they might be expecting an imminent threat."

"Are they already expecting a *threat* then?" Rauf retorted angrily.

"What is your problem?" Zaki argued back. "I have scouted every possible way in, and this is the only way. If you have an alternative, please share!"

"Rauf is right," Ghasif defended his lieutenant.

"Of course he is!" Mukhtar defended his brother. "You would side by Rauf if he was speaking *backward!*"

"Listen to yourself!" Ghasif snarled. "If they are already expecting a threat, then we must turn back. It's too risky!"

"No!" Mukhtar retorted blatantly. "We do not turn back. We focus on our mission and see it through!"

"If Thamir's aide suspects us in the slightest, we will be dead before we even begin!" Rauf argued.

"We need a way in," Mukhtar declared. "She will grant us a way in, and we will do what we came here to do! Have our guests arrived?" he asked Zaki.

Zaki shook his head. "I witnessed Yusri Abdi conversing with Thamir a short while ago, but have yet to see the others."

"Is that the aide?" Rauf nodded toward the kitchen doors.

Zaki turned. "It is."

She was tall and slim, looking no older than Mukhtar or Rauf, and she walked with a stride that construed condescension. Her hair was sleek, a deep shade of black, rich with streaks of light henna, loosely held back with embedded jewelry. It fluttered in the breeze to adorn her glowing porcelain-like skin, rosy cheeks, and full lips. Her walk was elegant and proud, and even though she had to lift up the hem of her immaculately embroidered robes to avoid the dirt, her stride did not break nor falter. Her head held high, she approached them with a handful of her robes covering her nose to ward off the steam and smoke from the kitchen. Her almond-shaped hazel eyes were lined with dark *Kohl*, imposing a tenacity expected from someone who bore the responsibilities laid out for her by the wealthiest merchant in Khalidah.

As she came closer, the air around them smelled not of food or spice, but of an unprecedented, sweet scent of exquisite *Bakhoor*. "You have done well, Kazimi," her lips curled into a minacious grin.

Mukhtar suddenly realized a most crucial flaw in their plan.

"I recognized this one," Kazimi pointed a fat finger at him, "when they chased him through the *Souk*."

A sudden image of a large man tumbling to the ground with a basket of vegetables, crossed Mukhtar's mind, and he could do nothing but stare with disbelief.

"Give me a reason why I should employ Assassins of Ghuldad," her eyes shifted from Ghasif and Rauf to Zaki, "a traitor of the Red-Army and…" her gaze rested on Mukhtar, "… an escaped *slave!*"

Mukhtar held his breath. Beside him, Ghasif stiffened, and Rauf choked and immediately coughed to cover his reaction.

"Yes. I know who you are," she stated with an air of smugness. "I know where you hail from. My agents have followed your every move."

Zaki made an instinctive gesture to draw the dagger under his sleeve, but the aide did not seem in the least intimidated.

"Draw that blade, Red-Guard," her voice lashed like a whip, "and you will be rained upon by a thousand arrows before your stroke fell!"

Shadows slithered across the grounds, and Mukhtar glanced at the parapets above. Several archers filed the deserted parapets, bows held steady, arrows drawn and targeted at them. He could tell from the navy-blue tunics under their armor, that these were not city guards.

Ghasif's shoulders tensed, and aside from a twitch on his temple, Zaki remained impassive, but the disbelief in their eyes was undeniable.

"Nothing to say?" she mocked, and indeed they could do nothing but blink back. "Very well," she stated after a long empty silence, filled only with the cries of the seagulls circling overhead, drawn by the aroma of food. "Then you will listen. And you will listen intently," she looked at each of them as she spoke. "Your presence here at the feast, attempting to sneak in through the kitchens like *mongrel slaves* and *servants,* is of no concern to me. Perhaps you are here to steal something, perhaps you are here to prey upon one of Thamir's gluttonous guests, I care not. Here is my proposal; I will allow you to leave here tonight—*alive*— and in exchange, I want you to kill someone for me."

Their bewilderment could only be escalated. They all spoke at once.

"*What?*"

"His name is Ghulam Mirza," she replied, her beauty undiminished by her sudden malignity. "He is a guest tonight, and he has crucial information. Information which he will only divulge over his dead body. Need I elaborate more?"

"What information is this?" Ghasif enquired. "Are we to torture it out of him, or will the simple search of his dead corpse suffice?"

"You did not listen, when I said *'listen intently',*" she frowned at him hysterically, as though thinking him rather dimwitted. "Do what you must. Retrieve this information for me, and redeem your lives. Kazimi will arrange for you to mingle with the guests as servants, and I will arrange for Ghulam to be alone when he needs to be."

"What foolishness is this?" Zaki snarled at her, and Kazimi stepped forward menacingly. "You do not command us!"

"You will do as you are instructed, Red-Guard," she scoffed blatantly. "Or should I say *'traitor'?*"

"Say what you will," Zaki remained unmoved. "We do not answer to you or your ilk!"

"Perhaps we can come to an agreement," Rauf attempted to bargain. "You may find that our interests are aligned, and we can achieve so much more as allies."

"You are in no position to negotiate, assassin!" Kazimi growled.

Again they fell silent. Ghasif flashed a look of warning at the others, informing them that they should accept the aide's terms.

"Do as you are instructed, and you will live," she continued. "Refuse, or try to squirm your way out…" she glanced at the parapets above with narrowed eyes, "…I believe we understand each other."

She turned on her heels and left, flaunting the same arrogant stride with which she had first approached. Mukhtar watched her go, piercing the back of her bejeweled head with hateful eyes.

Kazimi ushered them into the chaotic kitchen, past steamy, brewing pots over fiery flames, and into a back room where he handed them uniforms just like the one worn by Zaki.

"Are we your prisoners then, Kazimi?" Zaki rounded on the large man.

Kazimi did something no one would ever dare do. "Silence, *traitor!*" he swung his arm and struck Zaki on the back of his head.

Under different circumstances, he would have lost both his hands. Zaki's ears reddened, but much to Mukhtar's surprise, he did not erupt into the dangerous temper he was known for.

"You and the Ladyship seem to have thought everything through in this little ploy of yours," he said, rather calmly and with a tone that suggested praise. "How, I wonder, did you know who we truly are?"

One would have expected Kazimi to swing his enormous arm and hit Zaki again to silence him. Instead, he put up a smug face and said, "Did you think your frequent comings and goings were unnoticed? As soon we suspected something, we had you tailed. We knew exactly who you were when you returned to the House of Zafar. From then on, it took very little to learn of your desertion from the Red-Guard." He wiped off a build up of sweat on his brow from the heat of the kitchen. "Your brother, however... I had heard that a son of Zafar had been taken captive and sold as a slave to Ghuldad," he smirked at Mukhtar. "It was only until I saw him today did I realize the day he was chased in the *Souk* like a chicken! He had run into me, capsizing my basket of supplies."

Mukhtar stared at the large man with disbelief. This coincidence was so bizarre, he was rooted to the spot, unable to sense his limbs.

"You are prisoners of your own motives," Kazimi's smug voice brought Mukhtar's senses back and he continued to gape at the man. "The guests have all arrived. You will mingle as servants and offer refreshments, all the while keeping a civil tongue and stature. When your target has been drawn away, you will be alerted. Now move!"

When they were dressed and armed with their clever contraptions concealed under their sleeves, Zaki and Rauf were handed a rag and sweeper each, and guided out of the kitchens to their delegated duties. Mukhtar was given a silver tray with several porcelain bowls filled with a variety of olives, dried fruit, and nuts, among various other refreshments for the guests. He glanced at Ghasif, who was the only one left without a duty that would disguise his true self.

"He will work in the kitchens where I can keep an eye on him until your task is complete," Kazimi responded to Mukhtar's concern. "If you fail, or stray but a little, he will be executed without mercy. None will question the death of an assassin."

Mukhtar wanted nothing but to use his dagger and wipe the smirk off his face. Instead, he clenched his sweaty fists and exerted all his effort into maintaining calm. There was a task that needed to be done. Kazimi and that arrogant aide could be dealt with after. He caught a glimpse of Ghasif's reassuring nod, before he was forcefully evicted from the kitchen and into the courtyard beyond.

SEVENTEEN

THE FEAST

The festivities were already underway. Mukhtar navigated his way around the guests in the main courtyard, feeling ridiculous in his navy-blue uniform, tall hat, and silver tray. They felt shabby and dirty, compared to the elegant outfits of the guests, who wore finery imported from faraway lands. Their trailing robes were intricately embroidered with expensive silk threads, and unlike the majority of Khalidan residents, they looked well fed and very healthy.

They were chattering loudly, and laughing even louder, over the sounds of *Uds*, *Santurs*, *Rebabs*, and *Tefs*. Certainly, there was no shortage of food and refreshments, spread in lush variety and mountainous quantities in large golden dishes upon velvety cloths, set at regular intervals around the courtyard. Servants maneuvered between the guests, carrying silver trays like his, offering refreshments such as sweetbread, olives, and various delicacies along with assortments of wines and *Sherbets*.

Unlike the steamy kitchen, the courtyard was open and airy. The marble floor spread evenly across, interrupted by the occasional island of a flowerbed or an exotic sprout. Polished stone columns held up intricate archways and balconies, above which more guests mingled and feasted. In the center was a large fountain that made Mukhtar's look like the village borehole. Stone pedestals were erected in the pool of water around the fountain, supporting exotic dancers who were twisting and turning their bodies to the music.

There were dancers all around the courtyard, women, pirouetting and revolving to the tunes played by musicians stationed below a grand balcony. Mukhtar's gaze moved up the balcony where a familiar figure overlooked the courtyard. Abunaki, a former customer of Mika'il. So, *he* was in charge of the evening's security. His eye was transfixed on a particular dancer who was moving faster with the tempo, glistening with perspiration below her sheer silk outfit, as the guests around her raised their hands, cheering the instruments into a crescendo that built and built, until the very air seemed to vibrate.

Disgusted at the sight, Mukhtar turned away. He spotted Rauf, looking disgruntled, mopping up after a guest had just spilled the contents of his wine glass.

"Try holding the liquid *in* your glass or *in* your belly!" Rauf complained loudly.

"You cannot *speak* to me that way!" the man declared defiantly. "Do you *know* who I *am?*"

"A pompous fool who never learned to drink out of a cup?" Rauf retorted.

Mukhtar reached out and hastily pulled Rauf aside before the matter escalated. "Take it easy, brother," he whispered, cautiously glancing at an archer above them.

He caught Zaki's eye, and nudged Rauf. His brother was tucked away against the inner wall of the courtyard, where the light from the elegant lanterns barely touched the stone. Mukhtar and Rauf split up to give a false impression, blended in with the crowd, and made their way to Zaki.

Rauf looked like he wanted to punch him. "See what you have brought upon us?" he growled.

"Watch yourself, *assassin!*" Zaki warned.

"We are exposed!" Rauf hissed and glanced around to ensure no one was listening in. "You had but *one* task— to find us a way into the feast, *undetected*. I *told* you, we cannot trust that aide!"

"*Think,* Rauf!" Zaki argued angrily. "She has ensured that the guards will keep out of our way. Not only has she eased our task, but she has also unknowingly surrendered herself to our mercy!"

"How can you possibly think that?" Rauf scoffed.

"Did you not listen?" Zaki explained. "Kazimi betrayed their secret. They are acting solely on selfish motives, which means we have every advantage at our disposal."

"How foolish can you be?" Rauf retorted. "Do you honestly believe that they will allow us to stroll out of here once Ghulam is—" he lowered his voice upon Mukhtar's caution, "—Ghulam is dead?"

"Which is why we need to be two steps ahead of them," Zaki stated. "How were we to know of her deceitful intent? This was an unforeseen circumstance, and we are caught in it. She, and that overgrown servant of hers, do not know our true intent. They only want to take advantage of our presence here. Should we disband our unity and quarrel amongst ourselves, or should we focus on our task? Let that pompous aide live under the illusion that she has control. We will do what we came here to do."

"And then what?" Rauf enquired.

"I will pierce Kazimi's gut with my blade!" Zaki growled angrily.

Rauf became infuriated, and Mukhtar pulled him away from Zaki before daggers were drawn. They parted and vanished amidst the feasting guests.

Ahead of him, by the fountain, a squabble had broken out between two drunken men. It appeared as though they were quarreling over one of the dancers. The dancer was disheveled and frightened, as the squabble mutated into a fistfight, and two guards had to leave their posts and intervene.

Rather than carry on with his menial task of serving refreshments, Mukhtar lingered to watch the comical fight. The drunken men attempted to throw misguided punches at each other, somehow eluding the grasps and pleas of the guards, while a small crowd gathered and cheered on.

"Ghulam is here," Rauf spoke close to his ear, and he jumped.

Following his gaze, Mukhtar spotted the Chief of the *Souk As-Silaah* over the way.

"The aide has sent a messenger to draw him away from the feast," Rauf said. "We are to meet her in the Grand Hall." He pointed to a set of large oak doors open on the far side of the courtyard. "She will show us where to strike."

"Not '*us*'," Mukhtar corrected him. "You and Zaki must find a way to free Ghasif from the kitchens!"

"What about –?"

"I will meet you at the cabin," Mukhtar assured him. He knew Zaki would not give in to blackmail, nor would he back away from a fight, but he also knew that his brother had made a grave mistake, and he no other choice but to do what was necessary to rectify it. Be it to risk his own life to save theirs. "Nabiha Altaf will regret the day she threatened us!"

"What is the matter with you?" Rauf snarled. "What if something goes wrong?"

"If anything does," Mukhtar gave him a stern look, "I trust you and the others to complete the task. Make haste to find an escape. I will handle the rest!"

Rauf became red with anger. "Damn you!" he growled. "Your stubbornness will be the death of you! You *and* your brother!"

"I did not endure the tribulations of Ghuldad to be coerced by the likes of that woman!" Mukhtar responded with equal cruelty. "Nor do I appreciate being patronized by you, your Captain *or* your rebellious leader. I will further my quest alone if I have to!" He walked away without a second glance and made his way to the Grand Hall.

The Grand Hall greeted him with lush rugs spread over the entire dark-marble floor. Puffy cushions of vibrant colors served as comfortable accommodations for the guests. The large, domed-room was brightly illuminated by overhanging chandeliers and ornamental lanterns, while *Mabkharas* emanated the sweetly scented smokes of incense, *Oudh,* and *Bakhoor.*

The feast here was several elevations higher than the courtyard. The music was more elegant, soothing, and ecstatic, designed to enhance and intensify the inebriation and intoxication of the *Hashish,* wine, and *Khat* served in abundance. There was certainly no shortage of exotic dancers, wearing minimal clothing, covered in what appeared to be gold paint, so that they looked like animated golden statues. The guests wore robes so rich, so immaculate that he felt himself diminish with every step he took.

Maintaining his focus, he gently navigated his way past the guests, and up the large marble staircase. With a clear view of the Grand Hall from atop the balcony, he scanned the entire crowd, his eyes searching for any familiar faces. He spotted Thamir's aide, Nabiha, mingling with the guests while keeping a hand over the feast's running. She caught his eye and gave a curt, subtle nod.

Thamir was sprawled on a large puffy cushion, entertaining three men. The multiple folds of his chin quivered up and down, a thin stream of grease drooling out of the corner of his lips, as he chewed on his food. His left arm, as thick as a club, occasionally reached up to his lips with a golden goblet of wine, while his other arm clutched a glistening piece of roasted meat. He was wearing a silk waistcoat over his meaty inflated torso and when he laughed, his stomach wobbled like a large bag of water. Standing beside them, looking utterly miserable, a servant worked a large peacock-feathered fan to keep them cool.

The man responsible for humoring him was General Aarguf Babak, whose deep booming voice carried over the sound of music. He was laughing along, looking respectable in richly embroidered robes of a sky-blue shade, sporting a long white turban with a gleaming, roundish, red gem highlighting its facade. It was a stone widely known as the Sacrament of Sovereignty, an adornment boasted by those deemed worthy successors to the throne. In their company sat an older, gaunt man whom Mukhtar knew to be the High Chancellor Laban Varda. There was a fourth man whose back was turned, and he looked much younger than the other two. He emptied his wine goblet and turned around to signal a servant for a refill. Mukhtar held his breath.

General Aarguf Babak's only son, and nephew to the King, Adil Babak was dressed in a similar manner to his father, but for a jewel on his turban.

He had not yet earned that right. It felt strange to Mukhtar, seeing Adil in rich and immaculate robes. Perhaps it was because Mukhtar never really saw him as royalty, but as a friend with whom he always shared his own thoughts and ideologies. His lip curled bitterly as he looked upon his best friend, suddenly realizing the immense distance that had grown between them.

From where he stood, Adil seemed just as aristocratic as all the other noblemen he sat with. A split second passed during which he looked up, and their eyes met, but the moment passed impassively, and Adil did not seem to recognize Mukhtar in his tunic and ridiculous hat.

There was a small cough behind him, and he turned sharply. "You are alone?" Nabiha asked.

"He is one man," he responded.

"Quite confident of ourselves, are we?" She eyed him dubiously, then gave a small nudge for him to follow, and led him further into the mansion, holding a single candle to illuminate the way.

"Why us?" he asked simply. "With a host of guards, the unmatched skills of Abunaki, and all the political power and influence of Thamir at your disposal, eliminating Ghulam is as simple as a finger-click for you. And yet you choose to blackmail us to do your dirty work for you."

"Do you really need to ask?" She gave him a cynical look and continued to lead him along a wide corridor with hanging drapes and lush rugs, much like the ones in the Grand Hall.

Mukhtar scowled at the back of her head. She did not care. They were expendable. Her response confirmed one thing— the chances of escape after the deed was done, were very thin. He had done right by instructing Rauf to leave with the others. Within him rose a conflict. How would *he* escape?

They arrived at the end of the corridor, and she stopped. To her left was a room and to her right hung a large tapestry of intricate patterns. "Ghulam will be here shortly. He has been asked to meet an anonymous prospect with a promising trade. You will be that prospect. Kill him however you wish, search his body, and bring me what you find."

"What do you expect me to find?"

"Do not ask stupid questions," she threw him an irritated look. "Focus on your task."

Mukhtar rolled his eyes. "I need to know what I should look for!"

She gave a small sigh. "A piece of parchment containing names of slave traders in Khalidah and Din-Galad."

Mukhtar frowned. "Why would you be seeking such information?"

"Every slaver on that list will face his death," she replied coolly. "I believe you would approve of that, would you not? Now, get on with your task. Find me when the deed is done."

He watched her stroll away in an almost casual manner, as though the feat of what she hoped to achieve, hardly troubled her conscious. As though such things came to her as naturally as breathing. The glow of the candle vanished with her as she turned a corner, and Mukhtar was left alone, submerged in the darkness of the corridor. He reached out with his free hand and groped his way into the room. When his eyes adjusted to the darkness, he was able to make out his surroundings.

A thin beam of faded moonlight, tearing through the dark, painted the opposite wall with a shadow of a tiny window's architectural pattern. The room was small and simple, furnished with a spindly table, plain rug and a wardrobe. He placed his tray on the table and took off his ridiculous hat so he could move with flexibility. After calculating his options, he decided to hide behind the door. He released the dagger under his sleeve and caught it before it fully escaped, ready to strike. The air was still and quiet, and if he could hear his own heartbeat, he was sure to hear any footsteps approaching, which would give him the moment's notice he needed to prepare.

The minutes swam by as he waited patiently in the dark room, all the while calculating what was inevitably approaching, and how he would escape the aftermath of it. Had Rauf heeded his stern instructions? Had they escaped? He doubted that very much. If anything, he was sure that the Assassins and his brother may have only gotten into another meaningless squabble. His wandering thoughts were brought back to his environs when he heard footsteps coming down the corridor. He steadied his breathing, remembering everything he had learned from their reconnaissance trips on Ghulam.

'Ghulam is a trained swordsman. Avoid any form of open conflict with him.'

The footsteps grew louder…

'His strength is his sheer size. Avoid his grasp.'

…and louder…

'Steady yourself, don't be hasty. Calculate your reach carefully. You have only one chance— make it count!'

An orange glow grew closer and brighter as its bearer approached. Mukhtar readied himself silently behind the door, and remained still.

'Aim for the neck. Do not slice or swing. Stab!'

The footsteps stopped. Mukhtar peeked through the crack of the door to make sure he had the right target. There he was, the man he despised, the man responsible for the death of Hassin.

Tall and bulky, with a short brown beard, wearing elegant robes of dark turquoise and a ceremonial, jeweled sword. His thick, ringed fingers were wrapped around a brass candlestand. He took a quick glance down the corridor, and stepped into the room, unaware of his predator lurking behind the door. Mukhtar breathed in slowly, as beads of sweat formed on his brow, and he squeezed the handle of the dagger between his sweaty fingers. He found an opportunity in the moment when Ghulam was placing the candlestand on the table and was reaching out to some raisins while his back was turned.

Mukhtar stepped forward.

And froze.

The hem of his ridiculous tunic had caught on a rusty nail protruding behind the door, and the sound of ripping fabric almost deafened him.

Ghulam turned around sharply, astonished, bewilderment etched on his face. "You!"

Mukhtar became dumbstruck.

"I should have known not to trust that pompous girl!" Ghulam growled, his eyes shifting between the dagger and Mukhtar. "What is the meaning of this?"

Instinct took over him.

While Ghulam fumbled for the ceremonial sword at his side, Mukhtar sprung forward.

And struck.

When he pulled back, his dagger was embedded into Ghulam's belly, and its prey was at a loss for words.

"Wh— *why?*" Ghulam stumbled back against the wall, one arm reaching out for support, the other wrapped around the dagger, blood gushing forth through his ringed fingers.

Mukhtar trembled where he stood. "Because you deserve nothing less!"

"I—" Ghulam sputtered, his eyes became bloodshot, "—do not

understand—" he stumbled and crumbled to the ground, upsetting the table and all its contents. Mukhtar instinctively reached for the candlestand before it fell over.

"You are the reason why Hassin is dead!" he growled. "The reason why many continue to lose their lives!"

Ghulam pulled himself up and rested his head against the wall, heaving. "Vengeance will lay waste to your soul!"

"Justice. Not vengeance," Mukhtar replied harshly. "Justice for those whom you have oppressed!"

"You know very little, child!"

Mukhtar shook with hatred. "The artisans you overtax. The citizens you oppress. The sons and daughters you have robbed from them and sold to slavery! I know more than you think!"

Ghulam forced a laugh. "How very little you know. By my death, you have opened a door to wicked men!"

"Liar!" Mukhtar remarked. "Your lies will not save you now! You are an advocate of evil!"

"You have become—" Ghulam coughed more blood, "—as deluded as your father!" A dark scarlet stain had spread all over the front of his robes, and his skin was becoming paler and colder by the passing minute. He had very little time remaining.

Mukhtar was startled at his statement. "Speak then," he urged.

Ghulam shook his head defiantly.

Mukhtar reached for the dagger and gave it a little twitch. The resultant was a strained scream from Ghulam. "You have spent a lifetime serving the needs of wicked men. By your dying breath, redeem what little honor you ever had, or pass into the unknown, a traitor and an advocate of the *Shaytaan!*"

Ghulam coughed and spat out blood. His life was fading, and Mukhtar could see the conflict etched on his pale face. His eyes skirted over Mukhtar's shoulder for a brief moment, and Mukhtar gave a solemn nod to assure him that they were alone.

"Your father— made a grave mistake," Ghulam sputtered, and Mukhtar's eyes narrowed. "The Eye. The Doorway. The Amulet. All evil."

"What mistake?" Mukhtar urged again. "What did my father do?"

"Find— the Keystone, boy!" Ghulam struggled with breath, choking and drooling darkened blood. "The weapon to defeat them— lies beneath the Keystone."

"And the Amulet?" Mukhtar grabbed his robes and shook him desperately. "What of the Amulets?"

"They— will use the Amulets—" he croaked, "to reign— with the powers— of Pagan Gods. United— the Amulets will open—"

A cough. A sputter of blood. A final breath. Ghulam's head fell and hung to the side, his eyes cold and empty. Dead.

Mukhtar took two steps back, slid down against the opposite wall, and stared at Ghulam's dead body. Weapons under a Keystone? Doorway? Eye? What was happening? *What was happening?*

Mukhtar shook his head violently. The more answers he uncovered the more questions that arose. How long he sat there, he did not know. He searched the body and found what he was looking for. The piece of parchment contained a list of names, including those of Haim Tuma and Ghadan Lahib, among many others he did not recognize. He tucked the parchment into his tunic, and with great effort, dragged and heaved Ghulam's heavy corpse into the large wardrobe by the corner, after which he sunk back against the wall and thought deeply about his next move. The hours swam by, and he waited patiently, hoping that the others had escaped successfully.

He heard footsteps approaching, and he hid behind the door again. The footsteps were light, evenly spaced, and brisk. He knew whom they belonged to.

The scent of her exquisite *Bakhoor* reached his nostrils before she entered the room, and he emerged from the shadows, gripping his dagger firmly.

"You were to find me!" she turned and confronted him. "Is it done?"

There was a reason why Mukhtar had chosen to wait for her instead. Impatience led to recklessness, which led to error. He intended to use that to gain an upper hand.

Calm and composed, he held forward the bloody dagger.

Her lip twitched slightly. Other than that she showed no signs of satisfaction. "Where is the body? Did you search it? Did he have anything on his person?"

Mukhtar smiled inwardly and did not reply.

"Speak, murderer!" her voice became harsher.

He turned and shut the door, bolting the lock in place.

"What is the meaning of this?" she demanded.

"This is retribution," Mukhtar replied simply. "This is what you miscalculated when you decided to hold us ransom."

"Do you think you can threaten me, *murderer?*" She held up a ringed finger at him. "Do not forget, your brothers are still my captives."

"Is that what you think?" Mukhtar challenged.

"It is what I know!" She removed three daggers concealed in her silk robes, and placed them on the table. Zaki, Ghasif, and Rauf's daggers. "Are you willing to gamble their lives?"

"Are you willing to gamble yours?" Mukhtar struggled to maintain calm in his voice. "Tell me, your *Ladyship*, how did you know what Ghulam concealed in his pockets?"

"Do not toy with me, *peasant!*"

"You really should consider how you respond," Mukhtar removed the piece of parchment from his pocket and held it closer to the candlestand on the table. "I can assure you, *I* am not one to *toy with!* You will answer my questions, or I will turn your precious parchment to ash!"

She fell silent, watching him with hateful eyes.

"Why does an aristocratic woman, such as yourself, seek such information?" Mukhtar went on. "Seek it with such determination as to kill a man, and gamble with the lives of so many others, including her own?"

"Why do you care?" she asked scathingly.

"Your motives are questionable," Mukhtar smirked. "It cannot be for justice. It certainly is not for the betterment of humanity. Which only means you seek vengeance. The real question, is *why?*"

He watched her expression transcend from hatred to horror.

"They *took* something of yours," he pressed on, "or *someone,*" he edged the parchment an inch closer to the candle.

She bit her lip, eyeing the flame of the candle and the parchment. "My sister," her whisper was barely audible.

Mukhtar eyed her suspiciously. "You are *lying!*"

"I am not!" she remarked.

"And you just *happened* to discover that the man responsible for your sister's enslavement is your master's guest?" Mukhtar stepped forward menacingly. "That is why you blackmailed us into doing your dirty work, and since you did, you *will* speak the truth, or I *will* burn the list! Now tell me, did Ghulam serve Ussam Bashiri? Does Thamir also serve the assassin warlord? What do you know of the Keystone?"

She raised her eyebrows and gave him a vindictive look. "What absurdity is this?" she asked, and Mukhtar tried but could not detect a lie.

He sighed and shook his head slowly. "You are masking the misdeeds of evil men," he tried to sound solemn, "I urge you, your *ladyship*, disband your aristocracy and humble yourself, or such men will reign atrocity over innocent lives! Did you think our presence tonight was mere chance? Did you think we were merely here to prey upon your master's wealth?"

A stony silence lingered. She stared at him with hatred in her eyes. He stared back impassively, maintaining his composure.

"Last night," she said finally, "I woke to a letter embedded into my bedpost with a dagger, stating the whereabouts of my sister and the man responsible for her enslavement. Earlier today, one of my spies confirmed that Ghulam had a list of his slavers on his person."

Having witnessed Haim Tuma and Ghadan Lahib's brutality first hand, he was almost compelled to empathize with her. He gazed at her for a long while, reading her. Despite her stony expression, there was a piercing glint in her eyes that he could not particularize, a fierce beast hiding behind an irrevocable beauty, and he tried his best not to allow it to divert his focus. There was still the matter of his escape, and he would not allow her a victorious hand on him. He extended his arm and allowed the candle's flame to caress the parchment. It seared and set ablaze. Fragments of dark ash fell to the floor, and the air stank of acrid smoke.

"The parchment!" She gasped and started forward. "You said—"

"I lied!" he challenged, and the look of exasperation on her face was almost satisfying. "I read the names and etched them in here—" he raised a finger to his temple, "— and as I see it, you have but one choice. My brothers and I will walk out of here, untouched, and—"

She made a quick motion for the daggers, but Mukhtar was quicker. He had already moved forward with his own dagger, pinning her against the wall, the scent of her *Bakhoor* toying with his nostrils.

"Do not test me!" he growled.

She heaved, her eyes wide in horror. "Kill me and your brothers die!" she croaked.

"Is that so?" He pressed the blade on her neck.

"Wait!" she gasped. "I know what haunts you!"

He loosened his grip ever so slightly.

"I know what haunts you!" she repeated. "I know about the voices and the dreams."

He relinquished his hold and took several steps back. Now he wore a look of utter bewilderment.

"How did you—?"

"You reek of tainted witchcraft!" She eyed him shrewdly. "There is a presence about you that casts a dark aura!"

His eyes were wide. His expression betrayed everything.

Eighteen

False Piety

The city was still. The waters of the Hubur, calm. The darkness never-ending. Low-hanging clouds foretold a day of downpour. Dogs howled in dissent against the rhythmic croaking of river toads, as the distant yelps and cheers from taverns and brothels, carried across the city.

Their escape had been successful. Rauf had reluctantly heeded Mukhtar's instructions, and he and Zaki had managed to free Ghasif from Kazimi's grasp. It had been a simple of matter of distracting him while Ghasif slipped away. The Assassins returned to the cabin. Exhausted, Zaki had fallen asleep in the courtyard, awaiting Mukhtar. Rather than wake him and indulge in a lengthy conversation, he decided to climb the roof to seek some solitude.

It was close to dawn. He paced in a small circle, his thoughts drawn far from his environs, as the events of the night unfolded in chronological order.

Falling for Nabiha's contrivance was an unprecedented contingency, but a miscalculation on her part. Or was it just an abrupt decision; an impulsive response to a fortuitous opportunity?

A rather short-lived fortune, Mukhtar thought.

A salty breeze shuffled the leaves of the overhanging palm trees, caressed Samiya's lavender pots, and carried their scent to his nostrils. In a strange way, it reminded him of his murky, filthy station, chained by the wheel in the large courtyard of Ghuldad.

He gave a small laugh and welcomed the scent, the fleeting moments of joy it had brought at a time when he had forgone all hope. It reminded him of the girl who brought him food and tended to his wounds, but spoke very little. Never had she provoked him. Never had she deceived him. Nuzhah, a young woman he knew very little about, whose every aspect remained veiled, but commanded all his respect.

He shook his head. *Being ridiculous!* She was no longer by his side. What must have become of her? Did Ussam Bashiri learn of her motives to help him escape? Was she persecuted for her act of goodwill? Did it even matter?

What mattered was the trail of bloodshed he found himself on, this endless cycle of the powerful oppressing the weak, and the rising tide of corruption and wickedness consuming everything in its path. He had to find a way of destroying the beast, the evil that had come to manifest itself in the likes of Ussam Bashiri. Only then could he ascertain a way of saving those like Nuzhah.

His thoughts went to the butcher and the guard. They had

anticipated Ghulam's death, even plotted it, and for reasons not so distant from his own, Nabiha also plotted the chief's death. Someone planted that note and dagger. Someone led her to believe that Ghulam was responsible for her sister's enslavement. Even if that were true, Mukhtar could not help but wonder— who else would benefit from Ghulam's death?

He yawned heavily. Exhaustion was dawning on him. His limbs tired and longed for rest. He glanced in the direction of the cabin, where Ghasif and Rauf were either asleep or huddled over in whispered conversation. He could picture them discussing Zaki's untimely flaw, and their complete lack of faith in the brothers' abilities.

Mistrust for the Assassins had manifested itself in Mukhtar since Ghuldad, and showed no reason to ebb. The secrecy behind which Ma'alim veiled himself was continuously aggravating his disappointment and frustration. Would the old man be pleased when he heard news of Ghulam's death? What other scheme did he have planned? What more to his rebellion did they need to partake? In truth, Mukhtar only entertained Ghasif and Rauf for as long as their interests were aligned. For as long as the truth about the Amulets and Keystones remained obscure.

He remembered what Ghasif had read from *The Disguise of the Unseen*. The Dark Prince. The Destroyer of Worlds. Harbinger of Evil. The very thought of the Hand of Azazil, whatever wraith or demon espoused that title, sent shivers up his spine. Whenever the horrid sights of Arammoria loomed into his vision, he wondered who, or *what* sat upon the throne of the ancient fortress.

There was a sound, and he froze. A distinct rustle on the ground, mere feet ahead of him, moving against the wind. It was artificial. Deliberate. Something was there.

His hand instinctively released the mechanism holding the dagger under his sleeve. It sprang forth with a distinct *click,* and he caught it smartly, twirling it in his fingers, ready to assail. Alert, he peered through the darkness, his breath held, waiting to hear the sound again. Was it absolute, or a mere figment of his already exhausted mind?

"Show yourself," he mumbled to himself.

'Here!' A voice whispered so close to his left ear, he swung the dagger wildly and aimlessly.

There was no one there.

"Reveal yourself!"

That laughter, that eerie, maniacal laughter, shifted with the wind and sent shivers up his spine.

'You already know what I am, do you not?'

"A deceiver! A spawn of the devil!"

'I sense a greater wisdom in you tonight,' she mocked. *'You have learned much, son of Zafar. You have seen much. Done much. The question is, how much more are you prepared to do?'*

The laughter faded, its decibels decreasing and vanishing with the wind. Mukhtar remained rooted to the spot, unable to establish his next move. He knew what it was, what the voice belonged to. The Jinn had been haunting him since his capture.

The sky was beginning to change shade. Dawn was approaching. He silently snuck downstairs to his room to change his attire and waited until sunrise before leaving for Saif's house. Saif had maintained a cold shoulder since Hassin's funeral, and Mukhtar had strongly avoided speaking to him, hoping to give him the time and space he needed to recover. But he was desperate. If anyone could help explain his asomatous problem, it would be Saif.

True, he could have just returned to Thamir's mansion and confronted Nabiha for the answers he sought. She did claim to have knowledge of what troubled him. However, he did not know how much he could trust her. Whether there was a purpose to her involvement or not, or she was just an unanticipated impediment in a much larger ploy, he did not know, but the less he involved her, the better.

A substantial amount of rain had fallen in the hour before daybreak, and the streets were muddy and runny in several parts. The populous was already showing their frustration, cursing and swearing, struggling to navigate through loose, slippery soils and sloppy, murky puddles.

He knocked on the tattered wooden door of Saif's house, and waited, contemplating the various approaches he would use to bring Saif back under his friendship, each one seeming less likely to succeed than the last. Unlike Adil, Saif was of a more calming, soothing, and ever-forgiving nature, as long as the other party showed their sincerity. Manipulation was not one of his traits, and he was intelligent enough to read it if it were tried on him.

"Mukhtar!" he gave a groggy and mildly startled mumble when he opened the door. "Salaam."

"Salaam, brother," Mukhtar greeted him with a solemn smile.

"What is the matter?" Saif asked simply.

"Must something be of concern for me to call upon my friend?" Mukhtar responded.

Saif raised an eyebrow. "It is barely past dawn, your *thaub* treks mud, your body shows signs of weakness, and your eyes are laden with sleep. Something must certainly be troubling you if you have chosen to visit this early."

Mukhtar sighed. "I need your help."

Saif stood aside and allowed him to enter.

The room was only as large as Mukhtar's own, but served Saif with every one of his requirements. A tiny door in one corner led to a lavatory, and in the opposite corner was a small fire pit where he prepared his meals. Against one wall was a prayer mat, and next to it sat a floor-desk with a few books and scrolls in its immediate vicinity. By the other wall was where Saif slept, a simple straw mattress with a few disheveled sheets. Above the mattress, Saif had hung all his garments, *thaubs,* and cloaks.

"Sit," Saif gestured at his mattress and opened a window to welcome the morning breeze.

After taking off his muddy sandals by the door, and wiping his feet on a sisal sack that served as a doormat, Mukhtar pushed all the sheets into a heap to make room, and sat on the edge of the mattress. Splashing sounds of water came from the lavatory, and Saif emerged a few moments later, wiping his face with a cloth.

"Have you eaten?" he asked. "I have already had my breakfast, but I can prepare some tea for us."

"You ate breakfast in *there?*" Mukhtar pointed at the lavatory door. "I thought you only went to wash?"

Despite his reserved attitude, Saif gave a small chuckle. "I ate when I woke for prayer at dawn. May I offer you bread and dates?" He held forward a small wooden plate of shriveled and dehydrated dates, and bread that was so dry, it could be crushed into crumbs.

"This is indeed welcoming," Mukhtar received the plate with humility, and indulged himself as Saif prepared a kettle over the fire pit.

Meanwhile, Mukhtar narrated his experiences with the voice in the darkness, describing its daunting approaches. He tried to recall the horrid dreams, while nervously glancing about, unable to shake off the shuddersome thought of something watching them.

Saif was abashed. "Jinn are known to harm humans if they feel threatened, or out of pure malice. Magicians are also known to use the powers of Jinn to bring misfortune upon their victims, and they tend remain adamant until they have results. However, this is unlike anything I have ever heard."

"Have I been cursed then?" Mukhtar became horrified.

Saif shook his head and shrugged. "I cannot say. This is beyond my knowledge."

They sat in silence until the water in the kettle began to boil.

"I have become helpless," Mukhtar rubbed his eyes and forehead, and leaned back against the wall. He felt heavily laden with sleep, and wished for nothing more than to just lay down on Saif's mattress, and shut his eyes.

Saif poured the tea into two cups, and pushed forward the plate of dates. Mukhtar hungrily helped himself to more of the sweet, dried fruit, and washed them down with short sips of the hot and spicy, ginger tea. As simple as the meal was, he could not remember the last time he felt such satisfaction.

"Rest now, Mukhtar," Saif gave him a concerned look. "Today, noon prayers will be held in mass. We can go to *Masjid Naqi*. I rarely offer prayers there, but I have heard that the *Imam* is knowledgeable in such matters."

Mukhtar nodded, and within moments, he had sunk into Saif's mattress and drowned into a dreamless sleep. He was woken after what felt like mere moments, and they prepared for prayers, Saif looking grim, but fresh and well rested. Mukhtar felt sore, looking like he had been subjected to an endless cycle of weariness.

Masjid Naqi was one of the larger and more elaborate places of worship in the district, magnificently built of marble and richly adorned with brass ornamentation. Its minarets rose high above the structure like tall, whitewashed towers, and the brass dome in its center was fabled to have a unique resonance that amplified the voice of the *Imam* to all corners of the *Masjid*.

Devotees were already gathering and settling in the courtyard, where long, lush carpets had been spread to accommodate the larger than usual numbers. Unlike regular prayer sessions, more guards had taken station in various locations around the *Masjid,* to ensure security, and despite the continuous buzz of the masses, the voices of the *Muadhin* and *Imam* were clearly heard.

"...*we must strive to protect our own!*" the *Imam* was saying in his sermon, and while most of the worshippers indulged in their own conversations, many still listened intently at his commanding and demanding voice.

"... *and for our sons and our daughters. To our leaders, our lives have become nothing but tools at their disposal, to govern and dictate every aspect of our existence. Their treachery knows no bounds...*"

Mukhtar and Saif found spots in one of the rear rows, and settled down to listen to the sermon. To Mukhtar's right was an old man with dark, shriveled skin, and on Saif's left was a much younger man who sat crisscrossed with his two-year-old son in his lap. Behind them, three men chattered away shamelessly, not paying any attention to the sermon, nor displaying an ounce of respect to the fact that they were in a place of worship.

"It is an insult to everything we believe in," the *Imam* went on. "An innocent man would wake at dawn, and walk the streets to the Masjid, without a worry in the world. He would walk with pride, with peace and assurance that his family was safe. But no more!"

Saif sat up upright and became stern, listening intently. Still laden with sleep, Mukhtar also tried to focus, but found his attention wavering.

"… have shown us their true colors! They have shown us what they are capable of! Should we stand aside and allow them to continue? Should we cower beneath our sheets and hope for the best? The infidels will take our homes next! They will dictate our every step! Govern our very breath! Are we to stand aside and allow the disbelievers to take away our very existence? Are we to bow down to their injustice?"

Beside him, Saif began making odd noises of discomfort.

"We must fight! We must shed our blood, and not our tears, for the sake of our future. For the sake of our children and their children. Never should they look back upon a world destroyed, and blame their fathers, and those before them, for doing nothing when the need arose!"

Saif shuffled where he sat, and Mukhtar gave him a curious look.

"What is the matter?" he asked.

"Listen," Saif responded, and Mukhtar heeded.

"We call upon our youth. The strong. The able-bodied. Join the cause of freedom. Stand up to these oppressors, and drive them back…"

"I hear nothing provocative," Mukhtar shrugged. "Is he not speaking what everyone is thinking?"

"Is he really?" Saif frowned at him. "Or is he planting a seed of his own ideologies? Inciting the youth to violence? Preaching upon their temperamental ages? He is creating unrest. Not preaching peace!"

"Saif, considering recent events—"

"Recent events instigated by the very same thoughts!" Saif argued. There was a hint of controlled anger in his voice. "Is it not what led you down that path, Mukhtar? Do not forget, that since Immorkaan implemented their curfew, much of the conflict has been between ethnicities and beliefs, most of it instigated by the likes of such apostates."

Despite the early morning downpour, the sun was searing upon their backs, but that was not the cause of the hotness he felt around his neck and ears.

"Listen, Mukhtar. *Listen!*" Saif urged him again.

"Before we stand for prayer," the *Imam* continued, *"we must come together and contribute to the true cause of this Masjid. I stand before you, brothers and sisters, humble and contrite. Give coin to the Masjid, and let your blessings flourish! Come together brothers and sisters, pledge your wealth, and secure your place in paradise! Who among you is prepared to invest for the Hereafter?"*

"Look!" Saif pointed. Amidst the rows were several young men, moving from person to person, collecting money in sisal sacks.

"They are collecting for the upkeep of the *Masjid*," Mukhtar stated. "They are securing their place in the hereafter. What is wrong with that?"

"Faith without knowledge is ignorance," Saif said simply. "Through ignorance, people believe that by merely giving coin, they will be granted heaven, and such thoughts are always prone to extortion. Paradise is earned through devotion and worship of the Almighty God. Through true faith and belief."

Mukhtar raised both his eyebrows, following the motion of the collectors, while the *Imam* continued to call for pledges of donations.

"Do you see now?" Saif stated. "Do you see what has become of religion? Worship has become a playground for such men with false piety, deceiving the people, playing to their ignorance and extorting their wealth. In truth, the people have fallen prey because they simply refuse to educate themselves and learn the true essences of faith, religion, and worship. They set aside prayer to collect coin, to place material desires before divine ordinance, an act that is purely blasphemous in and of itself."

He shook his head in disbelief, and Mukhtar slowly began to understand. These were the true enemies of Faith. The ignorant advocates of Azazil. The devil did not need to wage open war when such men were already doing his work for him.

"Come away, Mukhtar!" Saif stood up swiftly, and Mukhtar looked up at his silhouette against the scorching sun. "I cannot supplicate behind such men, for my thoughts will continue to be distracted by their deception."

Mukhtar followed him past the last few rows, and they left the *Masjid* in haste.

"We should never have come here!" Saif muttered angrily.

"What now?" Mukhtar's voice gave a slight tremble of uncertainty.

"Do not be disheartened, brother," Saif assured him. "We will find no aid here. I was wrong to assume it. That man will extort every last grain from you before awarding you any guidance, which in itself will be hollow and meaningless. Come, brother. We will hasten to *Masjid Nur*. If we are quick, we will not have missed prayers."

Masjid Nur was a much smaller and simpler establishment of mud, brick, and wood, designed with traditional Khalidan architecture. It had a much smaller dome, whitewashed, and boasted only a single short minaret without any elegant ornamentation.

The *Imam's* sermon was simple but rich in both wisdom and knowledge. There was no talk of war, no incitement to violence. There were no pleas or pledges for donations, nor false vows and profound promises to heaven. Those who wished to give, did so with discretion, strengthening their bond with their Creator in true faith and confidence. Mukhtar and Saif joined the small mass of devotees prepared to stand in prayer on simple sisal mats laid inside and outside the *Masjid*. They followed the *Imam's* every calling, and made their supplications as the masses did. After the prayers, as the crowd began to thin, Saif and Mukhtar lingered close by, waiting patiently for the *Imam*.

"I am still confused," Mukhtar said to him.

"About what?"

"About what you said earlier," Mukhtar said. "About the falseness with which some religious leaders are extorting the people."

"I know," Saif nodded slowly. "It is so subtly and cleverly executed, it is almost impossible to discern their treachery. This has always been religion's most dangerous plague. Over time, people begin to stray from the truth, unable to distinguish the fine line between right and wrong. Between the permissible and the forbidden. People begin to question divine ruling. Fueled by the devil's whispers, they begin to dispute the sacred messages and oaths sent to them through countless messengers." He kicked a pebble and watched it roll away in the dirt, upsetting small clouds of dust in its path. "They begin to fabricate their own versions of faith, removing what they deem to be too cumbersome to follow and instating their own concoctions to suit their own conveniences of faith. Slowly but surely, they deviate away from faith, and the devil celebrates his achievement of leading mankind astray."

"But these are learned men!" Mukhtar asserted. "How can they be clearly versed in the ways of faith, and yet they choose to lead the people away?"

Saif gave a small chuckle. "After these men read and memorize everything they can from scrolls and scriptures, they simply forget the fundamentals and deeper wisdoms of true faith. They forget why they pursue this divine knowledge. They allow themselves to become elevated, filled with the arrogance that they *know* and others do not. They proclaim themselves as men of higher statures and they preach to the people— *'We are more knowledgeable, so follow what we say without question, or else seal your dooms to hellfire'*— and the people follow ignorantly. Such apostates are worse than sorcerers." He shook his head sadly. "Alas, very few men of true faith still remain, whom we can call upon to guide and educate us."

Mukhtar gazed at the doors of *Masjid Nur*, as the last of the devotees tied their sandals and made their ways back to their places of work. "From what you are saying, I would almost sooner ask a sorcerer about this Jinn, than trust one of those *Highly Knowledgeable Imams* and *Sufis*," he said bitterly.

To his utter surprise, Saif smacked his own forehead and gave a small yelp. Mukhtar gave him a very curious look. Saif's strangeness since that morning continued to intrigue him.

"What is it now?" he enquired.

"Jalil Ruwaid," Saif gasped. "Why did I not think of it before? Many know him as Sheikh Ruwaid."

"And what of him?"

"He has led today's prayers!"

"You sound very excited."

"Have you not heard of Sheikh Ruwaid?" Saif almost jumped with joy. "They say he is gifted with curing those ailed by the Jinn. He is known to be both wise and knowledgeable. Come, and let us pray we are not mistaken by trusting a false preacher."

NINETEEN

SHEIKH RUWAID

They waited until the masses had cleared away, and they crossed the street to a much smaller building that shared a wall with the *Masjid*. Saif knocked on the wooden door. An elderly man greeted them with a smile that was gentle, calm and composed, impressing them with a profound personality embedded with a generation of spirituality and knowledge.

"Salaam, Sheikh Ruwaid," Saif held out his hand.

"Salaam to you as well," Sheikh Ruwaid received the greeting with both his hands. His voice was slightly gruff with a deep and controlled resonance.

"I apologize for bothering you," Saif continued, "but my friend is troubled, and he seeks aid."

"Aid?" Sheikh Ruwaid shook Mukhtar's hand. "If it is lodging you seek, I can allow you to stay at the *Masjid* for a few days, but you must clear away during prayer times. Always maintain peace and purity in the house of God, and when food is served, you must show empathy for those with greater need."

Mukhtar held up a respectful hand and inclined his head to acknowledge Sheikh Ruwaid's kind gesture. "My needs are far more demanding."

Sheikh Ruwaid looked mildly confused.

"He is plagued by the mischief of the Unseen," Saif explained.

Sheikh Ruwaid raised his eyebrows. "You must come in then. Tell me everything!"

His hair was curly and silvery-gray, just like his beard. His black, hooded eyes had a distinct sparkle. Dark wrinkly skin and a stooping posture betrayed his age. His white *thaub*, cleaner than Mukhtar's by several shades, fluttered behind him as he led them into the living room with a strong stride.

"Sit, please," Sheikh Ruwaid gestured to the cushions in the room. "We will begin shortly."

He stood by the archway of the room, and called to someone. "Muneeb! Muneeb?" A young boy, about twelve years of age, appeared by his side.

"Ask your *Ummi* to bring some fruit," he told the boy. "We have guests."

Muneeb ran off, and Sheikh Ruwaid turned his attention to Mukhtar and Saif.

"Noble Sheikh, we do not wish to bring you trouble," Saif said apologetically, with regards to Muneeb bringing them refreshments.

"A guest is a gift from God," Sheikh Ruwaid smiled. "And a gift from God is not 'trouble'. Although, certain guests do tend to become troublesome," he added as an afterthought. "So tell me, what sort of trouble have you brought with you?"

Mukhtar could not help but smile. Barely moments ago, he was tense and nervous. Now he became calm and composed.

"Go on, son," Sheikh Ruwaid gave him an encouraging nod. "I do not claim to be all-knowing, for that power resides only with my Creator. But I will try and help you to the best of my abilities."

Mukhtar acknowledged his statement with a brief nod, cleared his throat and sat upright. Narrating his tale was a difficult affair, as he tried to filter out only the relevant pieces, taking care not to reveal anything about his previous night's experiences nor his journey through Arammoria with Ghasif and Rauf. There was no need to involve others in matters they were not concerned with. Sheikh Ruwaid's attention was fully drawn to him, and he occasionally gasped and recited a string of supplications when the tale took a turn for the dark.

When he was done, Sheikh Ruwaid nodded thoughtfully and pondered for a long, silent moment, his thoughts only disrupted when Muneeb appeared with a tray of grapes, sliced oranges, and a pitcher of *Sherbet*.

"Muneeb," Sheikh Ruwaid spoke calmly and politely, "go inside and stay with your Ummi. Do not come back here, understood?"

Muneeb nodded and left.

"He is my grandson," Sheikh Ruwaid explained. "His father

is on a trade venture to Hanan-Sula, and so he and his mother, my youngest daughter, are living with me for a few days. I would rather he not be here to witness this."

"Witness what?" Mukhtar asked sharply.

"Do not be fearful, son," Sheikh Ruwaid assured him. "Fear is the devil's advocate, and the very weakness that the Jinn love to manipulate. By your consent, I will subject you to a series of trials, to better understand the true nature of this being."

Mukhtar gave Saif a sideways glance, who returned a reassuring nod.

"Now, sit still before me," Sheikh Ruwaid filled a cup with water and placed it between them. "Remember, the Jinn will fear you only if you remain unafraid. Allow me to supplicate upon you, and have faith in your Creator that this obstacle in your life will be removed."

He began reciting rapidly, loud enough for them to hear. Mukhtar sat cross-legged, silently wondering whether Sheikh Ruwaid would pray for him until the Jinn became frustrated and fled. He turned Mika'il's ring on his finger, nervously rubbing the obsidian stone with a sweaty finger. For some reason, he was becoming uneasy, even though nothing in that room warranted any unrest. He thought he felt the Amulet, hanging from the chain around his neck, give a subtle throb against his chest, and he shuddered.

Concealed under his sleeve, he began to fidget with the mechanism on his wrist, toying with it, allowing the dagger to escape, stalling it just before it did. It felt as if it were a part of him now, and wondered if at all he would ever relinquish it. He frowned at his own strangeness.

Gradually, Sheikh Ruwaid's recitation began to irritate him like the annoying buzz of an irksome fly. In an attempt to keep his mind occupied, he looked around the *Imam's* humble abode. Potted plants brightened all four corners with their rich green foliage, and the rest of the room was lined with simple cushions of a brown shade, breaking the white of the plastered walls. He sat there, for what felt like hours, until he began feeling very drowsy. All he longed to do was to lie down and shut his eyes.

"Focus on me now," Sheikh Ruwaid spoke between his recitations, in a voice that seemed to come from far away. "Keep your eyes on me."

"So... exhausted..." Mukhtar sighed, unaware of his own speech, "... so... tired...."

"I need you to remain alert for me," Sheikh Ruwaid urged him.

Mukhtar yawned loudly. "I cannot!" he gasped. "I feel so tired!"

"Mukhtar!"

Mukhtar slowly shut his eyes, and Sheikh Ruwaid splashed water on his face, snapping him awake. He opened his eyes only to shut them again. Saif held him upright, and was speaking in his ear, but he could not understand anything. His head felt heavy, and at the same time felt light, like he was intoxicated. He giggled, somehow remembering that he did not even know what intoxication felt like. The room began to spin and sway, and he smiled to himself as though he was thoroughly enjoying this, but at the same time, he was not.

"Who am I speaking to?" Sheikh Ruwaid asked after he finished reciting.

Mukhtar made several blubbering and spluttering sounds, mingled with a handful of rude words.

"What is your name?" Sheikh Ruwaid asked again.

Mukhtar started rocking back and forth, singing an irregular, tuneless hymn under his breath. "My name is irrelevant," he then said. "What is *your* name?"

"Who are you?" Sheikh Ruwaid asked. "Where have you come from?"

"And why should I tell *you?*" Mukhtar smirked.

"There is no greater power than His. He is the One, who has created man from a clot of blood, and the Jinn from smokeless fire!" Sheikh Ruwaid recited. "By the command of the Almighty God, *tell* me your name!"

"*Who has created man from a clot of blood and Jinn from smokeless fire,*" Mukhtar mocked, cackling loudly and shamelessly. "Your piety can only take you so far!"

"I will use every weapon in my arsenal to send you back beyond the veil!" He splashed more water on Mukhtar's face, who cackled even louder.

"You have no *power!*" Mukhtar hissed, grinning menacingly. "You are but a simple *human!*"

"Not a *Ghul* or a *Sila*," Sheikh Ruwaid's eyes narrowed.

"Try again, old man!" Mukhtar scoffed brazenly.

"Bring that clay pot, and light some *Oudh*," Sheikh Ruwaid instructed Saif. "There is some sandalwood and incense in the tin beside it. Throw that into the fire as well."

Saif hastened, crossing the room to where Sheikh Ruwaid pointed, while Mukhtar continued to hum the same strange irregular tune, pausing at random intervals to clap his hands and pout his lips.

"What is happening to him?" Saif sounded frightful.

"We are no longer dealing with Mukhtar," Sheikh Ruwaid said in a stern voice. "Hurry with the *Oudh!*"

Mukhtar cackled. "Burn your incenses then! Do your worst!"

It took a few moments to light the coal, and when it was blazing, he fed it with a generous helping of *Oudh,* filling the room with its scented smoke.

"You are of a smokeless flame," Sheikh Ruwaid said, as calmly as though giving a lecture on the subject. "An entity of poison!" He brought the clay pot forward. "Breathe into fragrances of purity!"

Mukhtar was engulfed by the scented white smoke. "No!" he moaned in pain, shielding his eyes and waving his arms about in a frenzy. *"Remove this thing!"* he shrieked.

"A *Ma'arid...*" Sheikh Ruwaid smiled, "...interesting..." and Mukhtar was almost overcome with an urge to hit him, to wipe the smirk off his face, but the heat and fumes of the *Oudh* were so intensifying, he could not muster the effort.

"You are cruel!" Mukhtar screamed at him.

"You have not yet known my cruelty," Sheikh Ruwaid was no longer smiling. "Speak now!"

"I yield!" Mukhtar screamed, holding his hands up in defeat. "I yield!"

Sheikh Ruwaid drew back the pot, and placed it on the floor

beside him. Mukhtar eyed it, biting his lip so fiercely it began to bleed.

"What is your name?" Sheikh Ruwaid asked again.

Mukhtar's eyes darted back and forth, suspiciously shifting between Sheikh Ruwaid and the blazing coals. "Speak the truth, and I will stay the *Oudh*. Lie and suffer its wrath!"

"Talia!" Mukhtar mumbled. "My name is Talia!"

"And what are you?" Sheikh Ruwaid asked.

"Nothing of significance! A lowly *Ghul* from the barren Plains of Zarzara!"

"A liar is what you are!" Sheikh Ruwaid exclaimed, bringing the clay pot closer to Mukhtar, who began to whimper. "Speak! Or suffer!"

"Adva!" Mukhtar screamed. "My name is Adva!"

"Telling the truth now?"

"I swear!"

"Swear by your Creator!"

"I have no creator!"

"No creator? Name your father and your mother!"

"I have no memory of those who bore me as a child!"

Sheikh Ruwaid's nostrils flared. "Still telling lies, I see!"

The pain came again.

"Perhaps some more persuasion?"

And again. Agonizing and burning into her bones.

"It is the truth!" Adva screamed. *"I swear it!"*

Sheikh Ruwaid frowned. Adva twisted and turned in boundless torment. "Why have you taken over this person?"

"Not— possessed!" Adva spoke in a strained and horrendous

voice. "Not— yet!"

"And you intend to?"

Despite her shortened breath and pained expression, Adva grinned maliciously. "In time…"

"Why?"

"To serve a higher purpose. To free my kin!"

"You believe that this man has imprisoned your family?"

"Do you *mock me*, holy man?" Adva growled.

Sheikh Ruwaid's lips curled. "No, I do not mock. I only find it difficult to believe that a Jinn has been imprisoned by a human."

Adva laughed eerily. "You are so blind! So foolish! I know that which you do not. I know what you keep secret, *holy man*."

"Are you insulting me?" Sheikh Ruwaid pushed the sizzling *Oudh* closer.

"You are hurting me…" Adva sobbed pathetically, and then began humming, swinging Mukhtar's head in a strange fashion. Then she began to growl and glare at Sheikh Ruwaid, with deep loathing. "You are a vile creature!" She spat on his face.

Sheikh Ruwaid continued to smile calmly, and after wiping his face with his sleeve, he picked up the clay pot with burning *Oudh*, and brandished it before her. The scream was terrible, torturous, and agonizing with a culminating decibel. Sheikh Ruwaid and Saif, however, remained unscathed.

"You are blinded by your scriptures!" Adva screeched. "Your *faiths* and your *beliefs!* You know nothing but ignorance! The prophecy is as clear as morning dew. It is inevitable. The Jinn will rise to a power unlike any other witnessed on this earth. We will claim back the lands that were once ours before your creation. We will claim back our birthright!"

"That is an interesting speech, but it still does not explain why you are troubling this person. Why are you here? Where have you come from? Who sent you?"

"The boy is stubborn and uninviting, but his time draws close, and soon I will have him begging on his knees. He will succumb to his inner emotions, his weakness of empathy. He will succumb, and I will conquer."

"Name the sorcerer who commands you!"

"The prophecy does not lie," Adva ignored him. "He will rise— his time comes soon— I have seen *him*, the Hand of Azazil, the Unforgiven— arisen with scars— shall be made whole again— he will gather his armies, he will claim the Throne of *Ithm*— be warned, sons of Adam, your time draws to an end— he *will* wage his war!"

Adva laughed, but her laughter was irregularly coming and going. Her voice grew softer, and she uttered from an unknown language, and by the time it turned into a bare whisper, she had shut her eyes and fallen asleep. Sheikh Ruwaid splashed more water, and she grunted.

"Adva!" he called. *"Adva!"*

She grunted again. "Who is this Adva? And why is my face wet?"

Mukhtar was now awake. He wiped his face on his sleeve and tasted blood.

"Why is my face wet?" he asked again. "Why is my lip bleeding?"

"Did she flee?" Saif glanced about the room and then leaned

forward, eyeing Mukhtar quizzically.

"Did *who* flee?" Mukhtar leaned away from him with a curious look.

"The Jinn— *Adva*— she spoke *through* you!"

Mukhtar touched his bleeding lip and flinched.

"Do you not remember?" Saif gestured wildly.

"He will have no memory of it," Sheikh Ruwaid told him. "In order to speak to it, I forced the Jinn into an indefinite state of possession. Mukhtar was, in all sense, unconscious to the events, as is always the case when a Jinn possesses a human."

Mukhtar dried himself, while Saif and Sheikh Ruwaid explained what had happened. "Divine words will always incite fear in the wicked, and in such a state of dismay, the Jinn divulged some, if not all. Do not be afraid, Mukhtar," Sheikh Ruwaid eyed him closely.

"I am not," Mukhtar replied hastily.

"But you are," Sheikh Ruwaid imposed. "It is only natural. Being plagued by the Unseen is not a burden so easily endured."

"Has it been dispelled?" Saif asked.

Sheikh Ruwaid shook his head. "It appears to be far more convoluted than what I have encountered in my experiences. Alas, the Jinn are malicious, mischievous, and deceitful. They have roamed this earth before us, and were driven into the Unseen Veil because their corruption knew no bounds."

He plucked a few grapes from the bunch in the plate before them and urged Mukhtar and Saif to join him. Saif declined respectfully but Mukhtar helped himself to several cupfuls of the refreshing *Sherbet,* feeling incredibly dehydrated.

Sheikh Ruwaid

"It is an endless battle to dispel a Jinn," Sheikh Ruwaid went on, "and the stronger its hold, the more difficult the fight. However, as far I can tell, it is *trying* to possess you, but something is holding it back. An ethereal barrier, or some complex form of sorcery or incantation. It is difficult to say. Such things are, as sorcery is known to be, occult and unseen."

"*Curse* the sorcerer who has brought this misfortune upon Mukhtar," Saif remarked.

"Oh, pray that is not the case," Sheikh Ruwaid's tone became grim.

"Why is that?" Mukhtar frowned.

"The stronger the Jinn, the more dominant and vile the sorcerer," Sheikh Ruwaid said. "Sorcery is a sin so evil, the Almighty has declared hellfire upon its practitioners. Be wary of those who blow into knots and swear allegiance to the darkness, for theirs is sin and in it they shall abide."

Mukhtar struggled to suppress a shudder. Who could be so vile as to have done such wickedness upon him? Or was it otherwise? No vile sorcerer, no terrible curse... just fate?

"What of this prophecy?" Saif asked Sheikh Ruwaid.

"The world is riddled with falsified prophecies and presages," Sheikh Ruwaid replied with a nonchalant tone. "Soothsayers and fortunetellers always employ the powers of Jinn to make predictions of what may come to pass, and the Jinn have been known to fabricate their own tales to satisfy ignorant minds. However, the Jinn have a world of their own. They hold their own beliefs and convictions, which may be true to *them*, but in the world of man, prophecies are how the Jinn are known to spread lies and deceit."

Saif blinked. "But if such a claim is made with regard to our own lives, should we still be taking it lightly?"

"Lightly?" Sheikh Ruwaid gazed at him thoughtfully. "No. With grave caution. Years back, during the Great War, thousands of sorcerers were captured in Uduff, Din-Galad, and Ninya. They were subjected to torture, interrogated and forced to divulge what they knew about the Dark Prince. None had ever seen or spoken to the Dark Prince, but they all admitted to submitting to a Jinn of his picking. I know this, because I was one of the few who had been tasked by King Azhar Babak to lead the interrogations. I spoke to countless Jinn, who— after their contracts with the sorcerers had been nullified— chose to possess them. I would be lying if I said that none of the Jinn spoke any different than what we heard today. There may be some truth in this prophecy, or no truth whatsoever. No man has ever found this Throne of *Ithm*, nor the Hand of Azazil."

Saif's eyes were wide with awe and filled with interest. "These sound like tales of myth and fantasy. There is no such recollection in any script I have read, and I have read more than many."

"As have I, young Saif," Sheikh Ruwaid acknowledged. "But not all script is from the world of man. There is knowledge in the world of Jinn also, and there are many who would relentlessly pursue that knowledge, no matter the detriment. I, however, hold the belief that if such knowledge was meant for us, it would not be hidden. There is a *reason* why our worlds are disunited by a veil. The Realm of the Unseen is not meant for mankind, as is decreed by He who created both."

Mukhtar was not listening to them. His thoughts had strayed to the formidable blackened walls, the tall towering citadels, parapets swarming with archers, and the eerie orange glows in and around the gigantic fortress. He shut his eyes and re-imagined the hooded men who hunted him, and the symbol branded on their leader's arm.

There truly were others who sought what was beyond the Veil. Like the hooded men in Arammoria. Like Ussam Bashiri. Like Yusri Abdi. Like his own father and grandfather. The Amulet, the Book, the Keystone, and everything else they had discovered in the cabin and the study were evidence of it. Sheikh Ruwaid did not know this, but Adva had a greater purpose than a mere magician's whim. He was not certain of her motives, but he was convinced that she was not sent by any vile sorcerer. She was there by choice. She was there because of what his father had done, and what his grandfather had done before him.

"What else did the Jinn say?" he pressed, desperate for more information.

TWENTY

THE EAVESDROPPER

Demons and Jinn. Amulets and Keystones. Strange books and letters to a man presumed to be dead. Mukhtar was still unable to wrap his mind around what they had found in Harun's study, and what he had just learned from Sheikh Ruwaid filled his head to a point where he wanted to scream.

After they left the *Imam's* home, Saif pressed Mukhtar for every detail, and despite his hesitation, the matter was discussed at great length. Having reconciled with Saif, Mukhtar eventually decided to divulge at least part of the truth, but even then, he could not hold back the guilt and reluctance. It was not that Saif could not be trusted, but Mukhtar was slowly beginning to realize how bloody and destructive the path ahead lay. He had already lost one friend to a bitter discord, and another to a terrible fate.

"A tale of fantasy," Saif shook his head disbelievingly. "I would have called you *mad*, had I not heard the Jinn speak."

Mukhtar gave him an appreciative smile. Saif had done what Adil had failed to do.

"This... *prophecy*..." Saif said thoughtfully, "is deeply concerning."

"It is indeed," Mukhtar said. "Ghasif found a book which spoke of a *Throne of Ithm*. He who claims it, is named the Hand of Azazil."

"That is what the Jinn said!" Saif gasped. "Has it been claimed?"

Mukhtar gave him a dark look. "The fortress of Arammoria is not in ruin, nor as abandoned as we have been led to believe. Something festers there, something powerful and evil."

The sun was slowly approaching the western horizon, and the mud structures of Khalidah cast long shadows on the city streets, while the populous wound their day ahead of the scheduled curfew.

"This bodes ill, Mukhtar," Saif sounded panicky. "We *must* tell *someone!*"

"Who?" Mukhtar nearly laughed. "From guards to viziers, our leaders are either too corrupt or too arrogant to listen."

"Make peace with Adil," Saif suggested. "We can convince him to speak with his father."

"Adil will never listen!" Mukhtar scoffed. "Besides, what makes you think General Babak will believe us? You said so yourself, it sounds like a tale of fantasy."

"But we must *try!*" Saif argued. "There must be a way we can convince him."

"Adil scorned me!" Mukhtar protested. "Betrayed me! How can I trust him?"

"Mukhtar, when will you abandon this resentment?" Saif pleaded. "Do you not see? You are succumbing to the very whispers of the devil!"

"Is he not doing the same?"

"I know you, Mukhtar," Saif said. "I know you both. He despises this enmity!"

"Then *he* should seek reconciliation!" Mukhtar asserted. "As well as forgiveness for his foolishness!"

"Seeking forgiveness does not belittle anyone," Saif stated.

"Good!" Mukhtar commented. "We would not want *His Royal Highness*, Adil Babak, to *belittle* himself!"

Saif threw his hands up in frustration.

Mukhtar could not blame him for trying, but he did not know everything. He did not know about Ghulam, nor did he know that Adil sat in the company of Thamir and Laban Varda. "The enemy has infiltrated Immorkaan, Saif. We cannot trust *anyone!*"

"We can trust Sheikh Ruwaid."

"Perhaps. But you must speak to *no one* about this!" Mukhtar said firmly. "Do not despair. We will find a way. I must return home and rest my eyes. We will speak again, soon."

They parted along the way, and Mukhtar returned home with a throbbing head. When he entered, it was to find Zaki tending to his horse, Bisrah, in the courtyard. The black steed had occupied most of the courtyard and now called it home. Unwilling to take the risk of someone identifying his horse, Zaki had chosen to keep him at home. However, Mukhtar secretly suspected it was because Zaki was unable to afford the stables' charges, and was too lazy to work for it. He had already declared it several times, that a Red-Guard was not a laborer, even though Mukhtar constantly reminded him that he was no longer a Red-Guard.

Bisrah gave a loud snort and dipped his mouth into the pot of water Zaki had kept before him.

"How much longer will you keep him here?" Mukhtar asked aloud, and Zaki looked up sharply. "Ummi will have him removed eventually."

"Mukhtar!" Zaki hissed with a glance over his shoulder, making sure their mother was not about. "Where have you *been?*"

"With Saif," Mukhtar shrugged. "We went to the *Masjid* for prayers, and you will not *believe—*"

"Ummi is asleep!" Zaki interrupted with urgency in his voice. "I must speak with you. Come!"

Puzzled, Mukhtar followed his brother up the stairs to his own room, and shut the door behind them.

"What is the matter?" he opened the window to welcome the late afternoon breeze. Across the alley was the open window of Misbah's room. No shrieks or screams came through. Perhaps no one was home.

"Where have you *been?*" Zaki's voice was stern.

"I *told* you!" Mukhtar scanned the deserted alley below, and then up at the clear sky. "With Saif. We went to the *Masjid* for prayers. What is the matter, Zaki?"

"Ghulam is the matter!"

Mukhtar turned sharply, shoulders tensed. "What do you

mean?"

"We have not spoken since we left the mansion," Zaki stated. "What did Ghulam reveal? What did you find?"

Mukhtar sighed deeply. "A parchment with the names of mercenaries and slave traders. I used it to bargain safe passage from the mansion. Ghulam seemed to believe he was doing good. He urged me to search for the Keystone."

"What else?" Zaki pressed. "Did he reveal their locations? Did he reveal any names?"

Mukhtar shook his head. "He died."

Zaki eyed him and asked, "What of the other two?"

"You mean Ghasif and Rauf?" Mukhtar almost laughed. "They returned to the cabin, I believe."

"To converse about us," Zaki commented.

"Undoubtedly," Mukhtar agreed. "I question their motives."

"I question their leader," Zaki said.

"As do I," Mukhtar said. "Ma'alim continues to elude us. Perhaps he will reveal himself, now that Ghulam is dead. Ghasif will undoubtedly inform him."

Zaki nodded. "Keep them on a short leash," he said. "We may yet have use of them."

Mukhtar glanced at Zaki and said, "You have never spoken of your missions regarding the Assassins."

"Are you asking, or *saying*?"

"I am *asking*, you fool!" Mukhtar threw his pillow at him.

Zaki dodged the pillow and sat on the only stool Mukhtar had in his room. He took a deep breath, gazing at the wall before him, collecting his thoughts. "You remember Rafi Kataan?"

"The ink-maker from Aghara?" Mukhtar gazed at him curiously. "Abha's friend?"

"The very same," Zaki nodded. "He came to Aztalaan to marry his son to General Abidan's eldest daughter."

"Did you merit an invitation?"

"I would have perhaps," Zaki grinned. "But the wedding did not arrive. Two days after they agreed on the date, Rafi and his son woke to a pair of daggers embedded into their bedposts. The Assassins' way of warning them against going any further with the marriage."

Mukhtar raised his eyebrows.

"They were startled at first," Zaki went on, "accusing Abidan of some treachery. Abidan managed to convince them that *he* was not behind it, that there were others who sought to uproot his governance of Aztalaan and the Wall. He urged them to have faith and courage, that his enemies were only envious of his power, and that he would do whatever it took to bring them to justice."

"Sounds like he knew what he was doing," Mukhtar commented. "Were the culprits caught?"

"Barely a fortnight after," Zaki continued, "while he was announcing his son's betrothal to the masses, Rafi Kataan was assassinated in broad daylight."

Mukhtar gave a small gasp.

Zaki nodded grimly. "He had a silver throwing-knife in his throat," he said, "his son had an arrow in his chest, and all five of his personal guard were slain before a crowd of several hundred people in Aztalaan's largest market square. Witnesses reported a white-robed, turbaned and veiled assailant, who miraculously escaped by blending in with a procession of monks from a nearby monastery. Abidan was furious. He called together those he could trust, named me Captain, and gave us the mission to track down those responsible."

"Did you ever find them?" Mukhtar asked.

Zaki shook his head. "Elusive creatures!"

"So, in a fight between you and Ghasif, who would emerge the victor?" Mukhtar mocked.

Zaki threw him a scathing look, but did not respond to his question. "The Assassins do not honor the rules of engagement. They work in the shadows. Their existence has been described to the likeness of the Jinn. Ussam's tactics are infamous but effective. He has used a combination of stealth and agility with intoxicating herbs and sorcery to strengthen himself and his army. There is a reason why he has evaded siege for two decades. When Azhar was crowned King, he used Ussam to eradicate the few who opposed him."

"And when he was no longer needed…"

"Azhar declared him an enemy of the Empire," Zaki concluded. "I am surprised to see Immorkaan has not yet realized Ussam's ploy."

"What do you mean?" Mukhtar asked. "Perhaps they already have. Or perhaps they too have fallen prey to his deceit."

"Perhaps," Zaki nodded again. "Does it not strike you as odd, though? That despite all what has happened, Immorkaan's only response has been to ban any nightly activity?"

"The taverns and brothels continue to remain open," Mukhtar stated.

"To serve disloyal and unjust guards, yes," Zaki nodded impatiently. "It has been several days since the deaths of Ghadan and Haim. Immorkaan should have learned their true natures by now. They should have known that these men were serving Ghulam, and traced his allegiances to Ussam."

"In short, they should have known the Assassins are plotting to uproot the King's rule," Mukhtar added.

"Yes!" Zaki threw his arm forward, as though commending Mukhtar for finally being able to follow his thought.

"This does not make sense," Mukhtar stared at the wall. "Ma'alim approved our mission to kill Ghulam. The butcher and the guard seemed to think he had outlived his usefulness. Nabiha wanted him dead for her own personal gain. Judging by his final words, he believed to be serving a righteous cause."

"Do you think he served more than one master?" Zaki asked.

Mukhtar shrugged. "The speaker at the *Souk* accused Aarguf Babak of employing Ghulam. Do you think Adil's father might be plotting to overthrow the King? Mika'il said that much remained to be disputed between the brothers. Azhar did strip Aarguf of his power as Sultan, reducing him to a mere General. He would have more than enough motive to plot against him."

"I doubt that," Zaki said dismissively. "General Abidan has never spoken out against either of his brothers, nor has he ever declared any personal dispute."

"Perhaps he does not even know," Mukhtar suggested. "Everything has remained very obscure thus far. Aarguf could have been using Ghulam's influence and authority to strengthen his cause secretly until he is ready to mass an attack."

Zaki shook his head in discord. "Ghulam was bound to serve the General of the Royal Army by law. No... there must be another master. Another ploy or plot. Another obscurity we have yet to uncover. We must tread carefully, brother. Too much has happened and a lot more is still happening. It would be ultimately disastrous if we are caught flat-footed."

Mukhtar nodded grimly. It seemed very strange to him. Ghulam could not have lied, unless he was intentionally misleading them with his dying breath. And yet, the existence of the Keystone seemed undeniable. Haim's description, and the seal they found in Harun's study, were inseparable.

"Where is the letter?" he asked.

"Abha's letter? I have it here," Zaki removed the parchment. "It is strange that the man it is addressed to, is the same man you presumed to have died an infant."

"Strange indeed," Mukhtar painfully came to terms with what seemed to be an inevitable truth, but he made sure to keep his emotions concealed from his brother. "Unless Abha spread a rumor to conceal his existence from Ummi."

"It is even stranger that we have an uncle we did not know of," Zaki stated. "If he still lives. Abha speaks very highly of him in his journal."

"If he is still alive, then he is the only other person who knows about the Amulets, the Keystone, *and* the Book," Mukhtar said.

"And the journal," Zaki added. "You must read it, Mukhtar. There is so much of his life contained within those pages."

Mukhtar shook his head. "I do not wish to unearth my emotions at such a time. I have lived without knowledge of it and what it contains for all these years. Abha obviously wanted it to be a secret from all of us. I would rather it remain that way."

Zaki sighed heavily. "Very well," he said. "Be it your choice. Here," he showed Mukhtar their father's letter to Siyaad, "look at this."

"The mark of the Keystone," Mukhtar glanced at the symbol etched into the lower right corner of the parchment, beside his father's name; two swords, crisscrossing each other.

"We will need to journey to Uduff as soon as we are able," Zaki sounded distant and slightly nervous. He was pacing back forth, rather frantically.

"Has something happened that I am unaware of?" Mukhtar followed his pacing with narrowed eyes.

Frustrated, Zaki threw his hands in the air. *"Nothing* has happened! Unlike his dead accomplices, Ghulam's death has not even been announced. I have spent the day lingering about the *Souk As-Silaah*. No heightened security, not even a curious whisper."

"Did you anticipate one?"

"Naturally!" Zaki exerted. "Did you not?"

Mukhtar shook his head and stared at the cracks in the ceiling, focusing on a particular crevice on the whitewashed plaster. A spider's legs peered through, taking a feel for the world outside its home, and then disappeared within.

"Your confidence amazes me," Zaki stopped and stared at him.

"Your lack of faith in it, is questionable," Mukhtar responded.

"How did you really escape the aide?" Zaki asked simply. "You evaded me last night, you vanished all morning, and you haven't spoken a word of it since!"

"So why say it now?" Mukhtar replied without looking at him.

"Because the longer you keep it secret, the more suspicious it becomes," Zaki raised a dubious eyebrow.

Mukhtar gave him a sideways glance. "Have you lost your memory? I already told you what happened. She needed the parchment, and I used it to bargain our escape."

"As simple as that?"

Mukhtar frowned. "What sort of strange deception were you expecting from her? She underestimated us, and paid the price. She will think twice before she ever does so again."

"Do not mock me, Mukhtar!" Zaki warned.

"I am not," Mukhtar replied impassively.

"What are you hiding from me?" Zaki's tone became threatening, and Mukhtar became wary.

"Her sister was enslaved by Ghulam's mercenaries," he decided to divulge a portion of the truth. "She was desperate, and I used it against her."

"I find that hard to believe," Zaki sounded sarcastic. "And you left her alive?"

"I had every temptation to slit her throat," Mukhtar replied.

"So why didn't you?" Zaki sneered.

"I admire *your* confidence, brother!" Mukhtar said harshly. "Did you perhaps believe that we would leave the mansion by some other means? You are only upset because I barred you from taking your *revenge* on the fat man! And need I declare it to my own brother that I am not a cold-hearted assassin!"

"They are witnesses!" Zaki's nostrils flared. "What would it take for them to betray us?"

"They haven't!"

"Not yet!"

Mukhtar sat upright and glared at him. "*You* made the mistake, Zaki!" he remarked. "You should never have involved her. There were other ways of entering the mansion. I saw an opportunity to rectify your error, and I took it. We are free. Her mouth is shut. Leave it be!"

Zaki looked as if he wanted to throw something heavy at Mukhtar. It took a while before he calmed himself. Finally, he gave a deep sigh, "I was rash," he sounded apologetic. "It was a foolish mistake. She *knew* from the beginning. We were baited into her ploy, and I should have foreseen it!"

"Leave it be, brother," Mukhtar reassured him. "She is a devious woman!"

Zaki paused, eyeing his brother ambiguously. Mukhtar waited patiently, bracing himself for another lengthy and cumbersome argument, for which he truly did not have any energy remaining. He had not slept at all the previous night, and the short hours he had gained from shutting his eyes on Saif's mattress, had not awarded him any rest.

Zaki seemed to sense his brother's exhaustion, for he decided not to further the matter. "We will need to speak with Ghasif and Rauf again," he said instead.

"Concerning what?" Mukhtar raised his head slightly.

"The other targets. Yusri Abdi, Nizaam ibn Jalal, Rasha Bint Sumrah, and lest we forget, Thamir Ar-Rushdi."

"Can we not just *sleep* tonight?" Mukhtar sighed wearily.

"The longer we wait, the stronger they become!" Zaki urged him. "You said so yourself!"

"I must rest, Zaki!" Mukhtar pleaded and shut his eyes.

Zaki gave him an impatient look. "You have until nightfall," he stated blatantly. "At midnight—"

He did not finish, and Mukhtar opened his eyes to a look of pure horror on his brother's face. "What is it?" he asked.

Zaki did not reply. He was staring out the open window with his mouth slightly ajar. Mukhtar turned his head and sat up, startled.

Gizwani was staring back at them through the open window of Misbah's room, with a steaming cup of a hot beverage in his hands.

The cup fell through his fingers, and he vanished.

PART THREE

THE QUARTERMASTER

TEN YEARS AGO.

His senses were tingling, troubling him such that he could not focus. His hands trembled uncontrollably. Beads of sweat formed on his forehead and chest, dampening his brown *thaub* to a darker shade. *What have I done?*

Harun could not believe himself. He couldn't believe his own foolishness. He wiped his brow with the sleeve of his *thaub* and glanced around, suddenly very afraid.

The blackness of his study engulfed him, but for the tiny flame of a burning candle atop his floor-desk. On the desk lay a lengthy piece of parchment, a letter he had received only recently. It was slightly tattered and stained, mostly by the smudges of his own sweaty fingers. Part of it read—

...consider these events with utmost care, and pair them to those that have taken place since the Veil was last pierced. I assure you, all five seals will reveal themselves.

Now, with regards to the knowledge of the Jinn, this is not something that we humans can so easily comprehend. The manner in which time and space, fold and manipulate in their world, is nothing like our physical plane. Believe me, brother, very few have ever been able to transcend their realm— it is no small feat for mankind.

However, if you were to study the points where our worlds collide, you will be able to follow a certain pattern, and this will provide you with the evidence of what has destroyed every major civilization in the ancient world, because...

The rest of the parchment was obscured by an open book, its pages emitting a pungent scent of rotting eggs. The stench hardly bothered him, for it was an odor he had grown accustomed to whenever he would summon a Jinn or delve into the book's ancient and unprecedented text. He had only just been studying the vile and filthy chapters (both literally and figuratively), and he discovered something he had unknowingly overlooked in the past. A sudden realization of the mistakes he had made nine years ago, crashed down upon him in a rocky avalanche. How *could* he have been so *foolish*?

Panicking would avail nothing. He calmed himself. The damage could still be contained if he played his part well. But it could not be done alone.

Who could truly be relied upon, to help him undo all the wrong that had been done? The Sheikh had only spun riddling phrases of good and evil, of sin and deed, of fate and destiny. His words may have been wise and profound, but they hardly abetted a concrete solution to his current obstacles. In his most recent correspondence, Siyaad stated that one of the three had certainly betrayed him. He was, however, very vague as to who he thought this deceiver may be, leaving Harun to make wild assumptions. Was it Ussam?

The man always had a certain demonic aura about him, cold and eerie. He lacked ambition, however, and seemed satisfied within the confines of his fortress. Who then, if not him? Laban?

Perhaps. As far back as Harun could recall, Laban was the man who introduced them to the world of the Unseen. Then again, if Laban really was ambitious, why did he not step up as King? Why allow Azhar to take power?

Which then left Azhar. Azhar had become the presumed leader of their secret Order. An Order that was supposed to have liberated the people, brought them freedom. But their lives were no different from the enslavement of The Dark Prince. Freedom was just an illusion. The laws and legislations, drafted and enforced by Azhar's Immorkaan, had done very little to empower the people, if at all. The only persons who seemed to have tasted any empowerment by his governance were his politicians and viziers, and the wealthy merchants who donated generously to keep such corrupt leaders in their pockets. How could Azhar have allowed this to happen? Corruption had spread over the lands like an incurable disease, and the system intended for good had become a living, breathing beast, unchecked, uncontrollable, and unbeatable.

Harun gave a deep sigh. Just then, the door swung open, and in the light of the hallway stood a young boy of eight, looking sullen and disgruntled.

"Abha!" he called gloomily. "Zaki refused to play with me, and also, he took my toys and refused to give them back!"

Harun hastily wiped the sweat off his brow, and attempted to put on a calm and relaxed look on his face. "Mukhtar," he tried not to sound harsh, "how many times have I told you not to interrupt me here?"

"Many times," Mukhtar mumbled, swinging his arms, staring at his feet, "but Zaki—"

"Where is your mother?"

"In the courtyard," Mukhtar replied.

"Why don't you go and tell her what Zaki did?" Harun stated. "Abha has work to do."

"But Ummi said to tell you!" Mukhtar argued.

Harun sighed again. "Did you speak with your brother?"

Mukhtar nodded.

"Did you ask him politely?"

Mukhtar nodded again.

"Why then does he refuse to play with you?"

"And refuses to return my toys!" Mukhtar added angrily.

Harun broke into a warm smile. "And refuses to return your toys," he echoed.

"Because he is a bully! And a thief!"

"Is that so?" Harun's smile grew broader. "And who was it that stole Zaki's marbles only a few days ago?"

Mukhtar answered too quickly, "I meant to return them!"

"But you promised not to take them," Harun said calmly, "and yet you still did— without permission."

"It was not—!"

"Mukhtar," Harun asserted. "Remember what I told you? In everything we do, what must we show?"

Mukhtar murmured something.

"What was that?" Harun cupped his ear with his hand.

"Honesty," Mukhtar said.

"And—?"

"Sincerity."

"Honesty and sincerity, Mukhtar," Harun said. "These two things—"

"—will never lead you astray, *I know!*" Mukhtar completed the sentence. He gazed at his father earnestly. Then…

"But he chased me away! He *never* wants to play with me! Even yesterday in the *Madrassa*, he told me to go away. He is mean!"

Harun's chuckle eventually escaped him. His son could hardly be concerned about philosophies at the moment. He knelt down before him and held him gently by the shoulders. "Listen to me, Mukhtar," he said suggestively. "Go to your Ummi and ask her if she needs any help. And when — *listen to me* – when I have finished my work, we will sit to eat, and speak openly. Agreed?"

"Yes— but—!"

"No more arguments, Mukhtar!" Harun increased the decibel in his voice by a tiny fraction. "Now go!"

As stubborn as his father, Mukhtar refused to move from the spot. His father's assurance, without any action, was not enough. Harun would have to make an added effort to assuage his son.

"Mika'il told me you carved something on a brick while he was repairing the furnace," he stated.

Mukhtar nodded.

"Where did you see that symbol?"

Mukhtar pointed at the floor desk, and Harun understood.

"When?" he asked.

"When you were gone to the palace," Mukhtar replied.

Harun thought back. It had been several days since he met Azhar Babak at the palace. "You entered my study without permission?"

Mukhtar fidgeted with his fingers and avoided his father's gaze. "I came to find you."

"And when you did not?"

"I sat at your desk, and pretended to work, like you," he admitted.

Harun's eyes narrowed. "That would explain why my ink-pot was left open to dry up."

"Forgive me, Abha," Mukhtar's expression was of guilt and contrite. "I did not mean to disobey."

Harun nodded softly, and gazed at his desk for a while before saying, "Interesting. Coincidental, perhaps," he gave a small shrug, "but… very interesting… Go now, Mukhtar. I must return to my work."

Mukhtar shuffled out of the door, looking no happier than when he had entered. Harun closed the door gently and locked it securely. As soon as the darkness of his study engulfed him, his heart felt heavy, and he shut his eyes.

His sons, his weaknesses, and his strengths.

Their greatest strength was to show him that there was always a way, and his youngest son had done just that. The consequence, however, was detrimental, but if he played his part well, it could be averted. He could not do this without bringing utter ruin upon them. *Have I not already?* He shook his head. *That* could be dealt with when the need arose. *This had* to be done, and it needed to be done right, in order to ameliorate the disarray constituted purely because of his own involvement in the first place.

He steeled his nerves and gathered his wits.

"Urduk," he called aloud.

A *Ghul,* taking the form of a mere shadow in dark, emerged from the far corner. "Master."

"You heard what my son said?"

"Yes, Master," came the grappling, rasping reply.

"This is more than a mere coincidence," Harun stated.

"Indeed," Urduk agreed.

"You know what you must do then," Harun instructed with urgency in his voice. "Go! With haste!"

The *Ghul* dissipated into the very shadows it had emerged from, and its presence was no more.

Harun gathered his thoughts once again, and stooped to pleat the moth-eaten rug on the stone floor, revealing two painted circles. Inside each circle was a five-pointed pentagram with strange, unearthly symbols around the edges. He stood inside one circle, making sure to remain within the lines. Even an inch out of its boundaries could prove disastrous.

He had been careless, once before, to lose his balance and stumble out of the circle, and he recalled the cataclysmic event that had taken place in the derelict crypt where he had found that foul book. He was thick in the midst of binding a Jinn who guarded the Book, when a bat flew at him, knocking him off balance, and in that instance, all the spells and incantations were broken. The barrier had been lifted.

Had it not been for Adva and the Amulet, Harun would have been dead before he hit the ground. Incidentally, this was the same Jinn he was about to summon.

Once he was ready, he began reciting a string of incantations under his breath, in a language that was not remotely related to any human tongue. The temperature in the room cooled drastically, until mist poured from his mouth when he breathed. There was a distinct whiff of rotting eggs, followed by a faint *pop* and a light puff of dark smoke.

The smoke had materialized from the very air around him, thickening and conforming to shape. Drawn from the darkest shadows of the room, it writhed and slithered with a life of its own. When the last remaining wisps cleared, there stood before him a pale-skinned entity with blank, milky eyes. Gold rings latticed both his ears, gleaming in the candlelight.

The Jinn was shirtless, its sculptured torso glistening like it had just stepped out of water. The lower half of its body would have been that of a mule, hairy and muscular, complete with hooves for feet. It was so tall, it had to stoop, glowering at Harun, who had to crane his neck to meet its lifeless eyes. The climate readjusted itself and became warmer, and no one but the occupants of the room knew what had happened.

"Ba'al."

"Master," the creature spoke in a deep, growling voice. "You summoned?"

Unlike Urduk, a mere *Ghul*, Ba'al was not an entity he could simply call and dismiss upon a mere whim. It was a far more powerful and demanding Jinn. Which is why a summoning ritual was imperative. It needed to be controlled and contained, to be commanded only at the utmost of dire need.

"I did," Harun replied. "I have a task for you."

"Indeed?" The creature eyed him. "Payment..." it hissed. "I demand payment, sorcerer, as you very well know."

"You *dare* raise your voice before me?" Harun snarled. "You *dare* demand from an Amulet Master? Need I teach you the meaning of servitude, slave?"

The Jinn wrinkled its inhuman nose in contempt and displeasure, but said nothing. Harun allowed several moments to pass in silence before continuing.

"Hear my words clearly," he said, maintaining a stern and firm tone, "for I have decided to release you after your task."

Perhaps that was payment enough. "I am listening," Ba'al grinned. Three sets of razor sharp, drooling teeth were enough to make even the toughest man cower for life.

"Wipe that smirk off your face!" Harun said harshly. "It churns my stomach!"

It heeded reluctantly. It was not afraid of Harun. It feared the man's retribution. The weapons he possessed.

Harun sensed its apprehension. "They are hidden," he assured it. Fear impelled it into obedience, but he also needed its trust for the task that lay ahead. A task that no Jinn would ever dare to do.

It repositioned itself, its hooves *clunking* on the stone floor. "What is it then? Another quest to the Dead City? Another hunt for treasure?"

Harun shook his head, "No. Not this time. I have a more demanding task for you."

"Speak, and it shall be done."

Harun took a deep breath. "I need something concealed from all eyes. Of Jinn and man."

"Secrets!" Ba'al hissed. "What secrets would you be hiding then?"

"Some that concern Jinn-kind," Harun replied coolly. "Others that concern mankind. Many more beyond the comprehension of either being."

"Very well," Ba'al raised its scaly chin, "what task is this?"

"After my final entry in the Book," Harun explained, "I want you to seal it. Place on it a perpetual enchantment. I forbid you to alter even a single inscription, do you understand?"

"The Book's text is ancient and sacred to the Jinn," Ba'al's expression darkened. "Its desecration is detrimental upon all of Jinn-kind."

"Then I trust you will uphold those laws with whatever integrity courses through your essence!" Harun challenged.

The Jinn's blank eyes narrowed, filled with hate and loathe. "You *question* my honor?"

"I take issue with your very existence," Harun retorted.

The Jinn became infuriated, barring its gruesome teeth.

"Cast your hatred upon me all you want," Harun pressed into the wound, "but you have brought this upon yourself."

The Jinn looked away and Harun grinned inwards. He had it right where he wanted it.

"When you are done with the book," he went on indifferently, "I want you to bind Adva to the Amulet. You know the incantation, you know the ritual," he pointed at the floor-desk. Beside it was a small wooden box, bound in leather and embossed in gold embroidery. "You will find everything you need in there."

"You are asking me to imprison my own kind."

"And do you have a problem with that?" Harun raised an eyebrow.

"None at all," Ba'al replied. "Only curious. She has been of benefit to you; why imprison her?"

"Imprison is not the same as death, is it?" Harun asked. "All I need is for her to remain asleep, until such time as she needs to be woken. Now, if you are done questioning your master, shall we begin?"

"Certainly," the Jinn replied. "What of the Veil?"

"What of it?" Harun raised an eyebrow.

"Should I keep it open?"

Harun nodded.

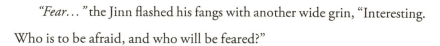

"And the key?" Ba'al asked.

"Fear."

"Fear..." the Jinn flashed his fangs with another wide grin, "Interesting. Who is to be afraid, and who will be feared?"

"That too is none of your concern," Harun said plainly. "Leave the veil open for her return, and let it be fear that breaks her bonds."

"It shall be done," Ba'al gave a short, reluctant bow. "The spell shall be bound on a scroll. You must keep all the items contained together. If the scroll is undone, the spell will be broken."

Harun nodded in acknowledgment. "Oh, and there is one other thing," he said before dismissing the demon. "The seal on the book must only be undone by Adva, and no other. Understood?"

"If it will earn me my freedom," the Jinn responded.

"You sound unconvinced," Harun stated.

It clucked its tongue, if at all it had a tongue to cluck. "Be warned, sorcerer. If you do not fulfill these terms, only death will undo the curse that will befall you and yours."

"Death is an uncertainty and an inevitability," Harun said. "I do not fear it."

"And the Ring Bearer?" Ba'al asked, to which Harun looked away and avoided its gaze. "He does not know, does he?" It smirked again, wider this time. "Oh, what *have* you done, sorcerer?"

Harun shook his head. "It matters not. The Ring was only meant to be used as a carrier. Complete this task, and you will have your freedom."

"If it is as you say, then it will be done," the Jinn said after a brief pause. "Too long have I lived in chains. I yearn to return to my realm."

"Freedom is an illusion," Harun stated. "A sympathy for emotion. A mask of delusion!"

With a final malicious grin, exposing its drooling teeth, the Jinn vanished in a puff of dark smoke, leaving behind a trailing scent of rotting eggs. Harun returned to his desk, picked up a quill and blank piece of parchment. His hand shook slightly, hovering an inch above the parchment for several silent moments while he collected his thoughts.

When he was ready, he dipped his quill into the inkpot.

> Siyaad,
>
> I pray this letter finds you in confidence and in good health. I have considered your proposal greatly, but for as long as our personal matters remain unresolved, we must keep our secrecy. Fragility endures between Suha and I, and such a notion will only shatter our relationship. I urge you to remain patient until we are ready.
>
> I have reviewed the notes and extracts along with the scrolls you sent me, and reexamined them with what the book has had to offer. As vague and unclear as the extracts have been, there can be no more doubt concerning the Dark Prince. There will always be another to claim the Throne of Ithm. You were right about the deception, and I now regret ever stepping into Azhar's tent. How I wish fate had brought us together much sooner, that I may have prevented this tragedy from ever happening. Unfortunately, very little can be done to prevent any further devastation.
>
> For now, all I can do is seal the Book and the Amulet, to prevent the inevitable, and as soon as I complete this tedious task, I will make haste for Uduff. Await my arrival after the next crescent moon.
>
> I will take my leave here, and return to my work.
>
> Farewell, and Peace be upon you.
>
> Your brother,
> Harun.

TWENTY-ONE

THE SILVER DAGGER

PRESENT DAY.

Zaki tore down the stairs and out the front door, Mukhtar on his heel. They emerged into the street just as the hem of Gizwani's brown *thaub* vanished around the corner.

"After him!" Zaki yelled, and together, both brothers began the chase.

Gizwani was agiler than anticipated. They could barely keep him in their sights. He led them halfway across the city, through the intricate maze of streets and alleys, before eventually attempting to lose them amidst the now retreating crowds of *Souk Al-Huda*.

Mukhtar and Zaki were faced with a difficult task, struggling to maintain pursuit while keeping clear of the city guards. They had only just entered the sheltered market when Zaki tugged on Mukhtar's shoulder.

"Wait," he said, and they slowed down. "Give him the illusion of losing us."

"And follow him to his masters!" Mukhtar agreed, and they kept a safe but visual distance, following him past the narrow, winding lanes of the market, up along an aisle that traded in silk.

Gizwani slowed his pace, and despite constantly glancing over his shoulder, he did not seem to spot either of his pursuers. Zaki lingered close by, pretending to be a shopper, while Mukhtar held back further behind another stall, peering through the gaps of long, colorful drapes hanging from the rafters. Even though the day was waning, the *Souk* was still a frenzy of assorted languages, bargains, arguments, shouts and cheers. The *Souk's* guards were moving from stall to stall, imposing their authority, alerting both shoppers and merchants to complete their transactions with haste and return to their homes.

Mukhtar watched Gizwani carefully, for he now appeared to be searching for something, or someone. His gaze hovered across, but did not seem to spot the brothers. Two men, carrying a large sack of goods, were passing through, and the crowd dispersed to give them way. They moved along the aisle, and the sack obscured Mukhtar's view. When they passed, Gizwani had vanished— again!

Mukhtar cursed under his breath and started forward, Zaki following closely.

"Where is he?" he growled impatiently.

"He slipped through the alley to the Incense Lane," Zaki nudged him forward.

The sweet fragrances of Incense Lane greeted them well before they emerged on the other side. Most of the shops were already closed for the day, and a handful of shoppers still hung about the remaining few, making their final purchases.

"I cannot see him," Zaki craned his neck over their heads.

"Neither can I," Mukhtar did the same in the opposite direction.

"Wait here," Zaki crossed the aisle, ran up the wall, and grabbed hold of a wooden beam overhead. He hoisted himself up in a single, swift motion, ignoring the curses and insults from people passing by. He squatted upon the beam like a bird of prey, and scanned both directions.

"Get *down* from there!" A guard, much further along the aisle, had spotted him.

"There!" Zaki ignored the guard's warning and pointed to the far side. "Close to the *Musalla!*"

Mukhtar looked. The *Musalla* was the very same prayer area where he had seen the hideous beggar, after which the slavers had begun chasing him. It occurred to him that he had not returned to the same spot since that fateful day.

A scrawny and disheveled man, highly intoxicated, appeared before him. The stench was unbelievable, his eyes were sunken and bloodshot, dry skin stretched over empty bones, and yet, with surprising strength, the man was able to grab hold of the front of Mukhtar's *thaub* and beg for a few coins, that he may be able to acquire and satisfy his next dose.

Mukhtar felt a rush of animosity. He forced himself free and pushed the man away in disgust, receiving nothing but curses and insults in return, until the man found another victim to harass.

Slightly ruffled, Mukhtar quickly recovered his bearings and spotted Gizwani, leaning in casual pretense against the wall on the opposite side. His brown *thaub*, drenched in sweat, was darker around his chest, and his brown-skinned face was glistening in the dimming light of the *Souk*. His stony eyes darted in every direction, brow furrowed in distress.

Zaki appeared moments after, panting slightly.

Mukhtar nudged his head in Gizwani's direction. "Who is he waiting for, I wonder?"

"We are about to find out," Zaki pointed, bringing Mukhtar's attention to a hooded figure approaching Gizwani from the opposite direction. The figure wore a white turban, simple robes, and a cloth wrapped over its nose and mouth, and although well-concealed, Mukhtar could distinguish the unmistakable signs of daggers and throwing-knives beneath its robes.

"An assassin of Ghuldad?" he whispered to Zaki.

"So it would seem," Zaki whispered back and nudged him forward. "He looks armed. Be vigilant."

They split up again and moved in closer, waiting patiently for what would follow. The figure approached Gizwani and they began speaking, but overhearing the conversation over the boisterous notes of the market was no simple task.

Gizwani's back was turned to them, and all Mukhtar could discern of his acquaintance were his piercing, light-green eyes. He leaned forward to whisper something in Gizwani's ear, and after a few moments, they parted, and before Zaki or Mukhtar could intervene, he had vanished among the people. Gizwani remained standing where he was, and Mukhtar, who was closest, approached him cautiously.

What followed was too abrupt and astonishing for him to immediately comprehend, and it was only instinctive that he caught Gizwani's collapsing body. His hands were clamped around his stomach, gripping the hilt of a silver dagger with an intricate pattern of a serpent on its hilt, protruding from a single spot where a crimson stain was already spreading. His mouth was frothy, and he trembled uncontrollably, his skin becoming paler as his life faded away.

Mukhtar's ears were ringing with an odd sound that muffled the screams and shrieks of the panicking crowd. He did not even realize Zaki calling to him, as he stared into the cold, dead eyes of his neighbor, the man he had despised for so long. And yet, in that moment, he could not help but be overcome with pity and remorse.

He looked up, lips trembling, eyes wide with horror.

"You must leave!" Zaki was saying. "Go! Now!"

Mukhtar fumbled with words, glancing from Zaki to Gizwani.

"Go!"

It took a moment for him to realize what Zaki was urging him to do. Guards were pushing their way through the aggravated and panicking crowd, approaching them with murderous intent.

As carefully as he could, he laid Gizwani's head on the ground and passed a hand over his eyes, before tearing through the resistive crowd. He escaped through the narrow alley, returned to the winding lane of silk merchants, and had already vanished before the guards had arrived at Gizwani's body. Whether Zaki had escaped or not, he was unsure, for his thoughts now lay on the assassin who had vanished with the winds.

The assassin knew their plans and their deeds, which meant it would not be long before Ghulam's death, and the names of his assailants, were made publicly aware. It was only a matter of time before Immorkaan would arrive at his doorstep to chain whoever they deemed guilty. Mukhtar shuddered at the thought of Suha, vulnerable and in harm's way. Something must be done, and with haste.

The only other person who knew about Ghulam's death was Nabiha, and he immediately altered his course for Thamir's mansion. He arrived at the western wall of the mansion and stopped to reconsider his options. When he was certain of what he needed to do, he scaled and climbed over the rough stone, and stealthily crept across the neatly trimmed grass, heading for the kitchens.

Dusk was already upon the city, the evening sky riddled with distant glimmers of stars and a fading orange haze across the western horizon. Palm trees swayed with the evening breeze, complimented by the calm and soothing caress of the sea upon the shoreline.

Just like the previous evening, the kitchen doors were left wide open to ventilate the steam and heat from the fire pits. Mukhtar spotted the bulking figure of Kazimi barking orders at the servants in preparation of the evening meal. When he caught his eye, Kazimi ushered the servants to continue working as he approached Mukhtar.

"Why have you come here, *slave?*" he asked rudely.

"Do not call me that," Mukhtar warned him. "I have not come to contend with you."

"Do not speak as if you have authority here, *slave!*" Kazimi snapped. "State your purpose, or begone before I call the guards!"

Mukhtar bit the retort he was itching to give back. Instead, he put on a more docile tone. "I must speak with her Ladyship. I ask that you call her for me."

Kazimi gave a loud chuckle, his bulbous belly bobbing up and down. "She will not speak with you, *slave!* Not after your treachery last night!"

"She will if she wishes to save her skin," Mukhtar said, impatiently abandoning his act of plea. "Now, be a good servant and fetch her for me. I will await her in the gardens."

He turned on his heel and walked away before Kazimi had any time to process his statement. He did not mean to insult, but with the turmoil of what was happening, and Kazimi's own smug demeanor, he did not really feel the guilt of doing so.

He hid amidst the shrubbery as the final glimmers of daylight dissipated into night, wondering whether she would truly show herself. Would Kazimi call for her, or merely ignore Mukhtar's heed and carry on with his duties as if he were never there? What if they ambushed him where he hid? He had not really thought of that either. He was nervously debating whether to continue waiting or to leave before it was too late, when she finally appeared, strolling barefooted, wearing night-robes of a bluish-white shade. Her head was covered in a loose, nearly transparent scarf, and much of her jewelry was missing except for her anklets, jingling with every step she took. Even without her adornments, her allure was not undefined, radiating despite the vanishing daylight. Mukhtar made sure she was alone before he made his presence known.

"What do *you* want?" She did not care to hide her displeasure, nor did she seem surprised to see him.

"I must speak with you!" he said urgently.

His distressed expression was enough for her to take him seriously, and she gave a curt nod, signaling him to follow. She led him across the gardens, and they arrived at an opening between a large flowerbed and the same wall he had crossed over.

She sat cross-legged on the grass. "You seem utterly distraught."

"Indeed I am," he sat before her, and began narrating what had happened at the *Souk*, all the while thinking to himself— what would happen next? Had Zaki escaped successfully? Had he returned home safely? Had the ill news already reached Samiya's ears? And what of little Misbah, now fatherless just as he was?

He wanted to weep, but just as when Hassin had died, he held back the tears. Held back the emotions. But he could not hold back the tremble in his voice. He could not hold back the anger and fury he had felt even then. Unlike before, however, he could not face this enemy with mere swords and daggers. He needed more.

"You said you knew what haunts me," he stated.

"I did."

"You spoke of tainted witchcraft, a dark presence about me."

"You reek of it," she gave him a disgusted look. "I fail to understand, what is it you want from me?"

"I want you to show me how to harness the power of this Jinn!" he demanded.

She laughed. Shamelessly and mirthlessly. "Turn back, Mukhtar," she then warned in an ominous tone. "You are too weak to sink into the dark depths of witchcraft!"

"I am prepared to embrace the darkness!" he declared, and even as he said it, he did not know whether he truly meant it.

"So you may enact your revenge?" she asked simply.

"So I may bring justice to these wrongdoers!" he claimed. "I must end their tyranny!"

"You *must?*" she sounded hysterical. "And who has tasked you with this mission? Oh, pray tell, the divinity that has dubbed you an emissary of justice!"

"Do not mock me!"

"And if I do?" she retorted back. "Will you knife me as well?"

"You vowed!"

"I lied!" she said blatantly. "What now, *murderer?*"

Mukhtar was abashed. What now? His last remaining hope was already fading away. Was there no end to her betrayal? His mind raced back a few hours, when he and Zaki were discussing in his room. They did not know how much Gizwani had heard, but it had clearly been enough to face his death. The assailant must have been Ussam's agent. What Mukhtar could not understand was why Gizwani sought out that particular person? An oblivious man would have alerted any city guard. So why that particular one? The only explanation was that he had been tasked to spy on them from the very beginning, and the only person foolish enough to have claimed so, stood before him.

"You!" he released the mechanism on his wrist, drew his dagger, and stood up threateningly. "*You* killed Gizwani at the *Souk! You* sent him to spy on us!"

"Sit down, Mukhtar. Before you alert the guards!" she said with a disinterested tone. "You are making a fool of yourself by jumping to conclusions. *Wrong* conclusions."

"How else did you know about my brother and I?" Mukhtar remained standing. "Gizwani has been spying for you all along. He spoke to you in the *Souk,* and since you no longer had use of him, you killed him."

"Yes, Mukhtar," she said in a bored voice and a false yawn. "You have uncovered my secret ploy and devious act. And right after I killed him, I hurried back, washed my hands, and decided to take a leisurely stroll in the garden to unwind my thoughts. Do you know how *ridiculous* you sound?"

Mukhtar gazed at her in bewilderment before realizing the facts in her words. Slightly red around the ears, he returned the dagger to its sheathing and sat back down.

"He wore simple robes," he tried to recall the assailant, "but the dagger... the dagger was made of silver, the hilt in the shape of a serpent. It was a poisoned blade. Gizwani was dead as soon it pierced him."

"The Seven Secret Serpents," Nabiha stated darkly. "The King's Elite Assassins. Protectors of the Inner Circle. Said to have been trained by

Ussam Bashiri himself. Your neighbor, it seems, was a mole for men of very high statures."

"So it seems..." Mukhtar narrowed his eyes. "You cannot help me then. I must find another way."

"You are distressed," she said. "I understand. But you must calm yourself before making hasty decisions, lest the wrong person suffer the consequences of your rashness."

He wrapped his arms around his drawn knees, and stared into the darkness for a long moment. "I am at a loss," he said finally.

"By your own doing," she stated plainly. "You chose this path, Mukhtar. You can blame no other for your loss."

He threw her a cautious glance. Not only did she speak what was true, but in a rather strange way, she almost sounded like Adil.

"I do not blame anyone but myself," he admitted bitterly. "My neighbor is dead. Witnesses suspect my brother and I. The true assassin has escaped with everything his masters need to know. It will not be long before Immorkaan arrives at my doorstep to place my brother and I in irons before my mother's very eyes. She endured it when my father was imprisoned. I cannot bear to see such grief burden her again. It will destroy her!"

"Why should I care?" Nabiha scoffed. "You are responsible for the consequences of your actions!"

"You do not understand!" he remarked. "How can you be so selfish and ignorant? This is greater than either of us!"

"You are a fool!" Anger blemished her pretty face. "Your arrogance will destroy you and everything you have come to know, and after the threats you made last night, what makes you think I will ever grant you allegiance?"

"How can you—?"

"I trusted you!" She had nothing but hatred in her eyes. "And you betrayed me by destroying my only chance of ever finding my sister again!"

"*You* betrayed us by *blackmailing* us!"

"You put a blade to my throat!"

"You invited me to!" he sneered.

What followed was unexpected. She uttered a string of phrases in a strange language and waved her arms furiously. A powerful gust of wind surged across the gardens, forcing the palm trees to bow to the ground against their will. It swept Mukhtar off his feet, and flung him several feet into the air. He fell hard and painfully, tasting dirt and grass in his mouth.

"Do not underestimate me!" she snarled fiercely. "I am not without protection!"

Mukhtar coughed, spat, groaned, and fumbled to get up, and despite almost losing consciousness, he laughed. "Where was your protection when you were at my mercy, *sorceress?*"

In an almost similar fashion, she waved her arms once more and the winds came again with an even fiercer intent, flinging him higher into the air and much harder onto the ground. He bumped, bounced, and rolled, until he came to lay flat on his back, the very breath knocked out of him, painfully aware of the many bruises he had accumulated.

She approached and stood over him in a most formidable fashion Even in the darkness, there was no mistaking the fiery gleam in her eyes. "I should have killed you and your band of miscreants when I had the chance!"

He coughed and drew breath, reminiscing the moment they were alone in the room. "Why didn't you?" he asked hoarsely, crawling away from her, allowing himself enough room to fling his dagger if another such demonic catastrophe were to arise. "What stayed your hand then, I wonder?"

"You *know* why!" she said scathingly.

"I *gave* you the names!" Mukhtar sat upright and drew more breath. He felt the ache and soreness from being tossed about like a sack of hay.

"The names mean nothing," she turned away. "I was deceived. The only reason why Ghulam had that list was because every slaver on it was dead, and now I have no way of knowing who was responsible and where she may be."

"He was covering his tracks..." Mukhtar's thoughts began to wander, "...*why?*" He gazed at her for a long moment, observing the manner in which a loose strand of hair swayed about the side of her face. He calculated his options. Would it be wise to make an enemy of her, or foolish to befriend her? Such a powerful ally was an asset indeed, but another soul he would be bringing into harm's way. *As if she wasn't already,* he thought. *What then did it matter if she walked the same path as he?*

"I too was enslaved," he said, maintaining sincerity in his voice. "I bear your pain. But it is time you chose the needs of others over your own. Help me fight this war, so that your sister and others like her can realize the freedom they deserve."

"You have the *nerve* to call me selfish, yet all you truly care about is saving your own skin!" She scoffed. "Is that not why you are here? Was that not why killed Ghulam? You only ever sought vengeance!"

Mukhtar felt anger rush through his veins, but he mustered himself. "Ghulam is dead, his mercenaries and slavers are dead, but his masters live on and they seek to overthrow the rule of Azhar Babak. They seek open war. They seek to destroy all that exists in culture and faith, and govern mankind under a singular ideology of their own. They will enslave or eradicate those they deem inferior, and empower those they deem superior. Thus doing, they will create a humanity to their perfection. It will be their New World without God."

The air was filled with the chirping of crickets, the subtle drift of the breeze, and rustle of leaves and branches. In the far distant, they could hear the dying sounds of the city, overcome by the calming waves upon the shoreline.

She was gazing at him intently. "Every politician seeks greater power. On any given day, there are at least ten who are plotting to overthrow Azhar Babak. Does it matter which fool wears the King's crown?"

"As I said, your Ladyship," he asserted, "it is time for you to choose a side. You can remain in ignorance, and assume they will have a place for you in their New World, but I can assure you, they will only destroy everything you know, to create their own. Nothing will be left, not for you, nor for me."

She was quiet, and the moments endured until Mukhtar felt he had no other option. He had hoped to gain an ally from her, perhaps even more. It had been a fool's hope. Eventually, he decided to abandon it, and approached the wall, preparing to climb over. He had to return home and contend with the foreboding of Gizwani's death. How would he explain everything to Suha? How would he relate with Misbah? How would he reveal to them that Gizwani was a spy for evil men?

"Wait!" she called, and he stopped and turned. "How can I be certain of what you speak?"

"You sensed a demonic presence about me," he stated.

"I did," her eyes narrowed. "I only assumed you were possessed by a Jinn."

"Were I to tell you the truth about this Jinn?" he took a step forward. "Were I to tell you of the devilish things I have witnessed, and the truth about The Dark Prince?"

"What do you mean?" her whisper almost dissipated with the wind.

He tugged on the chain around his neck, and pulled out the Amulet. In the darkness, it radiated, casting a hazy, mesmerizing, bluish glow over his hands.

Nabiha's gasp almost made her run out of breath. For a brief moment, she swayed on the spot and after regaining her composure, she approached him cautiously, eyes affixed on the Amulet, drawn by its mystical allure. She leaned in so close to look upon it, the scent of her *Bakhoor* filled his nostrils.

"It is true then!" she gasped. "The Amulets of Sihr exist!"

"Ghulam said that united, they would open something."

"The Doorway to *Almah-Zurah*," she spoke breathlessly. "The Eye of *Hurus!* The perfection of the human soul… in harmony with the body… inferior in every aspect, yet superior as created… *And ye shall witness the rising of the Hand of Azazil, the ultimate weapon of the Dark Prince… nay shall he be defeated… by the power of the five…* this bodes ill! This bodes ill for us all!"

TWENTY-TWO

THE PRIESTESS OF AFTARA

It was no secret among devout practitioners of sorcery. It was the myth of myths, the legend of legends, and ever sought by those who crave power. At least, that is how Nabiha described it.

He had climbed over the wall and waited, as per her instructions, in the dark alley across the mansion. Concealed in the shadows, he nervously fidgeted with the Amulet, pondering over what might happen next. An immense fear had overtaken him since he escaped the *Souk* earlier, and showed no signs of ebbing. Was he doing right by trusting Nabiha? What if she aligned with the enemy? She was, after all, Thamir's aide. What evidence did he have that she would not betray Mukhtar to him?

He withdrew further into the shadows as a large caravan of

several camels, horses, and mule-driven carts, thundered along the street, coming to a halt at the mansion gates. The camels and carts were laden with heavy sacks and overhanging bales of goods. The horses were mounted by both civilian tradesmen and soldiers, with several more escorting the large procession on foot. After a short interrogation by the guards at the gates, the caravan leader, clad in dark robes, gave a high-pitched whistle. The caravan slowly jolted into motion as the gates swung open to allow them entry.

More goods for Thamir to smuggle, Mukhtar thought bitterly, his lip curling slightly. *More to add to his already teeming hoards of wealth.*

Nabiha arrived a short while after the caravan had cleared away, marching briskly toward him. She had changed her attire to suit the journey ahead, and after ensuring they were not being followed, they headed north, beyond the inner wall and out of the city. Her status as Thamir's aide required no identification, and they strolled the city streets, past guard patrols and stations, unhindered. Those who dared to interrogate them, were left with shame, for she spared no expense in embarrassing them before their fellow soldiers.

"Almah-Zurah is the Forbidden Land beyond the Veil," she explained as they moved further into the outskirts of the city, continuing north in the direction of the cabin. "Said to host legions of Jinn, it is a barren stretch of fire, ash, ruin, and poison."

"And the Eye of Hurus?" Mukhtar asked.

Nabiha's loose scarf fluttered with a passing breeze. "The Doorway. A gateway to the other side. Because of the Veil, man cannot see into the world of the Jinn. The Eye of Hurus was built by the people of old. A very ancient civilization. The Western tribes of Arammoria are said to be descended from them. It was built to allow a human soul to journey to the other side. Almah-zurah is said to be only *one* of the many civilizations of the Unseen World beyond the Veil. No one knows where this doorway truly is, only that the Dark Prince Azazil has the power to unlock it and summon armies of Jinn to his bidding. Many, however, consider it to be just a myth."

"His fortress has been rebuilt," Mukhtar said. "I have seen it with my own eyes, if only from a distance. Nothing mythical about it."

She stopped, and so did he. Her expression had become terrified again.

"It is true," he affirmed.

"Then we must hurry!" She quickened her pace.

"Where are you taking me?"

They were well beyond the city's boundaries now, trekking along the Sultan's Pass into open farmlands. The air was cleaner, the breeze pleasant. Mukhtar could hear the distinct rush of the flowing waters of the Hubur as they passed the cabin. In the distance was a magnificent mansion amidst fields of wheat and barley on one side, and groves of date palms on the other.

"To one who is more knowledgeable than I," Nabiha replied. "She will help us better understand the Amulet and its Jinn."

"*She?*" Mukhtar raised a dubious eyebrow.

Nabiha nodded. "She is one of the Priestesses of our Temple."

"Your *Temple?*" Mukhtar raised his other eyebrow.

"Yes," she gave a brisk nod. "I serve the Temple of Aftara."

It was Mukhtar's turn to stop in his tracks. "You are a worshipper of a pagan god!" he remarked. "You bow to a demon cloaked as a deity! Aftara is a false god who serves the Dark Prince, and I will go no further with you!"

"Too pious to trust a sorceress?" she mocked. "Such hypocrisy! You wear an Amulet of Sihr like a medallion around your neck, and preach piety to others? Do you even know its true purpose?"

"I may have little knowledge of it," he said sternly, "but I am no fool! I will not risk bringing it closer to the Dark Prince's agents!"

"Which is why we are going to a High Priestess, and not to Ussam!" she said pointedly. "Now stop groping in the dark, like a *fool*, and pick up the pace!"

Mukhtar stood his ground. "Aftara serves the Dark Prince. *You* serve Aftara," his tone was steadily becoming darker and threatening. "Need I elaborate more?"

"You asked me to trust you," she said, "and I am asking you to trust me. What I will not do, is allow the likes of you to judge what you do not understand!"

"You are not too far from judgment!" he hissed menacingly. "Your false idols will burn, because they are nothing but. I will not allow you to guide me along the same impious path you walk, and I will certainly not allow the Amulet to fall into your wicked hands!"

She took a cautious step forward, hands held open in surrender. "Mukhtar... I beg you to trust me. I will not allow it either, you have my word, but you seek answers, as do I, and there is none other I know who can provide them."

Their eyes were locked, and behind the fiery gleam and mask of austerity, Mukhtar could somehow see a shadow of sincerity. Not evident enough to trust, but enough, perhaps, to take a chance. With caution.

"Be warned, *sorceress*," he snarled, "at the slightest shimmer of doubt, I will unsheathe my dagger, as well as the ravenous power of the Amulet," he chanced a bluff. "You, nor your High Priestess, will witness the light of dawn. This I vow to you!"

She gave him a cold hard stare, studying him, searching for a weakness in his staunch threat. She then nodded curtly and began walking again. Mukhtar followed cautiously.

He wondered why she had suddenly become so anxious and intimidated by him. Was it perhaps because of the Amulet? He had already witnessed her sorcery, perhaps a mere portion of it. How much more powerful was this Amulet, enough to incite fear in such a potent practitioner? Or was she not potent? Not even a practitioner perhaps. Was her display of vehemence merely that? A mere flaunt? An illusion? He could still feel the soreness of the bruises from being tossed into the air and hard onto the ground. Perhaps not. Still, he grinned inwards. He did not even feel the guilt. If he played his part well, he could turn the tide in his favor, even though he did not yet know how to harness the power of the Amulet.

"Where are we?" He peered through the darkness at the facade of the large mansion looming closer into view. Plastered and whitewashed, with glass windows and elegant wooden framings, it impressed him unlike any other building he had seen in the city. The architecture along the edge of the roof was ornamented with brass pikes. Dull orange glows in random windows, and around its perimeter, indicated that its occupants were still awake despite the late hour.

"The Sweet Orchards," Nabiha said after she had identified herself to the guards. They were escorted along a short, narrow road leading up to the mahogany front doors, where another pair of guards showed them inside. "This is the home of Rasha bint Sumrah."

They waited patiently in the open courtyard, floored with polished brick and bordered with stone archways under a balcony.

"Rasha bint Sumrah," Mukhtar's tone became stony when he repeated the name.

Nabiha gave him a nervous glance. "I urge you restrain yourself. Rasha is a perilous woman, but she has the resources we need. Be cautious."

Before he could respond, a man approached them. "Lady Nabiha. The hour is late," he spoke to her in an affluent tone and a polished Khalidan accent, wearing a clean white *thaub,* a flowing black cloak, and a white cap over his curly black hair. His short beard was oiled, glimmering in the light of the lantern in his right hand, while the left was held behind him as a sign of respect.

"Where is Sister Rasha?" Nabiha responded without much consideration. "I must speak with her."

"She is abed," he turned his gaze at Mukhtar, scanning his shabby attire with dark, *Kohl*-lined eyes. "Perhaps if you were to return in the morning, I can arrange for a meeting then. Or perhaps you are weary from your journey, and would prefer to stay the night? I can arrange for one— or two of the guest rooms to be prepared."

His oily voice and aristocratic diction was like the buzz of an irksome fly. The more he spoke, the greater Mukhtar felt the urge to knife him, but restrained himself with an aloof expression and remained silent, fidgeting with Mika'il's ring.

"Or perhaps you can *wake* her and *tell* her I wish to *speak* with her!" Nabiha pressed, her voice becoming rather dangerous.

"If you insist," the man gave a short bow, turned, and escorted them off the courtyard to a large room with an empty floor-table and large puffy cushions.

"You may wait here," the man bowed again and left.

Mukhtar had rarely seen luxurious abodes, and even the few he had, remotely came close to this one room. Highly polished dark oak gleamed beneath a rich and thick rug of intricate patterns and colors. The walls were finely plastered, and an elegant brass chandelier, with snake-like adornments and burning candles, hung from the ceiling.

Nabiha casually sunk into a cushion, while Mukhtar, not knowing what to do, remained standing in the furthermost isolated corner from the door. While they waited, servants appeared consecutively, bringing trays of food, random cutlery, and pitchers of wine. The empty table was bedecked with an assortment of glistening meats, succulent fruits, and shimmering drinks. Once again, Nabiha casually helped herself to whatever she fancied, as though she was a regular guest at the mansion. Mukhtar awkwardly refused whatever he was offered, ignoring the pangs of hunger in his stomach caused by the scrumptious aromas of the food. He kept his eye, instead, on Nabiha. She tried not to show it, but he sensed her stealing cautious glances in his direction. He knew that she was nervous and agitated, that he might lose his grip, unleash his anger and ruin whatever it was she hoped to achieve by bringing him there.

Incense was burned in two elaborate porcelain *Mabkharas*, and within moments, the room was filled with a hazy sweet smelling smoke. It was a long while before Rasha bint Sumrah presented herself, escorted by her handmaidens and the man who had greeted them earlier. As soon as she entered the room, Nabiha set aside her dishes and stood to greet her.

"Nabiha!" Rasha remarked in a shrill, high-pitched voice, and gave a casual wave.

The two women kissed each other on the cheeks, and Nabiha said, "I must speak with you. Urgently."

"Leave us!" Rasha instructed all her servants, and they hastened to obey. "You included, Fusan!"

Fusan narrowed his *Kohl*-lined eyes ever so daringly. "This is against the creed of the Temple!" he protested.

"And since when have you been one to question me, Fusan?" Rasha snarled at him.

"Not to question," Fusan gave another one of his short bows. "But to give… *fair warning.*"

"Go away, Fusan!" Rasha gave another casual wave at the door. "I can handle my affairs by myself!"

Slightly disgruntled, Fusan gave a final bow, and followed the rest of the servants, shutting the door behind him.

"Now…" Rasha said, once they were alone, "… what am I to make of this late intrusion?"

Nabiha responded with a slight nudge toward Mukhtar.

"Indeed," Rasha's gaze fell upon Mukhtar, and her thin lips curled into a rather meaningless smile, her cold eyes suddenly filled with interest.

Mukhtar saw her more clearly as she stepped forward. Older than either of them, Rasha still held herself in a manner that exhibited her elegance. Her pearly-white skin was smoothly stretched around her high cheekbones and a rather long neck. Her long beauteous hair hung in thick and dark locks. Silky night robes of a mint-green shade, fluttered as she approached him, coming to a halt barely a foot away. She was a few inches shorter than him, and carried with her an intimidating odor of stale wine. It was all Mukhtar could do to keep from wrinkling his nose.

"Mukhtar Harun Zafar," she parted her lips to display a rather provocative grin. "I thought Ussam had you gripped by your groin!"

Mukhtar's jaw was set. He forced himself to channel every bit of loathing in his stare. "Quite the contrary," he held his hands together in false pretense, but his fingers were slowly edging towards the dagger's mechanism concealed under his sleeve.

"Indeed?" She leaned back slightly and eyed him contemptuously from head to toe.

"He is crippled and aimless because of me," he bluffed. "Much like you, in that sense."

"So you think."

"So I know," his lips curled into a malicious grin.

She returned an equally malevolent expression. "Its seems the Sons of Zafar have finally grown to be as foolish as their father. Tell me, how do you intend on facing the might of Ghuldad with *nothing* between your *legs?*"

Mukhtar felt his blood boil, but he continued to display an aloof expression. "We have already sent his minions six feet into the ground. His world is slowly collapsing beneath him. If I were you, I would care less about him. His doom is sealed. How long do you think *you* will last?"

Her grin vanished. Her jaw was set, her expression became stony. Infuriated, she wheeled around to face Nabiha.

"He has found the Amulet, Rasha!" Nabiha stated. "Aftara smiles upon us!"

"Oh, save your false piety for the Council of Sages and Priestesses!"

Rasha shrieked. "You do not care if Aftara smiles or weeps. Rather, you do not believe if Aftara exists at all!"

"Rasha!" Nabiha gave her a bewildered look. "This is hardly the place, or the time, to bring up such—"

"It is you who have brought him here! And a *foolish* thing you have done!"

"I had no other option," Nabiha pressed. "If the Four Sahir come to know—"

"Then you will have led them to *my* doorstep!" Rasha screeched. "Your foolish endeavors continue to reign misfortune upon me!"

"We *must* prepare him!" Nabiha raised her voice to press her argument.

"Prepare him for *what*? The *prophecy*?" Rasha threw her arms open in frustration. "The tall tales of *slaves* from another world?"

"Prophecy or not, the truth cannot be denied!" Nabiha shrieked.

She and Rasha locked threatening looks. Mukhtar did not care for their domestic discord, but at the sound of the prophecy, he was urged to intervene.

"What is this prophecy?"

"Nothing but a tall tale and a false rumor!" Rasha denied scornfully. "Much like the Amulets!"

"The Amulets exist, Rasha," Nabiha gasped, staring at her with disbelief. "How can you deny that? You believed in them! It was *you* who told me of their existence, and when one walks through the door, you choose to deny it?"

Rasha glanced at Mukhtar uncertainly. "The Council *will* hear about this, and they will see it as a betrayal."

She approached the table and poured herself a cup of wine. She then collected several herbs from their various containers and served them to the *Mabkharas,* where they burned and discharged lingering, acrid, and spicy whiffs that clouded the sweet-smelling incense. *Whyever would she do that?* Mukhtar wondered.

"Sister Rasha, the Priestesses are as deluded as their beliefs," Nabiha pleaded with her. "They are heathens and idolaters, you have said so yourself. Are we to cower in fear of what they *might* do, while the fate of mankind falters upon the edge of a blade? The Amulet has come to us in the hands of one who is willing and able to brave the wickedness of the Dark Prince, and you would simply turn him away?"

Rasha eyed her for a brief moment, then laughed, loudly and shrilly, and Nabiha reddened with anger.

"Do you *hear* yourself?" Rasha lazily raised a bony finger at her. "Your conceit knows no bounds! Holier than thou, you march, in search of what? Valor? Glory?" She drank deeply from her cup and poured herself some more. "Very well then. Speak, O' Pious One. How do you intend on saving mankind from eternal damnation, when it is only damnation that awaits us in the end?"

She drank and poured herself even more wine, eventually draining the pitcher. "You, who has never held our beliefs. You, who is a *hypocrite* and a *charlatan*. Give me a reason why the Council should not sentence you to your doom. Give me a reason why *I* should trust you!"

Nabiha was utterly dispirited. Tears filled her eyes, and Mukhtar decided he had heard enough. A click on his wrist released the dagger, and in one swift step, his arm had engulfed Rasha from behind, an edge of steel touching the stretched skin on her neck.

"Mukhtar! No!" Nabiha gasped, clasping her hand over her mouth.

"Apologize, *witch!*" Mukhtar growled in Rasha's ear.

"Unhand me!" Rasha gnarled her teeth. "My death will not go unanswered!"

"You were already dead when you pledged allegiance to Ussam!" Mukhtar said. "Just like your ally, Ghulam. Pray to your *heathen* goddess. Tonight, you breathe your last!"

She trembled slightly and for a brief moment, Mukhtar thought he had truly intimidated her. But when she started cackling mirthlessly, he was suddenly filled with fright. "Perhaps there is benefit to be drawn from this—"

"I said *apologize!*" Mukhtar tried to maintain his dominance by increasing the pressure on the blade.

"—you have sealed your own doom, Son of Zafar!" Rasha continued to cackle and a nauseating odor filled his nostrils. "There is no turning back now. You thirst for what lay beyond the Veil? Witness now what has endlessly destroyed the bloodline of Zafar for generations!"

Despite all his efforts, Mukhtar's hands began to tremble. The dagger slipped and cut her slightly, but she hardly flinched as her blood was drawn, steadily dripping and staining her nightgown.

He unwillingly relinquished his hold on her, staggering away awkwardly and clumsily, feeling lightheaded and weak, trembling uncontrollably as the acrid scents of the herbs and incense more than overwhelmed him. They absorbed him, engulfed him, and slowly but surely, his vision blurred, then darkened, and he crumbled to the floor.

Sounds of thunder deafened him, flashes of lightning blinded him, and the sands shifted with fury, rising and falling against the wind, against the very storm itself. Mukhtar struggled to stand, surrounded by this unearthliness, but more so with uncertainty and doubt. Fear and despair.

He knew this landscape. He knew it all too well.

The erupting sands began to change their shade, and slowly they changed their texture, and before his very eyes, they became water. Droplets of water, waves upon waves of water. It was now an ocean. He stood upon the waters as if on solid ground, and as soon as he realized it, he was engulfed. The depths darkened as he descended, crashing down upon him. He was drowning in it, unable to make sight nor sound.

'This is my world, Mukhtar,' the voice came as eerily as before, as shrilly as ever. 'Here I am, Queen and Pauper. Here I am, most powerful, most weak. Here I am, your worst tribulation and your utmost absolution.'

Mukhtar mustered his courage. He would not be intimidated. He knew who it was— what it was. He would show no fear.

"You are an abomination of the Unseen World," the words escaped him, resonating through the darkening depths of the waters. "I fear you not, for I am guarded by He who has created you and I. By His command, you can never harm me!"

'Indeed I am,' Adva replied. 'And will forever remain.'

"But you would seek a different path?" he asked. 'You would delve to the depths of wickedness?'

'To free my kin, I will seek to world's end,' came the reply.

'Are you prepared to journey the same?'

"Indeed, it is only by His will does the moon wane and the sun rise," he said. "By His will, give me your power, and let me bring you your freedom. Show me what I must know."

'It is yours to command, son of Zafar,' she said. *'But do not hope to find contentment. Do not hope to find forgiveness. Forbidden is every pact between our kinds. Woe unto those who blow on knots and invoke the defiled. Theirs is Sin. Theirs is the Abysmal Flame, and in it they shall abide.'*

Mukhtar woke sharply, heavily drenched in sweat. Head throbbing, eyes watering, he was sprawled over the cushions in the same room with Nabiha, hunched over him looking deeply concerned, and Rasha, seemingly enjoying herself in some sort of mystic trance.

"I drowned—" he gulped and gasped for air, "—I saw—" he choked and coughed.

"What did you *see?*" Nabiha pressed.

"Water—" he gasped.

"You saw water? The Water Demon?"

"Must— *drink*— water!" he choked.

"No water!" Rasha scooped up one of the porcelain incense burners and brought it close to him. "Breathe... *breathe* and dream!"

The smoke of the acrid incense engulfed and drowned him once again into darkness, and he shut his eyes, falling into another dream.

TWENTY-THREE

SORCERERS AND SLAVES

A lifeless hum filled his ears, and his vision blurred in an array of dull, dancing colors. It was a strange feeling indeed, for he did not know if he was standing or sitting. He could not sense his limbs, could not feel his fingers, could not for that matter, feel any part of his body. In existence he was, but without a vessel to carry him.

As his surroundings became apparent, he found himself within the boundaries of engraved white lines and markings of a five-pointed star inside a circle of occult symbols.

The flames of lit oil lamps swayed in unsynchronized patterns, causing the shadows to come alive. A steady, rhythmic dripping of water resounded somewhere out of sight. He ran his gaze along the mossy damp walls, beyond stone columns of similar texture. Above him, the ceiling faded into darkness, but the height and size of the chamber became apparent enough when a crisp clear voice spoke from somewhere ahead of him, drawing his attention.

"Adva, of the tribes of Undomi'an, from the Seventh Plane of the Unseen World," the figure was partially devoured by the clinging shadows, but its form was evident enough. It was a human.

"What is the meaning of this?" Adva hissed in a feminine, high pitched voice. "You dare summon me?"

The man cackled and began a string of incantations, chanting in a language Adva had long forgotten; a dialect of the ancient world, not of human, but that of Jinn. The room, which was stifling and humid when she had first materialized as a formless spirit, now became colder and drier by the passing moment.

The effects of his chanting came in successions. First was the painful, forceful tribulation of assuming form. Human form. A form Adva despised above all other creatures to roam the earth. She, a Jinn, a being of smokeless fire, pure and unbound. Man, a hollow shell of mud and clay, driven by temptation, sustained by ignorance. It was torturous to be subjected to such impurity. She was forced to grow bones, to breed flesh, and stretch skin over a bloody and messy transformation.

Several inferior Jinn materialized in the room, and bound her in infernal chains. They were Shayateen, betrayers and traitors of Jinn-kind, worshippers of the wickedness of Azazil, and they spared no expense in bringing her malice. Ruthless they were, as they pierced her flesh and pinned her to the ground.

It was done. The process was complete. The contract was set.

The man, equally exhausted and depleted, still managed to speak in a voice that demanded her subjugation. "You have heard the incantations, the terms of our contract, and are bound to enslavement, until such time as—"

"Vile creature!" Adva screamed at him. "I know whom you truly serve, Ahumai!"

Sahir Ahumai cackled mirthlessly. "Then you know what torment awaits you, should you fail to obey my every command! Now, kneel before your master!"

Adva's unclad human form felt anger surge through its veins. She made to step off the platform, longing to fly across the room and sink her demonic fangs into the man's flesh, tear him to bits, and devour him until he was no more. Her arms gave a malevolent twitch, and with a single command, all the moisture in the room was drawn into the pores of her skin. The water condensed around her hands, like thick gloves. Her intent was murderous, her retribution remorseless.

However, she could do no more than cast loathsome profanities.

"You will obey!" Sahir Ahumai waved his hand, and several infernal whips crackled in the air, illuminating the room in bright flashes.

Adva screeched in pain as her human body was scorched with painful lashes. She struggled and thrashed like a wild animal in a cage, but could not transcend beyond the boundaries of the circle and the pentacle star. She *was imprisoned behind an invisible, intangible barrier, and the infernal chains painfully contracted with the slightest movement. When she could flail about no more, she sobbed, breathing deeply, the realization of being enslaved, burying her beneath an inevitable truth.*

Sahir Ahumai's soft cackle was strangely becoming distorted. Amidst the obscure laughter, she was able to distinguish other sounds, other sensations, like the smell of burning incense tinged with acrid herbs, and voices murmuring in the distance.

As soon as Mukhtar opened his eyes, he felt a jolt around his navel, and tasted bile. Uncontrollably, he rolled over and vomited on the side of his cushion, soiling the expensive rug beneath. His hands trembled, eyes watered, and head throbbed.

"What did you see?" Nabiha kept urging him relentlessly. "Mukhtar! *What did you see?*"

"The summoning—!" he croaked, groaned and vomited again, "—Sahir Ahumai— Adva—the demons—!"

He felt the world darken again. His eyelids felt heavy, his head felt intoxicated. Strange images flashed through his mind, and even stranger still, dark figures appeared to be slithering across the dimly lit, smoky room. His breath had shortened, and his chest and stomach hurt with every effort to remain conscious. Nabiha's concerned face loomed closer and the acrid incense was replaced with her sweet *Bakhoor*. He wanted her to remain there. Like a shroud. Like a protector from the evil shadows slithering in the distance. A shadowy figure crept up on her unsuspectingly. His heart beat in a frenzy, his eyes wide in horror, a sudden constriction in his throat. He wanted to shriek a warning, but could not muster the strength. She screamed as she was shoved aside brutally.

Her soothing scent vanished, and the acrid stench returned, seeping and permeating deep into him. He struggled to push himself up and go to her aid, but could not for the life of him, even lift a finger. Rasha's face swam into view, cackling with a demonic likeness. She fueled the *Mabkharas* with a daunting zeal, and the fumes intoxicated him until he succumbed once more into strange dreams.

> *It was just as dim and hazy, but the climate was different. It was no longer a dark and dank, stone chamber, but a warm, brick-walled room.*
>
> *She was, once again, in her natural form. A smokeless spirit hovering a few inches above the stone floor, within the confines of a circle and a pentacle star crudely streaked with occult markings and otherworldly symbols.*
>
> *A flame swayed in the fireplace to her left, and before her stood a young man, straight-backed, with handsome features and skin that had only recently sprouted facial hair. His pale complexion suggested a detachment from the outside world for a very long time.*
>
> *The adolescent boy was muttering feverishly under his breath, and Adva hovered patiently in her circle, knowing what this was. She had been summoned, and was now being read the details and clauses of a new contract.*
>
> *Strangely enough, she no longer dreaded what was to follow; the excruciating transformations, the binding infernal chains, or the forceful eviction from the Veil.*

She had a feeling, a riveting and peculiar feeling that this boy, as amateurish as he seemed, knew what he was doing. Did he, though? To breach another sorcerer's covenant, a sorcerer as powerful as Ahumai, a sorcerer who adhered to the will of Azazil himself. Such a breach was beyond any man's capabilities, not to mention the atrocity that would befall him should Ahumai learn of this treachery. So, how did this adolescent boy, greedily drawn by the Dark Arts, come to bear such strength as to conquer the allegiance of an Elemental Jinn bound to an Amulet of Sihr?

Behind him, a rooster shuffled noisily and nervously in its cage. It had already sensed its doom.

The boy seemed uncertain and nervous, straining to get his words and specifications right. Inexperienced in sorcery, or perhaps he had never before summoned a Jinn as powerful as her. He was probably one of the young apprentices favored by pagan practitioners, and learned from them the Dark Arts deep within the Cedars of Zila. As an apprentice, he probably got by with managing a docile Ghul, perhaps a lowly Khubuth, or a mediocre Khizab. But she was a far superior being, a Ma'arid of the noble Tribes of Undomi'an. She was an Elemental Jinn, more powerful than a thousand Ghul, and a thousand more. She gazed at the young sorcerer, with fiery intent, studying him closely.

His aura was unnatural, emanating ambition, greed, power, and a heightened sense of distraught. The boy was troubled. Why was he troubled?

'Salim, son of Wasif, son of Zafar, why would you perjure your bloodline, and succumb to the wickedness of sorcery?' Adva pondered deeply. 'Do you not know what monstrosity awaits you? Do you not know how cursed you will become?'

The boy stammered a little, and Adva tensed. 'Keep going,' she thought slyly. 'Only a few more words.'

There were no further impediments, and the boy completed his incantations to the final word. He picked up a brass pot on the table beside him, and drank from it. Then he turned to the rooster's cage, opened it wide enough to slip his hand in, and with surprising reflex, grabbed the frightened bird by its neck in a single attempt. Then he removed a knife from his belt, its blade gleaming in the firelight, and held it against the rooster's neck over his head. The bird screeched endlessly, flapping and struggling to free itself. Muttering devilish incantations and salutations under his breath, the dagger flashed and sliced off the rooster's head, allowing the blood to pour freely, covering him in a scarlet tint.

That seals the deal. The contract was set, the agreement was done, and Adva was now enslaved to this strange boy, a true master and conqueror of the Amulet. Were he a direct descendant of Ahumai, he would not need a ritual, but he had braved the impossible. Perhaps, he did indeed know what he was doing.

'Adva, of the Ma'arid tribes of Undomi'an, from the Seventh Plane of the Unseen Realm,' the boy spoke in a smooth, soft, and charming voice, 'you have been summoned and bound to the Amulet by the laws of witchcraft. The incantations spoken before you, clearly define the terms of our contract. You will serve my every need, want, and desire, to whatever end and cost.

Thereafter, you will serve my sons, and their sons, and by this bond, you will remain ever...'

The room was becoming hazy and distorted, as the real world rematerialized around him.

"Wait!" he groaned loudly. "No... wait! I must know!"

It was not as tasking as before. He was not as lifeless and helpless. His senses were more aware. His vision was less clouded. His mind more open. His eyes pierced the room nervously, searching for the devilish, shadowy creatures he had witnessed before.

Illuminated by the oil lamps, through the hazy trail of the acrid incense, emerged a face with pale-white skin and black eyes with icy blue, snakelike pupils. Its thick hair was so dark, it seemed to absorb all the light in the room. Blackened lips peeled over a snarling mouth, revealing several rows of razor-sharp, bluish fangs.

Mukhtar screamed, frightfully scrambling over the cushions and against the wall. "What is it?" he gasped. "What *is* it?"

"Mukhtar!" A voice spoke next to him and he recoiled against it. It took a moment to recognize Nabiha by his side. He shifted his gaze.

"This creature!" he gasped and pointed.

"What creature?" another voice sneered to his right, and his nostrils were met with a revolting stench of stale wine. "The only creature here, is the illusion of your mind. The reckoning of your dreams!"

The creature was there before him, as clear as anything else he could see. It grinned widely, snakelike eyes peering over their heads, gazing upon him with mild interest and a strange sense of self-satisfaction. *What devilry was this?*

"Breathe…" Rasha unexpectedly brought an acrid smelling *Mabkhara* under his nose, and he could not avoid inhaling it. Again it took effect.

She stood, or rather floated, a mere inch off the ground. She was upright, with form and structure, bound to the Amulet, and her human form.

She floated past a foggy mirror and caught her reflection. White robes flowed to the ground, shredded and tattered, but otherwise unnaturally clean. Think, long, black hair hung past her shoulders, down along her spine and over her subtly heaving chest, creating a curtain that partially obscured a pale-white face with thin, blackened lips and high cheekbones. Black eyes with icy-blue, snakelike pupils, pierced the very surface of the mirror, lifelessly returning her gaze. She stared at her reflection, contemplating how much she despised it. Despised it to its very core. It was a symbol of a degradation to the murkiest depths of her being.

Behind her reflection was a swaying flame in the fireplace, and a simple wooden floor-desk atop a sisal mat.

Her gaze was drawn to a shimmering blue light emitted by an ancient stone entrapped within its glistening golden frame. The Icy-Blue Amulet of Sihr. On the table beside it, was a cluster of strange objects. A pair of short-swords with jagged edges and silver hilts were laid next to several silver throwing-knives, a pair of rings with red and black obsidian stones, and a book.

Bound in darkened, tattered leather, as thick as a brick, as large as a slab of stone, and covered in stains of blood and worse. Of all the objects that lay there, the book drew her closer by a mystical bond, uncanny and unexplainable. Its existence affirmed how she came into servitude. Its sacred sanctity was responsible for the transgression of her bond and allegiance, from a vile sorcerer to a most inconceivable one. Be it as it may, it was servitude nonetheless. Enslaved to man.

From the corner of her eye, she glanced at the man sitting cross-legged in the far corner of the room with his back turned. He was entranced in meditation. Or so it seemed. She chanced forward, her footstep a mere glide over the stone floor.

"Ever so daring, my dear Adva," the man spoke.

Adva froze, shoulders slightly tensed. He knew. He had sensed her motives as he always did. If she were not bound to the Amulet, whether he wore it or not, the man would have suffered a most terrible adversity, a most disastrous infliction upon his living soul. Such was the hate she felt for him. But he was master, she was slave. And to slave was to obey and protect said master.

"Daring, yes," she responded. "But curious, also."

"Ah..." the man sneered, "... you wish to know your fate?"

"And of my kin," Adva replied curtly. "Of Avira. Of Ard and Agni. My brothers and sister are enslaved by your ilk, no less than I."

"And you seek answers from the Book?"

"The Book contains much more than just answers," Adva replied. "Its weight cannot be realized over a thousand lifetimes, and a thousand more. Its sanctity is sacred to Jinn-kind."

"Which is why it must be destroyed," the man spoke softly, as if only to himself. "To breach its verses into the world of man, only paves the way for wickedness to prevail."

"To destroy the Book is not without destroying all else," Adva warned, unable to keep her voice from quivering.

"It would destroy you as well, yes. And your brethren," the man said. "A shame and a loss indeed."

"Free us then!" she remarked. "Speak to your fellow sorcerers, and convince them. There are other ways to cripple the Hand and his master, Azazil. The Four have the ability to—"

"Do you take me for a fool, precious Adva?" the man chuckled. "I will never, in an eternity, risk the Amulets within a thousand leagues of the Four Sahir!"

"They no longer need the Amulets!" Adva stated. "There are other ways to open the Doorway."

"Indeed?" the man glanced over his shoulder. "And what of the Book?"

"We will take it with us," Adva suggested desperately,

"and hide it in our world. We will guard it for as long as we exist."

"Beyond which it will become unprotected," the man responded and stood, taking a step out of the shadows and into the firelight. "And another will rise to claim the Throne of Ithm, and he will bear the mark of Azazil. He will gather all the armies of the Jinn, and the book will once again fall into evil hands."

He was just as pale as ever, with streaks of white in his jet black hair and brown, wrinkly eyes. His beard, also black with white streaks, had grown longer than his collarbone. He was slouched and gaunt, looking like a man who had aged greatly in a very short time. It was strange indeed, for Adva had known him no more than a decade.

"I have never trusted you," he said simply. "Nor your kind. I never will. The Book will be washed from existence. To bar Azazil from furthering his vile ambitions, it must be destroyed. That will be its fate!"

Adva was most displeased. She glared and barred her razor-sharp teeth menacingly. "Fool!" she shrieked. "You think you can hoodwink Azazil? Mankind is weak! Time and again, he will conquer you! It his destiny. It is the very essence of his being!"

The man reached for the Amulet. A string of incantations escaped his breath, and the effect was immediately pronounced. The room was filled with thick, billowing smoke, engulfing everything into nothing.

When he woke, it was with another furious frenzy of vomiting, groaning and cursing. His senses returned to him in a rush of painful memories, and when his vision cleared, it was to find an awestruck look on Nabiha's beauteous face, and a most condescending grin on Rasha's.

There was another face among them. A pale face with darkened lips and piercing, snakelike eyes, dark hair flowing in thick long strands, just like her tattered white robes.

Mukhtar grimaced, and glanced furiously between Rasha and Nabiha, torn with disbelief.

"They cannot see me," Adva spoke in an eerie, shrilly voice. "They cannot hear me."

Mukhtar's gaze froze in the gap between Nabiha and Rasha's heads.

"The ritual has begun," Adva went on. "You must save him. You must save my brother, or he will be wiped from the existence of this world and the other."

She vanished in a blink, and Mukhtar gave a start. Searching the room availed nothing. He groped for the Amulet on his chest, recalling every dream he had just been forced to see. Had he indeed witnessed a memory of his grandfather?

"I must leave," he stood, and started forward. Pins and needles pricked his legs with every step, causing him to stumble awkwardly.

"But—" Nabiha tried to help him, "— you cannot just leave!"

"I can!" he replied determinedly. "And I will!"

"You must tell us what you saw!" Nabiha protested.

"No!" he pushed her aside clumsily. "Get out of my way!"

"Leave him be, Nabiha," Rasha clucked in a most offensive

way. "He is just as ungrateful and selfish as his father."

"Do not impugn my honor, *witch!*" he yelled at her, drawing his dagger as he did. "You know *nothing* about me!"

Rasha remained unmoved, and almost seemed to be enjoying herself. "Humble your heart and listen, child. Listen intently to what I am about to tell you about your bloodline."

TWENTY-FOUR

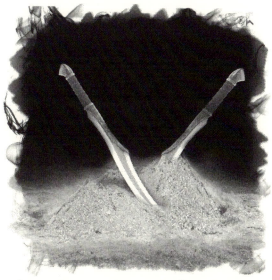

THE KEYSTONE

The hour was close to midnight. Dark, heavy clouds were swelling across the inky-black sky, blotting out the distant stars. Rasha escorted her guests out of the stifling room into the open courtyard, and an air, heavy with the scent of rain, filled their lungs as they crossed to the other side. The guards pulled open the front doors for them, and they walked along the dirt path, while Rasha explained what Mukhtar had long been itching to hear.

"The Amulets are very ancient," she said. "Almost as ancient as the age of the earth itself. Some claim they descended from the heavens, relics brought to earth by Azazil when he was cast out. No one knows their true origin, but they are famously associated with the Dark Prince's Four Sorcerers, Sahir Idumea, Sahir Eth,

Sahir Elzafaan—"

"And Sahir Ahumai," Mukhtar finished her sentenced grimly.

"They are of the Western Tribes of Arammoria," Rasha wrinkled her nose, looking slightly irritated at his interruption, "devout worshippers of the Sun God. Their people built magnificent tombs, in replication of the Amulets, to immortalize their gods. According to their scripts and beliefs, the Sun God had a son named Uzuris, and he was the guardian of his father's secret armies of Jinn. He entrusted this right to his own son, Hurus, who built what is known as the Eye of Hurus, the doorway to the Other Side. The Four Sahir, misguided by the whispers of Azazil, devised a way to harness this army."

Mukhtar exchanged a nervous glance with Nabiha. Rasha seemed to be enjoying herself. She spoke of the occult with a deep fascination in her tone, and hardly a trace of unease. The cut on her throat had stopped bleeding, but she had not even bothered to clean the traces of blood. Nabiha had been right in describing the priestess as *perilous*.

"Dispelled from the heavens," Rasha went on indifferently, "Azazil swore vengeance on mankind to the end of times, and will stop at nothing to achieve it. In their quest to attain power, the Four were tasked by the Hand of Azazil to serve his Throne of *Ithm*. Arrogant and corrupted by power, they recklessly discarded the Amulets deep within the caves of Simnia."

"Who is the Hand of Azazil?" he pressed curiously. "I keep seeing the name in scripts and scrolls, hearing his name uttered in frightful whispers."

"Azazil's most trusted," Rasha said. "An ancient Jinn with

incredible powers, said to be the most devious and malicious of their kind. His true origin is vague and obscure. No one has ever set their eyes upon him and lived with sanity."

Mukhtar stared at the cloudy night sky and breathed in the moist, chilly air. "But he is only a Jinn," he said. "How can he be so powerful as to be feared even by men of utmost spirituality and holiness?" He recalled how Sheikh Ruwaid had spoken of the Unseen. Although he had seemed certain of himself then, Mukhtar had still sensed a suppressed trickle of dread in his voice.

"A Jinn can defile everything with its sheer will," Rasha went on. "Jinn have not an ounce of good in them. They denote the pinnacle of all that is evil. Do not underestimate him, Mukhtar," she added grimly. "One cannot even *begin* to comprehend how he has earned the right to claim Azazil's Throne of *Ithm,* and become the Dark Prince's most trusted. His wickedness corrupted the Western Tribes, and he used them to wage his war on the world of man."

"The war endured because the Amulets lived on," Mukhtar filled in the gaps, "but without them, Azazil's ambition was crippled, until my grandfather and his companions chanced upon them," he remembered the book that sat upon the table in the dark room. "What of the Book, though?"

"The Book of *Kufr* is fabled to contain a thousand and one days of the knowledge of the Jinn," Rasha replied with a trail of fascination in her voice, as though she longed to hold it in her hands. "A day beyond the Veil is a thousand lifetimes in our world. Your grandfather, intelligent as he was, deciphered its text and used its knowledge to awaken the Amulets."

"Until he realized what he had done," Mukhtar stated, gazing across Rasha's date-palm orchards, while dark clouds continued to loom overhead with unnatural zeal.

"He destroyed the Book," Rasha continued, and Mukhtar eyed her cautiously. If this was true, then what they had found in the study may not have been the same book. But if this was only an assumption...

A thundering of hooves approached them, unearthing clouds of dust billowing with the winds. The rider dismounted his horse and rushed forward, breathing heavily, drenched in sweat.

"High Priestess," Fusan bowed curtly.

"What news?" Rasha demanded.

"Thamir has left his mansion in the company of Ussam Bashiri and another," he spoke feverishly.

Mukhtar tensed.

"Who?" Rasha asked sharply.

"Never have I seen him before, and they did not call him by name."

"They must have called him by *something!*" Rasha remarked.

"They only called him 'Master'."

Rasha cursed loudly.

"Who is this 'Master'?" Mukhtar asked her desperately.

She shrugged and shook her head disappointedly. "He has evaded my spies for too long. What else?" she asked Fusan.

"They were escorted by a host of Assassins. I followed them to the gates of the Royal Palace."

Rasha cursed again.

"They intend an attack upon the palace!" Mukhtar growled.

"Far worse," Rasha stated grimly.

"I saw a caravan arrive at Thamir's mansion," Mukhtar said. "It must have been Ussam!" He turned to Nabiha for confirmation.

She blinked, then shook her head. "I saw the caravan, but did not see Ussam. Kazimi covered my tracks while I slipped out through the kitchens."

"How could you *not* have seen him?" Mukhtar remarked. "I could have ended him there and then!"

He turned away in frustration and gazed into the dark silhouette of the Sweet Orchards.

"And what would you have ended him with?" Rasha mocked blatantly. "That rusty blade under your sleeve can barely cut through cabbage!"

Mukhtar did not argue with her. From the corner of his eye, he noted Nabiha looking slightly crestfallen, and he wished he hadn't shown his disappointment. It was not her fault.

"What more can you report?" Rasha demanded from Fusan.

"They were barred entry into the Palace," he said. "Thamir went in alone and requested an audience with Azhar, and after a short while, the King welcomed them as old friends. Our man at the palace reports that Ussam presented himself to negotiate a treaty with the King."

"The deluded fool!" Rasha cursed under her breath.

"Indeed," Fusan said.

"This makes no sense," Nabiha said. "If it is a treaty they seek, why is the Elder Council not included?"

"They may be, for all we know," Fusan replied. "Our spy did not mention any members of the Council, save for the King. This only means one thing."

"That the King has been deceived into Ussam's ploy," Nabiha stated.

Rasha shook her head. "No," she said in a distant voice. "Not Ussam. Ussam is no threat to Azhar. He commands an amulet, as does the king. They are bound to their Order. However, his other man they call 'Master'... There is a greater ploy afoot here. You know what you must do?" she added to Mukhtar.

Mukhtar gave a curt nod.

"You must not let them further their cause," she warned. "If they succeed this night, then all is lost. If the King falls under their reign, nothing will stop the Hand and the Dark Prince."

Mukhtar gave her a steely look. "I will need that steed!" he turned and reached for Fusan's horse.

"This is my finest horse!" Fusan protested angrily and tried, but failed, to wrestle back the reins.

"He is indeed a fine steed!" Mukhtar gave him a victorious grin and mounted the horse.

"It is a Mare, *peasant!*" Fusan glared at him. "And her name is Riah!"

"Come, Riah," Mukhtar kissed her affectionately on the neck, and whispered in her ear. "We must ride with haste!"

He tugged the reins, and just as he was about to turn, Nabiha called, "Wait!"

As she approached, he was drawn to the frightful expression tarnishing her dainty face. The wind was gaining strength, and a passing gale fluttered the unbound locks of her sleek hair in a most graceful manner. She hesitated at first, then said, "I thought you to be a hollow and selfish man. I was wrong. Forgive me."

He could not help but smile. "You need not seek forgiveness from me. It is I, who must beg your forgiveness."

She returned a smile of relief. "I now see the grave path you walk. I wish you strength and courage in overcoming your battles hereon."

"Do not despair, Lady Nabiha," he tried to assure her. "If you know your enemy, and trust in your Creator, you need not fear a thousand battles. This is only the beginning."

He rode with nothing but the wind howling in his ears, urging Riah to double her efforts. She was a strong mare, elegant and beautiful, obedient and ardent. She gave him the confidence to further his quest, but as his destination came closer, he realized the gravity of his task. Charging into the Royal Palace was a foolish and impulsive thing to do. He was unprepared for such a feat. He needed guidance. He needed his brother.

He was not enthusiastic about it, but he also needed the skills of Ghasif and Rauf. A reconciliation was imminent whether he desired it or not, and he guided Riah past the farmlands and through the shrubbery that hugged the Hubur.

They navigated the narrow winding trail with slight unease. The engulfing darkness and silence amidst the shrubbery, swaying palm trees and tamarisks, carried an air of gloom and stank of death. When he emerged into the clearing, he was greeted with a sight that confirmed all his fears.

The wind rustled the branches overhead, and the branches shook their leaves in an eerie melody of death and destruction. The fading stars and orange flicker of light from the cabin, did nothing to conceal the bodies sprawled over the uneven ground.

Horrified, Mukhtar dismounted Riah and clumsily sprinted up to the porch, where two more bodies lay, one hanging over the railing like a limp sack, blood dripping steadily into the ground below. With every step he took, the wood screeched uncannily, devilishly adding to the already pernicious symphony of the creaking branches. Arrows stuck out of the wooden walls and poles in odd angles, and the front door hung delicately off its hinges. A soft push and it gave in with a moan and a creak, falling to the cabin floor with a deafening thud.

The inside of the cabin was in utter disarray. The bed was overturned, the mattress ripped to shreds, its insides scattered all over. The ancient chest that stood beside the bed had been ransacked, its contents displaced. The floor was littered with ripped parchment and desecrated books. Dark traces of blood were splattered across the floor and walls, and the air hung with the foul odor of death.

If he had felt fear in the dark and dingy cell of Ghuldad, it was nothing to what he was feeling at that moment. Lightheaded, he swayed on the spot, threatening to collapse.

He picked up the only source of light in the cabin, a knocked-over lantern. Cautiously, he searched the cabin and spotted a crossbow with the Aztalaan insignia of a wolf on its stock.

Zaki was here! He thought. *He must have escaped the Souk and returned to the cabin to await me.*

He slung the crossbow over his shoulder and rushed out of the cabin to search the bodies. He must ascertain that Ghasif, Rauf, and Zaki, were not among the dead, and he moved from one to the other, overturning the bodies. Each one filled him with apprehension and dread, followed by immense relief, as none yielded any familiar faces. In addition to the two on the porch, he counted five bodies on the ground.

Captured? He thought. *Or escaped?*

They could not have escaped. The cabin was in disarray, the lantern was not extinguished. If Mukhtar was certain of one thing, they would not leave the bodies lying about. If anything, they would have dumped them in the river.

Captured, then. By whom? The host of assassins accompanying Ussam and Thamir to the Royal Palace? But these were not assassins.

He knelt down to reexamine the body closest to him. Although blood had stained the tunic under the armor, he could still distinguish the difference in shade from the one he was used to seeing on Adil. His eyes widened when he remembered where he had seen the navy-blue fabric. It was the same shade as the tunic he had been forced to wear, and the very same worn by the guards at Thamir's feast. These were Abunaki's men.

Mukhtar collapsed to the ground and buried his face in his hands. It felt as though he no longer knew who, or what, he was dealing with. His hope was to seek his brother's counsel along with Ghasif and Rauf, but if Abunaki's men had taken them captive, and Abunaki owed allegiance to Thamir, then that could only mean his brother and the others were being held captive at the palace.

How would he penetrate the Royal Palace by himself? It was an impossibility. Even the notion of seeking his brother's help now seemed far-fetched. Alone, the battle would be short-lived. He would not make it past the front gates.

He stood up. Now was not the time to falter. Zaki was in need. Ghasif and Rauf were in need. Ussam had to be stopped, and if he did not muster the courage to do what needed to be done, the evil of Azazil will endure. He knew what he must do.

He needed weapons. And he already knew where to find the perfect craft. He left Riah at the cabin and continued afoot. He felt terrible leaving her amidst the dead bodies and desecrated cabin, but it would be easier to navigate the city without her.

The city was quiet and asleep, and a later hour meant that much of the city guards and archers would most likely be groggily unaware at their posts. Even so, he swept his feet stealthily, creeping in the shadows like a predator. The streets were calm and deserted, devoid even of guard patrols, save for stray cats and dogs, and homeless citizens hurdled in dark corners and alleys, covered in rags to keep themselves warm.

Breaking into the forge was simpler than anticipated. The vicinity was suspiciously unguarded, warranting crucial investigation, but he was desperately pressed for time. Even so, he maintained caution as he slithered towards the rear entrance of the forge. He required very little effort in overcoming the lock on the door. Cautiously, he stepped into the stale but familiar scent of his former workplace. In the darkness, he made his way to the front counter and groped for the corner where a torch bracket usually hung. With its tip ignited, he familiarized himself with his surroundings.

He gasped. It was just as abused as the cabin, save for the dead corpses and puddles of blood. Every inch had been violated, from the tools on the benches to the storage crates under them. Every object in the forge was sprawled over the counter, benches, and the floor. Ghulam's men had searched desperately for the Keystone and what it concealed, but they seemed not to have found it. The reason was apparent enough to Mukhtar. They did not know what he now knew. They were driven by greed and hunger for power, blinded by their own arrogance, which prevented them from looking in the right place. Prevented them from seeing what he saw.

He glanced at the cold, damp furnace in the corner of the forge and could not suppress a shudder of excitement. Childhood memories flooded into him in a rush of emotion, making his heart beat in a frenzy. Unattended for so long, the coals had burned to cinder and ash. Regardless of Mika'il's claim, since the forge was first built, the furnace had run cold on only *one* other occasion. Mukhtar remembered a time when Mika'il and Harun needed to replace the bricks around its mouth. He was constantly running in and out of the forge, screaming and yelling with an excitement elevated from playing with his peers. He remembered Mika'il angrily brandishing a long wooden stick kept specifically for the purposes of discipline. He had chased away his friends for causing too much commotion, distracting him from his work.

Mukhtar could not help smile, gazing at the spot under Mika'il's bench, where he remembered hiding away, distraught after his uncle had scolded him. He remembered Mika'il softly ushering him to come out from under, and when he stubbornly refused, his uncle handed him a pair of carving tools and a freshly baked brick, urging him to channel his creativity in a more constructive manner.

He gave another chuckle as his heart skipped a beat, picturing his youthful self. He had pushed aside the tools and the brick hatefully, wanting no pity from his uncle. Mika'il had walked away, leaving him be. After a long while, Mukhtar's limbs had started to ache, his backside feeling sore. But his pride prevented him from coming out. In an attempt to shun away the boredom, he pulled closer the brick and tools, and decided to give his uncle's suggestion a try.

Mukhtar turned his gaze away from the counter. With the torch held high, he approached the furnace, taking caution with every step. Mere inches away, he ran his hand over its open mouth, large enough to comfortably accommodate a small man. The textured brick at the apex of the furnace was blank, but as his fingers moved further in, he felt something.

On the inside of the brick was a small gaping hole, about the size of his finger, and felt triangular in shape. Below the hole was an unmistakable indentation of two lines, crisscrossing each other. He turned around, leaned back into an arc and slid his head through, carefully bringing the torch with him. His head rested on a pile of undisturbed ashes, taking short and controlled breaths to avoid inhaling the toxic dust. Above him, the furnace dissipated into a dark chimney, beyond which a discreetly howling wind attempted entry.

The blackened brick, endlessly scorched by the furnace for years, would reveal nothing to an unsuspecting eye, but to him, it was as clear as he first remembered it. Fingers trembling, heart hammering against his chest and a sudden clench in his stomach were all but a fraction of the excitement and nervousness he felt. He pressed two fingers on the indentation and waited patiently for a dramatic event to follow.

Nothing happened. He exerted more effort on the entire Keystone, and yet nothing happened.

Frowning, he brought the torch closer to look upon it with better light. With his free hand, he reached for the Amulet on his chest and brought it closer to the Keystone. Both were exactly the same shape and size. He inserted the Amulet, maneuvering the golden chain to make a perfect fit, and pressed it into the hole.

There was a click and a groan.

The furnace gave a threatening tremble and he jumped, nearly breaking his back. Dust and debris rained down on his face, and he withdrew from the furnace instinctively, almost setting himself ablaze with the torch.

A few moments passed and the furnace continued to vibrate with an aggressive admonition of erupting with fury, and suddenly, two objects descended, successively rooting into the mound of ash, prominently proud in a perspicuous incarceration of an engraved symbol.

Eyes wide and gleaming, heart furiously hammering in his chest, he took a cautious step forward with his arm outstretched. Both blades stood, crisscrossing each other, twins in every aspect. He returned the torch to its bracket and pulled out the swords, fingers trembling, steeling the tingling sensation coursing through his body. He gazed at the silver, engraved handles, jagged but sharp edges, and nearly wept. The Keystone was true. The first of the otherworldly weapons had been revealed.

It was long before he remembered his true purpose, and hastily gathered his thoughts to further his ploy of infiltrating the Royal Palace. He groped for the Amulet still embedded into the hole in the brick, hung it around his neck, and searched the forge for more wares that would aid him.

He sifted through the littered and desecrated forge, picking out usable armaments such as sheaths and greaves, braces and an array of throwing-knives, all in preparation for his toughest battle yet.

An hour later, he had scaled up to the minaret of a two-story building across the street from the large iron gates of the Royal Palace. Lightning flashed, thunder roared overhead, and moments later, heavy droplets fell like pebbles from an enraged sky. Mukhtar was drenched within seconds, but regardless of the bleak deluge, he grinned with confidence and touched the Amulet on his chest.

TWENTY-FIVE

THE PALACE

Rain fell in torrents. Thunder boomed overhead. On the street below, a dog slithered away, whining in protest of the deluge. Across the city, oil lamps and lanterns were lit by the occupants of the mud and brick structures, as Khalidans were woken to address the detriments of the abrupt deluge upon their properties.

The pattering rain formed gushing streams, and in the distance, waves crashed upon the shoreline in a sudden turn of the tide. Anglers and sailors alike would pull into the harbor the following morning, with substantial damages to their vessels and wares. If at all they would survive what the night threatened.

Mukhtar drew his gaze away from the harbor, and scanned the stronghold of King Azhar Babak, chinking away at the sheer might of the force that guarded it. Small fires were lit every few feet, illuminating even the darkest corners. The large engraved oak doors that linked the palace to the grounds, were shut and well-fortified. The tall citadel cast a gloomy duress on the lesser guard tower and prison hold beside it, and the plush grounds stretched out far behind to the kitchens and slaughterhouses all enclosed within an expansive perimeter of a ten-foot thick and forty-foot high wall. The Palace served, not only as the Royal Family's abode on the eastern front, but as barracks for the Royal Army and the City Watch on western side, along with its arsenal and weapons-hold, prison-holds, war chambers, accommodations for resident dignitaries, and Immorkaan's court and council chambers. This was stronghold that had governed the Empire of Ahul-Hama for close to two decades.

From his perch, he observed with a keen eye. Visibility may have been greatly reduced due to the stormy deluge, but there was no mistaking the perpetual and heightened sense of activity and security. Rasha had cautioned him against Jinn guarding the palace, but the human guards alone were enough to make even the bravest man lose hope. Unperturbed by the deluge, archers crept silently along the parapets and battlements, scanning their surroundings as far out as possible. Sturdy and alert, armed guards moved in batches of eight or ten, each patrol spaced just a few feet away from the next.

Every archway, every corner, doorway, and pathway was guarded by upright soldiers armed to the teeth. Several more moved around in random patterns, and Mukhtar realized his futile visions of penetrating the palace. It would take weeks, if not months, of reconnaissance just to study the guards' movements, let alone work out a strategical plan of slipping in and out unnoticed, without possibly getting lost in the maze of rooms and corridors of the massive structure.

However, impossibility was not a word he could afford at this 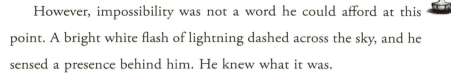 point. A bright white flash of lightning dashed across the sky, and he sensed a presence behind him. He knew what it was.

"I need your powers," he demanded.

'Yours by right of birth,' she replied slyly. *'Your thoughts are my command.'*

"If you betray me, I will destroy the Amulet and you with it!" he threatened angrily.

'Many have said the same before you,' she sneered.

Another flash of lightning, followed by thunder, and her presence vanished. A third flash illuminated the palace and its grounds, giving him enough time to spot a weakness in the fortifications.

He descended from the minaret, slow and steady, and as soon as his feet touched the ground, he set off toward the eastern walls of the palace, his swords and knives tingling softly, as he sprinted in the gloomy shadows. Guided by the sounds of gushing waters, he arrived at a point where a narrow man-made stream flowed under a low arch that allowed the Hubur to run through.

He stood at the edge of the bank, and stared into the dark waters. He had no intention of climbing the walls and risk being spotted by the archers, nor did he look forward to the alternative. His sandals sunk into the muddy slope, and he fumbled to keep his balance. With a quick prayer, he shut off his mind, took a deep breath, and plunged.

Every nerve in his body screeched in dissent. The water was cold, its icy chill drilling into his bones. The current was strong, and it put up a difficult fight. Only his determination to remain alive drove him forward, but it was not long before his lungs desperately cried for air. He pushed, kicking his legs as rapidly as he could. Two more feet of struggling against the current and he felt his lungs deplete whatever oxygen was remaining. Even though it was truly dark under the water, tiny spots began to appear and disappear before him like floating bubbles of light.

A rush of water, almost as solid as a human hand, grabbed him by his hair and pulled him upward. Coughing and sputtering, he tore through to the surface, taking in huge gulps of air. He swam for the bank and grabbed hold of a rock, resting his arms, breathing in deep. His teeth chattered against the cold and his body begged to be retired.

From between the rocks and shrubbery, he scanned his surroundings. There were no guards in the vicinity, but there was no mistaking the patrols in the distance, and the archers on the parapets far above.

The landscape was level but uneven due to the exquisite and exotic flowers, plants, neatly-trimmed bushes, and trees, adorning the fictitious replication of a paradise that served the Royal Family's recreational strolls. Several illuminated pathways and walkways cut through the gardens in random directions.

'How can the lanterns burn in such a deluge?' he thought.

'They are not flames of this world,' Adva warned. *'Caution, Mukhtar. Follow the pathways, but stay away from the lights.'*

The closest illuminated pathway stretched into the distance, and through the grainy screen of rainfall, he could see, though not clearly enough, several distant figures in motion.

'I can use the trees, bushes, and statues for cover.'

'Stay away from the lights,' she repeated.

He pulled himself out of the water, crawled over the bank, and did not stop moving until he was hidden behind a large stone statue of a rearing horse. Leaning against the foundation of the statue, he shivered uncontrollably, as the cold water clung to his skin, aggravated by the searing wind.

Taking care not to be seen, he peeked around the corner of the statue to peer through the darkness and rain, and map out his course. In the far distance, the illuminated facade of the Royal Palace stood firm and resolute under apocalyptic skies.

Something moved just a few feet to his left, and he tensed. His hand edged slowly to the sash around his waist, and pulled out a throwing-knife. It moved again, rustling the grass beneath its feet. Mukhtar was able to roughly estimate its position in the dark, just behind a bush ahead of him, and he readied the knife, holding it by the tip of its blade. He was on the verge of flicking his wrist, when the thing came into view, and he was caught in awe of the magnificence of its snowy white tail feathers, glowing despite being drenched in the rain. It was a peacock, strolling with an air of sovereignty, proud and boastful of itself.

Rather than slither away, it stared at him for a long while. There was a peculiar moment when Mukhtar's hooded brown eyes were locked into its proud black ones. It seemed to read his thoughts, studying him carefully before turning away and disappearing among the shrubs.

The storm roared above him, louder and more sinister than ever. A bolt of lightning streaked across the sky, reaching for the earth, threatening to set ablaze anything in its path. Time was running short, urging him to keep moving. Steering clear of the main trail proved more difficult than anticipated, as the illuminated pathway twisted, turned, and bridged into a network of winding lanes around the landscape. Several times, he was forced to either stop dead in his tracks, or alter his course entirely to avoid encounters with randomly strolling creatures, employed by the King to roam free in his garden.

He saw more peacocks about, exotic birds on high, sheltered perches, even a fox, and what he suspected may have been a sleeping panther on a low branch, which made him back away slowly and cautiously, and map out an alternative route. At one point, his foot fell into an unsuspecting pond, and he woke a sleeping alligator that nearly snapped his foot clean off, causing him to scramble away to safety.

The immaculate guise of the marble and brass-adorned palace walls, loomed closer into view. Elegant lampposts illuminated the lower levels well enough for him to see how difficult it would be to gain entry through the front.

Peering through the bushes, he watched how alert the guards stood, sturdy and brutally armed, prepared to cleave any who dared challenge them. Their counterparts, equally armed and alert, patrolled the area in pairs of twos or threes, pausing every now and then to gaze out over the gardens. Whether this was how they normally functioned, night after night, Mukhtar did not know. Clearly discernible from the burgundy of the Royal Guard, hooded and clad in white robes under light armor, were Assassins of Ghuldad and the unmistakable navy-blue mercenaries under Abunaki's employ. Mukhtar's suspicions had been true. Ussam's corruption, it seemed, knew no bounds, if assassins and mercenaries mingled freely with the King's guard.

He drew away from the bushes and mapped a path to the rear of the palace. Protruding from the smooth wall was a rough, stone

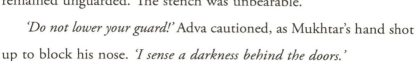

structure with a thatched roof, door-less and windowless. Only when he came closer to the structure, did he understand why this area remained unguarded. The stench was unbearable.

'Do not lower your guard!' Adva cautioned, as Mukhtar's hand shot up to block his nose. *'I sense a darkness behind the doors.'*

'What is it? Jinn? *Shaytaan?*'

'I cannot be certain. Tread carefully.'

"Tread carefully," Mukhtar muttered sarcastically, as he cut through the slaughterhouse, trying to keep from stepping into muck and animal waste. Large iron hooks hung from wooden beams above shallow pits where the animals were slaughtered and hung until their blood ran out. The air was heavy, putrid, and filled with the buzzing of flies.

At the end of the slaughterhouse, Mukhtar became still and silent. A shimmer of light peered through the tiny crack under the wooden door. He paused, heart hammering against his chest, dreading what he might find beyond it. Dagger at hand, firm but flexible enough to yield, he edged closer to the door.

I pray to thee Almighty, the most Beneficent, the most Merciful. Guide my soul through all atrocities, and protect it from the evil beyond this door. He took a deep breath and opened the door by a tiny crack. The room beyond was empty. He stepped through the door and shut it.

The light was coming from a dying fire pit to his right. To his left was an expanse of the royal kitchens, the far wall dissolving into darkness. Pots and pans hung from the ceiling. Cutlery, fruits, and vegetables lay upon large tables. Heaps of various colored spices and seasonings sent appealing aromas up his nostrils, and the air hung with a distinct scent of a scrumptious meal only recently served.

Before taking a step further, he was struck by a sudden notion.

He held out his hand, shut his eyes, and focused all his thought and energy on his clothes, imagining what he wished to be done to them. Adva had said that his thought was her command, but it was no simple task. It drained him of his energy, but he was determined, and just as the thought became clearer, so did it materialize.

He felt the water part with the fibers of his apparel, accumulate before him in droplets suspended in midair. The droplets fell to the floor, and he had to suppress a yelp of awe at what he had just accomplished, as his clothes became warm and dry again.

However, the sense of power and exhilaration was only short-lived.

'Someone approaches,' Adva's hiss made him jump.

His eyes darted to the door. Swiftly, he blended into the dark stone wall, drew his dagger, and waited. The door creaked open, slowly, steadily. A figure stepped in, a few inches shorter than him, covered from head to toe in long, dark, and sweeping robes. Mukhtar held his breath. He moved forward stealthily, a mere shadow in both appearance and motion. But he was not unnoticed.

The figure turned with speed and agility. There was a flash of silver, and Mukhtar had but his instincts to defend him, as he raised his own dagger to ward off the attacker. A clash of steel reverberated across the kitchens, but his attacker was an amateur, and did not possess the ability to fortify the strike.

Mukhtar wrestled with the assailant, twisted, turned, and pinned the cloaked and veiled figure against the wall of the kitchen. Large, almond-shaped eyes gleamed back at him in the dull firelight, horrified and terrified, fearful and hateful. He stared deeply into them, but it was not the eyes that aroused his senses. It was the flowery scent of lavender and *Oudh*.

Something was indecisively wrong. When he left the cabin, every step was unforeseen, unpredictable. He expected the unexpected, but this was a paramount turn of events. For several long moments, he remained rooted to the spot, staring at the one individual whose presence there was utterly inexplicable.

She was breathing hard, her chest heaving, yet her gaze refused to leave his.

"It cannot be!" he gasped.

'I see it now,' Adva filled the silence in his thoughts. *'It writhes and coils itself, caressing her soul. A phantom of fire and shadow. A Qa'reen is bound to every human by divine link. To break the link bears horrendous consequences. The girl is not a sorcerer, but she has done something terribly wrong. She is alive for as long as the contract lasts, but she will be consumed in a most inhumane manner once it is fulfilled. Be wary. Such a monstrosity is not to be trifled with.'*

"What have you done, Nuzhah?" he asked, as calmly as he could.

"Step away from me!" she growled and brandished her dagger.

Mukhtar took a step back and lowered his guard, sheathing his dagger.

"I mean you no harm," he said. "You once helped me. Let me help you."

"You cannot help!" she shrieked, "Step away!"

"Nuzhah!" he raised his voice but a little. "There are powers here beyond your control. You must listen to me! Do you understand what you have done?"

Her horrified eyes began to fill with tears. She slid back against the wall and collapsed to the floor. "Ussam forced me to partake in the rituals!"

Mukhtar's expression was stony. "Where?" he asked simply.

"In the Throne Room. They were drinking, intoxicating themselves and indulging in— in— *horrifying* acts of—"

She fell silent. Mukhtar noted the distressed tone in her voice. He gave her a moment.

"What then?" he pressed.

"I was overcome with delirious thoughts and illusions. Then, something spoke to me, as if from within my mind. I was frightened. I ran. I must leave this place! You *must* take me away from here!"

Mukhtar stepped forward and leaned in. "My brother has been taken prisoner," he asserted, more forcefully than intended, "along with Ghasif and Rauf. Do you know where they are being held?"

Her eyes shot up to him in disbelief. "If they are Ussam's prisoners then they must be held in the dungeons!"

"Can you take me to them?"

"No!" she shrieked even louder than before, and Mukhtar shut his eyes, praying that no one heard it. "There is evil within these walls! You cannot ask me to remain here!"

"You would let them perish?" he pleaded. "You would let Ussam spread his darkness? If we cower, then countless others will fall prey to his wickedness. We must be strong. Muster your courage. Help me as you once did, Nuzhah. You must!"

"No!" She shook her head in frightful plea. "You cannot ask me to return to those *horrors!* You *cannot!* I beg you!"

Mukhtar felt a rush of empathy for her. Whatever it was that had driven her to such terror, he was strongly overcome with an urge to reach out, grab her hand and take her away from the palace, somewhere far, perhaps far from the city, even further away from the

Empire. However, the evil afoot could not be ignored. Could not be run away from. He needed to muster his courage. He needed to take the step forward. He needed his brother and his friends, and for that, he needed her in sobriety and sound of mind.

"Nuzhah," he lowered his tone to its utmost humility. Her gaze moved up to meet his. "I have always known you to be stronger than many. Stronger, even, than I. In times of darkness, you were a beacon of hope to me. I still see that beacon, even now. I too am filled with terror and uncertainty over what lay ahead. But if I do not take a step forward, if I do not overcome my fears and brave this evil, by God Almighty, there won't be a corner left on this earth to seek sanctuary. I plead your allegiance now, more than ever."

She eyed him for a long while, gazing deeply into his eyes. He could not help but reminisce the chains that bound him to the wheel, and those fleeting moments of her precious company that almost seemed to make them vanish, almost forget his enslavement. She gave a brisk nod, severing the unseen link between their eyes.

She led. Mukhtar followed. Or rather, Mukhtar took cautious steps forward, while she trailed behind, pointing him in the right direction. As they lurked the dark and silent but magnificent hallways of the Royal Palace, Mukhtar could not help but wonder if he had done right by asking her to accompany him when she was so prepared to escape.

Was it selfishness to want her by his side, as he walked toward what felt like doom? Perhaps her presence helped overcome his concealed fears. Or perhaps she had yet a purpose to fulfill, one that would determine the aftermath of this night.

Adva made no objection regarding his decision in allowing Nuzhah to stay, and he suspected why. With regards to Adva's warning about the Qa'reen, Nuzhah's involvement in the night's activities may have some significance, and her separation from its confines could critically destroy her unless the predicaments were resolved. She silently guided him through the palace, surprisingly versed with its layout.

"When did you arrive at the palace?" Mukhtar whispered.

"Ussam sent us ahead several days ago," she replied in an equally hushed tone. "A handful of servants to attend to his personal delegates. He and his host of Assassins arrived tonight."

"I witnessed their caravan earlier," Mukhtar nodded. "They entered a wealthy merchant's mansion close to the harbor. We have been following a trail of conspiracies and plots to overthrow Azhar Babak's rule. This must be their final ploy. Whatever they intend, it will happen tonight, and I must do whatever it takes to stop them."

"I caution you, Mukhtar," Nuzhah's voice shook slightly, "much has been happening in Ghuldad since you left. I have not an ounce of understanding what it is, but I cannot free myself from the unsettling feeling that this is beyond any of us. I strongly urge you to escape while we still can."

"I have known you to be strong of faith," Mukhtar eyed her, "and those strong of faith must always be willing to stand up against evil. How can you choose to abandon hope now? Have you forgone your faith?"

"Do not judge me, Mukhtar," her voice became stern with warning. "Do not patronize me. You know not what I have been through!"

He fell silent. She had agreed to aid him thus far, and he knew she was on edge. To push her over would be a most foolish thing to do. It was true, he did not truly know what she may have been through.

He was to blame. He had left her in Ghuldad, purely because he had not wanted to jeopardize his own freedom, and the guilt of doing so had been boring into him since.

"Forgive me," he said solemnly. "I did not mean—"

"Don't," she interrupted. "You are right. I am overcome with much right now. I have no intent of abandoning my faith. I only pray for strength to carry me through."

"I pray the same," he muttered, almost to himself.

They continued along dark corridors in silence, passing lavish rooms with lush rugs and silk drapes, open halls with marvelous displays of art and sculpture, further and deeper into what appeared to be a suspiciously deserted palace.

"Where are all the guards?" he asked, questioning the absence of arm-bearers within the walls. "I spotted some outside, assassins and mercenaries mingling with the Royal Guard."

"All the guards were sent away to await further orders," she replied. "All the servants were ordered to partake in the rituals."

"Why?" Mukhtar enquired. "What rituals are these?"

"You will soon see," she replied grimly. "As much as I know, the King possesses something of value. The rituals are meant to force him to willingly relinquish it."

"Amulet," Mukhtar muttered. "And what of Ma'alim?" he asked. "What does he intend on doing about all this?"

To his utter surprise, she nearly laughed. "Ma'alim has not been sighted for months! Not since your escape from the fortress."

Mukhtar froze in his tracks. "How can this be? He sent Ghasif a letter, not ten days ago. He had a plan to end Ussam's vile ambitions. Is it that he has forfeited his profound quest for liberation?"

"Perhaps," Nuzhah replied, urging him forward. "He has been unheard of, and many have lost their faith in him. Whatever his efforts, they have failed to prevent Ussam thus far. He disbanded us when we needed him most."

Mukhtar gave her a puzzled look. "You believed in him as your leader, and now you mistrust him?"

The corridor they were stealthily creeping along, opened out to a grand balcony with marble flooring, polished railings, and silky drapes, all overlooking a large Entrance Hall lit with intricately designed lanterns on either side. Tall, circular, stone pillars held up the high ceilings, garnished with Khalidan architectural carvings that were even more pronounced by the dancing lights of the lanterns. Large stone statues, of both man and beast, filled in the gaps between the pillars, casting deep shadows on the silk-draped walls behind them, and the marble floor was bedecked with expensive and exotic rugs.

Nuzhah's footsteps slowed to a halt and her voice trembled with a distinct dread. "I know not what to believe anymore," she raised a shaky finger, and pointed.

TWENTY-SIX

OF SIN AND THE SINNER

Mukhtar was drawn away from the allure of the Entrance Hall, to two magnificent doors of highly polished mahogany inlaid with gold. A deep rumbling chant, effortlessly blending with the rhythmic procession of musical instruments, was pouring through the open doors. The symphonies were dark and daunting, clawing and gripping his heart with terror. It sickened him, but the feeling was nothing compared to what he felt when he approached the doors and peeked around them to connect sight with sound.

The Throne Room was much larger than the Entrance Hall, similarly embellished with silk drapes, palatial ornaments, and opulent artifacts on grandstands and pedestals, with several exquisite rugs and exotic animal skins spread out over the gleaming marble floor. The King's throne was erected atop a raised platform of several steps at the far end, set in stone between two large pedestals boasting elegant flames of a bright fire.

None sat upon the throne, but below it, at the foot of the steps, four hooded figures in dark robes were gathered around something, engaged in some sort of devilish worship.

Intricately embroidered cushions were sprawled all over the entire floor, their occupants male and barely clothed. He spotted ministers and viziers, members of the King's Court, prominent figures who had made several public appearances and even more false promises to the betterment of their people. Hovering above and around them, were women of even fewer garments, swaying to the sinister symphonies of the instruments and chantings, serving the occupants with varieties of wines and an array of intoxicants, or else indulging them in acts of prurience and salacity. The air was heavy with the scents of *khamr* and *khat*, and smoke from *hukahs* impaled with opium and *hashish*.

It was repugnant and outrageous, unlike anything he had ever seen. He averted his eyes and leaned back against the wall, breathing heavily to combat the nauseous feeling. Is this what had truly become of those who ruled this nation? How then could a dark storm not gather over such evil?

"Have you seen enough?" Nuzhah's voice trembled.

"I do not see Ussam," he craned his neck slightly. "Nor the King."

"Will you not leave now, while your sanity still permits you?"

"I will not leave without my brother!" he responded, rather harshly. "Take me to the dungeons!"

She threw him a scathing look, and led him to the lower levels of the palace, through hallways and corridors that may not have been as lavish as the upper floors, but were surprisingly just as destitute of guards and soldiers. The rough stone-walls were lit by torches on brackets, and the air felt cooler and damper the deeper they went.

The smell of human waste and decay informed them of their arrival at the dungeons. Despite her veil, Nuzhah still held up a handful of her robes to mask the stench. They stopped at the end of a long and wide corridor with several narrower ones branching out in either direction. Mukhtar picked up a torch from its bracket and began his search, while Nuzhah kept watch.

He crept stealthily, from cell to cell, peering through the bars for a familiar face. Prisoners, both young and old, some asleep, others shivering in the cold, some quiet and sound, several others beyond the grasp of sanity. Those unaccustomed to light, shied away into the deeper shadows of their cells when he passed them with his lit torch. Mukhtar wondered what these souls may have done to be barred in the dungeons beneath the palace, rotting away in filth and gloom below a carnal splendor so close yet so far beyond their reach. What heinous crime differentiated them from those locked away in the prison tower outside, where the convicts at least had a tiny window to bring them light and air, a ray of hope that perhaps freedom would one day come. The further in he ventured, he could not help but wonder where his father may have been held. Which was the infamous cell he had mysteriously vanished from?

Row after row, cell after cell, every step forward was breathtaking, horrendous, and frightening. Every gaunt and withered face squinting at his burning torch was a pitiful sight, yet disappointing that none of them yielded any familiarity, until a voice spoke from a cell behind him.

"Took you long enough!"

He turned and peered through the bars. "You seem disappointed!" he grinned.

Zaki's hair was matted with blood, a dark bruise under his left eye, and Ghasif was sporting a bloody nose. Beside him, Rauf looked the worst of the lot, with several cuts and bruises on his face, and what appeared to be a twisted left ankle.

"I will find the keys," Mukhtar stated.

He searched around and found a large wooden board pegged against the wall of the main corridor. On rusty old nails, hung rusty old keys, sequentially arranged to correspond with the cells. Mukhtar hurried back and counted the number of corridors and cells to the right one, then back to the board where he found the key, and after a loud clanging of heavy bolts being undone, the iron bars swung open with a grinding, screeching squeal.

"Alas, the scent of freedom!" Rauf remarked as he limped out, leaning on Zaki's shoulder.

"We were only in here for hours!" Zaki said pointedly.

"What happened?" Mukhtar asked him.

"Abunaki's men," Zaki said. "They must have followed me from the *Souk*. We fought hard."

"So I see," Mukhtar eyed their injuries. "The fight will only be harder from hereon," he unslung the crossbow and returned it to his brother. "Ussam is here with Thamir and Abunaki, and the one they call Master. They are all gathered in the Throne Room, in an evil ritual of witchcraft and sorcery. I know not what they mean to achieve, only that we must end this devilry before it is too late."

"How many guards?" Zaki asked.

"Many," Mukhtar replied simply. "A host of assassins and Abunaki's mercenaries are stationed outside with the Royal Guard. Whether they are deceived or allied, I do not know, but for now, we can only assume that any man bearing a sword is our enemy. I passed an armory on the way down. We can arm ourselves and prepare for battle. Come. We must make haste!"

He started forward, only to realize after a few steps that none were following. Not even his brother. He halted and turned to find them exactly where they were, and his eyes widened with disbelief.

"We are heavily outnumbered," Ghasif stated, glancing at Zaki then at Rauf. "How can we possibly survive such a battle?"

"I am not one to shy away from a fight, but to battle in our current state would be foolish," Rauf said.

"How can you *say* that?" Mukhtar walked back toward them. "This not the time to act like cowards!"

"*Look* at me!" Rauf unhooked himself from Zaki's support and took a forceful limp forward, wincing from the pain in his leg. "Look at *us!* How far into the battle do you think we will survive?"

"It is wiser to escape these morbid confines and regroup to better prepare ourselves," Ghasif said solemnly. "This night may be beyond our reach."

Mukhtar desperately wanted to dispute. He looked to his brother for support, but Zaki said nothing. He was adjusting the strap of his crossbow, with a slight twitch of his shoulder caused by a pernicious injury.

"There is evil afoot that cannot be allowed to endure," Mukhtar said sternly, working up the courage to meet their eyes. "I cannot force you to stay and fight, but I will not allow Ussam to succeed in his venomous endeavors. This ends tonight. If not, then I do not wish to live in a world filled with his wickedness. With that, I look forward to embracing death with honor."

He understood their reluctance. They were weary. They were injured. Indeed, Rauf spoke the truth— how would they survive another battle? He met his brother's eye. Zaki's expression had changed. It had become humbler, slightly shameful with a shadow of guilt. He swallowed. "When I deserted the Red-Guard, I had vowed never to leave your side. Your battles will always be mine. I will fight with you."

Mukhtar's spirits began to rise. He looked to Ghasif and Rauf.

They were both staring at him, astounded and taken aback by his statement. Like Zaki, they were both well-versed in combat, hardened by years of blood and sweat in battle. Their refusal to join him was not from cowardice, but from a calculable approach to fight. It *would* be better to escape, regroup and prepare to fight another day, but they had not seen what he had. They had not witnessed the nefarious affairs taking place on the floors above.

"Lead the way to the armory," Ghasif gave a strong nod.

"We have come too far to desert you now," Rauf limped forward. "Lead the way, brother. I too will stand by your side, be this my final stand in life!"

The armory was large and well equipped, with wares that made Mukhtar's poorly maintained short-swords shrink away. He secretly held on to his own weapons, while the other three armed themselves. He longed to tell them what he had discovered, but realized the weight of the matter. He was afraid that if Zaki was to learn of the Amulet's true nature, and that which resided within, he would utterly refuse to go any further, as would Ghasif and Rauf. He needed them. Perhaps it was foolish not to arm them with that knowledge, but they did not need it then. It may have been a gamble he was taking, but the only thing that mattered to him then was to end Ussam's ritual above. All else could be dealt with later— if at all they survived the night.

They reunited with a frightened Nuzhah and convinced her of their plans to make a stand. It took no small measure of pleading with her and in the end, Mukhtar vowed to see her to safety before they began their attack. She agreed to lead them to an isolated corner of the palace, further away from the Throne Room, where they could discuss their next approach and leave her in safety. As soon as they emerged into the Entrance Hall, however, all manner of hell erupted.

Amidst the chaotic screams of half-naked bodies running around in fright, they had but an instant to evade the large statue thrown across the hall. Nuzhah shrieked, and Mukhtar instinctively pushed her out of its projectile. It landed with a thundering crash, where they all stood only a moment before, fatal chunks of loose rock, stone, and debris expelled in every direction.

Several of the occupants, who had partaken in the occult rituals only an hour before, lay crushed beneath the rubble. Blood and innards sprawled across the marble floor. The rituals had ended and there was some sort of retaliation or retribution taking place, where the ritualists were now paying for their deeds with their lives. It was not long before a host of assassins and mercenaries engaged them in combat, and Mukhtar found himself facing three men with spears, charging toward him with murderous roars.

Impulse and adrenaline took him, as he pulled out the short-swords from their sheaths on his back, and prepared to face them.

The first man, large and baby-faced, swung forward with immense strength, nearly shattering Mukhtar's arm as he tried to parry the attack with one sword. The man struck again, but Mukhtar was ready for him. He dodged with agility and thrust forward, driving his blade deep into the man's belly, but did not stop to watch him die as he pulled back the blade. Two more mercenaries were already on him. He dodged several strikes from their consecutive attacks, receiving a fair share of blows and cuts. He conquered them with a mid-air twist, swinging left with one blade and right with the other. He caught one, with a powerful swing on his chest, tearing the man's leather amour through to his flesh, and slicing the other's neck.

Nearly breathless, he stood back and tried to find his friends and brother amidst the chaotic crowd. Assassin archers, on the grand balcony above, were raining down arrows upon anyone who moved, and several of the ritualists cowered behind the stone pillars, all manner of intoxication forgone by fear and adrenaline. Those who had weapons, or somehow managed to salvage one, made every attempt to survive by warding off the attackers.

Mukhtar watched Rauf dispose four archers at the top of the stairs, who were trying to get a good aim over their targets. Nuzhah was crouched beside him, tossing bits of rock and rubble at the mercenaries. Her aim was not perfect, nor was her reach, but she succeeded in distracting them long enough for Rauf to press his advantage and fire a steady shot. Zaki was fending off four assassins by himself, and Ghasif, after successfully disposing of his own opponents, rushed forward to help him

"*Ghasif, you traitor!*"

Mukhtar spun around wildly to see Shahzad the Impaler charge toward Ghasif, leading a fresh batch of assassins down the marble steps. Ghasif responded with a battle cry and charged to meet them, shortly joined by Zaki, and Mukhtar watched with horror as both men struggled to fend off Shahzad's forces.

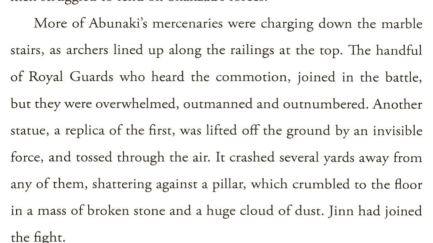

More of Abunaki's mercenaries were charging down the marble stairs, as archers lined up along the railings at the top. The handful of Royal Guards who heard the commotion, joined in the battle, but they were overwhelmed, outmanned and outnumbered. Another statue, a replica of the first, was lifted off the ground by an invisible force, and tossed through the air. It crashed several yards away from any of them, shattering against a pillar, which crumbled to the floor in a mass of broken stone and a huge cloud of dust. Jinn had joined the fight.

"Adva!" he called desperately. "Help us!"

The words had barely left his lips, and she materialized before him, hovering an inch off the ground, brandishing a strangely shaped blade. Her dark lips peeled back and revealed a razor-toothed snarl behind a curtain of long dark hair.

"What is attacking us?" he gasped, his eyes searching for the invisible forces.

"The *Shayateen* reign freely. Turn your attention to Ussam. They obey his command. Kill him and they will flee! Look to the Throne Room," she pointed above the stairs.

Mukhtar faced the Throne Room. "I will not allow Ussam to see the light of dawn!"

Below the grand balcony, Zaki braced himself to face five assassins, who, after seeing the dead bodies of their fallen comrades, approached with greater caution. Ghasif was engaged in a fierce clash of steel with his adversary, Shahzad, corresponding skill for skill, blade for blade. Nuzhah and Rauf took cover behind a large stone chest, arrows scattered all around them. The archers on the grand balcony had painted him as a greater adversity, and Mukhtar could see why. The balcony was riddled with several dead assassins, their blood dripping steadily onto the marble floor below. Mukhtar watched with awe, as Rauf leaned over the stone chest, took aim, and fired two arrows with such speed, he was a mere blur. He did not even find the need to confirm his shot, as the arrows struck their targets. The archers keeled over the balcony, and fell with horrid splats onto the floor below.

"Clear me a path to the Throne Room!" Mukhtar instructed Adva.

She responded by effortlessly lifting a large boulder and throwing it over the balcony. Some of the archers scattered, and those caught unaware were buried beneath the rubble.

Twirling both blades skillfully, Mukhtar started forward, building up his momentum from a jog to a sprint, fighting his way through the advancing assassins and mercenaries. Three archers took aim and fired. One of the arrows found its mark and sheared through the flesh of his right arm, throwing him back several feet. He screamed and recoiled in pain, urging himself to keep moving.

Mustering his strengths, he tossed a few throwing-knives without really aiming, and succeeded in critically wounding two archers and a guard at the top of the steps. Rauf's arrows took out two more, as another massive stone block shattered over the heads of four others, clearing the way for Mukhtar.

He chanced a glance back, only to see more assassins and

mercenaries flood into the Entrance Hall, advancing toward the others, their battle cries elevated. Mukhtar's limbs tired, his body ached, and he groaned on the verge of losing all hope. He hesitated for a moment, torn between advancing to the Throne Room, or turning back to help his friends.

His shoulders tensed, the grip on his sword handles tightened, as the elegant oak doors of the Entrance Hall burst open with a thunderous clap, and a larger host of soldiers marched through, spears held high, shields upright and firm, swords and scimitars, bows and arrows at the ready. Mukhtar nearly fell to his knees dispiritedly, until he realized the leader of the host.

Aarguf Babak, clad in armor, brandished his jeweled scimitar and barked orders at his men. Behind him, looking overwhelmed and mildly frightened, was Nabiha. She took one glance in Rauf and Nuzhah's direction, and ran forward to join them.

Aarguf's men charged forward and clashed with the assassins and mercenaries in battle. The Entrance Hall was ravaged by a fresh batch of shrieks, screams, and clashes of steel as petrified and injured civilians scampered to safety.

Mukhtar, whose attention was drawn to Aarguf's timely entrance, had failed to realize that the doors to the Throne Room had also opened. He caught a brief glimpse of fluttering dark robes before he was struck in the face by a strong fist. The impact swooped him off his feet in a backward arch, and he was flung down the marble steps, landing heavily on his back. Every part of his body groaned in pain, as tiny balls of light hovered before him, and his jaw felt loosely detached from the rest of his head. Through blurry eyes, he saw a strong set of legs running down the steps toward him. He raised his head just as a powerful kick struck him in his midsection, and he felt his guts force through his mouth.

"How I have longed to cut you open since I saw you sneaking through the feast!" the attacker exclaimed viciously.

Mukhtar vomited and gasped for air. Clutching his stomach, he forced his eyes open, and had but a moment's notice to roll over and narrowly avoid a trampling stomp.

Now is not the time to let them tread over you! He thought to himself desperately. *Get up, Mukhtar!*

He forced himself up, swaying slightly on his feet, gripping his swords firmly, ready for the fight.

Abunaki charged forward with his scimitar and a look of pure hatred. Mukhtar raised his own swords to deflect the powerful strike, forcing him to take several steps back. Abunaki charged repeatedly, relentlessly, and with an animosity Mukhtar had never witnessed of him. It was all he could do to fend off the attacks of the skilled and seasoned warrior's power and strength. But he was not prepared to give in so easily.

He learned and adapted to Abunaki's strong and weak points. Abunaki had all but forgotten who always sharpened and repaired his weapons. Mukhtar knew that scimitar well. Its weight gave him a powerful strike, but slowed his recovery from every swing. Mukhtar's short-swords were lighter and made him agile. He skillfully dodged and parried Abunaki's strikes, while inflicting him with minor cuts and slashes wherever he found an opening. Abunaki's frustration mounted with every strike, making him reckless, and Mukhtar wasted no effort in manipulating it to dominate the fight. It was not long before he had Abunaki at the bottom of the steps, bleeding, hurting, and holding up his hands for mercy, his scimitar several feet beyond reach.

"Redeem yourself, Abunaki. Repent for your sins!"

Abunaki pointed a bloody finger at him, and began to laugh, choking on his own blood. "Fool! You walk to your doom! Return to your mother's lap, child!"

"I once held you in high regard," Mukhtar gave him a disappointed look. "Now I only see a coward!"

Abunaki laughed mirthlessly, "Sometimes, cowards do survive!"

"And a coward you shall remain!" Mukhtar snarled.

A blinding, dazzling light overhead, made everyone in the hall cease the battle and watch with awe. Adva was engaged in a furious battle with another *Shayateen*. It had taken the human form of a muscular man, and they were both floating in mid-air, close to the high ceiling, firing detonations among other spells at unnatural speeds.

Their energies were unleashed with unimaginative force, shattering the stone-walls and ceiling, showering the humans below with rubble and dust. There was a fleeting instance when Mukhtar became afraid for her. A powerful force threw her across the hall and she crashed into a stone column. Everyone within the vicinity cowered for their lives, as the column crumbled to the ground. He was relieved to see her emerge unscathed from the cloud of dust, and respond with an energetic spell of her own, which involved several whips of a bright blue flash that tore through her opponent's body. Chunks of body parts and innards fell to the floor, showering those below with splatters of blood and organs. There was an icy gleam in her snakelike eyes, a deep satisfaction of having enjoyed the fight

 immensely.

Zaki and Ghasif rejoined Nuzhah, Rauf, and Nabiha, defending them from rogue attacks. Aarguf's forces continued to engage Ussam's in an enraged battle, but despite their efforts, many more non-combatants continued to fall in the crossfire.

Mukhtar struggled to bring his focus back to the task at hand. He felt deep remorse and regret for not paying heed to Zaki, Ghasif, and Rauf's pleas. They were indeed outnumbered and out-manned. Their blood spilled was on his hands. There was only one way to end it all. Cut off the head of the snake and the body will die.

He rushed up the stairs and before the doors of the Throne Room, he paused. His targets lay beyond, clad in flowing dark robes. Taking deep breaths, he repositioned the twin short-swords and stormed over the threshold. Several assassins charged forward, and he became occupied for a long while before the skirmish was won. When his final opponent, a short and stubby man with a scimitar, fell to the floor, clutching the open wound on his neck, Mukhtar was able to turn his attention to where the ultimatum of the night's events was taking place.

At the foot of the steps leading up to the Throne, a figure was sprawled with his arms and legs spread, bleeding and bruised, dressed in royal robes. Towering above him were two men, one short, the other tall. The short one was easily recognizable as the potbellied Thamir, and his companion, therefore, was Ussam Bashiri, the leader of the Assassins of Ghuldad.

Mukhtar's presence in the hall was not unnoticed. Ussam wore an expression of mild interest, as though he had not expected Mukhtar to have come this far. Thamir reacted without thinking, abandoning all manner of restraint. He wore a look of pure loathing, his bare chest and meaty face glistening with sweat.

"You!" he exclaimed, stepping forward. "Miscreant! A fool of Zafar, you are! You have caused us great misfortune, you vile spawn of—!"

Mukhtar did not allow him to speak any further. He sheathed the short-swords, drew a pair of throwing-knives, and swung them sequentially at Thamir's bulging mass. The first blade struck him on his chest, while the other wedged itself in his left eye socket. His final words escaped him in a muffled screech, and he keeled over, a bloated mass on the hard marble floor.

Ussam glanced at Thamir's body, and a shadow of horror momentarily flashed in his dark eyes. He displayed no further emotion, affirming the depth of his wickedness. He did not even care. He did not even dismay. He was a hollow shell of an egregious being.

"Lie there in silence," his hoarse whisper carried across the room. "You have served your part." He turned to face the king, and Mukhtar followed his gaze.

Azhar Babak was softly moaning in pain at the foot of the steps.

"Our work here is nearly done," Ussam said more audibly. "There is nothing you can do now. His soul fades into the great beyond, where lies an endless torture to world's end. So shall he pay and suffer, for he blew upon knots of conjury, invoking upon that which is forbidden. So shall he pay... and suffer..."

"Your work will remain undone for as long as I breathe!" Mukhtar yelled and unsheathed his short-swords. "Draw your sword, Ussam, and we shall end this!"

"You will not survive this night," Ussam stated, as calmly as though he were welcoming Mukhtar as a guest.

"I assure you, I will fight you to my death!" Mukhtar responded boldly.

"There is no sense in killing you—" another voice echoed off the walls.

It struck him like a bolt of lightning. In his rush to battle Ussam, Mukhtar had failed to notice the gaunt old man who stood beside the throne, stroking his long gray beard, watching the events unfold with interest in his deeply sunken eyes. He wore a black cap, which held his equally long gray hair in place. His long dark robes swept the floor as he stepped into the light of the burning pedestals on either side of the throne, the wrinkles on his wizened face bringing into effect the distinct shadow of a once fierce wolf.

The old man leaned against the throne, ringed fingers lightly tapping on its elegant gold ornamentation. Mouth slightly ajar, Mukhtar stared into those sunken eyes. They tore into him, unearthing a most tormentous statement from the deepest trenches of his thoughts.

The devil has sworn to haunt mankind with his wickedness.

TWENTY-SEVEN

THE TEACHER

Wordless. Speechless. Thoughtless. Mukhtar felt his world darken. His vision blurred and refocused. His mind deadened and sprung back to life with a rush of memories, and he realized all his suspicions and doubts about the elusive leader of the rebels of Ghuldad. He recalled the wizened man tending to his wounds. Staging his escape. Urging them forward to further a rebellion. A revolution.

"Bind him!" Ma'alim hissed, and Ussam took a brisk step forward, raised his arms and brought his palms together viciously. The magnificent mahogany doors slammed shut with a thunderous clap, deafening the battle cries from the Entrance Hall. He waved his arms about in several more fiendish gestures. Ferociously clanking and echoing across the throne room, heavy, iron chains flew forth from the dark shadows in every direction. Forcefully, they attacked Mukhtar, gripping and binding him firmly. His short-swords

cluttered to the floor. His limbs were bound together, utterly immobilizing him. He felt constricted, gasping desperately for breath. He fell hard on the floor, screaming himself hoarse. Thrashing and flailing about like a wild animal was all he could do until he ran out of breath and strength, and lay there on the floor, staring at Ussam through watery eyes with nothing but loathe and hate.

Unable to move, unable to speak, he continued to struggle desperately, hoping and praying that this was only a dream. An illusion. A vivid and horrid replication of the many nightmares that have haunted him since he was a child. The air felt thin and cold. It chilled the sweat clinging to his skin. The fire on the pedestals burned fiercely. They blinded him when he glanced at them. It all felt all too real to be ignored. The truth— the thunderous, mind-numbing truth, descended upon him with an irrefutable reality.

Ma'alim stepped forward and sat on the Throne with an obvious display of frailty, jolting Mukhtar's mind to reality. "There is no sense in killing you," he said, eyeing Mukhtar with mild interest over his laced fingers, adorned with jeweled rings gleaming in the firelight. "Your purpose has yet to be served."

"This is all *your* doing?" Mukhtar managed to utter with a slight quiver in his voice. "Flaunting your righteous fight for freedom while using your *puppet* Ussam to spread your doctrines of war!"

"You *dare* call my son a puppet?" Ma'alim asked calmly, his expression impassive, his eyes inscrutable.

Son? Bewildered, Mukhtar looked from him to Ussam. Had Ma'alim not declared it, Mukhtar would not have been able to distinguish the likeness, if but one was older than the other.

"My *bastard* son," Ma'alim explained to him as though they were friends of old, meeting after long years. "Conceived during a ritual. His mother, a Galadian *whore,* died while giving birth to what was only meant to be an object of payment to a most powerful entity. Who could have foreseen his triumphs?" He raised his chin proudly. "Fate saw him conquer the fortress of Ghuldad. Fate saw him reunite the Amulets. *Fate,* Mukhtar. Who knew, that four decades later, we would be reunited, with a world amiss and a chance to rebuild!"

Mukhtar was dazed. His neck cringed and pained, and he allowed his head to fall to the floor for a moment as he tried to piece together what Ma'alim was saying. "You are *deluded*, old man!" he finally mustered the courage to respond.

"Deluded?" Ma'alim sneered. "There is no delusion, Mukhtar. Open your eyes and you will see. Or shall I open them for you?" The old man was nearly skipping with excitement. *"Fate!* Fate saw me captured by slavers, and fate brought you to me!"

"My actions are my own!" Mukhtar yelled. "I walk this path by choice!"

"Fate and destiny are always intertwined, Mukhtar," Ma'alim said. *"Fate* has set you upon this path, but destiny is yours to shape, and you *chose* to unlock the cage and set me free! Think, Mukhtar, *think!* Do you see it now? Had you chosen to leave me to my fate, I never would have escaped those slavers to reunite with my son!"

Silence deafened him. The fire on the pedestals blinded him. He became lightheaded again. The chains constricted, tightening their hold, threatening to absorb him into a dark abyss. It could not be! It was not possible! How could he have been so *foolish* not to have foreseen this? *Haim Tuma's slaves?*

Mukhtar wished the chains would just swallow him whole. Erase him from this world. He wanted to turn his face in shame and defeat, and brood over how his ignorance had brought about all this death and destruction. He caught Ussam's cold eyes and saw malice in them. The sorcerer seemed to be reading his thoughts, controlling the chains with his sheer will. They coiled and curled over Mukhtar's neck and head, forcing him to face Ma'alim and the throne, and he remained there, drained of all energy and pride.

He could do nothing. Say nothing.

The old man's deceit had conquered and triumphed. Only moments remained until the King died and Ma'alim claimed the Throne.

No! Mukhtar desperately tried to strengthen himself. The time to brood over his mistakes will come, but now was not it. The King's brother was battling his way to them. There was still a fight to be had. He only needed to keep the old man talking and distracted long enough.

"So what is your intent then?" he tried to keep his voice steady. "What do you mean to do with the King?"

"Not just the King, Mukhtar," Ma'alim responded in a tone that suggested mockery. "Every living man, who has ever come to bear an Amulet of Sihr, shall endure what the King endures."

"Your son as well?" Mukhtar challenged.

Ma'alim gave a delirious chuckle. "Alas, my son has already fulfilled his purpose. Ard, the *Ghul* of Earth, serves my will." He held up his hand and allowed a golden chain to drop and suspend from his fingers. Held within the glimmering gold frame was a stone of emerald glow. "He willingly surrendered his Amulet to me and embraced the Mighty Azufil," he went on. "An ancient being. A behemoth among the Jinn. With the aid of its powers, as the ritual comes to an end, Agni, the *Ifreet* of Fire, will be forced to abandon the King and his Amulet, and succumb to my command, and I will bring upon mankind what it has long deserved."

His vision blurry and tilted to the side, Mukhtar eyed the Emerald Amulet with a distinct dread. "More death and destruction?" his voice was clipped and filled with a dark rage.

"*Order,* Mukhtar! Control!" Ma'alim emphasized. "Have you learned nothing since I freed you from your holds in Ghuldad?"

"You imprisoned me in the first place!" Mukhtar struggled with animosity.

"To *teach* you the true meaning of freedom!" Ma'alim argued. "To teach you the true meaning of power! Man has never truly had the right to rule. Man has always abused power. People need order, need to be *ruled*, to be controlled and *commanded*."

"Even if it means sacrificing your own blood?"

Ma'alim gave another cold chuckle. "Even if it means sacrificing mankind itself!" he declared.

Ussam's dark eyes were cold, icy, and lifeless, even though he stood upright. What gazed at Mukhtar, with heinous raptness, was no man. It was Jinn.

A cold chill crept up his spine. Struggling to keep his fears contained, Mukhtar turned his attention back to Ma'alim. He needed to keep him talking, and despite his situation, he could not help but ask the questions that have plagued him for a long while. "Why did you free me when you *knew* who I was and what I had?"

Ma'alim laced his fingers again, gazing at Mukhtar thoughtfully. "Yes, I did indeed know who you were. Unlike my son and this false king," he gestured at Azhar's limp body, "you did not truly possess the power of the Amulet. You were, however, bound to it. This bond kept it concealed from all eyes, in this world and the other. I tortured you to awaken the protection of the *Ma'arid* of Water. To break that bond, and force it to reveal itself."

Mukhtar's bewilderment was a reflection of Ma'alim's.

"Curious, yes. Very curious," Ma'alim said. "But necessary. The Ma'arid was protected, guarded by something so dark, so powerful, it was beyond my abilities. I was forced to summon the Four Sahir," he coughed heavily, clutching his chest, bearing the burden of old age. "It was an uncalculated gambit. A desperate one. The Four are ruthless, merciless. They do not owe allegiance, but unto *he* before whom they bow in worship. Azazil. *Iblees.*"

He turned his head to look at either pedestal for a moment, then at the King and again at Mukhtar, tapping his fingers with a subtle hint of nervousness. Mukhtar understood immediately. Even this ritual was beyond the old man's abilities. It was yet another of his desperate gambits.

"It was only after, that I realized the complex sorcery your father had done," Ma'alim went on. "In order to awaken the Jinn, I had to imprison and torture you, to incite fear within your deepest and darkest thoughts. However, to truly summon the Jinn, I needed to set you on a path of trial and tribulations, and give you the free will to make your own choices between good and evil. I set you loose before the Four arrived to take possession of what they believe to be truly theirs."

Once again, Mukhtar found himself trapped in a void of Ma'alim's deception. "You did not set me loose!" he denied with bitterness and disbelief. "I chose my own path!"

"Indeed, you did," Ma'alim assured him. "To kill Ghadan. To plot against Ghulam. You were faced with a choice, and you chose to murder! It was far simpler than I had anticipated," he gave a small chuckle. "I only needed to guide and aid you, to remove the barriers in your path. Did you think it mere chance that your uncle's forge was unguarded tonight? Mere good fortune that nothing hindered your path, that you were unwatched and unseen? I observed your every step, marveled at your determination to save your kin and your conviction to stand in battle tonight. You persevered through all trials, emerged a victor through all tribulations. You have become a man driven with reprisal, your hands soaked in bloodshed, your mind confounded with vengeance. You walk a sinner in body and soul. Do not flatter yourself, Son of Zafar. You were never a master of your own destiny.

You are merely a pawn in a much greater, cosmic ploy of deception and chance. Such are the fundamentals of sorcery. Illusion. Deception. I merely set the stage, and watched you do the rest!"

Mukhtar wished that the ground would just open up and swallow him whole. Every word pierced him with poison, tearing his insides. An even greater remorse was slowly beginning to seep into him. All along, he had been led to believe that Ghulam was an agent of Ussam. Ma'alim himself had sanctioned his death. Who then did Ghulam serve? Was his death truly deserved?

The sounds of battle in the Entrance Hall reverberated behind the shut doors of the Throne Room, which meant that Mukhtar would have to keep Ma'alim in conversation a while longer, until the reinforcements arrived.

Ma'alim stood and descended the steps, bringing his attention to Azhar Babak's limp body. He muttered a few words to Ussam, who nodded curtly and shut his eyes, as if falling asleep where he stood.

A sudden chill swept through the Throne Room, and lingered for a while, nearly dousing the flames on the pedestals. The moment passed, and they burned brighter and fiercer than before, restoring warmth in the room.

Another trick of Ma'alim's, or a true feat of sorcery? Mukhtar was not sure, but he had an ominous feeling the answer would reveal itself soon. Perhaps this was the opportunity he sought. With Ussam, or the demon Azufil absent, he might be able to come free of the chains and prevent Ma'alim from progressing any further.

Vision tilted and angled, his head and neck pained and ached. He could no longer feel the rest of his body. The marble floor spread out before him, riddled with stained and desecrated cushions, discarded wine pitchers and *hukah* vials, all left behind when the ritual turned into a massacre. The Teacher stooped to look closely at Azhar Babak's body, and Mukhtar took the opportunity to try and free himself. He writhed and struggled, but the chains only seemed to tighten their hold.

He paused to catch his breath, keeping an eye on Ma'alim and Ussam's seemingly absent self. He tried again to free himself, clenching his jaw, summoning every fiber of his body to fight. The chains fought back, constricting tighter and tighter. His world darkened as he was subjugated against his will. His eyes darted across the Throne Room, searching for anything that could aid him. Ussam still stood lifelessly, his father was still stooped over Azhar's body, neither paying him much attention. The bright fires, burning yellow and orange, were slowly changing their shade to emerald flames, becoming larger and fiery.

Ma'alim's lips curled into a malicious grin of self-satisfaction. He held up a gnarled hand, and pointed at them. "Look!" he whispered hoarsely and Mukhtar's eyes darted to the lambent, scintillating flames. "A testament to my accomplishment. Years it has taken me to achieve the impossible, and now… witness the union of the Elements of Creation, bound with sacrament and infinite power!"

The flames turned into a sparkling, raging shade of red, and grew even larger, reverted back to a green blaze, and again to red. Mukhtar had a strong hunch as to why that was.

Ma'alim was speaking to himself, but Mukhtar could hear every word. "Together they will open the Eye of Hurus, and he who commands the doorway, commands the forces of Azazil. The Prince of Darkness. The Destroyer of Worlds. He who welcomes the devil, only welcomes the end. He who has sworn to haunt mankind…"

"*This* is your *madness*," Mukhtar could not help but answer him. "*This* is your *insanity*."

Ma'alim sprung on his heels like an overexcited child, cackling loudly and mirthlessly. He squatted beside Azhar, and continued to examine him, all the while squinting up at the flames and muttering to himself, "...Earth bears all... Fire consumes all... When the King has served his purpose..." he pointed at the pedestals, "...chained as you are, in ethereal bonds, and I will draw from you the *Ma'arid* of Water, as poison is drawn from a wound. You will endure heightened pains. You will attain the pinnacle of penance. Alas, like your father, your sacrifice will pass into the unknown."

Mukhtar felt the decimating heft of a mountain crushing down upon him. His mouth became dry. An icy cold feeling dropped into the pit of his stomach, shock and awe etched on his face. Ma'alim continued to destroy him with words alone, tearing him bit by bit.

Without an ounce of remorse, the old man pierced the wound deeper. "In his final days, he sought me out, weary unlike any man I had ever seen, claiming to have been deceived and betrayed. He placed his suspicions on Laban Varda, the only Arammorian among them," he laughed mirthlessly. "Little did he know, it was *I* who discovered the Amulets with your grandfather! *I* urged him to reform the Order of the Four Horsemen, and claim the powers of the Amulets! We could have achieved the impossible!" he spoke with loathsome ferocity. "But your grandfather lacked the nerve and ambition. He claimed to have found piety! He claimed to have *found* divinity! Determined to destroy the Amulets, and expunge the book from existence. Your father set out to right his wrongs, but in the end, even *he* outlived his usefulness!"

"Murderer!" Mukhtar screamed at him.

"I am many things, Mukhtar," Ma'alim did not care to show subtlety. "But never a murderer! I bear no guilt, nor remorse, for he who decimates his own soul. Sorcery is not for those bound by righteousness," he said in with utmost condescension, "and those who bear not the strength, the weak and fragile, the *cowardly*, falter and face only annihilation."

Mukhtar was unable to think anymore. Blood boiled in his veins, and he trembled uncontrollably, with a rage he had never felt before. Such was the hate and loathe tearing through him, he failed to notice Ussam's body awaken. Ma'alim uttered several incantations, turning all the jeweled rings on his fingers. As a result of his conjuring, despite the tall and fiery flames on the pedestals, the air in the room became cold and bitter.

Mukhtar could only think of murder. The murder of Harun Zafar, his father. The murder of Salim Zafar, his grandfather. And the murderer who stood before him. How he desperately hungered to drive his short-swords deep into Ma'alim's gut, to sink his teeth into the old man's throat, to make him pay and suffer for what he had done.

Something else was afoot in the Throne Room. The air stank of death and decay, as entities of another world emerged from the shadows and enclosed him. Their dark skins glimmered like oily reptilian scales. Their tall and towering bodies hunched over him like hungry predators, brandishing their long, steely talons, gnarling inch-long fangs, their yellow, snakelike eyes beholding him with a grotesque plague.

These were not just Jinn of the Unseen World. These were monstrous deformities of Ma'alim's own doing, by-products of his vile attempt at playing god. A horrible breed of animal and *Shayateen*, of beast and demon, given physical form through satanic powers.

"Bring him to me!" Ma'alim's hiss reverberated across the walls and pillars.

Mukhtar was gripped with a fear that almost became tangible, raising the fine hairs on the back of his neck. He writhed and squirmed, doubling his efforts to come free of his bonds. The old man cackled at his helplessness. His Jinn-possessed son smirked mirthlessly, and Mukhtar felt his strength failing, his hope fading, his will abandoning him, the grim and dark prospect of death, or worse, dawning upon him inevitably.

A scathing, steely talon caressed the exposed skin of his neck and face, reaching further along his enchained body, sinfully plunging his dignity to abysmal depths. His eyes burned with woeful tears, his heart sinking to forlorn fathoms. Would this truly be his end? Would everything he had accomplished thus, mean for nothing, if his death came under subjugation at the hands of one as vile and wicked as Ma'alim?

No! He was a son of Zafar. He bore his father's weaknesses, but his strengths too. He would not succumb to Ma'alim's will without a fight. To die on his feet, than to live on his knees. He felt his strength returning, his will inspiriting. *Protect me, O' Almighty, from the malice of Shaytaan, empower me to withstand this wickedness.* He shut his eyes, embracing the inevitability, realizing one thing. When he infiltrated the palace, he had forsaken every intent of surviving the night. He *was* prepared to die.

Show them no fear.

As such, he did not even flinch as one of the demons leaned in and breathed ferociously, barely an inch from his ear, spraying him with acidic spit that burnt his hair and scalded his skin. The nauseating scent of his own burning flesh reached his nostrils and triggered an inner instinct.

"Adva," he called confidently. "Come to me!"

A cooling sensation came over him, and she whispered from within, words that were not of any human tongue.

'Will you help me?' he reached out to her. 'Will you free me from these infernal chains?'

'I am you, as much as you are me. By the will of He who grants us life and death, I now bleed through your veins.'

The chains began to ice up. He could feel the cold seeping through his skin and flesh, deep into his bones. Frozen beyond their will, they were no longer alive and they shattered to bits, relinquishing their hold. Life flooded into Mukhtar's body in painful pulses, tingling and prickling. He submitted to the pain, revering the freedom it came with.

"This cannot be!" Ma'alim's disbelief aroused Mukhtar's inner fortitude.

He felt a strange sensation fire through his body, and a sudden strength came over him, a lethal force, balancing ardently on his fingertips, itching to be unleashed. It was a sensation unlike anything he had ever felt before. Was this the power of the Amulet? Is this what it felt like, to have another entity fill his body with its essence? He adored it. He loved it. He would never part with it.

He stood and braced himself for a fight. This was it— there was no turning back now.

'To death!' he whispered to himself.

The demons attacked in unison, surging with unnatural speed, their powers unrivaled, their intentions fierce.

Time slowed down for him. He saw their every move, their every strike, slicing and cutting through the air. He sensed their attacks before they even thought it. He smiled. This power was prodigious, colossal, and monumental. It was intoxicating.

His instincts told him exactly when and where to strike. He pulled out two throwing-knives and flicked his wrists. He did not wait to see if they made impact, for he was certain of striking down two, before turning to the others. The demons moved, and he moved with them, matching their lightning speed with his own. They thought him a mere human; he was far more than that now.

He picked up his fallen the short-swords, twirled them skillfully and exerted his attack. Their steely talons clashed with his blades, sending fiery flares into the air. He dodged their swift and powerful strikes, but could not evade them all, suffering several cuts, searing through his flesh. He chose to ignore the pain, keeping his focus on his prey, returning fire with powerful strikes of his own, inflicting painful slashes on all within his reach.

Several of the demons now fell back in fright, while one of them boldly swung from behind him. He sensed its scaly arm approaching, and ducked just in time to elude the foot-long talons from cleaving his head. He bent low, swung around, and cut through its mid-section, its scream of agony mounting a decibel so high, it shattered the glass panes of the high windows.

Two more demons were already on him, and he stepped back, throwing one of his swords forward with a powerful swing. It struck the first one on its skull, and he watched its essence bleed through the cut, its fiery, snakelike eyes wide in horror. His free hand drew out a throwing-knife with speed he had never felt before, and flung it forward. It struck home, deep into the chest of the second demon. The force of the impact, crashed it into a stone column.

Five demons now lay dead on the marble floor. Several others were acutely wounded. Their essences oozed onto the rich and lush rugs and animal skins, burning with an acrid and putrid odor. They backed away, their snakelike eyes fixating on Mukhtar with loathsome glares.

"No!" Ma'alim screamed beside the still body of Azhar Babak. *"Stand and fight! I command you!"*

The demons refused to obey. Did they fear Mukhtar more than their master's whip? One by one, they vanished into the dark shadows, with putrid stenches of rotting eggs. They were abandoning him.

"You will all burn for your disobedience!" Ma'alim was beside himself with rage. "You *will* be punished for your insolence! *Attack him!* I am your master, and *I command you!*"

Mukhtar's confidence rose, and he strode forward fearlessly. "They flee because they know, as well as I, how this will end. Who then will you send in your stead? Ussam? And after I have killed your son, will you pick up a sword and face me? Will *you* then beg for mercy?"

'Do not exert yourself,' Adva warned. *'I can only hold you together for so long. We must flee while we can!'*

'Do not fear for me,' Mukhtar assured her, and hastily wiped the darkcrimson trickle down his nostril. 'The battle is not over. I will see this to the very end. Stay with me, Adva.'

"Bring me the Amulet," Ma'alim's whisper in Ussam's ear, carried across the room. "Destroy him!"

There was a flash. An empty moment. Ussam, or as Ma'alim had claimed before, Azufil the demon vanished, and Mukhtar blinked as fear gripped him once more.

A searing pain tore through his left arm, deep and gouging, forcing him to drop his swords and scream in excruciating agony. Azufil's blade had pierced his arm, almost cutting all the way through. His eyes burned and blurred with pain, searching the shadows for the balding man— or Jinn.

'Slow your mind.'

Mukhtar calmed his breathing and tried to ignore the blood trickling from the wound, and the searing pain that rippled through his arm. He picked up his swords, barely able to hold them steady, and scanned the room for his adversary.

He felt it before he could even see it. Azufil's blade cut through the air, creating ripples that his senses picked up, and he turned instinctively to meet the steel with his own, barely an inch away from his neck. Sparks flew, as both swords clashed in the air, and Mukhtar's fiery eyes met with Azufil's hateful ones.

The fierce battle shook the very walls of the Throne Room, fracturing and shattering the marble and stone. They exchanged lethal blows, unpredictable feints and parries, their swords swinging with grunts and ending with clashes. Azufil attacked, and Mukhtar dodged and blocked. Mukhtar attacked, while Azufil did the same, neither yielding to the other; neither prepared to surrender. Mukhtar exerted all his efforts in fighting back, but his body was wearing out faster than his opponent's. Soon he began to tire, but now was not the time to give in to exhaustion. Now was not the time to step back with debilitation. Now was the time to push harder and faster than ever.

Azufil dropped its sword, drew its arms out and clenched its fists, as if summoning something. Indeed it was. Dark powers.

Two columns closest to Mukhtar, exploded in a colossal outburst. He cowered to protect himself from the debris, but the damage was still detrimental, lethal fragments of rock and stone raining upon him with calamitous propulsion.

He was not without powers of his own either. When he recovered from the aftermath of the explosion, he focused every fiber of his body on his surroundings, and felt Adva's abilities surge through him. Moisture was drawn, and the air in the Throne Room became misty, as droplets of water gathered before him and formed into razor-sharp icicles. With a wave of his swords, the icicles were flung through the air.

Azufil defended itself by using its powers once more. Upon mere gestures, all the rubble from the collapsed columns flew forth and formed a temporary wall to protect the demon from the icicles, shattering them upon impact.

Mukhtar took his opportunity before the wall fell.

He threw both his short-swords into the air, and with unmatched agility and velocity, he sprinted in their wake, while simultaneously pulling out all his remaining throwing-knives and flinging them at Azufil. As its defensive wall crumbled, the startled demon picked up its sword, swinging it wildly, in an effort to ward off the knives rippling through the air.

With increased velocity, Mukhtar sprung into the air, in wake of his short-swords. He reached for them by their hilts and swung forward, his body bent in a graceful arch and a brilliant display of athleticism. Using every ounce of potency left in him, he thrust forth both swords. All within a fraction of an impulsive moment, Azufil's eyes widened with dread, terror, and apprehension, as it witnessed the approach of death. Mukhtar's blades reigned down and sunk deep into its upper torso.

Their screams were mingled. The pain mounted and blood splattered, as Azufil twitched violently, life detaching itself from its body, its essence pouring out of the open wounds, and they both crumpled to the ground.

It was over, Mukhtar thought. It was all over. The puppet was dead, the puppeteer screaming in disbelief. It was *his* turn now. Mukhtar only needed a short moment to catch his breath, then he would rise up again, and Ma'alim would face his own death.

However, he was having trouble breathing. The air felt thin and hollow. He coughed and gasped, desperately trying to draw air, as the pain attained heights beyond his imagination, driving him to the brink of insanity.

A deafening crash echoed off the walls. The flames on both pedestals died out, plunging the Throne Room into darkness. A faint light emerged from somewhere else and all around him, he heard screams and shouts, mingled with the thundering of heavy footsteps. Someone was crying. Someone else was cursing. Mukhtar choked and spat out blood. His vision blurred, becoming steadily murky, and within moments, he was engulfed by an even darker abyss.

TWENTY-EIGHT

THE SECRET SISTERS

A blinding white light brought pain to his eyes. He could discern no shape nor form. No shadow. Not a flicker. Nothing but an endless sear of whiteness tearing into his eyes. What was this new form of torture, and what had he done to deserve it?

He tried to blink, tried to shut it out, but could feel nothing, do nothing. It was certainly strange, a strange kind of strange, one he could not comprehend, and curiosity jolted his mind to work for some answers.

His first thought, his only thought— was this death? Is this what it felt like to look through his soul instead of his eyes, just a blinding white light? Is this what it felt like to linger without a body? If this be death, then he wished nothing but to remain there, untethered, unburdened, and untroubled— that *wretched, abhorrent light!*

It pained. It confused and disappointed him. If he was dead, how could he feel pain? This made very little sense. Perhaps he was mistaken. Perhaps it was so dark that it was light. But that made even less sense, just another infuriatingly unhelpful thought. Darkness is inexistent. Darkness is an immeasurable and unquantifiable anomaly, merely used to acknowledge the absence of light. Just as cold is a void for warmth.

He applauded and commemorated himself for his wit and continued contemplating the existent and nonexistent, that he simply strayed from his current conundrum. Light. Energy. What *was* energy? How could one relate to something that existed in so many forms? Heat, strength, speed, power, the forces of nature. What then was the purest form of energy? He pondered over this for a long while, before the answer came to him. It was light. Intangible, unbeatable, the fastest, most accurate thing in the world, for without light, how could man see? How could man discern and comprehend his own existence, and all that prevails around him? *That damned light!*

In an effort to shield himself, he felt something. He felt his eyelids. It was a strange and unexpected feeling. Could a soul beyond death, feel its body? What *was* the human soul? It was a question, so simple, yet so extraordinarily empyrean. A phenomenon beyond the grasp of man's comprehension. Knowledge divine.

He pried open his eyes by a tiny fraction, exposing them to the light. They burned and watered. Various colors blurred beyond the tears. The blurriness faded. The tears flowed through and dripped down the sides of his head.

In what appeared to be a distant horizon, set against a white-washed background, was a series of dark lines, crooked and webbed like the tangled branches of a withered tree against the pearl white of the moon. His gaze followed a long and thin zigzagging line across the ceiling to where it met with the wall, a section that was notoriously infamous for concealing spiders. He stared at the crevice for a long while, until realization dawned on him. It was the same crack. The same ceiling. The light came from the same window. He was in his own bed, in his own room.

No wonder he felt so comfortable. Life slowly tingled through his body, touching his fingertips, igniting his bones, arousing his senses. Yet he remained there, motionless, strangely afraid of what would follow.

He felt the soreness, the searing burns and cuts, the overwhelming fever, and he became restless, trembling where he lay.

"He is awake!" someone whispered. "By God Almighty! He is awake!"

"Send word to Sheikh Ruwaid!" another whispered, a little louder, more commanding, more demanding.

A door slammed. Something was knocked over. Someone yelped. Someone else spoke angrily.

Vivid images flooded into him in a rush of memories, and his vision blurred again. His head pained beyond reckoning, blackness threatening to engulf him. He could not allow it. He *would not* allow it.

A pair of soft hands reached under his head and lifted him up. Instinctively, he struggled and fought back. Even softer hands touched his chest and held him back. A flowery scent of lavender and *Oudh* cosseted his nostrils, persuading him to cease his struggle.

Words were spoken, instructions were given. Footsteps thundered about, yet no one did anything about the accursed light, endlessly burning his eyes. The door opened and shut again, the sound of it reverberating through his head like a thunderclap.

Enough was enough. He *had* to find peace, and if no one there was willing to grant him bliss, he would have to reach for it himself. His attempts were met with resistance. Whoever was holding him down, did not seem to understand his need.

His limbs felt heavy, laden with soreness and exhaustion. His body screamed in agony. Still he struggled. It was his stubbornness, the infamous stubbornness inherent of the Zafar bloodline. He only surrendered to the calming, soothing fragrance of lavender and *Oudh,* sweet in its intoxication, euphoric in its vivification, taking him back to that blissful place.

He abandoned his skirmish and allowed himself to be pushed back onto the bed. A wet cloth was placed over his head, cool water dripping down the sides. Despite the soreness, despite the aches, he felt serenity. His fever eventually subsided and his mind focused. When the cloth was lifted, he opened his eyes slowly.

Mika'il's face swam into view, slightly scruffy and deeply concerned. His arm was wrapped around Fariebah's tense shoulders, whose puffy eyes were a sign of tears and several sleepless nights.

Beside her, Suha dipped a cloth in cold water and wrung it thoroughly before placing it on Mukhtar's forehead. Eyes as teary as her sister's and a smile just as warm, she gazed at him with the fondness of a mother, and within his heart arose an aching sorrow. How long had she remained awake, weeping and begging the Almighty to save her son? Tears burned his eyes. Wearily he shut them, succumbing to a dreamless sleep.

When next he woke, it was night. Rain hammered against the shut window. He raised his head slightly and scanned the dimly lit room. An oil lamp in the far corner spirited a flame meek enough for him to trace the voices conversing in hushed whispers.

Rauf sat on the floor, massaging his foot, his staff set against the wall behind him. Ghasif and Zaki were seated beside him, sporting identical bandages around their heads. Nabiha wore a loose scarf, partially covering her sleek hair. She was deep in conversation with Nuzhah, whose veiled face revealed only her almond-shaped, *kohl*-lined eyes.

Saif was seated on a low stool beside the bed. When he realized Mukhtar was awake, he reached forward and slid a pillow beneath his head.

"I praise the Almighty for your betterment," he whispered.

Mukhtar responded with a weak smile. "Water," he requested in a dry and hoarse whisper.

Saif brought the cup close to his lips, and he drank heartily. The others abandoned their personal engagements and surrounded the bed, wearing looks of concern and relief.

Mukhtar was struck by an immense pain in his chest when he tried to sit up. Saif and Nuzhah reached forward and straightened the pillows for him. While they did this, he ran a hand to trace the source of pain and realized a swollen, bandaged region in the middle of his chest. It stung at his touch and he winced in agony.

"You were pierced," Ghasif told him. "We found Ussam's sword deeply entrenched into your chest."

Mukhtar stared at him with a horrified look. Indeed, he had difficulty remembering much, and any attempt to trigger his memory, aggravated the pounding in his head.

"And Ussam?" he asked.

"Dead," Zaki replied.

"And his father?" Mukhtar's voice became hoarse again, and Nuzhah helped him drink some more water.

"Father?" Ghasif frowned at him. *"Ussam's* father?" He shook his head and curled his lip. "There was none other when we entered the Throne Room."

"Then he has fled!" Mukhtar became agitated, giving rise to his wounds. *"The coward!"*

"Whom do you speak of?" Rauf furrowed his brow.

Merely thinking of it, brought him pain. "Ma'alim," Mukhtar gritted his teeth in agony, clutching his chest.

In an icy, stony moment, they stared at him with looks of pure disbelief. Both Nuzhah and Zaki attempted to ease his pain, while Nabiha rushed to bring more water.

"I ask your forgiveness, brother," Saif was first to break the silence. "The hour is late, and I must return home."

Mukhtar did not want him to leave, but he understood, more than anyone, why it was important. The less he involved Saif, the better. "I wish to see you again. Soon."

"If the Almighty wills it," Saif said, raising a finger to the heavens. "At dawn, I will inform Prince Fa'iz of your recovery. He had expressly urged me to alert him when you woke. I believe he wishes to meet with you."

"How did you come to be the Prince's messenger?" Mukhtar gave a quizzical look.

"It was without choice, I assure you," Saif stared at Ghasif, Rauf, and Zaki. "More capable individuals were tasked with the same, but declared themselves— if I were to use their own words— *not the domestic hirelings of a pompous, pampered brat of the Royal Family.*"

Mukhtar could not help but give a light chuckle, desperately fighting through the pain in his chest.

"From what I gather, the Prince was not pleased," Rauf commented sarcastically.

"Well, what did you expect?" Saif gave him an annoyed look. "You were *civilized* enough to declare it in the presence of his Royal Guards, his servants, *and* his courtesans!"

Mukhtar laughed and grimaced in pain. "Inform the Prince that I will be honored to meet him when I am able," he managed to say when the searing in his chest lessened.

Saif bade them farewell and left. Nuzhah occupied his seat and eyed Mukhtar ambiguously, as though she could not believe he was alive. Nabiha stood beside her, wearing a similar expression. Rauf settled in a cushion against the wall beside Ghasif and Zaki, resting his foot on a much smaller one.

"Can you be certain it was Ma'alim?" Ghasif was still frowning at him dubiously.

"Do you *doubt* me?" Mukhtar challenged him.

Ghasif looked mildly offended, and Mukhtar gave an arduous sigh. "Forgive me. I did not mean to insult."

"No one here doubts you, Mukhtar," Ghasif assured him. "Not after what you have accomplished."

"He revealed his true self," Mukhtar replied without meeting their eyes. He was not quite sure why he felt ashamed, whether it was because he failed, and Ma'alim escaped, or the mere fact he, Mukhtar, was responsible for releasing the beast.

"You knew," he said accusingly, glancing at Nuzhah. They all followed his gaze with confused expressions. Behind the veil, her expression was horrified. She looked to the others with anxiety, unsure of how to reply. "I freed you both. The wicked, and the righteous. You were enslaved along with General Masri and Ma'alim."

"I did not know until it was too late," her voice was barely audible.

"But you conveniently *kept* it from me!" Mukhtar accused.

"*I couldn't—*"

"*Couldn't?*" Mukhtar demanded harshly, and a sharp pain rose in his chest. "All the while I was chained to that accursed wheel, you uttered nothing but *lies!*"

"Caution, Mukhtar!" Ghasif raised his voice.

Mukhtar's eyes widened, not because of Ghasif's warning, but because he suddenly realized what he had done. The consequence of his outburst.

Nuzhah's eyes were teary and hurtful.

"Forgive me!" Mukhtar gasped, horrified, and the pain in his chest arose again.

She shook her head briskly, and just as she had done in the palace, she refused his apology, purely because she once again chose to take the blame upon herself. In doing so, she only left him with an undeserving, overburdening shadow of guilt.

Her breath shortened, her voice shook. "When we escaped," she explained, "we sought safe sanctuary. Kaden Talal, the fourth who was enslaved with us, spoke of Ghuldad and its open doors to those who were lost to the wilderness. Penniless and desperate, we slept in an alley that night, but when next I woke, we were before the gates of Ghuldad, pleading sanctuary."

"*Sorcery!*" Zaki, Ghasif, and Rauf said in unison.

Nuzhah nodded somberly. "Ma'alim's campaign to liberate the Assassins began soon after, and he strongly warned me not to speak of our enslavement. He did not want the assassins to know—"

"That he was a slave, and nothing more!" Rauf growled and uttered a string of curses under his breath.

Nabiha squeezed her shoulders, and Mukhtar tried to give her a reassuring look. He tried to tell her that she was not to blame, that she should not bear his guilt. It was *his* fault. *His* shame. His foolishness had brought about all this atrocity, had brought him enslavement, had forced him to sever friendships, and lead others to their death. He wanted to say so much more, but could not bring himself to utter the words. "What of the King?" he turned his gaze to the others.

"He lives," Rauf replied in a distant voice, pulling his gaze away from Nuzhah. "But only just. His healers tend to him, while Immorkaan convenes to decide upon his successor."

"Would that not be Prince Fa'iz?" Mukhtar furrowed his brow.

"Prince Fa'iz is the rightful heir to the Throne, yes," Nabiha spoke for the first time, and all eyes fell on her, "but he is not the only one with a right to claim, and by the laws of the land, only the Elder Council can name a successor. It is how Azhar Babak structured his governance. He did not want his Empire to be torn by a power struggle between his heirs."

"Absurdity!" Rauf remarked. "Ever has it been that power transcends to the next of kin. A true heir. A bloodline. How can the Elder Council be the one to judge a worthy ruler?"

"One *must* wear the Sacrament of Sovereignty," Zaki reminded them, "The stone marks he who is has the right to rule."

"The stone is merely an adornment," Nabiha argued. "A claim to the throne requires more than a symbol. An heir to the bloodline has the right to arise a king, but only if Immorkaan deems it worthy."

"The prince does not wear the stone," Zaki said pointedly.

"Does not mean that he is unworthy," Rauf stated.

"You place too much faith in the little princeling, brother," Zaki mocked.

"He is not a *child*, Zaki," Ghasif replied in a rather bored tone.

"For all we know," Rauf gave a snicker.

"If the wearing stone has no merit," Zaki said airily, "then Princess Layla also has a claim to the Throne. She is currently under the care of her uncle, General Abidan, but upon hearing news of her father, she will return to Khalidah."

"She has no claim," Ghasif denied openly.

"She *is* his daughter," Zaki argued. "Her mother was his first wife. She only needs to prove her worth, as you said."

Ghasif gave a ridiculing snort. "How can the Empire be ruled by a woman?"

"Why not?" Nabiha gave him a scathing glare. "Aghara is ruled by a Queen. Why not Ahul-Hama?"

"Aghara can do as it pleases," Ghasif said plainly. "The rule of an empire is unbefitting for a woman The Elder Council will never allow it. The throne will surely fall to Aarguf or Abidan Babak. Only *they* wear the Sacrament of Sovereignty."

"Which will only give rise to bloody feud," Rauf stated.

"And the people will pay the price," Mukhtar said grimly. The thought of Aarguf Babak being crowned king was not as troubling as the thought of seeing his once best friend as the Crowned Prince. It was, however, the least of his concerns as he exchanged a discreet glance with his brother. It felt too premature to cite, but it almost felt as though Aarguf Babak's secret ploy and pursuit of power was slowly taking a direction desired by the king's elder brother.

Mukhtar desperately tried to shake off the thought, condemning it to be the result of the devil's whispers. What gave him any right, to accuse a man of such conspiracy, without an ounce of evidence? He felt shame and guilt when he remembered how Aarguf had stormed the palace to come to their aid. The conviction with which he and his men had battled Ussam's assassins.

"And what of the Assassins?" He brought his thoughts back to the room. "Is there talk of besieging Ghuldad?"

They exchanged grim looks, and Mukhtar narrowed his eyes suspiciously.

"Immorkaan claims to have no substantial evidence to condemn Ghuldad," Zaki stated.

"No evidence?" Mukhtar sputtered, clenching his chest as the pain returned, and Nuzhah reached forward to try and comfort him.

"Perhaps the reason why the Prince wishes to speak with you," Zaki replied. "He wants to ascertain for himself."

"Why are you all speaking in riddles?" Mukhtar was becoming irritated. "What of all the dead? What of all the bloodshed and destruction within the palace walls? Have they not seen enough of an aftermath?"

Again they exchanged grim looks, and Mukhtar became even more agitated. "Speak then!" he yelled and contorted in pain.

"But you have said so yourself," Rauf told him. "They have only witnessed an aftermath. An aftermath of a destroyed palace, a dying king whose body lay only feet from yours, and the corpses of a wealthy merchant and an exiled General, among most of the King's viziers and ministers."

Mukhtar stared at him with a baffled expression. The rain continued to pound against the window and the shutters rattled when the wind forced itself upon them.

"Immorkaan claims that Ussam was there to negotiate a treaty with the King," Nabiha explained. "Until the King awakens, none can revoke this claim, not even Aarguf Babak's testimony, and the Royal Army will not risk open war without absolute cause."

"As the rightful heir, the Prince can—" Ghasif began.

"This again!" Nabiha scoffed at him. "Fa'iz is *not* the *rightful* heir, not until the Elder Council convenes and passes judgment!"

"But— there must be *someone* whose voice can be heard?"

"We do not even *know* where the council's allegiances truly lie!"

Mukhtar allowed his thoughts to wander while they argued amongst themselves. How could this have happened? How much more bloodshed did Immorkaan need, before they realized their call to duty?

Everything they had fought for thus far, arriving upon the brink of destruction, *everything* was simply being cast aside by the very institution they had risked their lives to save. He felt disgusted and angered. Did their ignorance and corruption know no bounds?

His eyes rested on Nuzhah for a while and remained there, lost in thought. She blinked and he averted his gaze. Nabiha was still arguing with Zaki and Ghasif, while Rauf occasionally expressed his own thoughts that were not too far from the general consensus. He pondered over how they had all come to be there, in that very room. Was it fate, as Ma'alim had described?

Each one from a different background, a remotely different circumstance. How strange it was that Ghasif and Rauf had chosen to escape with him from Ghuldad? He gazed at Nabiha. How strange it was that the very same person who had blackmailed him, armed him with the knowledge to defeat Ussam?

He turned his gaze back to Nuzhah. It was truly a bizarre set of circumstances, that he had unknowingly rescued her from cutthroat slavers, and it was by her assistance that he had escaped from Ghuldad. That her mere presence at the Royal Palace had guided him to Zaki, Ghasif, and Rauf. Fate, it seemed, was truly intertwined with destiny. As much as he loathed to acknowledge it, Ma'alim's profound claim was slowly beginning to shed light upon everything that had led him thus far. The death of Hassin, the vengeance upon Ghadan Lahib and Haim

Tuma, and the assassination of Ghulam Mirza.

Nabiha had wished Ghulam dead because she believed he was responsible for enslaving her sister. He looked deep into her eyes, pierced her gaze, and tried to read her thoughts. He remembered how she had abandoned all when she stormed the palace with Aarguf and ran to Nuzhah's side. There was something here that he had missed, something dire. A murky link of events that had somehow twisted and intertwined itself in his life, guiding and maneuvering everything that had led them thus far.

He decided to leave it be. There was no sense in wasting thought and energy over aimless presumptions. Had he not already accused and condemned others without any substantial proof? If it was a secret, let it remain a secret until it revealed itself.

Almost as though they were reading his thoughts, the women exchanged nervous glances, and Nuzhah acknowledged Mukhtar with a soft nod. "Nabiha and I are sisters by birth," she declared.

Zaki and Ghasif's argument ended abruptly, and Rauf gasped. Feeling lightheaded, Mukhtar opted to lay back down. He focused his gaze at the crack on the ceiling, and listened.

"I was journeying from Aghara to Khalidah with the hopes of visiting Nabiha, my older sister," Nuzhah said, her eyes were focused on the cup of water by Mukhtar's bedside. "Our caravan was raided on the road past Din-Galad, and those who survived were taken prisoner."

They turned to face Nabiha. "I did not know—" Nabiha started and broke off.

"Until Ma'alim sent a crude message, revealing to you that Ghulam knew her whereabouts," Mukhtar completed her sentence. "Ghulam profited from the sale of arms to mercenaries, as well as an acquaintance with several slave traders who helped him move his merchandise. Ghuldad was his largest buyer. Weapons and slaves to build Ussam and Ma'alim's army. For some reason, Ma'alim was threatened by Ghulam," again he exchanged a discreet glance with his brother, receiving a stern warning not to disclose too much. "He used us to kill him, and instigated Nabiha, among others," he recalled the butcher and the guard's conversation outside the *Souk As-Silaah,* "if we failed."

Ma'alim had indeed been threatened by the Chief of the *Souk*. He had discovered something, and what he had revealed to Mukhtar with his dying breath, had been true. Had Ghulam secretly served a righteous cause under a cloak of allegiance to the wicked? Mukhtar felt a sudden constriction in his throat and said nothing more, unwilling to dwell on the matter. He did not wish to contend with a revelation that he may have killed an innocent man, if at all Ghulam was innocent.

Nabiha eyed him cautiously, sensing his burden, and she attempted to divert their thoughts. When she spoke, her gaze turned to her sister and lingered there all the while. "Our father and mother died when we were only children. We lived on the streets. Orphans. Begging and pleading for alms to survive. One day, there was a procession in Imar. King Azhar was visiting Aghara. The festivals spanned the entire road between Imar and Nihar."

"Nabiha and I always held hands," Nuzhah continued, and all eyes turned to her veiled face. "But the King's advance fomented a riot, and in the chaos, we were separated."

"When night fell, I was lost in an unfamiliar part of the city," Nabiha said. "I was preyed upon by villainous men and ran in search of a place to hide. They chased after me. Close to the city gates, a caravan was being loaded with large baskets. I hid in one of them. They were still searching for me, so I remained still. I was scared. Frightened. Eventually, I fell asleep and did not realize when dawn came. The carts were loaded, baskets piled one atop the other. I was trapped for two days until the caravan arrived at Aztalaan. When they discovered me, they had a quarrel. Some of the guards wanted to sell me at the slave market. Others wanted to have their way with me. Unfortunately for them, it was Huda Babak's caravan, and when word reached her, she rescued me before I was ruined. She brought me to Khalidah as one of her servants. As a child, I bonded with Princess Layla, and as our friendship and sisterhood grew, so did Huda Babak's fondness for me. She called me her daughter. She adored me as she did her own."

There was a long moment of silence.

"You were raised in the King's household!" Rauf remarked. "You were raised as Royalty!"

Zaki wrinkled his nose. "Why does it surprise you?" he spoke with a mild tone of defiance. He had not yet forgiven her for extorting them during Thamir's feast, and Mukhtar suspected his brother would not relinquish an opportunity to enact his revenge on Kazimi for striking him.

Nuzhah's expression was hidden behind her veil, but Mukhtar could see the anger flash in her eyes. Nabiha was slightly rifled, and when she spoke, it was not to retaliate, but rather to shed light on what she saw as Zaki's ignorance.

"Royalty only recognizes bloodlines," she said sternly, exerting every word with clarity, "as it has ever been since the dawn of time," she glanced at Ghasif. "My ties to the Royal Family only existed for as long as I could see a mother in Huda Babak. I still do, and I forever will. After her death, the King remarried. His new wife gave him a son, Prince Fa'iz. I was not of Azhar Babak's blood. I did not belong in his house. She refused to have me as a member of her family, branding me as a stain to the Royal Bloodline. She called for my head. Only by solemn oath was I spared."

Along with a throb of emotion in his throat, Mukhtar felt subtle spasms of pain searing through his chest, and his head hurt as he tried to process this new knowledge. He also felt a surge of guilt when he remembered how he had taken her for granted, branding her a sinner. He was wrong to have judged her as he did, and he longed to seek her forgiveness but could not bring himself to speak it. "What oath?" he asked instead, exerting as humble a tone as he could, with the hope that his unspoken words will be understood.

"The King's oath," she replied, giving him an empathetic look. "The King's pledge to his dying wife. He swore not to bring me harm. But she was not there to defend me anymore. His house was torn after her death. He sent Layla and her younger brothers to Aztalaan, under the care of General Abidan. I was exiled from the palace, but he granted me livelihood with Thamir, keeping me within reach. He fulfilled his pledge. To this day, my childhood has remained a secret between my sisters, Layla, Nuzhah, and I."

TWENTY-NINE

THE ROYAL REQUEST

Mukhtar grew ever so restless, confined to his room to recuperate from his injuries. Sheikh Ruwaid had restricted him from venturing any further than the lavatory, until he had fully recovered. He was often visited by friends and family, his most frequent company being Suha, who brought him freshly prepared meals of his favorite foods. They ate and chatted merrily, but whenever Mukhtar was alone, he found himself brooding over uncertain and unknown matters, and one question continued to plague him— *what next?*

For months, he had thought of nothing but defeating Ussam Bashiri, and yet, as he lay recovering from the victorious wounds, he could not find peace. He continuously ruminated over Ma'alim's deception and betrayal, and the true cause of his father and grandfather's deaths. He tried his utmost not to succumb to retribution or revenge, and struggled with the conviction that sooner or later, the urge would overpower him.

Coming closer to a full recovery, Prince Fa'iz Babak visited him, escorted by his personal guards and viziers. Upon seeing the entourage, a lengthy discord ensued in the courtyard and the street outside. United, Suha, Fariebah, Mika'il, and Sheikh Ruwaid, confronted the Prince's viziers and personal guards, denying them admittance. In the end, Prince Fa'iz humbly accepted Suha's terms, and entered the house with five of his Royal Guard, who were only allowed as far as the courtyard.

"Lion of Khalidah!" The prince announced himself, entering the room alone with his arms spread open.

Mukhtar raised a dubious eyebrow. "That is not my title."

"Those who have attested to your deeds, have named you thus!" Fa'iz pointed out. "I am afraid you have no choice!" His broad smile exhibited white teeth that complemented his handsome features, glittering green, *kohl*-lined eyes and aptly trimmed, well-oiled hair and beard. "It is most comforting to see your good recovery, and an honor to make your acquaintance."

Mukhtar was not sure whether to acquiesce or rebuke the prince's claim. He was propped against his pillows, trying his utmost to appear respectful. "The honor is mine," he gave a welcoming nod, and put on a solemn tone, "How is your father?"

"Alas, he still lingers beyond revival," Fa'iz replied gravely. "He shows no signs of life. Does not respond to sight or sound. Yet his heart beats and his lungs draw breath. The healers are perplexed by his condition, and have yet to find a cure."

"He has suffered an ordeal far greater than any of us. I pray the Almighty grants him a quickened recovery."

"As noble a heart as I have been led to believe, Son of Zafar," Fa'iz gave him a broad grin. "I wish you the same."

Mukhtar acknowledged the compliment with a smile. "How fare the affairs of the Empire? In your father's absence, who assumes his rule?"

The Prince's smile faded. "As per our laws, the Elder Council retains stewardship of the Throne, until the rightful heir is declared."

"But *you* are the heir to the Throne!" Mukhtar argued. "Are you not? Is it not *your* rightful place—?"

"To assume his throne," Fa'iz interrupted, "without abiding by the proper protocols, would injustice my father's reputation and the laws he has struggled to constitute and uphold for two decades. However, I can assure you, I will do all within my power to restore order, and reign justice upon those who have perpetrated and conspired to dethrone the prosperity of our empire."

He spoke with absolutism in his voice. His posture, tone, and facial expressions, all construed authority, and did not at all strike Mukhtar as the pompous, pampered prince he had been led to believe. However, was he prepared to do what was necessary?

"Forgive my boldness, but I must know," Mukhtar asserted. "Has the council decided to pursue those responsible?"

"Who do *you* suspect is responsible?" Fa'iz asked.

Zaki was right. He wished to ascertain for himself, and Mukhtar was prepared with an appropriate response.

"You know, just as well as I, the atrocities that have befallen your father," he countered. "Have you not seen Ussam's corpse and the corpses of his dead assassins? Did your uncle not apprehend those who remained alive? How much longer shall we continue to ignore the truth?"

He had answered the Prince's question, and made clear his testimony. Fa'iz, however, did not accede nor demur. "The Council of Elders has yet to convene," he merely altered his former statement, "and decide upon a proper course of action, for there is much to uncover before a decision is made. This hierarchy of governance was put in place by my father, for a reason. To settle such affairs, lest the integrity of this great empire crumbles over a power feud. I am not alone in his succession. There are others, above and before me, those who were chosen by his hand, and have earned the right to wear the Sacrament of Sovereignty. That is the highest honor in the Empire, bestowed only upon those worthy to rule."

Mukhtar's jaw was set, and he tried to conceal his frustration. Perhaps he had misjudged the Prince's leadership abilities. He too displayed an intimidation to the dictatorship of Immorkaan. How much longer will this conflict endure? When will they realize the perils that lie ahead? Ma'alim commands the might of Ghuldad, and his allegiance with the monstrosity of Arammoria will grant him every opportunity to wage his war. A leaderless Ahul-Hama will surely fall.

"Mukhtar," Fa'iz tried to sound reassuring. "Do not trouble yourself with such matters. Rather, seek a hastened recovery. Needless to say, we may yet require your strengths and skills soon enough. Leave unto us the politics of Immorkaan, and have faith that the right course of action will soon be pronounced. Before I take my leave, I have for you a token of my appreciation and gratitude. I may not yet be king, but I do command the respect and influence of the Elder Council. Enough, perhaps, to bring you this." From within his royal robes of an emerald shade, he pulled out a scroll bearing the King's seal, and handed it forward. "It is an Order of Immunity, signed by myself and all the members of the Elder Council. It had come to my attention that a given individual foisted injustice upon you by wrongfully possessing your livelihood. Should you accept this, from this hour henceforth, none shall lay claim to your forge."

Mukhtar did not reach out a receiving hand. "I cannot accept this."

Fa'iz blinked. He had not expected a refusal. But Mukhtar was not declining it for selfish reasons. He did not think himself the rightful owner of the forge, even though it had first been built by his father. After nearly three decades of hard work and dedication, only Mika'il deserved the honor. "With your permission, may I ask that you bequeath the forge to its rightful owner?"

It took a moment for the prince to understand Mukhtar's humble plea. "I shall honor your request," he acknowledged with a nod and a small smile. "As per the state's scribes, you have always been the rightful inherent of your father's forge, but as you wish, I shall present it to your uncle on your behalf. I believe a celebration is in order, which brings me to my second gift," He pocketed the scroll and took a step back. "I wish to host a feast upon my father's recovery. I humbly extend my invitation to you, and during the feast, I also intend on announcing you as my Personal Adviser. Your courage and selflessness have shown that you are more than capable, and you have therefore earned my respect. It would be an honor to have you by my side."

Mukhtar slowly shrunk under the sheer weight of such a tremendous proposal. He felt hot and red around his ears. *The prince's personal adviser?* He did not feel competent enough to fulfill such a responsibility.

Fa'iz seemed to read the uncertainty on his face. "I will be personally offended, were you to decline," he said.

Mukhtar hesitated. "Prince Fa'iz, as great an honor as you have bestowed upon me, I am but one among peasants, and cannot fathom to see myself amidst royalty, nor have I the capabilities to toe against politicians and viziers. An empire's affairs are beyond my knowledge and comprehension. Perhaps such a position is better suited to one who is more capable than I?"

"You will not be running the empire, if that is what concerns you," Fa'iz chuckled lightheartedly.

"Prince Fa'iz, I—"

"Do I hear excuses?"

Mukhtar shook his head. "I fear my presence would only give your rivals an excuse to whisper falseness in your absence. It would stir a rebellion against your governance."

Fa'iz did not seem surprised by Mukhtar's statement. "I have given this decision careful thought," he clarified. "No matter what one does, there will always be something for them to say, for such people always confine themselves in ignorant affairs. I care not what they think or say, if their speech is riddled with malignity. I care only for the people of this nation. Yes, I pursue the throne. I have been groomed for it since I was a child. While the sons of my uncles only ever enjoyed the bounties my father provided, I have struggled to learn and prepare myself for the day I will lead our people into a better tomorrow. That day will come soon, and I know in my heart, that there can be none better by my side, than yourself, for I would sooner accept your simple and sound counsel, over the beguiling wisdoms of what would have been fair leaders of the Empire."

"Prince Fa'iz," Mukhtar argued, "what good would it do, if your opposers, and allies alike, come to learn that you have appointed a common man as your counsel? It would bring ruin to your reputation, and only hinder your path to kingship."

"You must not fear for my reputation," Fa'iz tried to assure him, "and instead look to a much greater purpose. Even if you were to decline as my adviser, your mere presence at the feast will serve a dire political need, and will bear strength for what we need Immorkaan to approbate. During the feast, I will speak of what transpired on the night the palace was attacked. With you by my side, the truth will be *known* to those who are misguided by false rumors. I implore you to consider these matters."

Mukhtar neither acknowledged nor rebuked the prince's plea, but he was making a statement of his own with silence. He did not wish to have any further involvement with Immorkaan. In truth, he had already thought out his true ambition, and he voiced his notions two days later, when Zaki asked, "What troubles you, little brother?"

"The feast," he said simply.

"As I thought it would," Zaki placed a tray of food on Mukhtar's bed, and settled into the stool beside it. "The Prince expressed his concerns before he left. He seemed disappointed."

"I care not for the politics of Immorkaan," Mukhtar reached for the large dish of buttered flatbread, shredded lamb, and a bowl of *Humus*. The spicy aromas sent overwhelming pangs to his stomach and he helped himself hungrily, joined by his brother. "Every passing day allows Ma'alim to become stronger," he said after a few mouthfuls and a sip of pomegranate *Sherbet,* "but the Prince believes in diplomacy before war."

"Is that not what he should do?" Zaki asked. "If he were of the other kind, we would already have bloodshed on our hands."

"Have we not already?" Mukhtar asked.

"Only but a taste of it, brother," Zaki replied grimly. "He is right in pursuing his current course, but I sense a more selfish reason of not accepting his invite."

Mukhtar raised an eyebrow, curious as to why his brother was suddenly upholding the prince's resolutions. "Fa'iz only wanted me to bolster his plea for the crown, and I *refuse* to be used as a *pawn* for this ambitions!"

"And I commend you for it," Zaki responded calmly. "Fa'iz may be pursuing the crown, but so is every other member of the royal family. The prince is only doing what is right by him. The true blame lies with Immorkaan. In all their glory, they failed to foresee such a tragedy. It is almost a pity to see that Ma'alim did not have to exert much effort to infiltrate the palace, and would have succeeded in his ploys had we not intervened."

"Yet they would not hesitate to use others as scapegoats!" Mukhtar said harshly.

"Shameful, indeed," Zaki shook his head in disappointment.

"What would you have me do?" Mukhtar asked, eyeing him

cautiously. He knew what Zaki's response would be, but he also knew that he could not pursue this quest alone.

"I sense you have already decided."

Mukhtar gave a curt nod.

"I strongly urge you *not* to!"

Although expected, Mukhtar still felt slightly abashed at his response. "Says the man who defied all counsel against pursuing Abha," he countered.

"And I would defy them all again, were there even a glimpse of him still alive." There was no denying the sorrow in Zaki's voice. Mukhtar had told him of Ma'alim's claim, and the death of their father at his hands. It had taken several days for Zaki to fully accept the bitter truth and make peace with himself. "I have come to realize my grave mistakes. Living so far away for so long, from you and Ummi, from Khal and Khala, I have come to regret the foolish decisions I made."

Mukhtar felt a forlorn ache at Zaki's humble and sincere pleas. "But I must," he argued, urging his brother to understand why, "and I cannot do it alone. I need you, Zaki. I *need* my brother!"

Zaki shook his head without looking at him. "I can no longer bear to see the despair in Ummi's eyes," he said. "Since my return, she has constantly been on edge, afraid that I might leave her again. Our mother is all we have, Mukhtar. I cannot bear to bring her grief. I do not *ever* want to. I have done enough."

Mukhtar's eyes narrowed. "What are you not telling me, Zaki?"

Zaki shrugged indifferently.

"Zaki!" Mukhtar's tone became stern. "Come clean with me. Dare we leave secrets between us that will one day destroy our bond. Dare that happen before Ummi's eyes. It will surely destroy her."

Zaki bit his lip. "The Prince has offered me pardon!"

Mukhtar threw his arms in protest.

"Listen to me, Mukhtar!" Zaki said sternly. "I took his pardon because it forgives my desertion. I no longer owe an oath to the Red-Guard. This is my redemption and I gladly accept if it will reunite me with my kin. This is my chance to finally be the son Ummi has always wanted of me. I understand your need, little brother, but I urge to understand mine also."

Mukhtar eyed him intently, trying to show empathy rather than disappointment. "I understand," he finally said. "I know now, I must journey alone."

Zaki nodded solemnly, reached forward, and laid his hand atop Mukhtar's affectionately.

"Then you must strengthen Ummi," Mukhtar asserted, battling the urge to give in to his emotions. It almost felt like his brother was bidding him grim farewell. "Until my return."

Zaki gave him a long, hard stare, gazing at him with the fondness of brotherhood. "I understand," he then said. "You do what you must. I will share your burdens and fortify your resolution. Indeed, there is little else left for you here," he added thoughtfully, "between a feud for the throne, Immorkaan's corrupt politics, and Ma'alim's vile ambitions, something must be done, and can only be done beyond the boundaries of the law."

Zaki's advice could not have been sounder, and they spent the remainder of the evening discussing politics. He was pleased to have Zaki by his side. The brothers were clear on the path ahead.

Yet, a distant troubling thought continued to nag him— what if he left, and they were wrong?

This thought continued to trouble him, up until his bandages were removed, and Sheikh Ruwaid declared him healed. Leaving home would not burden him, for Zaki would care for Suha, and Mika'il would provide for them through the forge. His departure, however, would raise even more questions.

Why did he leave? What, and *why*, was he hiding? He did not intend to hide, but instead pursue his father's treacherous quest— the Amulets of Sihr, and their true purpose on *this* side of the Unseen Veil. Understanding this, he felt, was the only way of destroying Ma'alim and his schemes to unleash his wicked ideologies.

Despite numerous attempts to call for her, Adva remained unresponsive. Zaki had secretly taken away the Blue Amulet from him when they stormed into the Throne Room, and only returned it after Mukhtar gained consciousness, but it only hung around his neck, as lifeless as it could ever be. Mukhtar had tried speaking to it, whispering Adva's name when he was alone, even occasionally rubbing it as one would rub an oil lamp from a fabled tale, but his efforts bore no fruit. The dread did not leave him. Had she perhaps died in the battle with Ussam, when Azufil's blade pierced him? And if it were true, then did it mean that the Eye of Hurus could no longer be opened?

Somehow, Mukhtar doubted that a Jinn as powerful as Adva could so easily be killed. Then again, he did not know enough about sorcery to be certain. Regardless of what may have transpired, he did not feel satisfied leaving the Amulet behind, and allowed it to remain around his neck. Even if it was no longer of any use to him, it had belonged to his father, and was one of the few remnants of his memory.

He had polished his short-swords for almost two hours on the eve of his departure. He admired them despite their poor state. They had been cleaned and oiled, but the jagged edges remained. He eyed the silver blades for a long while, recalling his furious battles with the demons and the Jinn Azufil, as well as Abunaki and all the assassins and mercenaries who had fallen to the otherworldly weapons. Carefully, he sheathed and packed them along with whatever else he thought he could carry with him, including some throwing-knives, a spare *thaub*, trousers, and a shirt.

Zaki had brought him some food for the journey, which he packed along with a goatskin water-bag. The brothers had agreed on a nightly departure. Mukhtar would leave at midnight, allowing him enough time to reach their grandfather's cabin unobstructed, where he would rest for the day and leave Khalidah under cover of darkness the following evening. Meanwhile, Zaki would remain behind and cover his tracks. Already he had prepared the cabin for his accommodation, and saddled Bisrah for the journey.

Sheikh Ruwaid arrived after dusk to inspect his wounds. Mukhtar remained silent for a long while, until he could no longer hold back the questions.

"I must ask you something, Sheikh Ruwaid," he said.

"Ask away, Mukhtar," Sheikh Ruwaid gave him a welcoming smile. "Or shall I call you, *Lion of Khalidah?*"

Mukhtar gave him a disgruntled look.

Sheikh Ruwaid chuckled. "Ask away."

"Nuzhah—" he began but hesitated, unsure of how to phrase

his thoughts.

"Ah, yes," Sheikh Ruwaid understood immediately, "she did indeed approach me with her concerns."

"Can anything be done?"

Sheikh Ruwaid shrugged indecisively. "Perhaps. Perhaps not. I could not sense any Jinn presence about her. Perhaps your intervention severed Ma'alim's vile incantations on her. Perhaps it is dormant, awaiting a vulnerability in her faith. Whatever the case, I have reason to believe that her trials will soon come. It would be unwise to further involve her in such matters. Let her faith flourish and strengthen her from within."

Mukhtar gave an acknowledging nod. "What of the rituals in the Throne Room?"

There was a brief glint of fascination in Sheikh Ruwaid's eyes. "The Ritual of *Zar*," he said, "from the ancient Kingdom of Zarzara. A most illicit form of sorcery, meant to revive and awaken a dormant, or otherwise bound Jinn, so long as no other enchantments exist. They are detrimental. Life-threateningly dangerous. Abuzahil must truly have been desperate."

Mukhtar's expression was puzzled.

"You did not think 'Ma'alim' was his name, did you?" Sheikh Ruwaid affirmed. "Yes. Abuzahil is his true name. One that very few know."

Mukhtar nodded slowly. "Yes, he was very desperate. He admitted so."

"It is no simple task to enslave an elemental Jinn," Sheikh Ruwaid continued. "In the case of Agni, the *Ifreet* of Fire bound to the King's Amulet, Abuzahil required a large host of willful participants, which as disconcerting as it is to acknowledge, were available to him in plenty. With song and dance, intoxication and adultery, they praised and chanted the names of unholy beings, declaring their unfaithfulness to the Almighty, and professing the worship of Azazil and his Throne of *Ithm*."

"Is that how the demons materialized?" Mukhtar asked.

"The demons who attacked you in the Throne Room?" Sheikh Ruwaid eyed him. "Perhaps. I was able to study one of them, before the bodies were burned. They are vile breeds of two most heinous and monstrous kinds of Jinn. The *Nasnas* and *Udhrut*."

Mukhtar did not know what an *Udhrut* or *Nasnas* was, but his encounter with the demonic beings was enough to deduce their monstrosity.

"Ma'alim claimed that Ussam was his illegitimate son," he said, "that a Jinn named Azufil had occupied his body and soul."

Again, there was a distinct glint of fascination in Sheikh Ruwaid's eye. "Abuzahil has had many illegitimate sons and daughters," he said, and Mukhtar raised his eyebrows. "An infant child is his most favored way of pleasing powerful and evil Jinn, from whom he draws sorcery. He did not care if his son were possessed. His only desire has always been power, and he did unto his son what he was doing to the King, and would eventually do unto you. Your swords killed both his son and his Jinn," he lowered his voice to a bare whisper, "cling dearly to those blades, Mukhtar. Their craft is beyond the Unseen Veil, and are two of the only armaments that can truly kill a Jinn."

Mukhtar stared at him for a long while before averting his gaze and focusing on the crack in the ceiling. Sheikh Ruwaid continued to remove his bandages and clean the remnants of spent medicine off his healed wounds.

"I know that look," he said, drawing Mukhtar from his thoughts.

"Ask not, for I wish not to lie to you," Mukhtar stated.

"Alas, the troubles of youth, to mention but a few," Sheikh Ruwaid stated. "I can almost recall my own days. How confusing I found my path. How disconcerting it was to distinguish fate from destiny. I was ambitious. I was energetic. I did much, but somehow, after all these years, I have achieved very little."

Mukhtar almost laughed. "I find that hard to believe."

"Fair enough," Sheikh Ruwaid gave a lighthearted chuckle. "What if I were to offer you counsel?"

"I have found your words to be as kind and comforting as they are perplexing," Mukhtar answered.

"Only if you choose to be perplexed," Sheikh Ruwaid eyed him thoughtfully and cleared his throat. "Years ago, before your father's unfortunate imprisonment and disappearance thereafter, he came to me for assistance. An honorable man he was, married with two children. But troubled. Very troubled. Perhaps more than I could have predicted of him. He begged my help in a field of study I was unfortunately well known for, just as I am to this day," he gave a heavy sigh. "He spoke of Jinn and Demons. Of artifacts and amulets. Of keys and doors. Of betrayals and regrets. He regretted many things, and he sought absolution from his sins. He cried before me, poured his feelings. Alas, I could do very little to ease his burden."

There was sorrow in Sheikh Ruwaid's eyes, and Mukhtar understood. "You persuaded him to abandon his quest."

"I tried," Sheikh Ruwaid nodded and sighed again, "but failed. And I have lived with that regret, for I had vowed never to abandon a troubled soul. I have always been saddened by seeing others walk the same path as I once did, concerning themselves with otherworldly matters. They embrace the occult with delusions of ascension, of becoming the Masters, the Rulers, the Kings and the Lords. What they fail to understand, is that certain things in this world are simply beyond our control, and no matter how much we believe ourselves to be the masters, we are but slaves on this earth. Our freedom, our true ascension lies in our abilities to seek and comprehend the purpose of our existence. You must ask yourself, what is *your* true purpose? Who are *you*, and what do *you* want? Our choices in life define who we are. Our destinies are those which we shape for ourselves. What has to happen, *will* happen, but *how* it happens is governed by our own thoughts and intentions. Always remember this though, in your quest to save the world, be careful you do not destroy yourself. Every action, every step we take has a consequence. Of sin and deed, we will pay and be paid, in this life and in the hereafter. Always remember that, Mukhtar Harun Zafar."

Sheikh Ruwaid bade him farewell, and left him to his thoughts. He lay back on his bed, staring at the ceiling for a long while before falling asleep, waking close to the midnight hour to begin his journey. He dropped his bag into the alley below his window, climbed over the sill, and lowered himself with ease, stealthily scaling down the rough stone using footholds and handholds in the wall.

An hour later, he trekked through the mild shrubbery

surrounding the cabin, and crossed over its threshold, stepping on to the creaking floorboards of the porch. Bisrah was tied to the railing, helping himself to a water trough and a mound of hay.

The cabin's door had been reattached to its hinges, well-oiled and unlocked. Once inside, he dropped his bag by the door, groped around the dark for an oil-lamp, and lit it to bring light into the tiny room.

A slight dampness hung in the air, but aside from that, everything had been neatly organized, clean and tidy. The bed had been restored and the sheets changed. All the books and scrolls lay in neat piles against the opposite wall, and the floor had been swept and scrubbed. Exhausted and laden with sleep, he shut the door and opened the window to bring in fresh air, then took off his sandals, got into the bed and shut his eyes, falling almost immediately into a deep sleep.

He rose late the following morning, feeling far more rested than he had for several days. Sunlight crept through the open window. A lazy breeze carried with it the chirping of birds and the scent of the forest. He wanted nothing but to lay there in serenity. Eventually, he forced himself up, washed, and after a good breakfast of flatbread and *hummus*, he began scrolling through all the books and parchments in the cabin, hoping to find something that would ease his quest. Much to his disappointment, however, nothing substantial surfaced, at least nothing he had not already discovered from the very same sources. After several hours of frustration, he sat back on the bed, and gave a small sniff.

Something crept up his nostrils, triggering his sense of smell, bringing back a memory. He sniffed some more, tracing its source to the trunk at the foot of the bed. Inside, wrapped in a ragged cloth, was a black, tattered, leather-bound book, reeking a strong, disgusting stench of rotting eggs. The Book of *Kufr*.

He spent a considerable amount of time flipping through every page, trying everything he could think of, including using the flame of a candle to force it into revealing something, but it simply refused to yield.

A tiny scroll had been squeezed into the binding of the book for safekeeping. It was the same scroll that had been handed to him with the Blue Amulet. The frayed string he had undone so many months ago, hung loosely around it. After eyeing it for a long while, he stored both the book and the scroll into his bag. Their usefulness might unravel upon his arrival at Uduff.

Dusk was approaching briskly, and he was running short of time. Looking through the cabin had taken the entire day, and he was just about to prepare for his journey, when someone walked in through the door behind him. He froze and cursed himself when he remembered leaving his swords by the side of the door.

"I thought I might find you here."

He recognized the voice and turned around. "Why are *you* here?"

Nuzhah was wearing long robes of a maroon shade, with a matching scarf and an elegant veil to adorn. Her shoulders were deliberately hunched, her head slightly inclined with a gaze that was warm and benign. Very unlike her sister, she was. In nearly every aspect.

"Might I ask the same?" She raised an eyebrow. Her eyes were attractively lined with *kohl,* deeply captivating and alluring in every way. "Everyone is looking for you."

"How did you know to find me here?" he asked. "I told no one, but Zaki."

"I asked no one," she replied, affirming the anomalous bond efflorescing since the day he freed her. "Your mother told me about your grandfather's cabin, and how you always came here to be alone. I could think of no other place that would bring you solitude."

Mukhtar looked away from her, busying himself with arranging all the books back into their neat stacks. He knew why she was there.

"Why are you so troubled, Mukhtar?" she asked kindly.

He hesitated.

"Is it so vital you pursue this course? Have you not seen enough, endured enough?"

So she knew. Or she had ventured a guess. He turned around sharply. "After all you have seen, how can you say that?"

"I have seen too much," she said bitterly.

"Then you know why I must leave," he said. "This tyranny must end. The oppression must end. A dark force gathers in the wastelands, and mankind rests upon the brink of destruction. I cannot allow it to endure."

"No!" she remarked. "You believe this to be your destiny, but it is not! This is madness! It is a fool's ambition! Your responsibility is to your kin. To those who love and care about you!"

Her voice trembled when she spoke the last few words, and Mukhtar suddenly understood. What he had felt before was not unparalleled. The memories of her tending to his wounds, bringing him food, kindling his hope when all else had abandoned him, and as much as his heart desired it, he knew that it was just not possible. Not upon the path that lay ahead.

"Nuzhah," he spoke in a kinder voice, reminiscing Sheikh Ruwaid's grave warning, "I urge you to understand. The sins of my fathers have followed me through the years, gnawing at me from beyond their graves. They have burdened me with a terrifying purpose. And where this path leads, you cannot follow. I have lived with the grief of losing my father for many years. Hassin, my friend, my brother, died because of I. Because of my foolishness and inability to do what was necessary. I cannot bear such grief anymore. I must end this, once and for all."

"I share your grief, Mukhtar," she asserted. "I sympathize the sorrow in your heart. Those before us, attest for the choices they made. Their actions were their own. Do you not see? Their burdens are not yours to bear. Their deaths were not by your doing, but by the will of the Almighty. They will be judged by what they did, and you will be judged by yours."

In all the time he had known her, she had not once faltered from her righteousness. Ever had she clung to her faith. Ever had her innocence overpowered him. However, there was much she did not yet fully understand. There was more to it than mere faith.

"There is truth in what you say," he urged her, "but I will also be judged if do nothing. If there is but a chance for me to redeem my father's worth, respect, dignity, integrity, and all the good he did, then I have an obligation by divine rule to seek it. Need I sacrifice my own life to do so."

Her head shook briskly. Behind her veil, her eyes began to show signs of weakness. "I assure you Mukhtar, it is not so. Your obligation is to those among your kin. Those whose bond is true to your heart and soul."

Mukhtar sighed deeply. "I understand your plea," he said. "Believe me, I have struggled with these thoughts time and again, and I know that this struggle will continue endlessly. It pains me, *believe me,* it pains me deeply. We did indeed share a bond, even if it remained unknown to us. But upon the path I now walk, fate will never allow this bond to endure. In those fluttering moments, in those troubled times, whatever we felt deep inside, was just a dream. A faltering dream. Nothing more. In truth, I cannot give you what your heart desires."

He avoided looking into her eyes. He did not want to, could not bear to, afraid that they might weaken him. She held up a *henna*-adorned hand and unclasped the knot of her veil, removing it to reveal her face.

"What is the meaning of this?" He stared at her, astounded. "Why do you unveil yourself?"

"You have seen my face before," her voice shook, her porcelain skin slightly blushed. "I want you to look upon me once more as you push me away!"

Mukhtar's heart sunk. He knew, understood the sanctity behind which a pious woman would veil herself. If Nuzhah had chosen to show her face, he knew deep down, she would never do so for anyone else. He sighed deeply and moved a step closer to her. Closer than he had ever been. He could have felt her warmth from where he stood, and he breathed in her scent, her flowery aura of lavender. It sent shivers up his spine and made his heart beat faster. Her face was glowing, her full lips trembled slightly, and her scarf fluttered in the slender breeze.

He gazed into her eyes. Her brown, almond-shaped eyes. She was an image of perfection. Would she have smiled, the world would smile with her. Would she have laughed, the world would laugh with her. But at the sight of her tears, Mukhtar became helpless and forlorn. It truly pained him, but he was right— where he was headed, she could not come. It was inevitable. She deserved more than a bedeviled son of a condemned bloodline. She deserved all the happiness in the world. She was elegant in her ethics, he was unpolished. She was flawless in her character, he was scarred. She was gifted and he was cursed.

"There comes a time when everyone has to make a choice," he tried to keep his voice from trembling, tried to keep the jolt of emotion in his throat contained. "A bitter and painful choice. For those we truly care, such a pain must be endured. It is in such moments, when a person's true nature is unveiled, their honor, their dignity, and nobility. A noble heart will always thrive, no matter how much it is suppressed, for its nobility lies in its virtue, its righteousness, and affection. Yours is a noble heart, Nuzhah, daughter of Altaf, and may it forever be filled with the benevolence and grace you have always shown me. You stood by me when no other did, and for that, I will forever remain in your debt. I wish we could have been, as we desired to be. I wish to have been the one, to enlighten your world, as you have always enlightened mine. I am bound to a resolute purpose, and on this path, my most tasking endeavor will be to lose you to a memory. But I will always adore you. I will always cherish you. Do not forget me, for I will never forget you."

She broke. Tears like pearls trickled down her smooth skin, her eyes filled with sorrow. He longed to reach out and embrace her, feel her warmth, place his hand upon her head and draw her closer into his arms. He fought the temptation with all his inner strength, crossed the room, picked up his leather bag and short-swords, and walked out of the cabin into the fresh air, where the sounds of nature masked away her soft sobs. He undid Bisrah's reins and guided his brother's steed along.

Painfully, he walked on. His purpose was true and firm, and where he was bound, she could not follow, for he would rather suffer an emotional pain that would fade away with time, than bear the grief of bringing her closer to harm, only to satisfy his own selfish desires.

Hanging from the chain around his neck, the Amulet pressed on his chest and gave a subtle, almost ephemeral throb, masked by his saddened heart.

He suppressed a sniff as he hiked down the narrow pathway that took him away from his heart's desire, away from the cabin, away from the tiny village, and would eventually take him away from the very sights of the Immortal City.

GLOSSARY

Abaya *[aa.baa.yaa];* Cloak for women
Abha *[aa.bhaa];* Father
Abu *[aa.boo];* Father of
Bakhoor *[baa.kkh.oor];* Scented wood
Banu *[baa.noo];* Descendants of
Bin *[bin];* Son of
Bint *[bint];* Daughter of
Falafel *[faa.laa.fel];* Fritters of chickpea wrapped in pita
Hashish *[haa.shsh.eesh];* An extract of the cannabis plant
Hukah *[hoo.kaah];* Traditional tobacco pipe and vial
Hummus *[hoo.moos];* A creamy dip made from chickpeas
Ibn *[ee.b.n];* Grandson or great-grandson of
Kaymak *[kaay.maak];* A creamy, buttery dairy product
Khal *[kkh.aal];* Maternal uncle
Khala *[kkh.aa.laa];* Maternal aunt
Khat *[kkh.aat];* Twigs of a plant used as a stimulant/intoxicant
Kohl *[kohl];* A black powder or paste used for facial beautification
Kitaab *[kee.taab];* Book
Kufr *[koo.fr];* Sin
Mabkhara *[maab.kkh.aa.raa];* Incense burner
Madrassa *[ma.ad.raa.saa];* School
Ma'alim *[maa.aa.leem];* Teacher
Masjid *[ma.as.jeed];* Mosque/ Place of Worship
Musalla *[moo.ss.aal.laa];* Prayer room
Muadhin *[moo.aad.dh.een];* An announcer for prayer

Oudh *[ood.dh];* Scented wood

Qadhi *[qa.ad.dhee];* Judge

Rebab *[rey.baab];* Stringed Musical instrument

Sahir *[saa.heer];* Magician/Sorcerer

Salaam *[saa.laam];* Greeting

Santur *[sa.an.toor];* Stringed musical instrument

Shaytaan *[sha.ay.ta.an];* Devil

Shayateen *[sha.aya.teen];* Devils (plural)

Sheikh *[sh.ay.kkh];* Nobleman/Scholar

Sherbet *[sh.arr.batt];* A cold drink of fruit juice with/without milk

Sihr *[see.hr];* Magic/Sorcery/witchcraft

Silaah *[see.laah];* Weapon

Shukran *[shoo.k.ran];* Thanks/Gratitude

Souk *[soo.wk];* Market

Tahini *[taa.hee.nee];* A creamy sauce made from sesame seeds

Tef *[tef];* Drum

Ud *[ood];* Stringed musical instrument

Ummi *[oo.m.mee];* Mother

Ustaadh *[oos.taa.ddh];* Wise and learned individual

Thaub *[tth.aw.b];* Single robe, worn by men

Aarguf [aar.goof]
Abaraina [aa.baa.raay.naa]
Abdi [aab.dee]
Abidan [aa.bee.daan]
Abunaki [aa.boo.naa.kee]
AbuZahil [aa.boo.zaa.heel]
Adad [aa.daad]
Adam [aa.daam]
Adil [aa.deel]
Adva [aad.vaa]
Agni [aag.nee]
Ahumai [aa.hoo.maa.ee]
Alulim [aa.loo.leem]
Anbar [aan.baar]
Ard [aa.rr.d]
Ar-Rushdi [ar.roosh.dee]
Avira [aa.vee.raa]
Azazil [aaz.aaz.eel]
Azhar [aaz.haar]
Azufil [aa.zoo.feel]
Ba'al [baa.aal]
Babak [baa.baak]
Babati [baa.baati]
Banu [baa.noo]
Baqil [baa.keel]
Barish [baa.ree.sh]
Bashiri [baa.shee.ree]
Bayzar [baay.zaar]
Bisrah [bee.s.raah]
Darr [da.arr]
Dymek [dee.mek]

Elzafaan [ell.zaa.faan]
Eth [eth]
Fa'iz [faa.eez]
Falami [faa.laa.mee]
Faraj [faa.raaj]
Fareibah [faa.ree.bah]
Farid [faa.reed]
Fusan [foos.aan]
Galel [gaa.lel]
Ghadan [ggh.aa.daan]
Ghasif [ggh.aa.seef]
Ghulam [ggh.oo.laam]
Gizwani [geez.waa.nee]
Gussar [goo.ss.aar]
Haddad [haa.dd.aad]
Haim [ha.aym]
Haleem [haa.leem]
Harun [haa.roon]
Harus [haa.roos]
Hassin [haa.ss.een]
Hitu [hee.too]
Huda [hoo.daa]
Hurus [hoo.roos]
Iblees [ee.blees]
Idumea [ee.doo.may.aa]
Iyad [ee.yaad]
Jaffar [jaa.ff.aar]
Jalal [jaa.laal]
Jalil [jaa.leel]
Jaul [jaa.ool]
Jawad [jaa.waad]

Jubair *[joo.baa.eer]*
Myrah *[mee.raah]*
Kaka *[kaa.kaa]*
Kanaan *[kaa.naan]*
Kashif *[kaa.sheef]*
Kataan *[kaa.taan]*
Kazimi *[kaa.zee.mee]*
Khoury *[kkh.oo.ree]*
Khurn *[kkh.oo.rn]*
Khuru *[kkh.oo.roo]*
Laban *[laa.baan]*
Lahib *[Laa.hib]*
Layla *[laay.laa]*
Ma'alim *[maa.aa.leem]*
Majtaba *[ma.aj.taa.baa]*
Masri *[maa.sree]*
Mika'il *[mee.kaa.eel]*
Mirah *[mee.raah]*
Mirza *[meer.zaa]*
Misbah *[mees.baah]*
Mukhtar *[moo.kkh.taar]*
Murad *[moo.raad]*
Nabiha *[naa.bee.haa]*
Nabun *[naa.boon]*
Nechem *[ne.chh.em]*
Nizaam *[neez.aam]*
Nuzhah *[nooz.haah]*
Qurais *[qoo.raa.ees]*
Rafi *[raa.fee]*
Rasha *[raa.shaa]*
Rauf *[raa.oof]*
Riah *[ree.aah]*
Ruwaid *[roo.wayd]*
Sabbagh *[saa.bb.aa.ggh]*
Saif *[sa.ayf]*
Salim *[saa.leem]*
Samiya *[saa.mee.yaa]*
Shahzad *[shaah.zaad]*
Shura *[shoo.raa]*
Sitra *[see.traa]*
Siyaad *[see.yaad]*
Suha *[soo.haa]*
Sumrah *[soom.raah]*
Surukh *[soo.roo.kkh]*
Talia *[taa.lee.aa]*
Tasseem *[taa.ss.eem]*
Thamir *[tth.aa.meer]*
Tuma *[too.maa]*
Ufuk *[oof.ook]*
Urduk *[oor.dook]*
Ussam *[oo.ss.aam]*
Uzuris *[oo.zoo.rees]*
Varda *[vaar.daa]*
Yael *[yaa.el]*
Yabis *[yaa.bees]*
Yusri *[yoos.ree]*
Zaki *[zaa.kee]*
Zafar *[zaa.faar]*

Aftara [aaf.taa.raa]
Aghara [aa.gh.aa.raa]
Ahul-hama [aa.hool.haa.maa]
Alhram [aal.h.raam]
Almah-Zurah [aal.mah.zoo.rah]
Alshura [aal.shoo.raa]
Arammoria [aa.raam.mor.ee.yaa]
Aztalaan [aaz.taa.laan]
Baghda [baa.gh.daa]
Din-Galad [deen-gaa.laad]
Dunhah [doo.haah]
Fashaan [faa.shaan]
Ghafa [Ggh.aa.faa]
Ghuldad [gh.ool.daad]
Hanan-Sula [haa.naan.soo.laa]
Hangai [haan.gaa.ee]
Haraldar [haa.raal.daar]
Hifa [hee.faa]
Hizak [heez.aak]
Hubur [hoo.boor]
Imar [ee.maar]
Immorkaan [ee.mm.or.kaan]
Ingha [een.gaah]
Khabara [kkh.aa.baa.raa]
Khalidah [kkh.aa.lee.daah]
Khamur [kkh.aa.moor]
Mirzaan [meer.zaan]
Mudanisin [moo.daa.nee.seen]
Murfaqat [moor.faa.qaat]
Nihar [nee.haar]
Ninya [neen.yaa]

Rhud [rh.hood]
Rhudah [rh.oo.daah]
Rhunga [rh.oo.gaa]
Sadh [saa.dh]
Samaan [saa.maan]
Shabb [shaa.bb]
Simnia [sim.nee.yaa]
Suria [soor.ee.yaa]
Uduf [oo.doof]
Undomi'an [oon.do.mee.aan]
Uzad [ooz.aad]
Zarzara [zaar.zaa.raa]
Zila [zee.laa]

ABOUT THE AUTHOR

My apprenticeship with Mika'il began nearly a decade ago, enabling me to scribe all my experiences with Mukhtar and Saif. It was during this time that my encounters with the Unseen took corporeal forms, wherein in the past, I had only read of them in books, or spoken of them in discussions.

There is nothing fictitious about the Jinn. Tread with caution.

Over the years, I compiled my recollections and thus began this journey. There is still much to unravel. Much to explore and discover. A greater adventure is still afoot, and I am purposed to see it to its destination.

To you, I reach a welcoming hand.

Let us make this journey together.

 www.abubilaalyakub.com

 @authoryakub

 @abubilaalyakub

 @abubilaalyakub

 abubilaalyakub

 abyakub.tumblr.com

Made in the USA
Columbia, SC
15 December 2018